Summerlin Groves

ELIZABETH CAMDEN

Historical Romances by Elizabeth Camden

The Blackstone Legacy

Carved in Stone

Written on the Wind

Hearts of Steel

Hope and Glory

The Spice King

A Gilded Lady

The Prince of Spies

The Empire State Series

A Dangerous Legacy

A Daring Venture

A Desperate Hope

Christmas at Whitefriars, a novella

Stand-Alone Novels

The Lady of Bolton Hill

The Rose of Winslow Street

Against the Tide

Into the Whirlwind

With Every Breath

Beyond All Dreams

Until the Dawn

From This Moment

To the Farthest Shores

Cover design and interior formatting by *Hannah Linder Designs*

ISBN (print): 978-1-7332225-4-9
ISBN (digital): 978-1-7332225-5-6

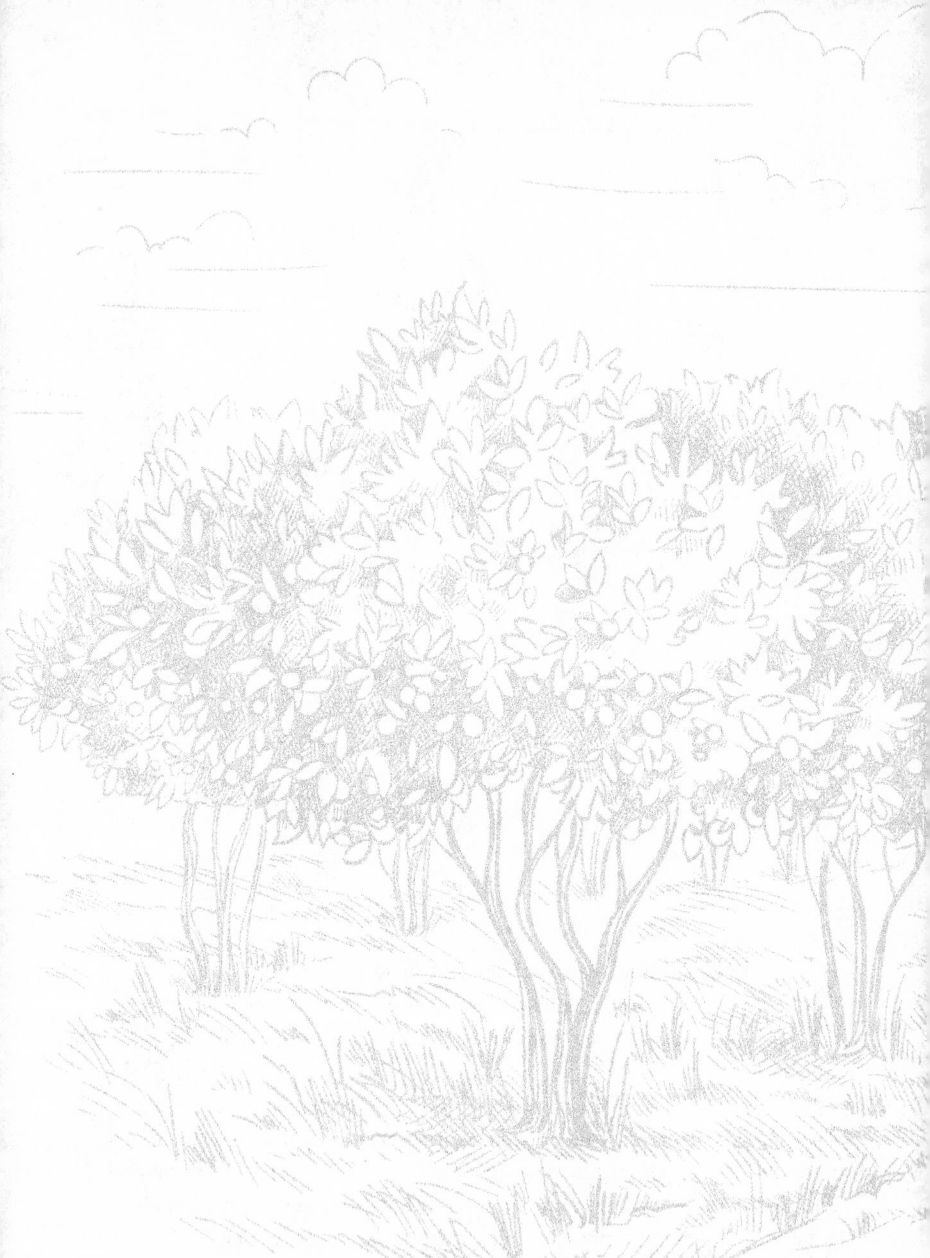

Chapter One

"There's a dead body in the west field," Hemingway said.

Jenny Summerlin straightened her spine and brushed the grit from her hands, squinting from the sunshine filtering through the orange grove to see if Hemingway was joking . . . although nothing that happened in the west field was a joking matter these days. Her field hand had just returned from dumping another load of stumps, and maybe he'd come across a dead possum or raccoon.

"What do you mean, a dead body?" she asked. English wasn't Hemingway's first language, so maybe he didn't understand the difference between a dead body and an animal carcass.

"A dead person," Hemingway clarified. "Human."

She stood motionless, unable to believe this latest catastrophe. "Are you sure he's dead?" It would probably be best to call an ambulance to be on the safe side.

"I'm sure," Hemingway said. "It's a skeleton, inside the hollow of a cypress tree down by the river."

Jenny took a steadying breath as she gazed toward the

river. This stretch of land was so immensely beautiful, and yet, some unknown stranger met a terrible fate right here on her property. Hopefully whoever that person was could be at peace now.

A skeletonized body wasn't an emergency, merely another blow in a string of disasters over the past eighteen months.

Eighteen months ago, she and her brother shared ownership of a spectacular orange grove in the middle of Florida. They were flush with cash. She was in love with a war hero who was ready to lay the world at her feet, and the future was alive with hope.

Now her brother was dead, she was broke, the grove was dying, and the war hero hated her. It seemed like each time she regained a hint of equilibrium, something rose up from the deep to smack her back down.

At least Hemingway had stuck with her. He was her last remaining field hand and always good for a laugh, even if he rarely buttoned his shirt or ran a comb through his white-blond hair.

She rubbed the small of her back where it ached from pulling stumps. The wind was picking up and the January morning was unusually chilly, penetrating her denim jacket.

"Aren't you freezing?" she asked Hemingway, who wasn't even wearing a shirt.

Hemingway scratched the tanned skin on his shoulder and sent her a lazy smile. "Sunshine Girl, you don't know what it is to freeze."

True, when a man was born and raised in Iceland, cold was a relative term. Hemingway had fled Iceland as soon as he finished his Ph.D. in English Literature and came to Florida in search of an outdoorsman's life like his hero, Ernest Hemingway. No one in Florida could pronounce his real name, so he simply went by "Hemingway." Jenny was probably the only citrus grower in Florida who had a former college professor working her land, but the arrangement suited them both.

"Show me the skeleton," she said, then climbed onto the back of the all-terrain vehicle they used for hauling stumps. Hemingway started the engine and drove them slowly through the torn-up acre of land that once had over a hundred orange trees growing on it. After they'd burned them down last week, all that remained was a barren, depressing mess of charred stumps and acrid cinders, but they'd have it cleaned up soon.

Hemingway drove faster once they reached the gravel path at the end of the row. They passed the farmhouse where she'd been born and raised, then the freestanding garage, then through the back ten acres where the trees were still healthy. At this time of year her oranges were still green and needed a few more months of sunshine before they would mature into heavy orange fruit ready for harvest.

Hemingway slowed the ATV as they approached the river, where a line of ancient cypress trees had been left standing as a windbreak.

"The skeleton is in the split cypress," Hemingway said as they both dismounted. The enormous tree had taken a lightning strike last summer, causing the trunk to split. Over the subsequent months, the split had widened as gravity pulled the dying tree in two, slowly exposing the hollow inside. The tree was over a hundred feet tall and fifteen feet wide at its base. It ought to have been cut down, but it would cost a fortune and Jenny didn't have that kind of money.

Besides, Jenny had good reasons for not wanting strangers in the west field.

Their boots sliced through the wiregrass as they neared the line of old trees. Spanish moss draped the tree limbs in a ghostly veil and knobby roots protruded from the soil. Her grandfather called them "cypress knees." They jutted straight up from the dirt like spokes guarding the mother tree. Some were only a few inches tall, but others reached three or four feet high. She and her brother, Jack, used to climb on them when they were kids, even though it drove her grandfather nuts. He thought the crooked roots were dangerous, but climbing on them was an irresistible temptation for two lonely kids growing up on an isolated orange grove.

"How long does it take for a body to become a skeleton?" she asked Hemingway.

"I don't know. My degree was in English."

And Jenny's had been in agricultural sciences with a minor in history. She chose the major for practicality, but the minor in history was for love.

The boggy soil sucked at her boots as she trudged closer to the tree. Everything smelled normal, just a piney green scent mingled with musty smells from the slow-moving river. She held her breath, bracing a foot on a knobby root to get high enough to peer down into the cavity of the tree. The bark was dry and crumbly as she grasped the rim, pulling herself higher to look into the exposed hollow below.

The skeleton lay curled in the hollow, its leg bones drawn close to its ribcage. She heaved a sigh of relief and hopped down.

"I think it's pretty old," she said.

"A lot older than eighteen months," Hemingway pointed out.

Now that she was thinking clearly, there was no way the skeleton could be associated with what happened eighteen months ago. For a week the grove had been crawling with law enforcement officers, and turkey vultures would have alerted them to another body.

"Who do you think it is?" Hemingway asked.

She and Hemingway were the only people living on the grove since Jack died. A work crew came through each April to pick oranges, but she rarely knew them well. Could the skeleton have been a migrant laborer from a past harvest? Or a homeless person who took shelter in the hollow of a tree and died?

An arborist once told her these trees were around six hundred years old. As cypress trees aged, their trunks eroded and hollowed out, gradually filling with decaying leaves and bark. It could be a tempting place to seek shelter or stash a dead body.

She climbed up for another look at the skeleton. It was in the fetal position, its chest cavity packed with dirt. The detached skull lay near its elbow. There was no sign of the lower jaw. This skeleton could have been here for decades. Maybe even *centuries*.

Hemingway climbed up on the opposite side of the hollow. "Do you see any sign of clothing?" he asked. Clothes would at least let them know if the body was male or female, a child or an adult.

She leaned in closer, holding her breath to avoid the grit swirling in the air. No sign of clothes that she could see, but clothing would rot quickly in the heat and humidity of central Florida.

She couldn't bear to look any longer and hopped back down to the ground. What a disaster. As soon as she reported this, there would be sheriff's deputies and investigators crawling all over the grove again, nosing into her business. Of all places, why did this have to happen in the *west* field?

"I think I found something," Hemingway said, one arm in the hollow of the tree. "It's hard and smooth. It seems manmade."

Curiosity got the better of her, and she climbed back up for a peek as Hemingway continued pawing at a small lump. He swiped away leaves and twigs, then something sparkled.

She gasped. Blue sparkles glinted from the lump near the skeleton's disarticulated hand. "Be careful," she cautioned as Hemingway angled to reach deeper into the hollow. The tree creaked, releasing a scent of damp, rotting wood.

"Don't touch it," she said. "Hem, this might be a crime scene."

"The entire west field is a crime scene," he said lightly.

Jenny wasn't sure if the fire she set last week was a crime or not. She was probably allowed to burn down whatever she wanted on her own land, but she couldn't risk consulting a lawyer to find out.

"Hemingway, please stop," she implored. "I'm going to call the sheriff's office, and we shouldn't be poking around in there."

"You sure?" Most of Hemingway's upper body now dangled into the interior of the hollowed-out tree, blocking her view. The loamy smell of damp wood and tree sap intensified as he pawed through the interior of the tree.

He finally began wiggling back up, struggling to hold something in his right hand. It was about the size of an apple and covered in dirt. He passed it over to her, then hopped out back onto the ground.

She swiped mud from the grimy ball, revealing smooth blue enamel threaded with traces of golden vines and flashing gemstones. Diamonds? She held her breath as she rotated the lump to clear away more grit and mud, barely able to believe her eyes as beauty emerged from the mud. She cradled it in her palms and looked up at Hemingway in amazement.

It seemed unbelievable, but . . . had they just found a Fabergé egg?

THEY TOOK the egg back to the farmhouse kitchen, where Jenny held it beneath a trickle of warm water to gently rinse the rest of the grime away, revealing peacock-blue enamel encircled by golden vines. This was probably a cheap knockoff and not actually a real Fabergé egg, though the craftmanship was beautiful and extraordinary even to her untrained eye.

Jenny knew very little about flashy gemstones. The only jewelry she owned was her parents' matching gold wedding bands she inherited after a car accident killed them both when she was eight years old. Her typical daily attire was a simple pair of blue jeans, a tank top, and work boots. During the summer, her long blond hair was almost as light as Hemingway's.

Hemingway stood beside her at the oversized kitchen sink as the magnificence of the egg came into view. Twining gold filigree looked like the branches of a tree encircling the luminous blue enamel. What looked like pear-shaped sapphires and rubies decorated the limbs like budding leaves. A thin band of diamonds circled the long edge of the egg. At the top were two tiny, entwined golden twigs.

"I think that's a clasp and the egg can probably open," Hemingway said. "Should we try?"

She shook her head. "I don't want to risk breaking it." She was afraid to even set it down. Hemingway lined a cereal bowl with a terrycloth dishrag, and she placed the egg inside as carefully as if it were a grenade with its pin pulled out. The still-damp egg glistened in the sunlight streaming in from the window, exuding a near-magical aura.

"Do you think it's real?" she whispered.

"I don't know," he said just as softly. Why were they whispering? Their voices wouldn't damage it, but somehow this moment deserved complete reverence. The unearthly beauty of the egg was a masterpiece.

Jenny had a solid understanding of Russian history, having grown up paging through her grandfather's old books about the mighty empire. Her favorites had been the books with pictures of the spectacular Russian landscapes, though there had been plenty about the revolution, featuring pictures of the last Russian czar and his beautiful daughters. He had a wife and a young son too, but Jenny had always been haunted by the photos of those four girls, dressed in matching white gowns with broad-brimmed hats, looking ghostly and lovely in those long-ago photographs. The entire family had been executed in a hail of gunfire, forever casting a shadow over their memory.

The books inevitably described the wealth of the Russian aristocracy, epitomized by the extravagant Fabergé eggs. Every year, the czar gave his mother and his wife a unique egg crafted by the famous House of Fabergé. Many of the eggs survived the Russian Revolution of 1917, but not all.

"Let's see if we can learn anything online," Hemingway said and headed toward the office.

The office was Jenny's favorite room in the hundred-year-old farmhouse. After her grandfather died, she and her brother decided they'd rather have a modern office instead of a formal dining room. They took out the dining table and ripped up the shag carpet to expose the original hardwood floor below. Jack installed cables and wiring for the computers and new overhead pendant lighting.

The only part of the dining room Jenny couldn't bear to part with was the old farmhouse table. The massive slab of walnut held ninety years of family history in its weathered planks. Generations of Summerlins took their meals around this table, propped their elbows on it, played cards on it, and talked long into the night. A few cigarette burns were mementos from the era when people still smoked, and the cracked leg happened after a hog got loose in the house when her dad was a kid.

Jenny sanded and sealed the wood with a coat of new varnish. She repaired the cracked leg instead of replacing it because the split made for a good story. Someday she'd have kids who would want to know about the family's brief, failed attempt to diversify into hogs. The dings and the scars were vestiges of her family's long history. An antique collector had once offered her $6,000 for the table, but Jenny wasn't interested. Her family's heritage wasn't for sale.

Now the table held two computers, a printer, and a weather monitoring system. Gone were the days when farmers stuck a hand into the wind to judge the climate. Jenny had access to weather alert systems, commodity prices, and online forums to trade information with fellow citrus growers. One monitor displayed live video feeds from security cameras posted at various spots throughout the grove.

Jenny set the cereal bowl with its treasure on the table and fired up her desktop. Hemingway already brought his laptop from the trailer where he lived on the edge of the grove, and they both started prowling for information on Fabergé eggs.

Jenny learned the House of Fabergé made fifty eggs that had been commissioned by the doomed Nicholas II. These were known as "imperial eggs" and were the most valuable of all the Fabergé eggs. Each egg opened to reveal a charming surprise inside. Some contained miniature portraits, or working clocks, or tiny replicas of palaces where the czar lived.

After the revolution in 1917, the czar's mother escaped to Copenhagen, carrying one of the imperial eggs with her. Other members of the royal family smuggled out a few as well, but most of the Fabergé eggs had been abandoned in Russia. As Bolsheviks plundered the Romanov palaces, those eggs were seized, stolen, or disappeared.

Several websites confirmed that forty-two of the imperial eggs had been located. Those eggs were heavily documented and photographed from every angle, but none of them looked anything like what sat on her table.

Eight imperial eggs remained lost to history. Had one of them just been found?

Another hour of searching the internet turned up written descriptions of the lost eggs, and one of them sounded exactly like the egg sitting on her terrycloth-lined cereal bowl.

Dubbed the Firebird Egg, it had been a gift from Nicholas to his then-fiancée, the princess Alexandra of Hesse, in 1893. After the wedding, Alexandra kept the Firebird Egg on a bookshelf in her private chambers for the rest of her life. It was one of the eggs that disappeared after the revolution.

Hemingway began to pace. "We need to call someone about that skeleton," he said. "The egg probably belongs to whoever that person is."

"Unless he stole it," Jenny said. "What kind of person walks around with a Fabergé egg in the middle of nowhere unless they are on the run?"

"*If* it's a real Fabergé," Hemingway pointed out, but its craftsmanship was too fine to be a cheap knockoff. A real Fabergé egg would be worth millions. Owning the property on which it had been found might entitle her to keep it.

And she could use the money. Last month she had to write a check for $1.2 million to settle a lawsuit. Though the grove was worth a little over two million, most of it was tied up in the value of the land, the buildings, and the equipment. The McAllister family sued her for every dime of her brother's estate. Jenny either had to sell the grove or take out a huge loan to pay the McAllisters for Jack's half. Rather than waste money and heartache on lawyers, she took out a $1.2 million loan and paid the McAllisters outright. Paying them had left Jenny with a debt she'd probably be stuck with until her dying day, but at least the matter was settled and done.

The rim of diamonds on the egg gleamed in the late-afternoon sun slanting through the window blinds. Hemingway looked mesmerized as he gazed at it.

"Are you thinking what I'm thinking?" she asked.

"Probably," he said. "We could sell this on the black market and be millionaires."

"Yup."

Selling the egg on the black market would avoid a snarl of court cases from potential claimants, but it would have a stink on it. She had no idea how the egg ended up in that old cypress tree, although it was surely quite a story. If the egg disappeared into the underground antiquities market, its story would be lost to history forever.

Sometimes it was terrible to have a conscience. Jenny smiled a little wistfully at the egg resting on its bed of terrycloth. If this truly was the Firebird, the world deserved to know how this egg got from Empress Alexandra's bookshelf, out of war-torn Russia, and onto an orange grove in rural Florida.

"I'd rather keep it legal," she finally said, and Hemingway flashed her a wink in agreement. He went back to his laptop, fingers flying across the keyboard as he dug up more research. It was getting late now, and she put together a couple of ham sandwiches while he continued working.

"Look at this," he said, turning the laptop for her to see. It was an article from a lawyer's website outlining the laws governing lost-and-found property in the state of Florida.

"According to this, if you find something valuable on your land, you need to make a public announcement, then give people ninety days to come forward with a claim."

She thrummed her fingers on the table. A find like this would garner media attention and provoke a stampede of people wanting to file claims.

It didn't matter. Telling the world was the right thing to do. She drew a fortifying breath and met Hemingway's gaze.

"I think we make that announcement," she said. "Maybe nobody else will be able to prove ownership, which means we get to keep it."

"We?" Hemingway asked.

"You found it. I'll split it with you."

Hemingway's eyes widened in astonishment. For the first time in the six years since she'd known him, he looked speechless, but splitting the proceeds with the man who found the egg was fitting.

A slow smile spread across his face. "You're a good friend, Jenny."

She smiled back, because they *were* good friends. Hemingway was possibly the best friend she'd ever had. People sometimes assumed she and Hemingway were a couple because he was drop-dead gorgeous, but she'd never been tempted by him. He reminded her too much of her brother, which was an instant turn-off. Jack and Hemingway both had a charming and irreverent outlook on life tinged with a huge dash of irresponsibility.

After Jack died, it was Hemingway who kept the grove operating when she'd been too devastated to get out of bed. He handled the flurry of initial paperwork and dealing with the sheriff's office. When it could no longer be delayed, it was

Hemingway who dragged her out of bed, forced her to get dressed and confront the world again. It was Hemingway who stuck by her side when she first ventured into town to brave the cold looks and snide comments. One lady literally spat at her. Hemingway gave the lady a courtly bow, then the middle finger.

The entire town still reviled Jack, and some resented Jenny, too. The skeleton was bound to stir up a new bout of suspicious hostility.

She'd let the sheriff worry about the skeleton, but the egg needed more care. Turning it over to the sheriff's department was a risk. For a prize this big, she wanted everything documented in triplicate.

First they photographed the egg alongside a copy of the morning newspaper to verify the date of the find. Then they took videos of each of them holding the dishtowel-lined cereal bowl with the egg inside. They stated where they found it, and their intention to report it to the Pierce County Sheriff's Department. If anyone at the sheriff's department tried to steal the egg for themselves, these videos would prove who had it first.

They downloaded the videos to Jenny's desktop and uploaded them into a secure photo-storing site in the clouds. There must be no doubt about who found this egg first.

The sun was setting by the time they finished documenting their find. It was too late to call the authorities about the skeleton tonight, but that would happen tomorrow morning.

Then the high-stakes game to claim ownership of the egg would begin.

Chapter Two

Jenny headed toward Hemingway's trailer first thing in the morning. She could have taken the gravel path that led to his trailer, but preferred the wide, sandy aisles through the grove. Walking among these trees made her feel connected to the generations of ancestors who'd farmed this land before her. It had been a good place to grow up. When she was younger, she and Jack used to spend endless summer days playing in the green-tinted world beneath the canopy of leaves.

Walking past the charred acre in the middle of the west field tugged at her conscience. She and Hemingway still had a long way to go in disposing of evidence, and the burned acre might raise questions from the sheriff she didn't want to answer.

A break in the trees gave way to a clearing dominated by the two storage barns, the pumping station, and the battered, single-wide white trailer. The beachy tunes of Jimmy Buffett leaked from behind the aluminum door, assuring her that

Hemingway was back from his morning fishing trip. She navigated around a couple of free-range chickens pecking at the ground to approach the trailer door. Hemingway answered her brief rap.

"Want some catfish?" he asked, then went back to wiggling a cast-iron skillet on the stove. Hemingway ate so much fish he'd probably sprout gills one of these days.

"Too nervous," she said as she slid onto the dinette bench. As always, the interior of the trailer was a mess of books fighting for space among mounds of clothes and dirty dishes. "We'll tell the authorities about the skeleton first, then mention the egg after things calm down."

Hemingway flipped his morning catch onto a plate before taking the opposite bench at the table. "Do you think he'll show up?"

There was no need for Hemingway to say Wyatt's name. Jenny's brief, exhilarating love affair with Wyatt Rossiter had flamed out eighteen months ago during their first real crisis. Even thinking about him triggered a pained thrill. Wyatt was nothing more than forbidden fruit. Six feet and two inches of whipcord-lean, darkly handsome forbidden fruit, but that was all over. She'd seen him around town a few times since their breakup, though he always looked away and made himself scarce before they had to speak to each other.

Mercifully, he wouldn't have any role in today's investigation. "Wyatt works for the Department of Agriculture, not the sheriff," she said. If anyone was trying to steal cattle, hunt during the off-season, or violate agricultural regulations, Wyatt would lead the investigation. Dead bodies and murder investigations fell to the sheriff's department.

As soon as Hemingway polished off his breakfast, he set his fork down and sent her a sympathetic look. "Ready?"

Not really, but delaying wouldn't help matters. "Let's go poke the hornet's nest," she said with a wink, bracing herself to endure the next few hours.

HEMINGWAY CALLED the sheriff while Jenny unlocked and opened the metal gates to Summerlin Groves, then they both returned to the farmhouse to wait on the porch swing for the authorities to arrive. Jenny wore her heaviest wool peacoat and still shivered. Maybe it was just nerves, because fifty degrees wasn't too terribly cold considering it was the middle of January, but it was still chilly for Florida.

Within fifteen minutes, two green-and-yellow cruisers from the sheriff's department arrived. The tires crunched on the gravel drive as they slowed down, then cut their engines at the front of her house. She hopped down the porch steps as a deputy got out of the front car.

It was Tommy Kasich. She remembered him from high school. Tommy played the trumpet in the marching band while Jenny had been in Future Farmers of America, so they both ran with the nerdy crowd. They didn't know each other well, but he'd always struck her as a decent guy.

That was a long time ago, and like most people in Pierce County, his attitude toward her was cool as he rounded the car. "Hey, Jenny," he said. "What's this I hear about a skeleton on the grove?"

"It's about a quarter mile away in the hollow of a cypress tree," she said. "You'll probably want to drive. I can show you the way."

Tommy nodded and gestured her to the back of his squad car. She didn't recognize the deputy in the front passenger seat, a skinny man with a thin mustache, who frowned at her as she slid onto the vinyl bench in the back of the car.

"Who found the skeleton?" Tommy asked after he started the engine and began rolling down the gravel path.

"Hemingway. Neither one of us know who it could be. We don't have any friends or family members who went missing. Neither of us know anyone who—"

"Did your brother have anything to do with it?" the skinny guy interrupted.

Jenny's breath froze, and Tommy sent the younger deputy an annoyed glance. "Shut up, Ames," Tommy muttered, then met her gaze in the rearview mirror. "Sorry, Jenny. Tell me again what you saw."

"Just turn left at the fork," she said stiffly. By now she ought to be used to the snubs because after Jack died, she was the only one left to blame. The car gently rocked across the uneven soil, and pebbles pinged the undercarriage as it rolled closer to the cypress trees.

"You can park here," Jenny said, pointing to a grassy spot. The other squad car had followed, so she waited until all four men were out of their cars before guiding them to the split cypress tree.

"That tree got hit by lightning last summer," she said. "The gap has been widening ever since, and the hollow opened up. We noticed the skeleton yesterday."

"You haven't disturbed the scene?" Tommy asked.

"I haven't," she said truthfully enough. It was Hemingway who found and disturbed the egg, not her. She watched as the men took turns stepping onto the raised cypress knees to peer into the cavity, then two of them started encircling the area with yellow crime-scene tape. Tommy spoke into the two-way radio anchored on his shoulder, and another deputy sheriff started taking photographs.

All of them were engaged in the scene. Nobody noticed the burned patch a few acres away in the west field, which was a relief. She headed back to the farmhouse since it sounded like Tommy was summoning more people to the grove. She and Hemingway had already agreed that one of them would ride in each car coming to the scene so the cars wouldn't take a shortcut through the grove and see the burned acre.

An hour later, a van with a sign on its side noting it carried mobile crime scene equipment arrived, driven by a woman from the Pierce County Sheriff's Department. Hemingway offered to take her to the scene, which was good. Women liked Hemingway because he was funny and acted like he didn't realize how good-looking he was to every female with a pulse. Jenny stood on the porch and monitored the action at the cypress trees through a pair of binoculars. Everyone seemed fully engaged in the scene, and a hint of misgiving arose. Her family had worked this grove for ninety years. She didn't know how long that skeleton had been there or how he died, but if he was murdered, the odds were good someone in her family might have been involved.

It didn't take long before Hemingway came jogging back. "Brace yourself," he said. "They're calling the fire department and a tree service."

"Why?"

"They can't get the skeleton out of the tree without disturbing a possible crime scene, and aren't taking any chances. They want to cut it down. One of the deputies kept mouthing off about Jack probably being responsible."

"That's ridiculous," she scoffed.

But it wasn't. No matter how much she wanted to deny the possibility, Jack *might* have done it. She never could have imagined that he would kill the mother of his child and the young social worker who'd been sent to help facilitate visitation, but eighteen months ago he snapped and did it. Two women dead, Jack's senseless suicide, and an orphaned four-year-old boy were all the result of Jack's hair-trigger temper.

She hadn't seen her nephew since that terrible night. Neither Jack nor his girlfriend, Miranda McAllister, had been stable enough to raise a child. Miranda's parents had custody of the boy since infancy, so at least there had been no jarring transition for the boy's living arrangements. And now they had a $1.2 million trust fund for him.

The fire engine arrived, kicking up clouds of dust from the gravel drive as the heavy truck came closer to the farmhouse. The siren wasn't engaged, but the emergency lights were rolling, twisting Jenny's nerves even tighter. A flatbed truck from a tree service company followed.

Hemingway hopped into the firetruck to lead it to the cypress tree, and a few minutes later another car pulled onto the grove. It was the squad car Jenny dreaded the most.

Captain Wyatt Rossiter's familiar white cruiser with a green stripe drove slowly down the gravel path toward the farmhouse. She walked to the porch swing on unsteady legs and sat, watching as Wyatt calmly unfolded his tall frame from the Agricultural Law Enforcement vehicle.

The sight of him packed a wallop. He wore mirrored sunglasses and his khaki officer's uniform. Tension crackled between them as he approached the steps, his mouth unsmiling in his hard, chiseled face.

"Jenny," he said tersely.

One word. After all they'd been to each other. After the way he disappeared without even telling her goodbye, all he could muster was a single word. She returned the favor.

"Wyatt."

The sculpted features of his lean face were expressionless.

He planted a boot on the porch step, hooked a thumb in his belt loop, and waited.

She wasn't going to make this easy on him. She rocked slowly, the chains from the porch swing grinding out a rhythmic squeak. The two of them used to spend hours on this porch swing. Sometimes they spoke of raising kids here; other times they held each other and kissed until they were both breathless.

She kept rocking and staring at the two tiny reflections of herself in his mirrored sunglasses. He'd once told her he wore mirrored sunglasses because they made people with a guilty conscience feel uncomfortable.

Everything about Wyatt Rossiter made her uncomfortable, from his six-foot-two frame to his wavy dark hair and the square jaw that looked like it was carved from a block of granite. She'd hoped the pull of attraction he provoked would have died by now, but no. Wyatt's aura of calm, controlled strength still held her in thrall.

Except . . . he wasn't always so calm and controlled. The last time they'd spoken to each other there'd been bellowing voices, things thrown, and tears. Before that afternoon she hadn't ever heard Wyatt raise his voice.

Now he was back to being grim and unruffled, with the corners of his mouth turned down in disapproval.

"You've got a sagging gutter on the side of your house," he finally said.

She shrugged.

"It's a safety hazard," he pointed out.

Repairing the gutter was a luxury she couldn't afford. She'd liquidated almost every asset she had to settle the lawsuit, so there wasn't money for things like repairing a saggy gutter.

"What brings you out here, Wyatt?" She managed a deliberately polite tone, rather than one laden with eighteen months of lonely anguish.

"I came over as soon as I heard a skeleton had been found on your land." He sounded genuinely concerned, which deepened her discomfort, but she strove for a nonchalant tone.

"The west field is already crawling with government investigators, so the situation is under control. You can leave."

"I want to see it anyway."

She didn't want him anywhere near the west field. So far, nobody had looked twice at the burned acre, but Wyatt might be different. He knew a lot more about citrus groves than anyone else on the scene today, and he might spot the trouble.

"Forget it," she said casually. "This is private property and I don't want you here."

He cleared his throat and braced a foot on the top porch step. He even took off the scary sunglasses to lean in and lock gazes. "You and I have good cause not to like each other, but I am an officer of the law and want to see what's out there."

His words hurt, though she refused to let him see it. She'd always vowed that when the inevitable day came when she finally encountered Wyatt again, she would be thoroughly decent. It was time to deliver.

She stood and softened her tone. "Drive down to the fork in the path, then turn left. You'll be able to see the split cypress at that point."

He got in his car without another word and closed the door with a click . . . not a slam like she would have done. Even the purr of the engine sounded soft and controlled as he put the car in gear and started down the gravel drive.

Of all the people on the grove today, Wyatt was the only one smart enough to figure out what she and Hemingway had been doing when they incinerated the trees in the west field. Wyatt was Sherlock Holmes, Clark Kent, and Captain

America rolled into one man. He was the straightest of straight arrows and would blow the whistle long and loud if he figured out what she'd done.

His car rounded the bend and she lifted her binoculars to track his journey to the cypress tree.

It would have been better if their first words to each other after eighteen months hadn't been so prickly. She'd hoped that maybe when they finally spoke again, he might apologize for abandoning her. Say that what happened wasn't her fault. Say that he wanted to patch up their wounded hearts and recapture what they had before.

What a pathetic fantasy. The loneliness of the grove made it easy to spin daydreams and then hope they might come true. She'd done the same when she was eight years old and prayed the car accident that killed her parents hadn't happened and they would miraculously come back to the grove. Silly, wishful thinking.

Wyatt's car turned left at the fork and rocked over the rutted path toward the cypress trees. The car rolled past the burned acre, and a faint smile curved her lips. The muscles in her neck relaxed and her smile grew wider. He hadn't noticed anything.

A second later Wyatt's car began to slow, and then it stopped. The taillights illuminated, and the car backed up several yards and paused, its engine idling.

Jenny's mouth went dry and her heart began to pound. Long seconds ticked by, then Wyatt got out of the car. He shaded his eyes and stared straight at the acre of cinders and burned stumps.

He only lingered a few seconds before getting back in his cruiser and heading toward the split cypress tree. Her heart continued pounding long after he arrived at the yellow tape and began conferring with the others. Her racing heart had nothing to do with grief over an old flame or curiosity over what the officials were learning about the skeleton.

It was due to the fact that if Wyatt figured out why she'd burned those trees, Jenny would lose the rest of her orange grove. He was the enemy now—and wouldn't hesitate to see her entire grove destroyed.

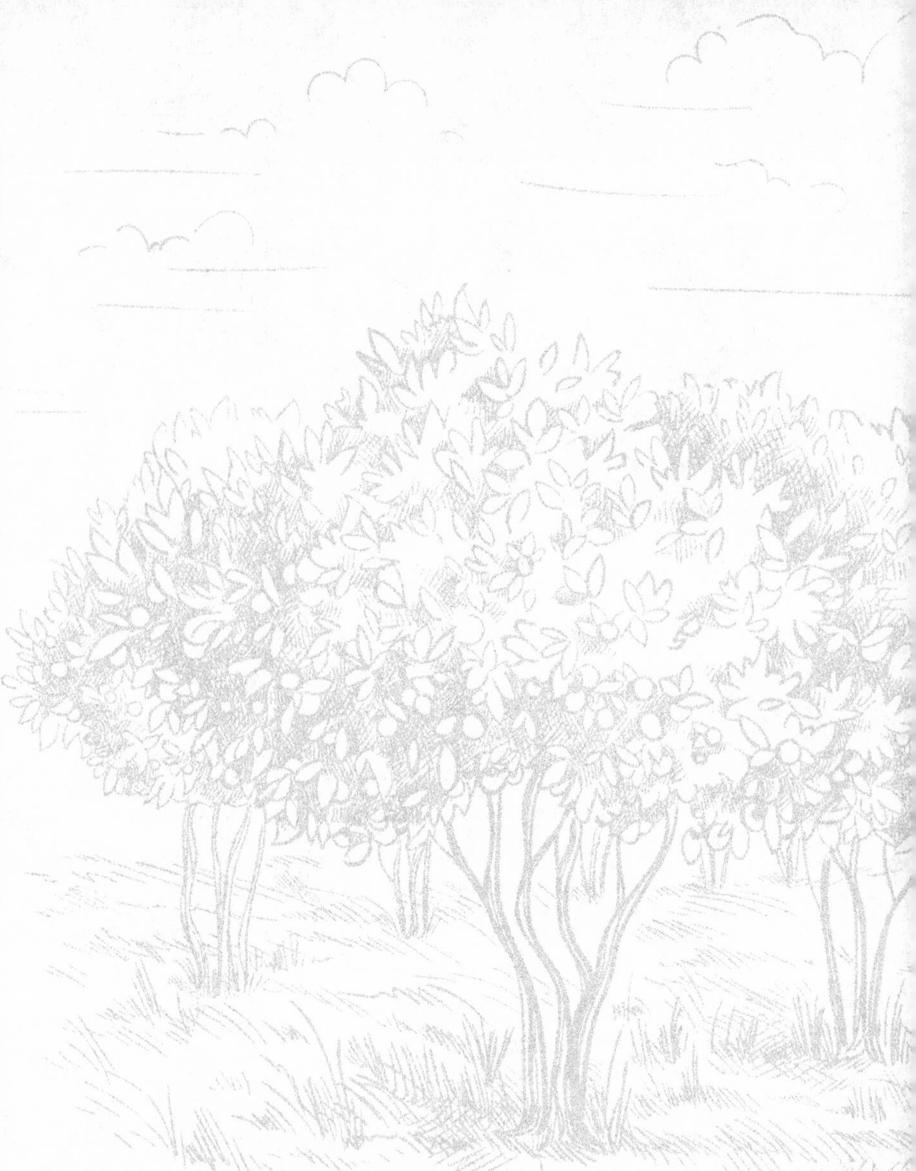

Chapter Three

It all began so innocently. She and Wyatt met through their jobs two years ago. She was at the Tri-County Orange Juice Plant to sign a new contract while he'd been there performing a routine inspection.

Like most citrus growers in Florida, Jenny sold her oranges to the frozen concentrate market. She could have signed an automatically renewing annual contract, but she enjoyed touching base with the business folks at the processing plant each year. It was a rare chance to escape the grove and mingle with townspeople.

After leaving the OJ plant with a newly signed contract, Jenny's triumph faded the moment she spotted the flat tire on her pickup truck. Normally she could change a flat while blindfolded, but she didn't have a spare tire with her and hunkered down to inspect the damage.

Wyatt was leaving the plant at the same time, and her first sight of him was like something out of a movie. The late-afternoon sun cast him mostly into silhouette, obscuring everything but his impressive height and broad shoulders tapering to a slim waist. He had a long, languid stride as he drew near. He approached slowly, as though not to alarm her because she still knelt on the asphalt beside the flat tire.

Who didn't love the sight of a man in uniform? It was a khaki uniform with a fully loaded duty belt and a shiny badge, but best of all was the expression in his eyes. He had deep, gentle brown eyes that gazed at her with empathy as he hunkered down beside her.

"Can I be of help, ma'am?" She could melt from the sound of his smooth, rich baritone and barely had the strength to stand. He helped her up, her hand slim in his large, firm grip.

"I've got a flat, but I can probably make it to the auto supply store."

"Hold on, let me make a call." He had one of those two-way radios in his service vehicle, and in short order arranged for someone to drive a spare tire out. It was hard not to gape at his handsome features as he took care of the problem.

"You don't have to wait," she assured him after he completed the call. "I've got a jack in my truck and can change it myself."

"You can?" He sounded skeptical, but Jenny's grandfather taught her all manner of survival skills, whether it was finding potable water, hunting and rendering a deer, or changing a tire. Suddenly she was grateful for her grandfather's crazy survivalist training because Wyatt seemed alternately intrigued and alarmed as she positioned the tire jack under the pickup's frame after the tire arrived.

"Ma'am, I really wish you'd let me help."

She started cranking the jack handle, then paused. Despite growing up in a male-dominated world and playing with Tonka trucks, GI Joes, and air rifles, she always secretly wanted a Barbie doll. While other girls in high school fussed over pretty manicures, Jenny cleaned tractor grease from beneath her nails. Her favorite movie was *Cinderella.* Was it so wrong to want to be sought after and adored? Or to feel feminine and pretty? She didn't need a knight in shining armor . . . but deep inside, she *wanted* one.

She stepped aside and let Wyatt take over. He carried out the task with quick efficiency, the muscles in his forearms tensing and releasing with each twist of the jack handle. His competence as he changed her tire appealed to a secret thrill of having a strong man look out for her.

They chatted while he worked, and it turned out they had a lot in common. They both grew up in Amity, Florida, and had the same fourth-grade teacher, though seven years apart. They both went to the University of Florida, except Wyatt majored in environmental science before joining the army and working all over the world doing environmental cleanup on military bases. After leaving the army, he took a job with the state's Department of Agriculture in the law enforcement division.

Workers were beginning to leave the processing plant for the day before her tire was changed. Wyatt retrieved an old rag from his service vehicle and slowly wiped the grease from his hands, but time went into slow motion as he gazed at her. She felt his eyes on her as she returned the wrenches to her toolbox, and didn't want their time together to end.

"You know, ma'am . . . I don't think I've ever seen anything sexier than watching you handle those tools."

Then . . . amazingly, he started to blush. He glanced away, shifted his weight a little, and went completely tongue-tied. She'd never seen such a handsome, powerful man get clobbered with embarrassment like this, but it was . . . well, it was rather wonderful. He stammered for a moment before putting a coherent sentence together.

"Could I . . . would you . . . Are you hungry? I know a

place a mile up the highway that makes the world's best smoked brisket."

He seemed as captured by the same magnetism that drew her the moment she spotted him striding across the parking lot toward her.

"I'd love smoked brisket, but please quit calling me ma'am."

He grinned and touched the brim of his hat. "Yes, ma'am."

A rush of joy bloomed inside. Some men were simply born and bred with those gentlemanly southern manners. She followed him to the barbecue joint, then went to his condo to watch an old Jimmy Stewart movie. Before sliding the DVD into the player, he scribbled a note on a slip of paper and tucked it into a pewter tankard that doubled as a bookend.

She loved that he had a fully loaded bookshelf. His entire condo featured vintage furniture with a Frank Lloyd Wright vibe. Leather sofas, craftsman-style tables, and prairie-style simplicity gave the condo plenty of old-school character. The tankard clanged as Wyatt returned it to the bookshelf.

"What's on the note?" she asked.

"Nothing." And yet, he couldn't meet her eyes and he was blushing furiously as he started the movie. It was *Mr. Smith Goes to Washington*, her first clue that Wyatt was as sappy and sentimental as she. They watched the movie, and at the end she got choked up because *he* got choked up. In short, it was the best date of her life. Before that day she hadn't known it was possible for two people to click together so perfectly, as though God himself played matchmaker.

She shouldn't have read so much into it. Millions of couples had magnificent first dates, but that didn't mean they were destined for the altar. She and Wyatt had a magnificent second date, too. And a third, and a fourth . . . actually, they had enjoyed a magnificent April, May, and June.

The more she learned about him, the more appealing he became. He earned his Eagle Scout badge and graduated from high school with honors. He was class president his senior year, and played wide receiver for the football team. He completed law school while still in the army and was studying to pass the bar exam in Florida.

With each date at his condo, she glanced at the tankard on his bookshelf and wondered if the note he wrote on their first date was still in there. He clearly didn't want to tell her what he wrote, but it plagued her.

And she never could resist a secret.

One evening when he carried a bag of trash to the dumpster behind his unit she reached up for the tankard and felt inside.

The note was still there. She pulled it out and read:

Today I changed a tire with the woman I'm going to marry.

Her hands trembled as she replaced the note. She hopped onto the sofa, hugging her knees to her chest. Sometimes the threads of one's entire world started weaving together into something magical. She loved everything about Wyatt's old-school manners and unabashed sentimentality. He was a man of the law as comfortable wielding a gun as writing a sappy, sentimental note to himself.

Then there was the appeal of Wyatt's family. His parents were happily married and they all doted on his kid sister, Lauren. They were a nice, wholesome family who went to church, paid their taxes on time, and had an actual white picket fence surrounding their home.

Meanwhile, Jenny's family was littered with broken

marriages, alcohol abuse, and a touch of mental illness. Not that anyone had ever been formally diagnosed with a mental condition, but proof of it was all over the grove. There were the two extra supply sheds built specifically to store objects of her grandfather's compulsive hoarding. They had an underground bunker stocked with supplies to survive the Armageddon. Her family were preppers before the word was invented. Wyatt knew about her crazy Summerlin family history and loved her anyway.

Then it came crashing down on a sweltering summer night eighteen months ago when Wyatt's sister was in the wrong place at the wrong time. Lauren Rossiter was the social worker who came to help Jack in his custody dispute with his child's mother. The argument had been vicious. The security camera out in the barn didn't have audio, but the murder was caught on video. Jack panicked after he shot his girlfriend, and when Lauren arrived on the scene five minutes later and tried to call 911, Jack panicked and shot her too.

All of it was caught on video. Jenny had been out of town at an orange growers' conference in Miami. If she hadn't seen that video footage with her own eyes, she couldn't have believed her charming and reckless brother could be guilty, but there it was. For a few minutes after the murders Jack curled over Miranda's lifeless body and sobbed, then he put the gun to his temple and took the easy way out.

The double-murder and suicide knocked her sideways and time stopped as grief crippled her. Belief in goodness and mercy evaporated. How could a loving God let something like this happen? Jenny would never understand how or why Jack fell into such darkness, but she eventually came to understand that his failings didn't give her permission to abandon her faith. The day eventually came when sunlight began to pierce the veil of grief. She got back on her feet and life went on, even if it wasn't quite as bright as before.

Another thing she lost after that terrible night was Wyatt. Their love affair collapsed even faster than it had blossomed. She wished it wasn't so, but Wyatt had good reason to hate everything about Summerlin Groves.

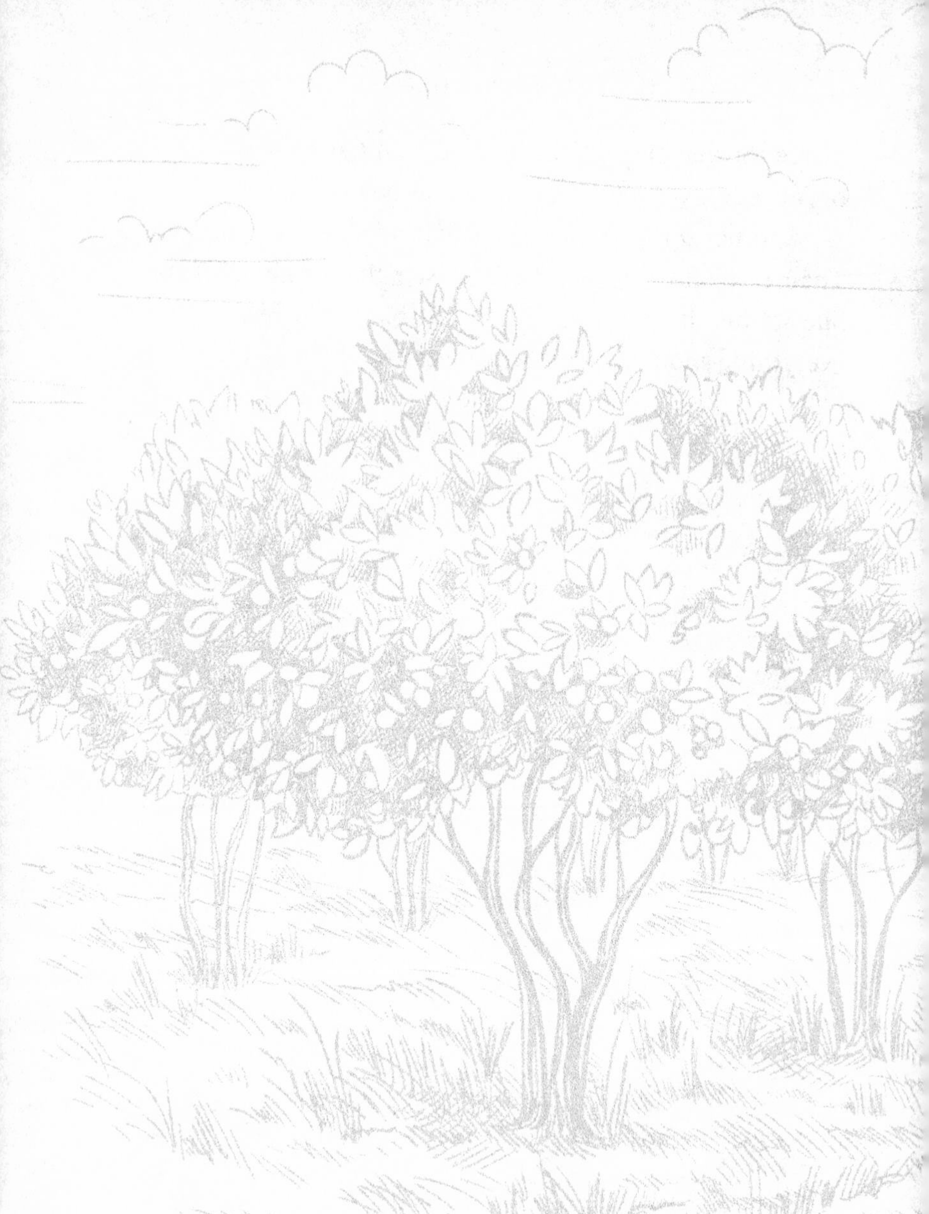

Chapter Four

Jenny watched from her porch as additional people from various state agencies showed up to investigate the skeleton. The sheriff wanted the cross-section of the cypress trunk housing the skeleton to be removed intact. The upper part of the tree needed to be cut down first, which was why six tree trimmers had arrived with climbing gear, chainsaws, and woodchippers. The raucous buzz of chainsaws echoed across the grove as limb after limb crashed to the ground. Soon, a crane on the back of the fire engine would lift the excised section of the tree onto the flatbed truck.

Jenny had been waiting for a break in the activity to pull Tommy aside for a quiet word, but the day got more hectic as the hours passed.

"When are we going to tell them about the egg?" Hemingway asked as he joined her on the porch steps.

"I've been waiting for Wyatt to leave."

Why was he still here? After briefly consulting with the sheriff's deputies, Wyatt retreated to watch the ongoing action from a distance. She zoomed her binoculars to study him as he paced around the perimeter of the yellow tape.

He didn't walk with a limp anymore. When they'd been dating, he still limped from a wound he got in Iraq when a roadside explosion flipped the jeep he'd been riding in. Wyatt had shrapnel embedded in his leg but still carried a fellow soldier over his shoulder to safety. It made his own wound a lot worse, requiring two surgeries and earning Wyatt a Bronze Star and a Purple Heart.

He seemed completely healed now, and if nothing else good came from this day, at least she had the satisfaction of seeing Wyatt completely healthy again.

"I'll go let Tommy know we need to talk to him," Hemingway said. "I'll ask him up to the house, where we can speak in private."

Hemingway began strolling toward the activity. She watched through the binoculars as he approached Tommy, both men putting their heads together. Hemingway gestured toward the house, and Tommy nodded, clapping him on the back.

A couple of the firemen joined them, and whatever Hemingway said must have been hilarious because others joined in to shoot the breeze even as Hemingway started typing something into his phone. A moment later she had an incoming text:

Tommy will be over in a couple of minutes.

She lifted her arm high to send Hemingway a thumbs-up, then dashed inside to unload kitchen dishes from the drying rack before Tommy arrived. If all went well with the egg, maybe she could soon afford a dishwasher for this old place, but in the meantime, she wanted it looking tidy.

Footsteps thudded on the front porch, then Tommy knocked on the screen door. She took a fortifying breath, bracing herself to confess how she and Hemingway took a Fabergé egg off that skeleton.

To her shock, Wyatt stood on the other side of the screen door, and he had the imposing sunglasses on again. She'd be tempted to turn him away except it would make her look like a coward. She steeled herself and opened the screen door.

He spoke first. "Yeah, Jenny, what do you need?"

"I asked for Tommy."

He shook his head. "The medical examiner just arrived, so he's busy. What do you need?"

Revealing the egg to anyone was going to be difficult, but doubly so to Wyatt, the most hidebound rule-follower on earth. She learned that on their first date when she tried to jaywalk across the street. He instinctively pulled her back from the curb, then walked with her to the end of the block. They had laughed about it at the time, but now his obsession with rules wasn't so funny.

She stepped back from the door and gestured for him to enter. At least he removed the scary sunglasses, sliding them into his shirt pocket as he stepped inside, glancing around the front room in surprise.

"You cleaned up in here."

A laugh escaped. "It was a big task."

Her grandfather had been a hoarder. She'd grown up in the jam-packed farmhouse, so overstuffed chaos seemed normal to her. After he died, it took years to clear everything out. Much of it was high-quality vintage collectibles, so it couldn't be quickly liquidated.

Wyatt scanned the interior of the parlor and dining area. "I never noticed how big this room was. It has good bones."

It did. Crown molding, large baseboards, and wainscotting

surrounded the family room. The original pine floors had been refinished, and she and her brother furnished the room with a new sofa, a rocking chair, and a couple of craftsman-style end tables. Sunlight filtering through the window blinds cast a glow over the walls newly painted in shades of ivory and soft beige.

An awkward silence stretched, and his physical nearness awakened a thousand dormant emotions. Wyatt's rolled-up sleeves exposed his strong forearms, something she'd always found intensely attractive.

She tamped down the memories and braced herself to get this over with. "Hemingway and I found the skeleton yesterday," she admitted. "We didn't call it in right away because . . . well, it obviously wasn't a medical emergency. We actually forgot to mention one tiny detail of what we found." Her mouth dried out and it was hard to keep speaking. Wyatt's jaw tensed, and his eyes went hard.

"What?" he asked, not in the friendliest of tones.

"There was a fancy jeweled egg right beside the skeleton," she said. "We took it out for a better look."

"You did *what*? Where is it?"

"Follow me." She never would have secured the egg in the gun safe if she'd known Wyatt would be the lawman on the scene when she turned it over. Wyatt had a whole slew of reasons he hated guns, even though he carried one for his job. He stayed on the far side of the mud room while she turned the dial on the gun safe.

Nervous energy caused her to flub the combination twice before she got the door open. Several antique rifles and guns were lined up beside the newer rifle she used for venomous snakes. The cereal bowl with the Fabergé egg sat on the top shelf. She used both hands to lift it down. The sapphires and diamonds flashed beneath the overhead light.

Wyatt looked gob-smacked as he paced inside the tight confines of the mud room. "That was in the cypress tree," he finally stated in disbelief.

"Yup."

"And you took it," he accused.

"I did," she said, starting to get angry too. She was doing the right thing by reporting it to the authorities, and he didn't need to sound so personally offended.

"You tampered with a crime scene," he accused.

"It didn't look like this when we found it," she said, walking into the front room to set the bowl on the coffee table. "It looked like a muddy rock. It wasn't until we rinsed it off that we got a good look at it."

"That's why you leave crime scenes alone," he bit out. "That's why you go straight to a telephone, call 911, and don't touch anything. A child knows that. What you did is called tampering with evidence and destroying a crime scene."

"Knock it off, Wyatt. What I did is called basic human curiosity. I found something interesting on my property and brought it inside for a better look. In the morning I called the cops."

"Now you might want to call a lawyer."

She scoffed in disbelief. "Are you kidding me?"

"You tampered with evidence."

"And you must have had your heart clinically removed and your brain lobotomized by the state. Have you never done something daring and impulsive? What about Morocco?"

"Oh, shut up about Morocco," he snapped, his temper threatening to blow.

Bringing up Morocco was a mistake, and she held her hands up in concession. "I take it back," she conceded. "Forget I said the word. It was a mistake and I'm sorry."

His mouth was a hard, angry line as he stared at the egg.

"I'll get Tommy to come up here, and don't touch that egg again."

The slamming of the front door echoed in her ears long after he left.

THINGS WENT DOWNHILL AFTER THAT. Tommy arrived with Wyatt in tow. There were no more volcanic outbursts like with Wyatt, but Tommy was clearly annoyed. She and Hemingway dutifully answered all his questions about the egg's location in the tree.

"Who else knows about this egg?" Tommy asked.

"Just the four people in this room," she said.

Tommy looked toward Wyatt, who leaned against the back wall, still in a snit. "I want to keep this quiet," Tommy said. "The medical examiner says the skeleton is at least a couple decades old. We don't know if foul play was involved or not, but this is a very cold case. We need to start gathering information, and that egg will bring the crazies out of the woodwork if news of it leaks." He looked directly at Jenny. "Don't tell anyone else about this egg. It will be secured in the evidence bureau, and knowledge of its existence will be limited to only a handful of people. Do the two of you understand that?"

His tone irked her. "I'm fine with staying quiet for now, but you should know that Hemingway and I intend to file a claim to keep the egg. It was found on my property, and according to Florida law, that means I'm entitled to keep it unless someone with proof of ownership shows up."

Tommy raised a brow. "I wouldn't be too sure of that,

Jenny. Once we identify the skeleton, the egg will probably go to his heirs."

The odds of the dead person being the legal owner of a treasure like this was slim. It made the news when rich people disappeared, and whoever was in that cypress tree hadn't caused a stir when he disappeared.

"I still intend to file a claim for ownership," she told Tommy.

"I've had enough of this," Wyatt grumbled as he pushed away from the wall. "Jenny, Hemingway, you're both obligated to follow the sheriff's order and keep silent about the egg."

He slammed out of the room without another glance at her. Tommy opened the flaps of an evidence collection box and lowered in the egg, still resting in its terrycloth-lined cereal bowl. He issued another terse warning regarding staying quiet about the egg before leaving.

"Somehow I don't think we'll be getting Christmas cards from them," Hemingway said after the rumble of Tommy's departing cruiser faded into the distance.

Jenny shrugged. She was already a leper in Wyatt's eyes, but perhaps the silver lining from his anger over the egg was that he hadn't glanced again at the burned patch in the west grove.

It was a good thing that she and Hemingway had thoroughly documented what they found last night, because as Tommy drove off, she had a worrisome suspicion that powerful forces would try to ensure she never saw that egg again.

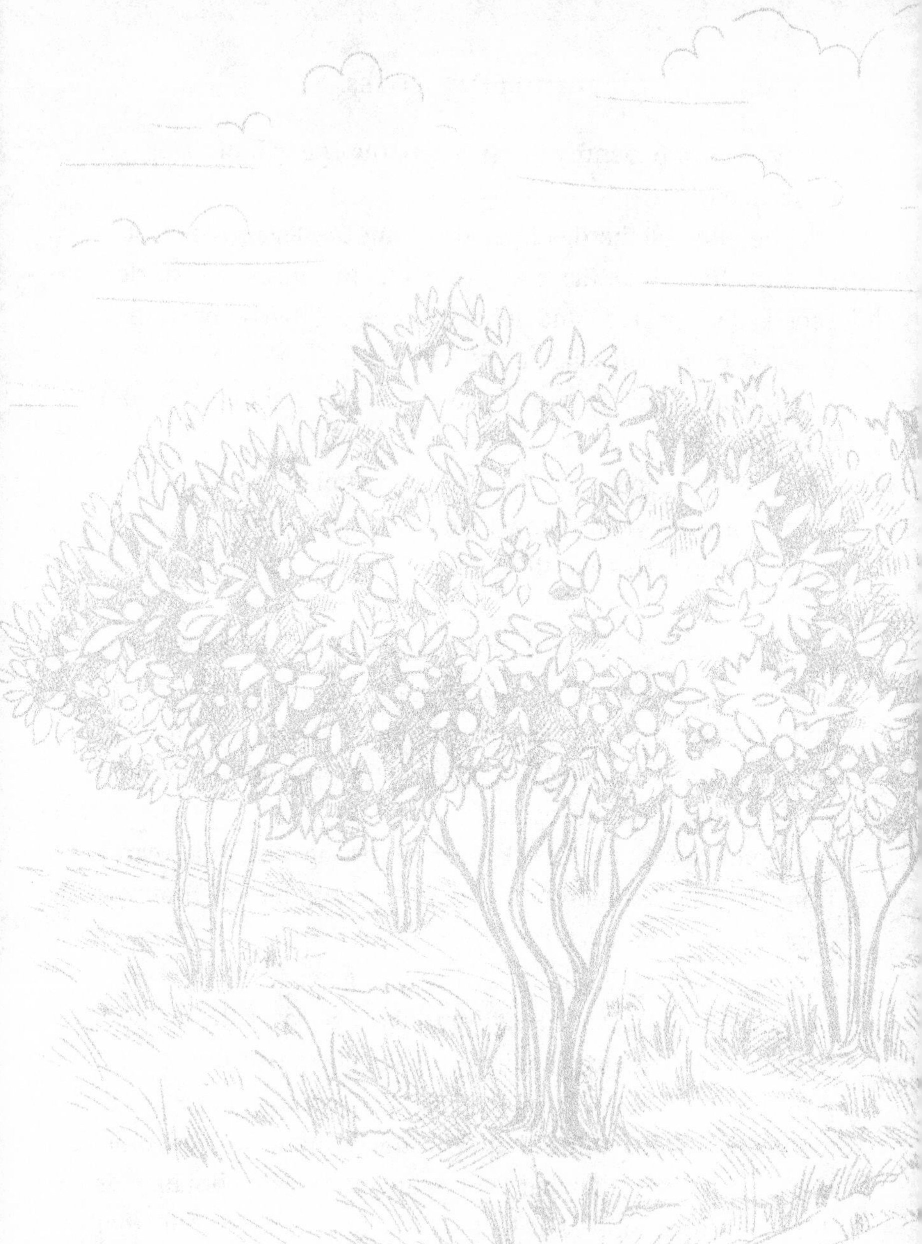

Chapter Five

Wyatt fought to regain his equilibrium after leaving Jenny's house. He'd been knocked off keel the moment he learned a body had been found on Summerlin Groves because the initial reports had been sketchy. Some said a dead body had been found, others said an old skeleton. Either way, he had to be certain Jenny was okay.

He should have reversed gear and sped back to town the instant he confirmed she was alive and well. Instead, he waited in the car until his pulse returned to normal, then made the monumental mistake of getting out to talk with her. Despite everything, Jenny still had the power to trigger a raw, primitive urge to swoop in and protect her.

The discovery of the skeleton was going to be blared all over the evening news, which meant he needed to warn his parents. They shouldn't hear about it from anyone else. It took a while to navigate around the vehicles clogging the narrow rural lane just outside Jenny's grove, but soon he was on the road leading back to town.

Besides, he had other news to tell his parents. He'd been

trapped in this town too long, and an avenue for escape had just appeared on the horizon like a shaft of sunlight breaking through the small-town gloom. Better still, it might even help his mom heal.

The drive to his parents' store was interrupted by a slow-moving train at the railroad crossing a mile outside of town. The nation's largest phosphate mine was right here in Pierce County, so trains carrying freshly mined rock were a common sight. Soon the lumpy gray rocks would be pulverized and mixed with a little nitrogen and potassium to turn them into fertilizer that was sold all over the world.

United Phosphate & Fertilizer was the largest employer in the county, with three thousand people either mining rock, staffing the factory, or working in the office. Could the body in Jenny's tree have been someone who worked at the mine? United Phosphate had been operating in this part of Florida for over a hundred years. Some of their workforce was seasonal, so it was possible a migrant laborer with no family had come here for a few months of work. Once the medical examiner narrowed down the approximate year the guy died, the mine would be the first place to check. Wyatt was friendly with the folks at the mine . . . after all, they'd once offered him a job in Morocco.

Jenny had a lot of nerve to bring up Morocco in the middle of all this. He switched on the radio to think of something else, scrolling through the preset stations, bypassing the ads, except one cheerful voice caught his attention.

"Are you worried that a loved one isn't eating properly?"

He paused, unable to move on to the next station as the advertisement continued.

"Our easy-to-drink, complete meals will give you peace of mind, and your loved one the proper nutrition for a healthy life!"

The ad ended with instructions on how to order the high-calorie drinks. He ought to order a case . . . anything to stop his mom from losing more weight. She claimed to be eating, but he didn't believe her. Now instead of travelling the world in a life of adventure, he monitored how many calories his mother ate and the number of hours she slept.

He jotted the website down on a notepad he kept in his car. He and his dad had tried just about everything to get Donna to eat, but depression was a strange beast neither of them understood. He was still thinking about it as he arrived at his dad's feed and farm supply store ten minutes later.

It was a relief to see both his parents' cars in the parking lot. They didn't actually need his mom's help at the store, but she couldn't be left alone anymore.

A bell dinged as he entered and the dusty scent of cattle feed awakened childhood memories of growing up here. His mom sat at a stool behind the front counter, sorting sales receipts. The cheerful sunflowers embroidered on her sweatshirt were in stark contrast with the gaunt hollows beneath her eyes. She hadn't bothered to shop for new clothes in eighteen months, and still wore tops printed with sunflowers, nesting bluebirds, and American flags. Her goofy clothes had always been her trademark but were now a sad reminder of her former self.

"Hi there, stranger," she said with a hint of a smile.

Relief trickled through him at the sight of that smile, though it would vanish once she heard what he had to report. He peeked his head down the aisles loaded with bags of fertilizer and pesticides.

"Is Dad around?"

"Right here," Ed said as he emerged from the irrigation aisle carrying a box of PVC fittings. Ed's lanky frame had become a little stooped over the past few years, but behind the horn-rimmed glasses his eyes were as kind as ever. "What's up, son?"

There was no point beating around the bush. "You need to know that I got called out to Summerlin Groves on a case this morning."

Donna visibly flinched, while Ed plonked the box of supplies down and went around the counter to join Donna. His eyes went steely as he waited for Wyatt to continue.

This wasn't going to be easy, and he gentled his voice. "A human skeleton was found in a hollowed-out tree trunk at Summerlin Groves, but I don't think Jack had anything to do with it. The medical examiner thinks it's been there for a long time, maybe even decades."

"That doesn't mean Jack couldn't have done it," Donna accused. "Or his crazy dad or crazy granddad."

Ed rubbed Donna's shoulders as he frowned at Wyatt. "Why does stuff like this always happen in that family? They're a bad lot, and always have been."

Wyatt didn't say anything, because, yes, the Summerlins had a wild, cantankerous history, even though Jenny never struck him that way. At the beginning, Jenny seemed pretty much perfect, and he'd overlooked her dubious family when he fell head over heels for her.

Ignoring his instincts had been a mistake. Family mattered, and when his sister stepped into Jack Summerlin's world to facilitate parental visitation, none of her training as a licensed social worker had prepared her for the violence she faced that night.

"Did you see her?" Donna asked. His parents had never been wild about Jenny to begin with, and now her name was anathema.

"Yeah, she was there," he admitted. "We were cordial, but

that's all. Don't worry . . . I won't start things up with her again."

Donna had been hospitalized for depression twice in the months following Lauren's murder, though she'd finally begun slowly stitching the pieces of her life back together. Nevertheless, Wyatt had learned from painful experience that it didn't take much to plunge Donna back beneath a suffocating blanket of despair.

Hopefully, his next bit of news would cheer her up. Donna hated that he carried a gun as part of his job. Working for agricultural law enforcement wasn't nearly as dangerous as when he was in the army, but she still worried.

"Roger Adkins died in office last week," he said, referring to Florida's Commissioner of Agriculture. Technically, Commissioner Adkins had been Wyatt's boss, although he'd never met the man. The Department of Agriculture was based at the state capitol up in Tallahassee. The department oversaw thousands of employees spread across a dozen smaller agencies for farming, ranching, water policy, and consumer affairs.

Wyatt continued, trying not to let his anticipation show. "There are three years left in Adkins's term, and the governor has decided to call a special election in June."

"Why so far off?" his dad asked.

"There will be a primary next month, then plenty of time for a head-to-head campaign between the two top finalists in June. I want to run for it."

The last time Wyatt had run for office had been for senior class president in high school. He'd never considered a career in politics until last week when Commissioner Adkins died of a stroke. For years Wyatt had been frustrated by the shifting political and economic forces that whittled into the livelihood of Florida's farmers and ranchers. It was time to stop grousing about it and *do* something.

"Doesn't it cost a lot of money to run for office?" Ed asked. The Rossiter family was comfortably middle class, but they didn't have a fortune to splash around on a vanity political campaign.

"I won't put much money into the race unless I win the primary, and I'm a long shot." The Commissioner of Agriculture was a stepping-stone to a higher office like governor or the U.S. Senate. It was a coveted job, and everyone who sat in the commissioner's chair for the past fifty years had been a career politician. They were slick, polished candidates with professional campaign advisors and the ability to raise millions in contributions.

Donna sat a little straighter on the stool. "I would love for you to have a good job where you didn't have to carry a gun." She nudged her husband. "Wouldn't you, Ed? I think we should do everything possible to get Wyatt elected."

"It seems an awfully big step," his dad warned. "Where did this come from all of a sudden?"

All of a sudden? A glance around this old store was proof of how sharply agriculture had declined in the state. Wyatt folded his arms and stared out the plate-glass window. "I'm sick to death of watching farms and ranches going under because of regulations imposed by politicians who cater to the city vote. Look at that thing," he said, pointing to a twirling metal rack filled with keychains and video games. "This place used to sell nothing but farm supplies, but now you sell video games to round out the business. The people who run the Department of Agriculture cater to tourism and land developers because that's where the money will come from when they run for higher office. That's not how it's supposed to be. Whoever is in charge of the department should be interested in pastureland, not parking lots."

Donna hopped off the stool to nudge his shoulder. "Oh,

Wyatt, I like that. *Pastureland not parking lots.* Can't you see that on a bumper sticker, Ed?"

"I see a lot of money squandered on a hopeless campaign."

Donna came from around the counter and reached up to tug the collar of Wyatt's uniform a little straighter, her smile reaching all the way to her eyes. It was the brightest he'd seen from her in eighteen months.

"Oh, Wyatt, let's do it!" she said. "You can dust off that law degree and have a nice job in an office building where you aren't getting shot at by cattle rustlers."

He'd only been shot at once, and it wasn't from cattle rustlers, just a drunk ranch hand siphoning gasoline from his employer. Still . . . bullets had been flying that night, and no mother wanted her son in the middle of that.

The odds were stacked against him in the coming race. He had no money or connections, just a solid grounding in agriculture and a desire to make a difference. His odds of winning were low, but he intended to saddle up and fight for it.

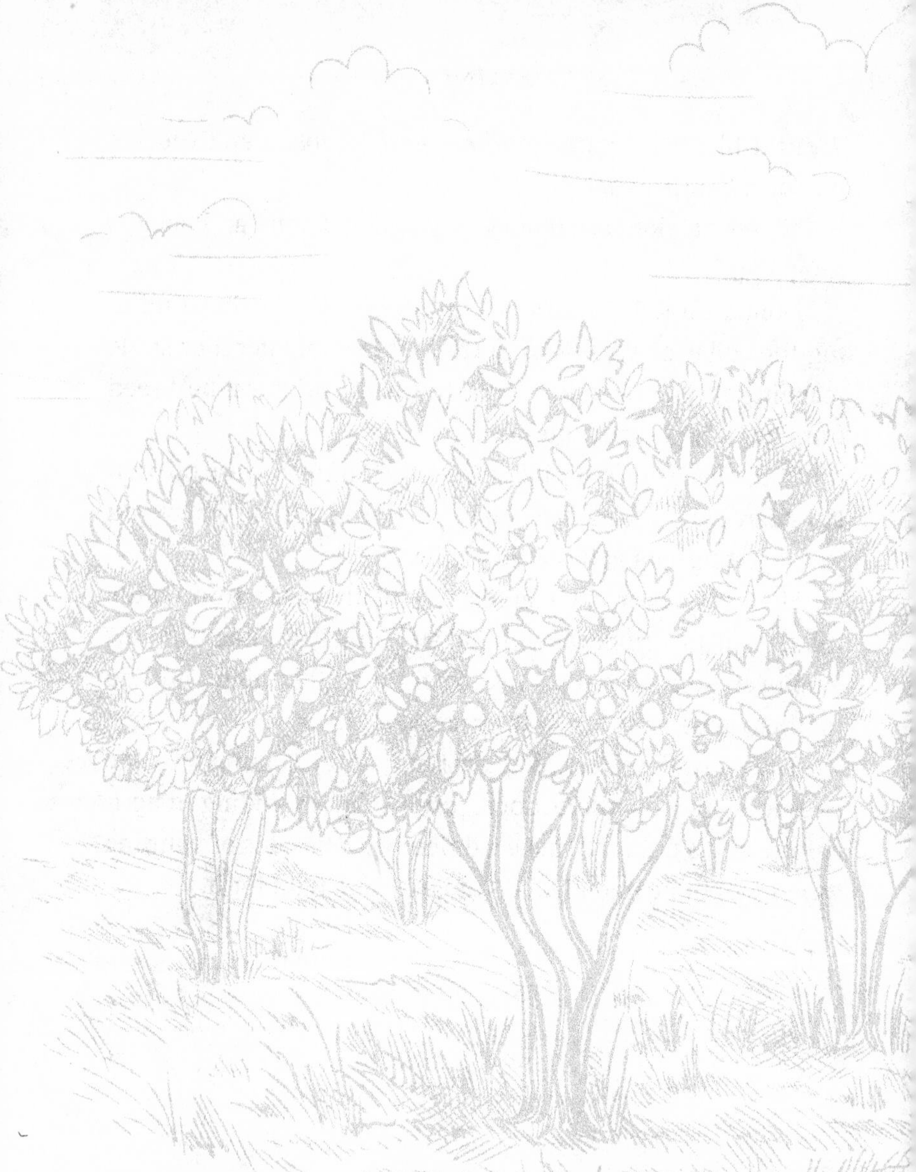

Chapter Six

Orange juice was a three-billion-dollar industry in the United States, and most of the revenue came from the sale of frozen concentrate. It was a highly regulated industry, and Wyatt's job today was to ensure the OJ processing plant was operating within the health and safety guidelines set by the feds. Unfortunately, yesterday the manager of the plant had blocked a surprise inspection, which meant Wyatt had been called in to provide security for the inspectors as they did their job. The food inspectors wore white lab coats and carried test tubes. Wyatt wore a uniform with a gun strapped to his hip. It tended to invoke a little more cooperation.

Wyatt leaned against the side of his cruiser in the parking lot to await the food inspectors, trying not to remember that this was the exact spot where he met Jenny Summerlin two years earlier. She'd been wearing blue jeans, a white tank, and her sun-kissed hair was tied up in a high ponytail. The image was permanently branded on his brain, the epitome of wholesome, healthy sex appeal.

He folded his arms and scowled. It was time to extinguish

the latent attraction that roared back to life the instant he saw her again last week. There had been no news about the identity of the skeleton found on her grove, but the medical examiner's report was due soon.

A little two-door hybrid vehicle pulled into the parking lot, and a perky young food inspector got out.

"Hi, I'm Abbie!" she said, striding across the parking lot with her hand outstretched. She had bouncy blond hair, a bouncy step, and bouncy Mickey Mouse earrings. "Are you the security guy?"

"I'm the security guy," he said, battling a smile at her bright enthusiasm. Abbie proceeded to tell him that she just finished her master's degree in biology and was only two months into her first job as a food inspector.

"The manager was pretty rude yesterday," she said. "He said they'd been inspected last month, but we're allowed to run an inspection four times a year, even if it's in the same quarter."

A full inspection took parts of the factory offline and was an annoying intrusion, but Abbie was right. If the department wanted to do an inspection, they were within their rights. They waited until the other two members of the inspection team arrived, then the four of them headed toward the building.

The processing plant was in a squat building that looked like any other factory except for the three-million-gallon liquid storage silo alongside it. Their inspection followed the same route a truckload of oranges would travel after arriving at the plant. Everything started at the unloading docks, where oranges were sent to conveyor belts for grading and sorting. Then the oranges were rinsed, peels stripped, flesh pulverized, and the juice pasteurized. The juice then went into evaporator tanks to be heated until it was reduced to one-sixth its liquid state. Nothing was wasted. Peel oil was used for cleaning products, and the leftover pulp used for animal feed. All along the way the food inspectors took samples, swabbed surfaces, and measured temperatures.

The manager of the plant wasn't happy to see them. Jed Hawkins had been working at this plant for thirty years, and answering to a pipsqueak like Abbie probably set his teeth on edge.

"We have to stop production and flush the pipelines every time she wants to take a swab," he grumbled. "All three tanks operate under the same conditions. Why can't she just take a sample from *one* line and not all three?"

"Rules are rules," Wyatt said. He understood Jed's aggravation, but enforcing picky health standards was the key to keeping the industry safe.

His cell phone vibrated with an incoming text message, and he took it out to read. The medical examiner had finished her investigation into the skeleton from Jenny's grove and was ready to present her findings. Wyatt needed to report to the sheriff's office at four o'clock this afternoon to go over the report.

Unless the skeleton related to agricultural theft or drug smuggling, this fell under the sheriff's department, not his. He stepped away from the noise of the evaporation tanks to call his departmental secretary and get her to beg off.

"The sheriff says you need to be there," Veronica replied. Wyatt glanced over at Abbie, who looked like she belonged in high school. Jed had calmed down, but Wyatt didn't like leaving her and the other inspectors on their own. More importantly, he didn't want to risk any further entanglement with Jenny or Summerlin Groves.

"Get someone else from the department to go," he instructed his secretary.

"Nope. The sheriff specifically said you needed to be there."

Wyatt would rather sit through a root canal than endure a debriefing about Summerlin Groves, but a disastrous love affair wouldn't derail his professional obligations. He set off for the sheriff's department as soon as another officer from the department arrived to watch over the inspectors. He would be professional, competent, and nobody at the debriefing would have the tiniest hint that this meeting was cracking open a gateway into the most painful episode of his life.

His footsteps echoed down the linoleum corridor in the sheriff's department as he headed to the designated meeting room, where laughter leaked from behind the closed door. He peered through the window slit to ensure he was in the right place before twisting the door handle and stepping inside.

Almost a dozen people crowded around the conference room table. Three deputies, two people from the medical examiner's office, an anthropology professor, and a couple of others he didn't know. Apparently, he'd interrupted an important discussion about college football, but Tommy eventually got around to introducing him to the people he didn't know, all of whom were faculty from the University of Central Florida located an hour away in Orlando. One was an expert in forensic medicine, and the other two were historians.

The Pierce County medical examiner was the only woman in the room. Dressed in a boxy white lab coat, she still looked remarkably feminine with a pink scarf tied around her neck. She smiled and stepped forward to shake Wyatt's hand. "Rebecca Lowenstein," she introduced herself. "We met a few years ago at . . ."

Her sentence trailed off to an awkward halt. Dr. Lowenstein handled the crime scene where his sister had been murdered, so their previous acquaintance hadn't been pleasant.

"I remember," he said. "You were a real professional that time. My family and I appreciated it."

Dr. Lowenstein gave him a sympathetic smile before turning to connect her laptop to an overhead projector. Wyatt claimed the last remaining chair at the table, still wondering why he'd been invited to this meeting.

"We've got a doozy," Dr. Lowenstein said as her first slide was projected onto the whiteboard. It was a wide-angle photograph of the skeleton's disarticulated bones arranged on an examination table. Cleaned of dirt and debris, the skeleton looked starkly different from the mud-encrusted remains he'd last seen curled up in the tree.

"I'll get straight to the point," Dr. Lowenstein said. "This skeleton is a woman who was approximately fifty years old at the time of her death."

Dr. Lowenstein reported that the woman had been Caucasian, and the condition of her pelvic bones indicated that she never bore children. She was probably fully clothed at the time she went into the tree, but aside from a few hooks, buttons, and shoe material, her clothing had completely disintegrated.

The next slide on the screen showed a closeup of the jaw and skull. "This woman's dental work is unlike anything that we use today," Dr. Lowenstein continued. "Her fillings and bridge work were common in the mid-twentieth century, but completely obsolete by the 1980s. Based on her dental work and the brittleness of her bones, my hunch is that this woman died in the early 1950s."

The next slide was a closeup of some tattered leather shoes. "These are a pair of round-toed pumps with a two-inch heel. They are consistent with styles of the 1950s. The word

'Trevolina' is stamped on the insole of both shoes. The brand was sold only in the Soviet Union."

She tapped the keyboard and another image came on the screen. It was a ladies' watch with a delicate face and a filigree metal wristband. "This watch was found in the cavity of the tree," Dr. Lowenstein said. "It's an Alpina watch, made in Switzerland, and is also consistent with the mid-twentieth century. The clasp was fastened, so it was probably on her wrist until the body became skeletonized and pulled apart. The band is gold-plated over stainless steel. It's not a cheap watch, but not terribly expensive, either."

A young deputy raised his hand. "Can we assume the motive wasn't robbery if whoever stuffed her in the tree left the watch?"

"You're assuming it was a murder," Dr. Lowenstein said. "I wasn't able to find a cause of death. There was no bullet wound or trauma to the bones. She could have been strangled or suffocated or drowned, but those things don't show up on skeletons this old."

"So no cause of death," Tommy stated.

"I'm afraid not," the doctor replied. "All the clothing has disintegrated with the exception of five resin buttons and six hook-and-eye closures, probably from a brassiere."

She clicked to another slide showing a closeup of yellow buttons and the bits of tiny, rusted metal hooks. Sad remnants of what had once been a woman left abandoned in a tree hollow.

"At this point I'm going to turn the presentation back to Sheriff Caleb Eckert," the doctor said, stepping aside as Caleb took her place. Caleb Eckert had held the top job in the sheriff's department for thirty years. He had the scowling expression of a bulldog as he looked at the professors from UCF.

"The next part of the discussion is being held tightly

under wraps," Caleb said. "Everything said for the rest of the meeting must remain confidential. It can't be discussed with your students or assistants or your family . . . and *especially* not the press."

Wyatt perked up, suspecting they were about to discuss the jeweled egg. It was the most baffling part of the entire case, but too crucial to hide from the investigators.

"This was the only other thing found in the cypress tree," Caleb said as he tapped the keypad to bring up a full-color photograph of the stunning, jewel-encrusted egg. There was a collective gasp from around the table.

"This egg was found with the skeleton," Caleb said. "We've had two jewelers independently examine it, and both believe it to be a genuine Fabergé egg."

A history professor leaned forward. "Aren't those incredibly rare? Like only a few dozen in the world?"

Caleb's voice was matter-of-fact. "According to one of the jewelers, fifty imperial eggs were made, although many were lost after the Russian revolution. Every few decades another one turns up, but eight are still missing. The jewelers think this may be one of them. Based on sales of recent Fabergé eggs, the experts predict it would bring between 35 and 50 million dollars at auction."

Fifty million? Wyatt gazed at the brilliant, high-resolution image of the egg. Professionally cleaned and illuminated, it was even more dazzling than when he'd seen it nestled in a dishtowel-lined cereal bowl.

The second photograph Caleb showed was a shocker. It showed the egg opened lengthwise to reveal a surprise in the interior. It contained a scarlet eagle with its wings raised and extended, its head tipped back, and a sapphire for an eye. It was reminiscent of the eagle emblazoned on the imperial Russian coat of arms. The inner shell was coated in a layer of royal blue enamel to simulate the night sky, with tiny diamonds to serve as stars.

The archaeologist gave a low whistle of admiration, and despite himself, even Wyatt was dazzled by the unexpected charm inside the egg. Did this treasure make the case more or less likely to have been a murder? No sane person would knowingly dump a body with a treasure that valuable . . . unless it had somehow been hidden on the woman? Her clothing had deteriorated. So might a cloth handbag or purse. The egg was five inches tall. It could have been overlooked if the woman was hiding it. He gazed at the photograph, trying to think of any other explanation than murder for her presence in the hollow of that tree.

The group gathered at the table batted around speculation about how she got there. Some thought she might have been an illegal art smuggler trying to sell the egg on the black market. Others speculated she might have been a high-end antiques dealer . . . but that theory was quickly dismissed. A wealthy antiques dealer would have had relatives or associates to raise an alarm about the missing egg.

"Could the woman be a descendant of the Romanovs?" one of the history professors asked. "Maybe we could get a DNA test?"

Dr. Lowenstein nodded. "Her teeth could probably yield DNA, but we'd need to find a Romanov willing to provide a reference sample. We'd also need the sheriff to fund some expensive DNA sequencing."

"Nope," Caleb said. "Not yet, anyway. I don't want word of this egg getting out and stirring up the crazies and the fortune hunters until we've exhausted the other possibilities."

"Have we asked one of the Summerlins if anyone in their family mysteriously dropped out of sight in the 1950s?" Dr. Lowenstein asked.

Tommy's tone was flat. "We asked; she won't answer."

Wyatt shifted uneasily. The "she" was obviously Jenny, the only Summerlin left to ask. Jack left a young son who was being raised by his maternal grandparents, but there weren't any other cousins or aunts or uncles. Suddenly, he felt the gaze of every person in the room on him.

"Wyatt," Caleb said in an artificially bright voice. "You know Jenny Summerlin better than anyone here. Maybe you could get her to talk?"

Every officer in the Pierce County Sheriff's Department knew of his history with the Summerlins, and it was surprising they'd even ask. "I'm not too keen on getting roped into anything to do with that orange grove," he said tersely. "Someone should consult with the HR Department at the United Phosphate mine. They were a big employer in the mid-twentieth century, and the dead woman could have been a seasonal office worker. Or married to someone who worked at the plant."

"But why would such a woman have a Fabergé egg?" Tommy asked.

It was a good question. Most of the people employed by United Phosphate were miners or factory workers, but there were office jobs, too. Phosphate was a billion-dollar industry, and the company used to boast about how their fertilizer made farms all over the world flourish. Growing environmental concerns and the unpopularity of strip-mining had caused the company to lower their profile, but they were still a thriving enterprise.

The sheriff agreed to ask the HR Department at the mine to search for employees who dropped off the radar in the 1950s, although it was a long shot. The quality of the woman's watch made it unlikely she had been a migrant laborer.

"Maybe a migrant prostitute," one of the professors tossed out.

"And someone paid her with that egg." A younger deputy snickered, and Wyatt shot him a surly glare.

"Show a little respect, please."

"Uh-oh, Wyatt the Weeper is on the march," Tommy said with a nudge, while Wyatt gave a terse grimace of acknowledgment. The problem with growing up in a small town was that it was impossible to outrun his past. Things he'd said or done decades ago were still ripe for teasing.

"Wyatt the Weeper?" Dr. Lowenstein asked in bemusement.

"Never mind," Wyatt said. "Can you show the slide with the woman's teeth? There are only a couple of dentists in town, and they might have records."

Dr. Lowenstein shook her head. "I've already asked around. No one in town has files from that far back."

The history professor came to his aid. "It's not too hard to do a search through ancestry databases or census records to search for immigrants from Europe who lived in this area during the years in question. I can help you out."

The purpose of the college professors being in this meeting suddenly became clear. Historians were good at piecing old information together based on fragmentary evidence. One of the professors offered to have his class search government records looking for female immigrants from Eastern Europe or the Soviet Union to this area during the mid-twentieth century. The other historian would search police archives in the surrounding counties, looking for old missing persons reports.

The meeting broke up after thirty minutes, although Tommy asked to speak with Wyatt privately. They went upstairs to the second floor of the building, where the Department of Agriculture had offices for eight employees. Wyatt's office was a plain room with a nice view of U.S. Route 17 out the window.

Like most government offices, it was furnished with a fake woodgrain desk, a credenza for files, and a couple of chairs. The walls were plain and the nubby beige carpet had seen better days. The only hint of personality was the cactus garden in a hand-thrown pottery dish on the windowsill.

It had been a gift from Jenny on their one-month dating anniversary. He had a brown thumb but she laughingly reported that scrubby cacti were impossible to kill, and his office needed a spark of personality.

She'd been right on both counts. The cactus garden was a painful reminder of Jenny and the world that might have been if they had eloped to Morocco. His mother's illness kept him trapped in Amity, but the cactus garden represented an escape, wings into a different world, far away from this dead-end hometown. Each time he started carrying it to the dumpster to finally get rid of it, he ended up turning around and bringing it back.

So here it sat, a bittersweet memento of the best three months of his life. When Jenny gave it to him, could she have had any idea it would someday come to represent all his broken aspirations?

Wyatt took a seat on the other side of the desk while Tommy flipped open a file. "Caleb is driving me pretty hard on this case," Tommy said, a hint of stress showing around his eyes. "I hate to ask again, but you're our best shot at getting Jenny to cooperate."

Wyatt glanced away. He'd figured this was coming, and Tommy's voice was respectful but pleading as he continued.

"Summerlin Groves has two outbuildings that are crammed to the rafters with junk hoarded by her grandfather.

The lady in the tree was probably connected to Summerlin Groves, and there might be something left on the property that will lead us to her identity. Maybe old farm records or appointment calendars. The judge says we don't have enough evidence to get a search warrant, so we need Jenny's permission to get onto the property. You could persuade her to let us poke around a little."

"No."

"Come on, Wyatt."

Thinking about Jenny was a torment he didn't need. They had both acted badly during the swift implosion of their relationship. He more than she, which was why everything to do with the grove remained raw with shame.

Wyatt leaned back in the chair and crossed his arms. "If you need Jenny's help, you'll have a better shot at getting her to cooperate than me. Sorry, Tom. I can't help."

He suddenly had another reason to win the race to become the next Commissioner of Agriculture: Moving to Tallahassee would get him away from Jenny Summerlin, her grove, and the danger she still represented to his heart.

Chapter Seven

Jenny headed to the west field to continue pulling the stumps of the trees she'd burned down earlier in the month. The cinders had been cleared away, leaving only the chore of stump removal. Orange trees didn't have much of a root system, so Hemingway scraped a few inches of the topsoil away from the stump, then she wrapped a chain around it, then the all-terrain vehicle pulled the roots free of the sandy soil.

Ever since the skeleton had been found, investigators from the sheriff's department had been trying to poke around the grove and pick her brain. She couldn't let them onto her land until the west field was completely cleared, but that didn't stop her from wondering who the woman in the cypress tree might have been. Jenny devoured every word of the medical examiner's report in yesterday's newspaper. She and Hemingway had been tossing around theories as they pulled stumps.

"Did your grandfather have a girlfriend?" Hemingway asked.

"He had a lot of girlfriends, but he liked them young," Jenny confirmed. Her grandmother died of cancer when Gus was in his early thirties. The lady in the tree was at least fifty. She would have been around twenty years older than her grandfather at the time, so a romantic link was unlikely.

Hemingway scraped more dirt from the base of a stump. "Could she have worked for him? Like a bookkeeper or something?"

"Maybe," she said, securing a chain around the remnants of the tree. The Summerlins had been poor for generations until her grandfather turned the family fortune around through clever grove management and stock market investments. A bookkeeper would make sense because although Gus was smart, he didn't have a formal education. As he accumulated money, he built the front porch and upgraded the electrical wiring in the old farmhouse with his own two hands. Later, he built two supply sheds and an actual fallout shelter during the Cold War paranoia of the 1950s.

"I don't think she worked for him," Jenny said after a little consideration. "Bookkeepers simply don't carry around Fabergé eggs."

Hemingway mounted the ATV and slowly advanced, dragging the chained stump forward, the ropey roots flinging a spray of sandy dirt as the root ball came free of the soil. By the time they moved to the next stump, Hemingway was ready with another theory.

"Your grandfather was a hoarder," he said. "He built two sheds to store the junk he collected from flea markets and yard sales. What if he found that Fabergé egg at a yard sale from someone who didn't know its value?"

It could happen. Jenny had once heard about an original copy of the Declaration of Independence hidden inside the frame of an ugly painting bought at a garage sale. It was the best theory so far.

"Maybe the lady was someone he hired to appraise it," Jenny said. "The lady figured out its value and tried to steal it. Gus was hot-tempered and wouldn't have tolerated anyone stealing from him."

"This still doesn't explain how she ended up dead in the tree *with* the egg," Hemingway said.

"Maybe she was hiding? Maybe Gus caught her red-handed trying to steal the egg and he came after her. She hid in the tree waiting for him to leave the grove."

"Hid until she died?" Hemingway asked skeptically.

"Maybe a snake got to her when she was hiding," Jenny said. Florida had its share of poisonous snakes, and if one bit the lady in the tree, it wouldn't take long for her to die in there.

If Gus legally bought that egg at a flea market or yard sale, she and Hemingway would be entitled to keep it. The last time an egg like that had gone up at auction, it fetched $33 million. After auction fees and taxes, she and Hemingway would probably clear ten million dollars each.

She squatted down to wrap a chain around the next stump. What would she do with all that money? At the very least, she'd hire someone to yank these stumps for her.

The honk of a truck startled her and she dropped the chain, turning around to spot a television news truck idling behind the gate at the entrance to the grove.

"Hey!" a female called out through cupped hands. "Can we come inside to get a little film about where you found that skeleton?"

It was Penny Danvers, a reporter for the local news station. It was probably uncomfortable to walk on a gravel road in high heels and a snazzy suit, but it looked like Penny was ready for an on-camera interview.

Hemingway handed her the shovel. "I'll take care of this," he muttered, bounding down the front drive toward the reporter.

The news crew was a nerve-racking invasion of her privacy. It was a miracle that none of the people who extracted the skeleton last week raised any questions about this burned acre. If the local newscast included video footage of this part of the grove, thousands of people would see it and someone might figure out what she and Hemmingway did.

It probably wasn't a crime. The state would howl about it, but most citrus growers would do exactly what she did if they found a case of the highly contagious citrus disease taking root in their grove. A smart grower would kill the infected trees immediately, then stake out a perimeter and burn everything nearby in case the infection had spread.

That wasn't how the state wanted it handled. According to Florida law, trees infected with citrus canker were to be reported to the Department of Agriculture, who would quarantine the grove and cut down everything within several acres of the outbreak. Given where the infection hit on the edge of the west field, that meant she'd lose most of her grove.

There was no cure for citrus canker. It caused ugly brown splotches on the leaves and fruit, then the tree would drop its leaves and die. She had to act quickly or the entire grove would die. She'd burned the infected tree and a large swath around it to protect the rest of the grove.

The problem was now solved. Maybe it was just that she was optimistic by nature, but even after the catastrophe of Jack's death and Wyatt's abandonment, she was going to be okay. Thirty acres was a lot for two people to manage on their own, but she and Hemingway had done it, and she was proud.

The odd thing was that the harder she worked, the happier she became. She and Hemingway had sweat bullets to keep this grove up and running, and it had become the greatest satisfaction of her life. It was proof that nothing was impossible. The immovable object could be moved. The tide could be turned. Hard work would be rewarded if she simply refused to yield to despair.

The past eighteen months had been filled with hardships and close calls. She came within a week of having the grove repossessed because she'd neglected to pay her property taxes. Jack had been an accountant at the phosphate mine and handled the grove's paperwork, so she never realized she'd missed several payments until an anonymous note appeared in her mailbox shortly before the deadline.

That note saved her from financial ruin and she often wondered who put it in her box. That last-minute note from a good Samaritan proved there were still decent people in the world. Most people were good, even if she'd seen too much of the bad side.

Hemingway came striding back toward her. "They're gone?" she asked.

"They grumbled, but they're gone."

She nodded and leaned down to secure the chain on another stump. The less attention Summerlin Groves got, the better. The McAllisters had *finally* consented to allow her a visit with Jack's six-year-old son. She hadn't seen Sam since before the murders, and time was growing short for her to reestablish a relationship with the boy before he forgot her.

The first time she tried to see Sam was only a few weeks after that terrible night. The McAllisters had blocked her telephone number, so she drove out to their ranch in hope of discussing the issue like rational adults.

It hadn't worked. Kent McAllister called the police and

threatened to take out a restraining order against her if she tried to see his grandson again. The restraining order never materialized, but there had been no thaw in her relationship with the McAllisters until last evening when a telephone call from Mr. McAllister tersely agreed to a brief meeting with Sam this weekend. She had no idea why he changed his mind but was too grateful to question it.

She and Hemingway successfully pulled two more stumps and then Hemingway let out a curse, and she followed his gaze.

The news crew *hadn't* left, and were erecting a scaffold right outside her fence. In all likelihood, they intended to take a birds-eye film of her grove, meaning they'd capture the ugly scorch mark in the west field.

"Are they allowed to do that?" Hemingway asked.

Jenny didn't know. They weren't allowed on her land without permission, but did the law allow them to build a scaffold to spy on her?

It didn't matter; she needed to make them leave. She hopped on the back of the ATV and Hemingway gunned the engine, carrying them down the front drive quickly. They parked the ATV on her side of the locked farm gate.

"You can't set that thing up here," Jenny said, gesturing to the scaffolding that was already ten feet high and perilously close to the narrow county road.

There were three people on the news crew. Two men in blue jeans and T-shirts, and Penny Danvers, the on-air reporter, whose sleek chestnut hair was arranged in a perfect coif that ran along her jaw. Penny's voracious ambition could devour half the state of Florida, and Jenny had dubbed her "Bad Penny" years ago.

"This is public land and we have a right to use it," Penny said.

"It's a safety hazard," Jenny retorted, mimicking the way Wyatt sounded whenever he spotted people doing something risky. "People come barreling down this road at fifty-five miles per hour. You're creating a visual distraction and it's dangerous."

Penny's smile was insincere. "Then let us on your land to film. If anyone is causing a safety hazard, it's you."

"I am entitled to a reasonable expectation of privacy on my own land, so I'm warning you not to shoot anything," Jenny said.

"Shoot anything?" Penny asked. "I guess your family knows all about shooting things. Have you gotten your guns back? Because I don't think a felon like you is allowed to have them."

Jenny was too stunned to summon a reply, but Hemingway came to her rescue.

"Jenny's not a felon," he said in a casual tone. "She plea-bargained down to a lesser charge."

Jenny kept her chin up, even though last year's brush with the law over a trespasser on her property still smarted. The gun charges against her had been completely unreasonable, but an aggressive district attorney came at her with everything in his arsenal. And yes, she had been in danger of going to jail on a technicality until someone in the county government talked sense into the D.A. She was lucky to escape with probation and a slap on the wrist.

Legal threats could go both ways. The United States was the most litigious country in the developed world, and threats of a lawsuit tended to bring corporations into line.

"If you broadcast images of my grove without my permission, I will sue you and your television station to kingdom come."

It was a bluff. Jenny didn't have the spare cash to consult a lawyer, let alone file a lawsuit, but she must have sounded convincing because Penny conferred with her two camera guys, and a few minutes later the men returned to the truck . . . but left the scaffolding.

"We'll be back," Penny said.

"Bad Pennies always turn up when you least expect them," Hemingway taunted. Penny's glare turned poisonous before she turned heel and stalked back to the news van.

"I have no idea what you ever saw in that woman," Jenny said.

Hemingway flashed one of his wickedly dashing grins. "She's actually a lot of fun. Penny can juggle shot glasses while mildly buzzed and improvise poetry in iambic pentameter. She's smart, determined, and ruthless."

"She seems like the kind of woman who'd sell her firstborn child for a promotion."

Hemingway scoffed. "Penny would sell her first, second, and thirdborn if it would get her a promotion to New York or London."

"Is that why you broke up with her? Penny's ambition?"

He shook his head. "I broke up with her because she cheats at cards. People who cheat when the stakes are low will never stick by your side when you need to storm the beaches at Normandy."

Jenny felt like she'd been storming the beaches of Normandy for the past eighteen months. Penny and her crew left the scaffolding in place, an indication their retreat was only temporary. They were likely to come back unless Jenny could figure out a way to scare them off permanently.

WYATT FELT lousy about his blunt refusal to help the sheriff's office make inroads with Jenny about the skeleton, but that body was dumped on the grove long before Jenny was born. She probably didn't know anything about it, although Wyatt knew who might.

Millicent Hawkins had been his fourth-grade teacher at Amity Elementary. In a town this small, half the people in Amity had Mrs. Hawkins as their fourth-grade teacher, and the other half *wished* they'd had Mrs. Hawkins.

Mrs. Hawkins grew up in this town and had a long memory. He couldn't guess her age, but everyone knew that once upon a time, Millicent Hawkins had been courted by the richest young man in town. Max Wakefield was heir to the United Phosphate mining fortune, and while in high school he and Millicent had been an item and foolishly believed that love could conquer anything.

The Wakefields might have been rich and powerful, but in the 1950s, a romance between the white son of a prominent family and the Black daughter of a postman wasn't going to be universally popular. Max's parents warned him against dallying with Millicent, and yet Max ignored their warnings. He and Millicent sat at the counter of the soda fountain in town. He even took her to the senior prom. Florida wasn't the Deep South, and most people could tolerate that sort of thing, even if it wasn't celebrated.

No one ever knew what caused their romance to fade, but after high school Max went to India to work on a charity mission before eventually coming home to attend Yale University. While he'd been gone, Millicent graduated from Bethune-Cookman College over in Daytona Beach. She became a teacher and married a dentist, then a few years later Max married the daughter of a stockbroker.

Millicent never said a bad word about Max Wakefield,

even as he climbed in the world of politics, first serving as a congressman and now in his fourth term as a U.S. senator. When the senator and Millicent Hawkins were young and in love, they spent plenty of time on Wakefield land, which bordered the west side of Summerlin Groves.

Which meant that Mrs. Hawkins might know something about the skeleton in the tree.

He headed to the town square to meet with her. Amity had once been among the wealthiest small towns in Florida, which was still evident by the town square with its statuesque courthouse and a copper-topped bandstand. Quaint, bow-fronted shops lined the east side of the square, while the adjacent street had a row of grand old Victorian homes. All of it had been built on fortunes made from oranges and phosphate.

Now the orange industry had competition from Brazil, and the phosphate industry competed with Morocco. The stately town square was showing its age. The sprawling Victorian homes had been subdivided into duplexes or turned into private businesses. The grandest of them was a bed and breakfast, one was a funeral home, and the two-story Victorian painted a sunny yellow was a dentist's office. After Dr. Hawkins retired, a new dentist moved into his office, but the Hawkins family still lived upstairs on the second floor.

Wyatt's footsteps thudded on the front porch steps as he approached the door. He pressed the doorbell to their unit and waited, eyeing the porch with a critical stare. It was worrisome to see old people navigating all these steps. He didn't even like ringing the bell because Mrs. Hawkins was liable to come downstairs to answer it herself.

She did. "Hello, Wyatt," she said fondly. Mrs. Hawkins was at least seventy, but still attractive. A spray of wrinkles fanned from her eyes when she smiled, adding to her air of genteel dignity.

He nodded to the potted geraniums. "You might want to cover those," he said. "I hear a cold front is on the way."

She nodded and held the door open for him. "Alvin says he's going to take care of it tonight," she said in reference to her husband. He was still "Dr. Hawkins" to Wyatt, just like she was still Mrs. Hawkins. He followed her up the staircase to her second-story home, where the original hardwood floors gleamed with a fresh coat of varnish. As always, it smelled like lavender potpourri. Mrs. Hawkins always loved lavender. She had a framed poster of the lavender fields of France in her fourth-grade classroom, and now that same poster held a place of honor over the mantel.

He was glad Dr. Hawkins wasn't here. This conversation might get awkward, and it would be easier without her husband nearby.

"You heard about that skeleton they found at Summerlin Groves?"

She nodded. "Have they figured out who it is?"

"Still looking." He filled her in about the few details he was at liberty to share. "I know that you were sometimes over at the Wakefield place during the fifties. Do you remember an older woman who went missing around that time?"

"The Wakefields had a lot of help," she said. "Housekeepers, lawn people, cooks. They were all Black. My own mother worked as their cook for twenty years. The Wakefields entertained a lot, so there were always lots of people around. High-flying people. Governors and movie stars. Princess Margaret came once. Those were the only times they asked me to stay away."

His mouth tightened. Society had come a long way, but a

woman as old as Mrs. Hawkins had living memories of being asked to leave the room or drink from another water fountain.

"Now don't you frown like that," Mrs. Hawkins said. "Karl Wakefield was very progressive for his time."

Karl was the senator's father and had been the wealthiest man in the state at the time. He died sometime in the 1980s, but he was internationally renowned as a philanthropist and even did a stint as the American ambassador to the United Nations. Mrs. Hawkins continued to defend the old man's memory.

"Old Mr. Wakefield was never a racist," she insisted. "He was a real gentleman and had lots of ideas about how the downtrodden should be lifted up and how the state had a duty to help the working people."

"That's because he was a communist," Wyatt pointed out. According to the history books, it was why he'd lost his appointment to the U.N. during the red scare of the 1950s. Karl might not have been an official member of the communist party, but his admiration for the Soviet Union wasn't something he ever denied.

Mrs. Hawkins was nonchalant about old Mr. Wakefield's political views. "He grew up in the 1920s when it was fashionable to be a communist." She leaned forward and lowered her voice to a conspiratorial whisper. "He was named after Karl Marx. His family got driven out of Russia before the revolution because they were communists. They changed their name from Vaykfildov to Wakefield, and never looked back." She smiled and straightened back up. "Anyway, being a communist in the early part of the twentieth century meant that you were a free thinker and cared about the little people. It meant that you didn't think people like me had to ride in the back of the bus."

Wyatt shifted uneasily. "Karl still didn't think you were good enough for his son."

Mrs. Hawkins gave him a gentle smack on his knee. "If Max hadn't split with me and gone to India, I never would have met my husband, so don't get teary-eyed over me, Wyatt the Weeper," she said, and they both laughed.

The site of his greatest humiliation happened in Mrs. Hawkins's fourth-grade classroom, and it haunted him to this day.

She used to read to the entire class after lunch. Mrs. Hawkins was convinced that good books could open a world of possibilities to children, and over that fourth-grade year they'd gone on all sorts of adventures as she read to them each day.

Charlotte's Web was twenty-two chapters, and she read a chapter to the class each day. Her rendition of the novel was masterful. Mrs. Hawkins could switch tones and voices with each line of dialogue, perfectly capturing the hopeful innocence of the farm girl, the brash cleverness of the rat, and the wild emotions of poor Wilbur the pig.

But Charlotte? Mrs. Hawkins used her own voice for Charlotte. It was fitting. Charlotte possessed a gentle, timeless wisdom layered over a core of steadfast strength. Each afternoon Wyatt looked forward to another chapter of *Charlotte's Web*.

It was always after lunch when Mrs. Hawkins read to them, and most of the kids laid their heads on their desk while she read. The room was darkened, and Wyatt was swept along with the story as the farm animals engaged in their improbable adventures.

Charlotte wasn't supposed to die. That wasn't the end he'd been waiting for. It took him completely by surprise when the wise, wonderful Charlotte gracefully slipped away as death claimed her.

He started crying.

He wasn't the only one. There were plenty of other sniffles in the classroom as it became obvious that Charlotte was going to perish after performing her great, selfless act of love, but Wyatt was the only boy caught blubbering. He tried to hide it, but it didn't work. His cover was blown the moment his gulping sniffle echoed in the suddenly quiet classroom.

So. Wyatt the Weeper.

The taunt was slung around his neck in the school hallways and in the lunchroom and on the bus ride home. The name followed him into middle school and high school. He was the best receiver on the varsity football team, and it wasn't unusual to hear people calling out from the stands, "Throw it to the Weeper!" Someone slipped it into the high school yearbook. The origin of the nickname was lost on a lot of people, but Mrs. Hawkins had been there that day. She remembered.

He cleared his throat and looked at Mrs. Hawkins. "I know you've always been a tough lady, but Senator Wakefield was a fool to let you go." *A racist fool*, he silently thought, though Mrs. Hawkins's intuition was sharp enough to read his mind.

"Look me in the eye, Wyatt," Mrs. Hawkins ordered, a note of steel in her voice. "Senator Wakefield is a good man. Leaving me behind wasn't easy for him, and I don't think he ever patched things up with his father for making him leave me. It was a different time, and I don't blame him for anything. Do you hear me? The two years I spent on Max Wakefield's arm are something I will never regret, but it ended. Most teenage infatuations do, and that's all it was."

"And you don't have any idea who that lady in the cypress tree was?"

Mrs. Hawkins shrugged. "They say she was a white lady, so that rules out the help on the Wakefield estate. And aside from Max and his family, I didn't mingle with a whole lot of white people back then."

Mrs. Hawkins would never lie, but her statement wasn't a definitive denial, either. She hadn't wavered from her calm, self-assured gentleness, so that meant she either truly didn't know who the lady might have been . . . or she had good reasons not to reveal it.

Chapter Eight

Jenny needed to learn if she had the right to stop a journalist from taking photographs of her grove, but asking the sheriff wasn't an option. There hadn't been a murder in Pierce County for thirty-five years before the night Jack went crazy, and Sheriff Eckert still resented having his pristine track record broken. Then there was the incident when Jenny fired a rifle to scare a trespasser off her land. Sheriff Eckert overreacted, and she was still on probation because of it. Now he was angry over her delayed reporting of the Fabergé egg, and she couldn't risk letting anyone learn what she was *really* hiding on her grove.

That meant Senator Wakefield was the best place to turn for help. Sometimes living next door to the most powerful family in the state had its advantages. Of course, "next door" meant a mile down a rural county lane, but that didn't stop their families from becoming entwined over the generations despite their different stations in life.

The Summerlins were salt-of-the-earth farmers, while the Wakefields were high-flying jetsetters who loved politics, business, and the limelight. Despite his wealth and prestige, Senator Max Wakefield had a folksy manner that made him popular both in Florida and on the national stage. His friendship with the Summerlins went back a long way. He grew up hunting and fishing with Jenny's grandfather, and even stood as godfather to both her and Jack.

The drive through the sprawling pastureland surrounding the Wakefield estate was a balm to Jenny's spirit. A person could drive through miles of this land and never realize it was owned by the Wakefields because they never boasted about their wealth. Some people assumed the Wakefields got rich off of land and cattle, but it was really their stake in the phosphate mine that made them rich.

It used to be called the Wakefield Phosphate Mine back when it was founded in 1890. After the environmentalists started coming after them, they renamed it United Phosphate & Fertilizer, which had a much more humanitarian sound to it. As the Wakefield family rose in the American political scene, the phosphate mine was a millstone around their necks. Open pit mining didn't project the image old Karl Wakefield wanted for his family's dynasty. He sold the mine decades ago to a multinational conglomerate, though everyone in central Florida remembered who once owned that mine. It had paid for high schools, hospitals, and an art museum that was the envy of cities five times the size of sleepy little Amity, Florida.

She parked her truck in front of Wakefield Manor, a sprawling country house that looked like it had been plucked from eighteen-century England. The honey-limestone walls were enhanced by a red tiled roof, mullioned windows, and a massive walnut front door. A kennel with thirty purebred English foxhounds was around back, and they yapped vigorously as Jenny crossed to the rear entrance of the manor.

The senator answered the door himself. He was seventy-five years old but still looked handsome and fit with a barrel chest and perfect posture.

"Jenny," his voice boomed as he wrapped her in a bear hug. "How's my favorite goddaughter?"

She returned his hug with affection. The senator was probably the person who had been looking out for her ever since the terrible night of the murders, even though he denied being the person who alerted her about the unpaid property taxes in the nick of time. It was the sort of benevolent, grandfatherly thing he'd been doing for her all her life.

He led her to the living room filled with comfortable leather seating. Photographs on the end tables showed various members of the Wakefield family posed alongside presidents and movie stars, and the painting over the fireplace was an original Rembrandt. The only thing that looked out of place was the Kashmiri tapestry hanging beside the bookshelf, a memento of the senator's time serving as a missionary in India.

"Anything new about that skeleton found on your land?" the senator asked as he handed her a glass of lemonade.

"They say it's a middle-aged woman who has probably been in there since sometime in the 1950s."

He nodded. "Anything else?"

The senator probably had enough clout to get all sorts of inside information, but did he know about the Fabergé egg? So far, its existence had been withheld by the sheriff and she was still sworn to secrecy.

"Not that I've heard, but people keep trying to nose around my grove."

He cocked his head. "What do you mean, 'nose around'?"

"Reporters have tried to get onto the property even though I posted a sign against trespassing. They set up a scaffold right outside the front gate and are threatening to come back to film a story so they can milk that skeleton for TV ratings. It seems like an invasion of privacy. Is there anything you can do?"

Instead of answering her, the senator gave a weary sigh. "I'm worried about you all alone out there. Don't you ever want to see something of the world beside the inside of an orange crate? I thought you wanted to spend a year in Italy after college. Whatever happened to that?"

"It was the year my grandfather experimented with pineapples," Jenny said and winced at the memory. Pineapples were a lot of work, and when their ten-acre crop began to fail, she cancelled the trip to Rome. They tried everything to coax the undersized and unappealing pineapples into health before abandoning the project. Jenny still sometimes hankered to see Rome, but that was okay. She'd heard the reality wasn't nearly so wonderful as the travel brochures made it out to be . . . but sometimes she still wondered.

Senator Wakefield obviously disapproved. "You're too young to be tied down to a grove, and I wouldn't mind expanding the ranch. I'd be happy to buy you out."

She cut him off before he could launch into his prepared speech. "My answer is the same as it was when you offered after Jack's funeral. It is very generous of you, but I'm not leaving the grove."

"I'll give you a good price. You could spread your wings and see something of the world."

There was a time when she might have been tempted by such an offer, but it was too late now. What would she do if she couldn't grow oranges? Changing careers would take degrees and certifications and training. She wouldn't even know where to begin.

"Thanks for the offer, but I don't want to sell. I just want things to stay exactly as they are."

Actually, she wanted to turn the clock back to eighteen months ago, back when she still had Wyatt. Back when she had a laughing nephew and a brother she could respect. The senator leaned over to pat her knee.

"Don't worry, Jenny. I'll put a stop to the television reporters. You have a right to privacy on your own land, and I'll make sure you get it."

She relaxed back into the cushions of her seat, comforted by the warm confidence in his tone. "Thanks," she said. "My life is finally getting back to normal, and gossip over that skeleton is the last thing I need. The McAllisters are even going to let me see Sam again."

"Oh?" the senator asked. "What made them change their mind?"

She held his gaze. The senator still owned a heap of United Phosphate stock, and Kent McAllister was now the CEO of the mining company. The connection was obvious.

"I thought you might have had something to do with it," she said.

He shook his head. "Kent McAllister is a mean son of a gun, but he loves the boy. Maybe he's finally realized you can't be blamed for what Jack did."

Maybe. Jenny was still fairly certain the senator had somehow leaned on the McAllisters to permit the visit, but she wouldn't look a gift horse in the mouth. The visit with Sam was going to happen this weekend, and she silently gave thanks for whatever strings the senator pulled to make it happen.

SENATOR WAKEFIELD MADE good on his promise to intervene at the television station. The scaffolding disappeared the day after Jenny's visit, making it one less thing she had to worry about as she geared up to meet with her nephew again.

Would Sam still recognize her? Eighteen months was an eternity to a six-year-old. It would have been better to meet with him at the grove to help jog Sam's memory, but this visit was at the McAllisters' discretion, and they picked the gazebo at the new public park for the reunion.

The two hundred acres of restored wetlands was part of United Phosphate's commitment to the environment. Twenty years earlier this stretch of land had been strip-mined into a barren white landscape that looked like the moon. Now Jenny waited amid the lush greenery at a gazebo overlooking a freshwater pond. It was stocked for fishing and a two-mile boardwalk meandered through lush wetlands. Long-legged storks poked through tall grasses and the call of wood ducks sounded in the distance. Fast-growing loblolly pines towered over the park, obliterating any clue that this land had once been strip-mined.

She tried not to fidget while watching people come and go from the boardwalk. Hikers navigated around mothers pushing baby strollers, but so far there had been no sign of the McAllisters. Would they actually show up? They'd been so nasty while fending off her attempts to see Sam, insisting Jenny had nothing to offer they couldn't provide.

There was no delicate way to put it, but Jenny knew the problems that came from being raised by a grandparent. She'd never breathe a bad word about Gus Summerlin, but he was sixty-five when she graduated from high school. Instead of having a mother teach her to cook or put on makeup, Gus taught her to bait a hook and which brand of arthritis cream was best. By the time she was twenty-four, Gus had passed away and she was on her own in the world.

Twenty-four was too young for anyone to be left without older relatives to provide wisdom and guidance. That would eventually happen to Sam once his grandparents passed on unless she could foster a relationship with him.

The McAllisters were ten minutes overdue and it was chilly. Just when she considered running back to the truck for a heavier jacket she spotted Kent McAllister's tall form striding down the boardwalk and her heart sank.

He was alone.

She stood, ready to face him. "Have you brought Sam?"

"Sam is in the car with my wife," Mr. McAllister said, looking tall, tough, and flinty. "I'm going to set the ground rules for this meeting. First, you are not to breathe one word about your good-for-nothing brother. My wife and I will be a few yards away, listening to every word you say. The best thing for Sam will be if he scrubs Jack entirely out of his memory, so don't attempt to instill any warm or tender memories of your brother. Is that understood?"

It didn't sound like she had much choice, and she nodded.

"What have you got in that bag?" Kent demanded, eyeing her canvas sack on the wooden bench.

"Just an activity to serve as an icebreaker," she said. A two-hour visit was a long time for a six-year-old unless they had a project to work on, and Sam loved to help. He used to follow Jack around the grove to pick oranges and loved helping Hemingway feed the chickens. Getting Sam engaged in a task would soothe the awkwardness of this reunion.

Kent tugged the rim of her canvas bag to inspect its contents. His frown never altered, but her activity must have passed muster since he gave a brisk nod, then called his wife's cell phone, saying all was in order and she could bring the boy.

Jenny stood at the front of the gazebo to watch Mrs. McAllister walk Sam down the boardwalk toward them. How tall he'd grown! The chubbiness of a toddler was gone, but his hair was still a stick-straight blond. Would he even remember her? She twisted her hands as Sam squatted to watch some ducks paddling beside the boardwalk.

Mrs. McAllister finally coaxed Sam to leave the ducks and continue toward the gazebo. Jenny beamed as he drew closer, but Sam ignored her as he ran ahead to give his grandfather a quick hug.

Okay, that was fine, too. It was good Sam was comfortable with his grandfather because Kent McAllister scared the dickens out of most people.

"Sam, this is your Aunt Jenny," Mr. McAllister said with stern formality. Sam didn't say anything, just peeked at her in curiosity through his big blue eyes.

She hunkered down to be eye-level with him. "Do you remember me?"

He shook his head, and she swallowed back a squeeze of disappointment.

"That's okay," she said. "I'm your Aunt Jenny. I live on an orange grove. And look! I've brought something from the grove for you to help me with. Would that be good?"

Sam glanced at Mr. McAllister as though silently asking permission, which he received. Jenny reached for Sam's hand and led him into the gazebo.

"We'll be right here if you need us," Mr. McAllister told Sam.

"We're not going anywhere," his wife called out, and both McAllisters settled onto a bench a few yards away at the edge of the gazebo. Jenny tried to ignore their glowering presence as she took the potted lemon sapling from the canvas bag. Then she set out pruning shears, a jar of grafting compound, and a set of damp paper towels.

"I need help building a magic tree," she said to Sam. "Do you think you can help?"

The child's eyes grew large. "What's a magic tree?"

"It's a tree that can grow oranges, lemons, and limes. With luck, we might even be able to get this tree to grow grapefruit someday. Can you be my helper?"

A hint of a smile tugged as Sam gave a tentative nod.

Yes! Jenny unwrapped orange and lime twigs that had been kept damp in the paper towels. It wouldn't take long to graft them onto the lemon tree. Even the McAllisters looked interested as she began preparing the lemon sapling by slitting a two-inch cleft into the trunk. She let Sam hold the bud from a lime tree, then began the grafting process. She slipped the bud beneath the flap of lemon tree bark, where it would hopefully grow into a branch that would produce limes in the years to come.

She let Sam have a try with the next bud. His little face screwed up with the intensity of a surgeon as he began the task.

"You're doing a good job," she said, helping him through the more delicate parts. "You seem like a natural at this. When I was your age, my grandfather showed me and my brother how—"

"Careful," Mr. McAllister barked from a few yards away, and she bit her tongue. The McAllisters held the keys to the kingdom, so she gave a single nod to acknowledge that she'd overstepped, then proceeded to show Sam how to wrap the bud union.

It was the last mistake she made. After finishing the tree project, they fed the ducks outside the gazebo while Sam asked a zillion questions. He wanted to know where the ducks slept at night and did ducks have to brush their teeth. Even the McAllisters seemed more relaxed as she supplied a steady supply of pellets to feed the ducks.

The easy relaxation abruptly ceased at the end of the visit when Jenny suggested Sam could take the magic tree home with him. The McAllisters lived on a thirty-acre ranch and could surely find a spot for the sapling. It would be the perfect excuse for her to start visiting and establish a relationship again.

Sam loved the idea and he looked at Mr. McAllister. "Can I?" he asked, his voice bursting with excitement. "Can I, please?"

Mr. McAllister frowned. "Of course not, Sam. We wouldn't know how to take care of it."

"I can come out and show you," Jenny volunteered. "It's not hard. Every couple of weeks Sam and I ca—"

"That's not going to happen," Mr. McAllister said. "Come along, Sam. It's time to get home and practice your Spanish lessons."

"But what's going to happen to the magic tree?" Sam asked, his voice brimming with such dismay that Jenny rushed to the rescue.

"I'll take it to my grove and look after it for you," she reassured him. "The tree will be fine."

"Come along, Sam," Mr. McAllister said, taking one of the boy's hands while his wife snatched the other. Sam had to trot to keep up with them as they headed down the boardwalk.

A tangle of emotions twisted inside as she watched the

trio walk away. The visit was mostly a success, wasn't it? And the McAllisters might let her have another visit. Anything was possible if she just refused to give up.

A gust of cold wind buffeted her as she reached her pickup truck. It snaked beneath her collar, sending a chill throughout her entire body. The wind carried pinpricks of icy rain, reminding her that the one thing she would never be able to control was the weather.

And for an orange grove, ice could be deadly.

JENNY LUGGED the magic tree onto the farmhouse porch because she still couldn't be certain the canker in the grove was completely gone. The sapling was young and vulnerable, but it might also be her key to establishing a renewed relationship with Sam. She was brushing grit from her hands after placing the sapling on the edge of the porch when Hemingway came driving up on the ATV.

"A cold front is coming in and there's going to be a frost tonight," he said.

The breath left her in a rush. Frost could wipe out her entire season's crop, and those oranges were worth $300,000. After deducting the operating expenses, she ought to clear a little better than half, and she needed every dime of it for the mortgage she'd taken out to pay off the McAllisters.

It would be suicide to ignore a freeze warning. "If you get out the smudge pots, I'll go into town for fuel," she said, dreading the next twenty-four hours.

Hemingway agreed, and they went into high gear. A line had already formed at the agricultural service station when she arrived. Growers from all over the county waited to buy oil for their smudge pots. Big orange groves had wind machines to blow warm air into the tree canopy, but small operators like her still used the metal pots with an oil supply to send clouds of warm smoke into the tree canopy. It was usually enough to buy a few more degrees of warmth and stop the trees from dropping their oranges.

Ned Wilkensen was in front of her in the line. He leaned against the side of his truck as a clerk filled his cannisters. Deep grooves were carved into his leathery skin, his face betraying no emotion. He'd been through plenty of cold snaps and was still in business, so she shouldn't be so worried, right?

"How bad do you think it will be tonight?" she asked him.

Ned shrugged. "Not too bad. Can't afford to get lazy, though. We thought the frost ten years ago wouldn't amount to much, but that one took everyone's crop down."

It wasn't the comfort she'd hoped to hear. She'd helped operate the smudge pots with her grandfather during plenty of frosts. Back then, she and Jack had looked on it as an adventure. The glowing smudge pots had flickered in the night sky like campfires as they darted from pot to pot, ensuring they didn't run out of oil. She'd never been confronted with a freeze as an adult, and Hemingway had never done it at all.

Soon it was her turn at the pump, and she watched the electronic numbers on the display climb at an alarming rate. This fuel bill was an expense she hadn't counted on. She went inside the station to pay and was stopped short by a poster hanging on the front window.

It showed Wyatt Rossiter in a denim shirt with his sleeves rolled up as he gazed confidently at the camera. The slogan on the sign was a shock:

Wyatt Rossiter for Commissioner of Agriculture. Florida needs pastureland, not parking lots.

Laughter bubbled up inside. Since when had Wyatt aspired to political office? And yet . . . he would be a good commissioner. He knew ag. He was trustworthy.

Pride mingled with anguish as she gazed at his image. If he won, Wyatt would leave Amity and move to Tallahassee. He would finally be completely gone from her life.

"*Oh, Wyatt*," she whispered as an ache bloomed in her chest. Maybe it was just as well that he had dumped her. Wyatt always had such big dreams, while she didn't belong anywhere except Summerlin Groves. Trying to keep up with Wyatt as he tackled the world would have exposed her inadequacies. The only thing she knew how to do was grow oranges. She was nearing thirty years old, and it was too late to learn anything else. Still, she gave in to the temptation to gaze at Wyatt's photograph for a guilty few moments before heading inside to pay.

Cory Messner stood behind the front counter. She'd known Cory since elementary school when he used to fry ants under a magnifying glass.

"That'll be three hundred and twenty-five dollars," Cory said, his voice carrying a hint of scorn as he took her credit card. He probably resented having to wait on a woman.

"Be a shame if this frost killed everyone's oranges," Cory said as he handed her card back. "Almost as bad as if two innocent women got shot because they crossed Jack Summerlin."

The words were a slap in the face. She ought to be used to the contempt by now, but it still hurt. Cory had said it too quietly for anyone else in the store to hear. Cowards were like that, hitting only when no one else was looking.

Jenny tucked her card back into her wallet. "Been great seeing you, Cory. You've always been such a class act."

She slid into her truck to head home. Small-minded people might always blame her for what Jack did, and it got worse after her own brush with the law.

It happened a month after Jack died. A trespasser came onto the grove wanting to poke into her family history. He was a little guy, with horn-rimmed glasses and a goofy smile. He claimed to be a genealogist and wanted insight into Summerlin ancestry. The goofball refused to leave when she asked him, and she ended up getting a gun to prove she was serious about not wanting to talk to him.

He *still* refused to leave. All she did was fire a single shot into the air, but it was enough to bring charges against her, even though she'd been on her own land and nobody got hurt.

The district attorney wasn't going to overlook any gun crime committed by a Summerlin, and he tried to make a name for himself by demanding the maximum penalty, which would have meant jail time.

Somebody pressured the district attorney to back off, and Jenny was allowed to plead guilty to a lesser offense. She was still on probation, but so long as she kept her nose clean for the rest of the year, she'd be fine.

That was in the past. She'd learned to live with the cold shoulders and snubs because no one could ruin Jenny's self-respect without her own consent, right?

Snubs could only hurt her feelings, but a real battle was brewing tonight when the blast of frost from the north could wipe out her grove for good.

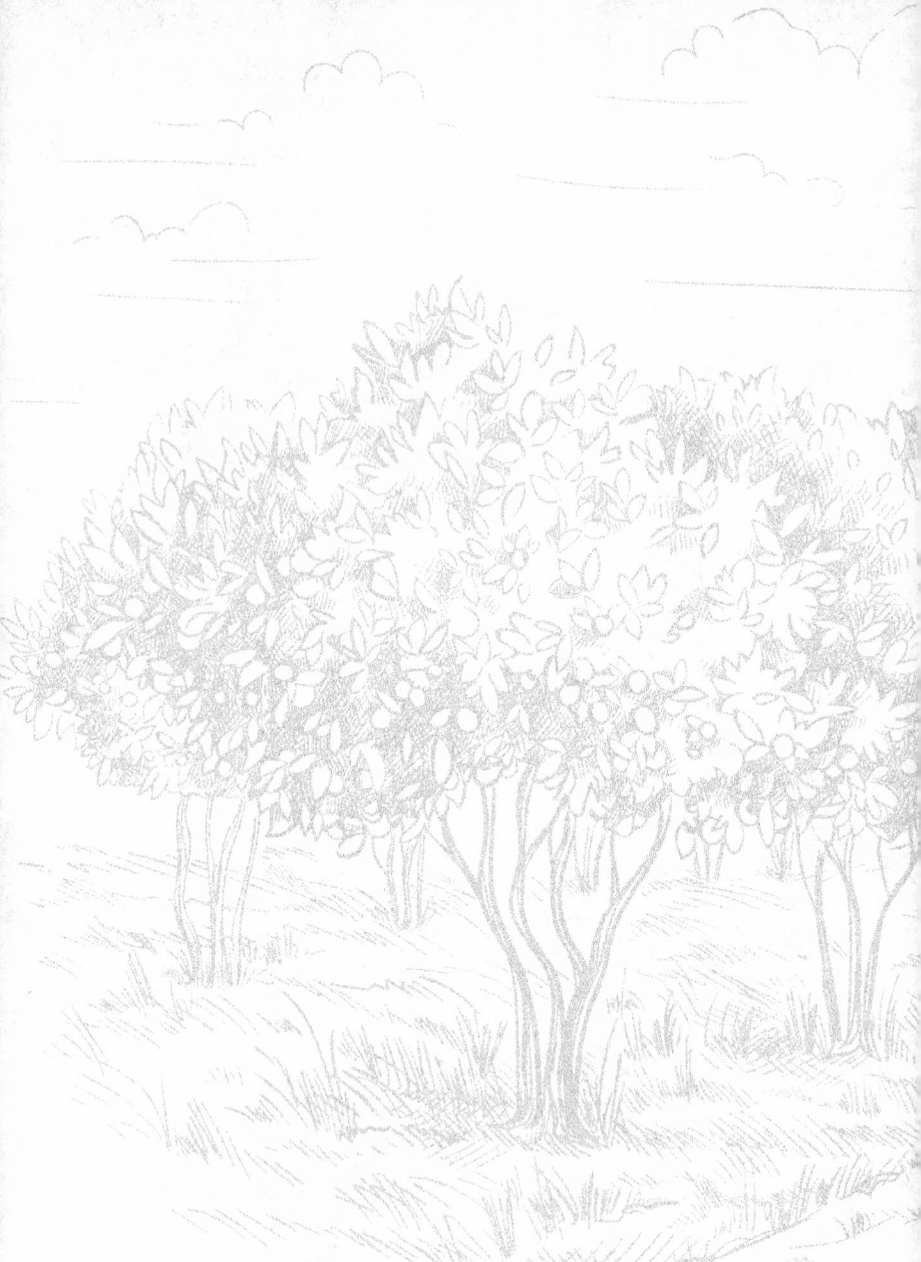

Chapter Nine

Donna Rossiter was Wyatt's biggest Achilles's heel. He's always been a mama's boy, and when she cried, it got to him.

"I can't do it," Donna sobbed over the phone. "I know everyone wants me to, but if I let go of the chest it will cut the last link with my precious girl."

She was speaking of the heirloom hope chest in Lauren's bedroom. Donna started filling the old cedar chest with things to set up her daughter's first marital home shortly after Lauren was born. The first item to go in was the family's antique baptismal gown. Over the years Donna created a binder of recipe cards and knitted baby blankets. Lauren helped because she loved girly things and crocheted lace table linens and napkins for the chest.

After Lauren's death, the hope chest became an obsession for Donna. Instead of joy, opening up the hope chest to air it out became a time for tears followed by days of suffocating depression. Wyatt's father finally convinced Donna to pass the hope chest on to another member of the family where it could be used for its intended purpose.

Wyatt hadn't realized this was the day his uncle intended to pick up the hope chest, and Donna was in a complete meltdown. It had been a normal Saturday morning at his condo when he got his mother's desperate call.

"Is Dad there?" Wyatt asked, his heart thudding with dread.

"He had to open the store," Donna said. "There isn't anyone else here today and I don't think I can do this. I can't, Wyatt. I just can't go on anymore."

He needed to get to their house immediately. "Okay, hold on, Mom. I'm coming over. I'm going to be on the phone with you the entire drive, okay?"

Donna gave a watery gulp. "You won't hang up?"

"I won't hang up." He raced for his keys and shrugged into a coat. It was so cold he could see his own breath as he hurried down the metal staircase outside the condo, his feet clanging the entire way until he reached the parking lot.

"Keep talking, Mom," he said once he started the car. He had her on speaker phone to monitor her mood as he navigated through the sleepy town. With luck he should be at his parents' house in five minutes.

His memories of the hope chest were different than Donna's. As a kid, he'd teased Lauren over her extravagant daydreams of marriage and the bridal magazines she put inside the hope chest. When she wasn't looking, he would replace them with issues of *Car & Driver.* It would usually take a while for Lauren to notice, but her shrieks could shake the rafters as she'd chase him down to demand the return of her magazines.

If only he could take those childhood taunts back. Lauren would never have her wedding day. The hope chest was the closest she would ever get to marriage, and helping Donna pass it on was going to be hard for everyone.

He parked on the tree-shaded street before his childhood home, a plain brick house that looked so ordinary from the outside but had been an extraordinary place to grow up. Rather than material riches, it was the bounty of love, faith, and acceptance that once made this home the envy of the neighborhood.

His Uncle Brian had just arrived in a pickup truck, ready to retrieve the chest. Brian brought both his kids with him. All three of them climbed out of the truck, stretching their legs after the ninety-minute drive from Tampa. Becky, the twelve-year-old girl destined to inherit the treasured family heirloom, was all elbows and knees, her chestnut hair in braids just like Lauren wore at that age.

Wyatt sent them a silent wave as he continued talking into his cell phone. "Brian and the kids just pulled up. Are you ready for them, or do you need a few more minutes?" It was freezing, but he'd keep them outside if Donna needed more time.

"I'm all right," she said in a thin voice. "They can come in."

Maybe this would be okay. He tapped the phone off and strode toward Brian. "It's been a rough day," he said as he returned Brian's handshake. "Letting go of that chest will be a big step if we can convince her to do it."

Uncle Brian understood the magnitude of the step, but his daughter was bursting with excitement. "Can I go inside and see it?" Becky asked, her eyes sparkling.

"You might want to pipe down a bit," Brian warned his daughter, then turned back to Wyatt. "Is Ed here?"

"Dad is at the store. Let me go up alone and be sure she's ready."

Once he was inside, the hardwood floor in the front hall made the same creaky squeaks he'd heard for the past thirty-four years. The familiar scent of lemon polish and the steady tick from the grandfather clock summoned a wave of childhood memories as he mounted the steps.

Lauren's bedroom door was open and Donna sat atop the hope chest, staring vacantly at the floor. A few crumpled tissues were scattered about, but Donna's expression was blank.

"I hate him," she whispered. "I hate that he took the coward's way out."

There was no need to ask who she was speaking about. Donna clung to her anger toward Jack Summerlin as tightly as she clung to Lauren's hope chest. It would be best if she could let both of them go, but one step at a time.

Wyatt sat on the other end of the chest. "Hey, Mom," he said softly. "Lauren is in a better place. Heck, Lauren was just about perfect, and if anyone's soul could fly straight to heaven, it was Lauren. Right?"

Donna's reluctant, half-hearted nod barely registered. It was something, at least.

"We had such a good life here," she said, her voice nearly reverent. "I once heard a pastor say that we live in an imperfect world, and can never really be happy because our hearts remember the echo of Eden. But I *was* truly happy. Maybe that was why it was all snatched away."

What could he say to that? Their family had been blessed beyond all reason, and none of them anticipated the tsunami that would smash their idyllic world to pieces. People always struggled with the age-old question of why a loving God caused innocent people to suffer. Wyatt had prayed long and hard about it, but still had no answer. The best he could do was lean on the passages from Revelation, promising that at the end of this age would come a time when there would be no death or mourning or crying or pain, for the old order of things will pass away.

Donna was in no mood for biblical wisdom. She preferred clinging to Lauren's memory rather than lifting her eyes to the good that remained in life.

"Brian is downstairs," he said as gently as possible. "He brought Becky and Ethan with him."

A fresh wave of grief rippled across her face. Wyatt kept his expression carefully composed despite the prickling at the back of his eyes. If Donna sensed he was struggling too, she'd start bawling. Was there anything worse than watching a parent weep? He'd become reconciled to Lauren's death, but Donna hadn't and probably never would. It was time to rip off the Band-Aid.

"Come on, let's go downstairs," he coaxed. "You don't have to watch."

The cell phone in his pocket vibrated with an incoming text. It was his state phone, not his personal phone. He often fielded work texts on the weekend, but he ignored it while walking his mother down the staircase.

Brian and his son headed upstairs while Wyatt started brewing a pot of coffee. The radio was on, a welcome distraction as the announcer talked about a new head coach for the Florida Gators.

"Maybe we'll finally have a winning season," he said, searching for something to distract his mother. Donna used to love the football season, hosting parties for half the neighborhood while she and Lauren cooked up a feast.

The football parties stopped after Lauren died, but his father wanted to start them up again in the fall. Would Donna be ready? Next July would mark two years since Lauren's death. Two years since he scrapped his plans to move out of state in search of a bigger challenge. He was only marking time in Amity, stuck in a dead-end town and growing older as his dreams grew fainter with each passing season.

Donna stared out the kitchen window at a tree swallow seeking shelter in a little wooden birdhouse Lauren made in Girl Scouts. Upstairs, the scrape and thump of the hope chest banged against the floor. Donna winced as though she'd been struck but kept her eyes fastened on the birdhouse.

His cell phone vibrated again with a second incoming text, and he yanked it out. It was an auto-generated alert telling him that a new message had been registered at the Suggestions Box on the Ag Law Enforcement website. Normally he wouldn't bother with something like this on a weekend, but it would give him something to focus on rather than his mother's grief.

He opened the message and blanched at the subject line: *Problems at Summerlin Groves.*

The rest of the message got worse. Citrus canker had been found on Summerlin Groves, and Jenny was trying to cover it up. The message linked to a series of photographs documenting the outbreak. One picture showed the burned patch in her west field, and others were closeups of citrus leaves with the distinctive brown splotches and yellow halo. It was the unmistakable sign of canker.

He braced his hands on the linoleum countertop, the blood rushing in his ears. This explained the burned acre on Jenny's grove. He'd been so distracted by seeing her again that he forgot about that burned patch as soon as he left the grove. Now the hint of fear he'd seen in her eyes made sense. She'd been burning trees in an attempt to contain the outbreak.

A spot fire wouldn't do the trick. Citrus canker was so contagious it could devastate the orange industry, and state regulations dictated *all* citrus trees in the vicinity be burned down, both healthy and diseased. Depending on where the canker was detected, Jenny could lose her whole grove.

Another thump from upstairs distracted him as Donna darted toward the base of the stairs.

"Be careful," Donna called up. "That chest is a hundred years old!"

"I got it," Brian grunted as he and Ethan took another step down the staircase. Donna breathed a sigh of relief when the chest arrived safely on the ground floor, and she followed them outside to load it into the truck.

Wyatt remained inside, the weight on his chest getting heavier as the implications of the text message sank in.

The laws for citrus canker eradication were unpopular and inflexible. Wyatt still remembered the heart-wrenching day he had to cut down an orange tree in an old lady's front yard because it was close to an outbreak on a nearby grove. The lady said her husband planted that tree on their first wedding anniversary. It was almost fifty years old and her husband had died of cancer the previous month when Wyatt showed up with a court order to destroy it. Her tree was healthy. There was nothing wrong with it other than its proximity to an outbreak in a nearby orange grove. The old lady cried when the state burned her tree.

A headache began to pound. Jenny didn't deserve this. No wonder she'd been on edge when he showed up at her grove.

He read the anonymous complaint once again. Who sent it? Anonymous complaints rubbed him the wrong way, and yet he was required to act on it. He'd bring in specialists to confirm the outbreak . . . and then it would be his duty to enforce the eradication order.

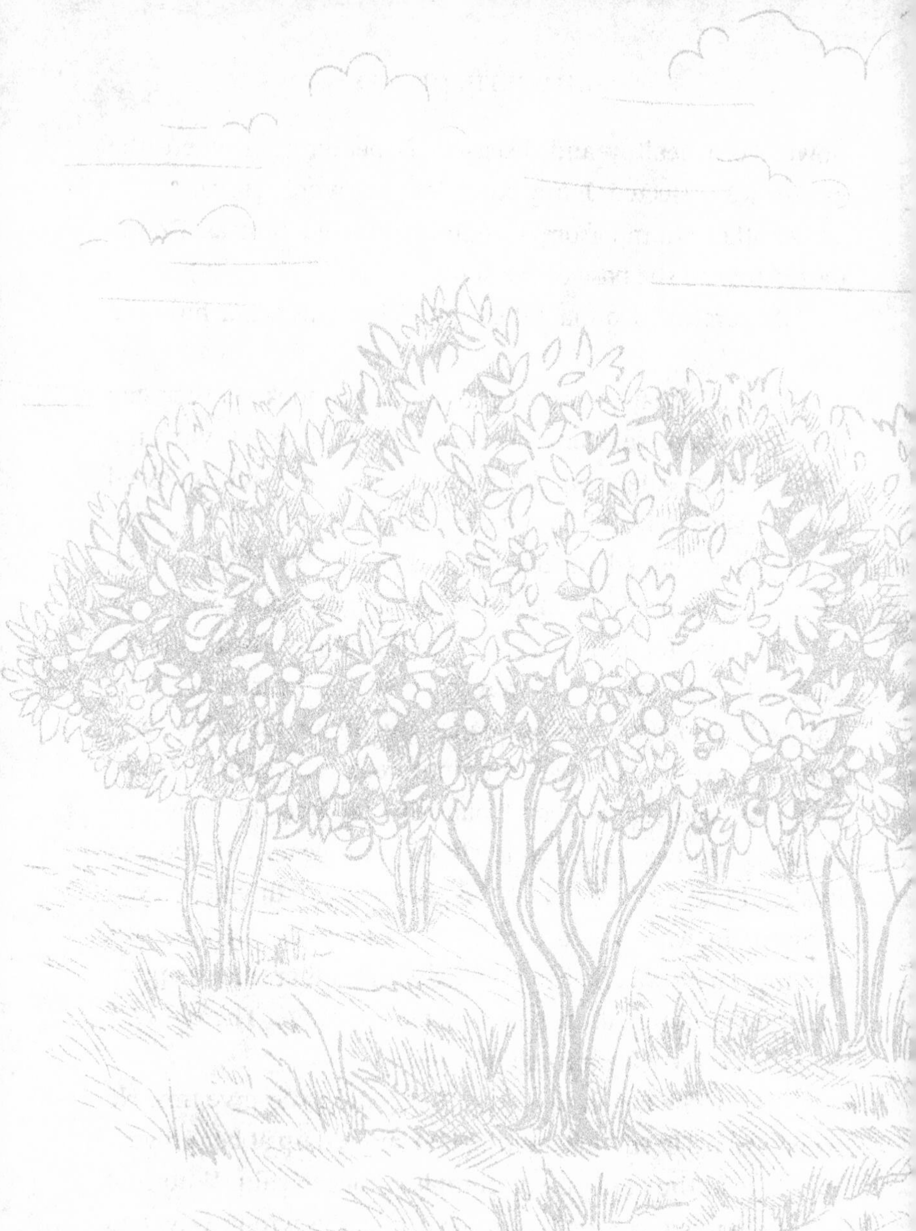

Chapter Ten

Country music crooned from the radio as Jenny sat across from Hemingway at the kitchen table, drinking strong coffee because it was going to be a long night. They had already distributed and filled the smudge pots throughout the grove earlier this afternoon and the temperature was dropping rapidly. It was only a matter of time before one of the electronic temperature gauges stationed at three different spots in the grove set off an alarm. Twenty-eight degrees was what she dreaded, the temperature at which fruit began to die.

"You deal the next hand," Hemingway said as he pushed a deck of cards toward her.

Jenny shuffled the cards while eyeing Hemingway's flimsy jacket. "Is that going to be warm enough?"

Hemingway snorted. "I suffered through two years in the Icelandic Coast Guard. You don't think I can cope with twenty-eight degrees?"

"You said that you quit the Coast Guard because you weren't cut out for it."

Hemingway narrowed his gaze. "How many people on the actual face of the earth want to live on a boat in the arctic circle?"

They both laughed as she started dealing the cards. Hemingway had a number of short-lived jobs during his colorful life, but in his heart, he'd always wanted to be a writer. He'd been at the grove for six years, spending his free time working on a manuscript for "the great American novel" and it was nowhere close to being finished. He took ghost-writing jobs on the side, which had been his only real form of income aside from the paltry amount she'd been able to pay him.

It was quite a step-down from being a college professor. Hemingway tried to pretend he didn't carry a grudge from being denied tenure. The students had loved him and he was a great teacher, but he refused to raise grant money or publish dry, tedious academic articles.

A warning buzzer sounded from the computer, and her heart plummeted. It was now twenty-eight degrees, and time to light the smudge pots.

"Let's go," Hemingway said as he shrugged into his flimsy jacket. She pulled on a hat and her winter coat, but the chill still made her shiver the moment she stepped outside. It was a moonless night and the grove was shrouded in darkness. She followed in the circle of light from Hemingway's lantern, the rhythmic sound of their boots striding through ankle-high grass the only noise as they headed toward the first smudge pot.

Jenny hunkered down beside it, unhooked the cap from the fuel tank, and ignited the flame with a long-barreled lighter. Smoke billowed from the three-foot exhaust stack, sending a warming cloud directly up into the branches. Hemingway secured the lid, then they walked to the next pot.

After an hour they both peeled off their jackets, their bodies heating up as they labored. Constant bending and lifting was strenuous work, and she started sweating despite the chill. Halfway through the grove her arms were aching and just walking felt like wading through sludge. Once she made the mistake of rubbing the sweat from her face and the sting of oil caused her eyes to scream in protest.

By the time all the pots were smoldering, they went back to the top of the grove to monitor the oil level in each pot. It was nearing four o'clock in the morning and the temperature was now twenty-six degrees.

"The smokestack on this one is cracked," Hemingway said as he tipped a pot toward her. Smoke seeped up the side of the stack, leaving an oily trail in its wake.

Jenny glanced up at the trees being warmed by the smudge pot. The crack was probably harmless, but she couldn't be certain. The oil might leak and start a fire. Better to lose the oranges from a few trees than to risk a blaze in the middle of the night.

"Let's choke it cold," she said.

"You'll have to show me how to do that." Hemingway had been so efficient through the night that she forgot this was his first experience with smudge pots.

She demonstrated shutting the hatch to cut the air flow. It took less than a minute to accomplish, but the sharp edge of the lid managed to slice through her cotton glove. She squeezed her hand against the sting, wishing she'd remembered to put on her leather gloves before fastening the caps like her grandfather taught her when she was a kid. At least her tetanus shot was up-to-date.

At eight o'clock the temperature was thirty degrees and would warm quickly with the rising sun. It was time to begin extinguishing the pots and saving as much of the precious oil as possible because the cold snap might go on for days.

She handed Hemingway a pair of old leather gloves and they settled into a routine. Hemingway lifted and fit the cap, Jenny fastened the hatch, then they walked to the next pot ten yards away. She was cold, tired, and hungry. Her feet hurt, her eyes stung from the grime and smoke, and she needed to go to the bathroom.

She looked at Hemingway, whose job lifting the lids was even harder. He had no ownership of the grove and was being paid peanuts for wages, but he hadn't complained once throughout the night. The sun had risen and she got a good look at his exhausted face for the first time in hours.

"You look like a coal miner."

His teeth flashed white against his smoke-darkened face. "You look like a dirt farmer."

Jenny smiled and forced her aching feet onward toward the next smudge pot. She supposed she was just a dirt farmer now, but that didn't diminish her love for this place. The sun crested the horizon and the melting frost glinted like diamonds on the leaves of her trees.

She straightened her spine and her muscles wept in relief as she rolled her shoulders. Acres of trees stretched across the land in perfect, orderly rows that sloped down the hill toward the river. It looked like heaven.

Euphoria caused her to stand taller. They'd done it! She was exhausted and so tired the bones in her face hurt, but she had saved her oranges.

JENNY SLEPT until two o'clock in the afternoon and was still groggy as she made her way downstairs to start a pot of coffee. The kitchen floor was cold, but she was too lazy to go back upstairs for her slippers. If she got rich from the sale of the Fabergé egg, she would add central heating to the house. She leaned against the counter, smiling at the sunlight filtering through the blinds and listening to the percolating coffee, drawing energy from the aroma. Maybe she'd buy one of those fancy coffee machines if the Fabergé egg paid off.

A knock on the front door broke her concentration. She must have accidentally locked Hemingway out because he usually just walked in.

Except it wasn't Hemingway.

Wyatt Rossiter stood on the other side of the door, looking tense and grim and something else. Worried? As usual, he was in the khaki uniform with a fully loaded service belt around his hips. The only thing that looked out of place was the legal-sized manila envelope in his hand.

"What's up?" she asked, feigning a casual attitude.

Wyatt looked away as though pained, then drew a deep breath and blew it out. "Can I come inside?" he asked. "It's cold out here."

She stepped back to let him in. Something was wrong. Instead of looking steely and annoyed like he did the last time she'd seen him, he seemed ill at ease and worried. Wyatt only took a few steps into the house before he closed the door, then turned to extend the envelope to her.

"I'm here on business," he said. "I got a report that you're hiding citrus canker on the grove."

It hit her like a kick in her chest. The breath left her in a rush and she crossed her arms, refusing to take the envelope from his hand.

"Who said that?" she asked, proud of how calm she sounded.

"It was an anonymous complaint. You've got a burned section in your west field. It looks like you're already taking steps to mitigate the disease, right?"

She clamped her mouth shut. Wyatt was a lawyer and could use whatever she said against her. She wouldn't admit anything.

He opened the manila envelope and withdrew a single leaf. It was scattered with brown crusty dots, each with a familiar yellow halo. He held it up without a word.

"You didn't find that on my grove," she said, praying it was true. She and Hemingway burned the infected patch until there was nothing left. They spent days raking through the ashes and cinders, ensuring all the infected leaves had been incinerated.

"I picked this off a tree five yards from the entrance to the grove," he said. He reached into the manila envelope again and took out another leaf, this one in a clear baggie. "This one came from the north field."

"No," she whispered in horror. Wyatt was many things, but he wasn't a liar.

She reached for the back of the chair to steady herself. After the skeleton was found, her life got so hectic that she quit inspecting for canker. It was a mistake. She'd gotten careless and assumed the danger had passed.

The leaf with the brown specks and yellow halos proved otherwise.

"I'll take care of it," she said. "I'll pull down and burn every infected tree."

Wyatt remained unmoved. "It's too late for that."

"No, it's not. I'll do a spot eradication and then everything will go back to normal. I know how to fix this."

Pity took root in Wyatt's gaze. He strolled deeper into the family room and pulled aside a white cotton drape from the southern-facing window.

"Look out there," he prompted.

Her mouth went dry as she joined him at the window. A line of pickup trucks was parked on the far side of the field, and half a dozen field agents walked through her grove, taking samples. There was no more hiding. They knew everything.

The disease had spread. All her work clearing the west field had failed.

"I didn't realize it had spread," she whispered. How pathetic she sounded. It was horrible for Wyatt to see her like this . . . a pitiful, pathetic failure.

"I'm sorry, Jenny. The state is going to take over and eradicate the disease."

She shook her head. There were ways to treat canker short of burning everything down. It might not work but she ought to be given the chance to try.

"The oranges are still good," she said. "The disease won't hurt the oranges. I can still have a decent crop in April."

"Jenny, I'm not going to let you harvest these oranges."

They were fighting words. "You're not going to *let* me? The fruit will be ugly, but who cares? It will still be fine for juicing and you know that."

"The law says—"

"Screw the law! I can use a fungicide to get it under control."

"That can only treat it, not cure it."

She swallowed hard, trying to keep a cool head. "The law is wrong. You people have no right to seize my entire grove over a few sick trees."

"Jenny, we can and we will," he said, not unkindly.

"I'm getting a lawyer," she snapped, and he nodded.

"That's probably a good idea. There may be some government programs to help you—"

"I don't want a government program; I want the government to mind its own business! I'll bring in an arborist to help." She glanced out the window at the strangers in uniform who wandered through her grove, taking samples.

"I want those people off my land," she said. "They've got no right to be here."

He sighed and reached into his pocket, removing a slip of paper and holding it out toward her. "This is the state statute that allows plant inspectors onto your grove. We'll take the samples back to the laboratory to confirm the outbreak, but you need to prepare yourself to lose the trees."

She folded her arms and refused to touch it. She wouldn't even look at it.

Wyatt set the paper on the coffee table. "Someone from my office will contact you later in the day with a report from the inspectors. Assuming they confirm my suspicions, the state will start clearing the grove within a week."

"How much of the grove?" she asked, trying not to shake at the freezing chill racing through her veins.

"All of it. I'm sorry, Jenny."

He left without a backward glance.

Chapter Eleven

Jenny walked the grove after Wyatt and the plant inspectors left. Sure enough, the tiny brown spots were just barely forming on a handful of trees scattered throughout the grove. The law was unforgiving. All citrus trees within a third of a mile of an infected tree had to be destroyed. Given the dispersal of infected trees, the entire grove would be plowed down.

She called Kenneth Tolland, the agricultural lawyer her family had used for years, and he confirmed her worst fears. Citrus was too important to the state's economy to risk an outbreak of disease.

"But the nearest citrus grove is three miles away," Jenny said. "My grove is no danger to them. Why can't I spot-treat the grove by taking out the infected trees and monitoring the rest?"

"The state is playing hardball on this one," Mr. Tolland said, regret heavy in his voice. "I know it's tough, but they will replace your trees."

"With saplings!" she said. "It takes four years for saplings to bear fruit. What am I supposed to do for income during those years?"

"Saplings won't require much of your time," her lawyer replied. "You could get a job in town. Try something new and exciting."

Jenny's shoulders sagged. Where could she get a job? Waiting tables wouldn't pay the 1.2-million-dollar mortgage she'd taken out in order to pay the McAllisters. Where could she earn that kind of money? The only thing she knew how to do was grow oranges, which wasn't exactly a transferrable skill. Just thinking about leaving the security of Summerlin Groves triggered a shaky feeling. This was where she belonged, and she would fight for it.

The next day she got a written confirmation from Wyatt that her entire grove would be quarantined, uprooted, and burned. The process would begin on Friday, a mere two days away.

She wouldn't give up. Her lawyer wouldn't take the case and the local agricultural extension office advised she become reconciled to starting over. She registered an appeal with the Governor of Florida but didn't have great hopes there. Her best hope was Senator Wakefield, who was back in Washington and had yet to return any of her frantic telephone calls.

The day before demolition she walked through the grove, the chilly breeze rustling the leaves. Sunlight dappled familiar patterns on the grass, but the peace Jenny normally found in the grove was absent, replaced by escalating fear with each passing hour. Her trees were going to be destroyed tomorrow, and Senator Wakefield hadn't even bothered to return her calls. She could only assume he hadn't gotten her messages. It was inconceivable he would have ignored her if he knew she was in trouble.

Jenny returned to the house, where sunshine filtered through the slatted wood blinds of the living room, illuminating glossy hardwood floors and character built into every line of the house. Four generations of Summerlins had lived here, and if she didn't figure out something soon, she would be the last.

A rude buzz broke the silence. Jenny's gut plummeted, wondering if she could be imagining this latest catastrophe, but after a thirty-second pause, the terrible alarm buzzed again.

It was a frost warning.

Exhaustion pulled on every muscle of her body as she logged in to the weather forecast. Temperatures were predicted to dip down to the lower twenties tonight, with frost warnings throughout the listening area.

She braced her hands on the table, sucking in gulps of air. She was either on the verge of laughing or crying but didn't know which. If a miracle didn't happen, this time tomorrow the tractors would be here ripping up her trees. Did she really want to spend the night filling smudge pots for trees that would be destroyed a few hours later?

There was still a possibility Senator Wakefield might come through for her. Or maybe the governor would order a stay. If she didn't light the smudge pots tonight, this year's orange crop would die. She couldn't let $300,000 of oranges freeze in exchange for a couple hours of fitful sleep.

She took a sobering breath and shrugged into her coat, then headed out to find Hemingway. The chickens pecking in the scrub outside his trailer didn't seem to mind the cold, and grudgingly moved aside as she strode toward the weathered wooden planks before his trailer.

She had to knock several times to rouse him from a late-afternoon nap, but his pale blue eyes crinkled with sad understanding when she asked for his help manning the smudge pots.

"Are you sure this is what you want to do?" he asked.

She barely had the energy to nod. "I still think there's a chance we can save the grove. I'd like your help overnight."

He stepped away from the door and beckoned her inside. He cracked open a beer before joining her at the dinette table. Several cans were already scattered on the countertop . . . a sad reminder that Hemingway was under stress, too.

He drew a long swallow of beer before speaking. "If the senator was going to help, you would have heard from him by now."

"I don't know what else to do," Jenny said. "Quitting isn't an option."

"Then we will fire up the smudge pots."

IT WAS two hours after midnight when the temperature dropped to the critical level requiring the smudge pots to be lit. Jenny and Hemingway had already established a routine from the other night, but this time there was no joking, no banter. Light the pots, inspect the smoke, check the oil levels.

A faint breeze rustled the leaves, the sound both comforting and familiar. If this was to be her trees' last night, at least they would have a warm blanket of smoke to ward off the frost.

It was silly to imagine the trees appreciated the warmth. Trees were inanimate objects that didn't actually feel the cold. The cold was piercing *her* gloves, *her* flesh, but the trees were made of xylem cells and didn't actually feel anything. Her brain knew this, and yet she still wanted to provide a warming smoke for her trees. Surely on some level the trees sensed the care she lavished on them. She had played beneath these trees as a child and started tending them as a teenager. She sometimes even *talked* to these trees when she got lonely enough. She wouldn't abandon them now.

They began extinguishing the pots at seven o'clock in the morning. Cap the smokestack, fasten the latch, move on to the next pot. *Maybe the senator will call. Maybe the governor will intervene.*

They capped the last smudge pot at eight-thirty. Nine o'clock was the deadline, the time the state would arrive with their tractors. She couldn't face it alone.

"Will you come up to the house with me?" she asked Hemingway.

His face was streaked with oily, black smoke, and she probably looked the same. He nodded, the pale blue of his eyes the only color on his exhausted face.

They sat on the porch steps and Jenny checked her cell phone for messages. Nothing. She'd left a dozen messages for the senator, but he clearly wasn't going to intervene. She dropped the phone onto the ground and put her face in her hands. In the distance, a rumble of approaching diesel engines and tractors sounded as workers from the state neared the grove. Hemingway slung an arm around her and pulled her against his shoulder.

"I don't know if I can face this," she whispered.

His arm tightened. "You can handle it, Sunshine Girl. You have more courage than any woman I know."

The ground beneath her feet blurred as she stared at it. "I'm a coward. I can't even look at those tractors." She could feel them, though. The ground was vibrating as the massive tractors turned onto her property. The tears pooling in her eyes spilled over.

Hemingway passed her a handkerchief. “Courage is being scared to death but saddling up anyway.”

She pressed the cloth to her eyes and sniffled. “Is that Ernest Hemingway?”

“John Wayne,” he said. “The other great American.”

If she weren’t so shattered, she would have laughed. Leave it to Hemingway to define America in terms of John Wayne and Ernest Hemingway. She wanted to say something funny to prove she wasn’t collapsing, but all she could hear was the ghastly rumbling of those tractors rolling closer.

The tractors stalled midway up her drive. It was ten minutes until nine o’clock. Her eyes strayed to the grove and its orderly rows of trees looking healthy and vibrant. *Please God*, she prayed.

Wyatt’s cruiser arrived, navigating around the tractors and work vans that perched like vultures on her drive. He parked his car, then strode toward her, stone-faced.

“Jenny, I’m here to ensure the proper procedures are observed. These are the official papers to begin the eradication process.”

The papers fluttered in the breeze, but she wouldn’t touch them and Wyatt didn’t push it. He lifted an empty geranium pot and slipped the papers underneath. “I’m sorry about this, Jenny. We’re ready to begin.”

Footsteps thudded as he walked down the porch steps and gave a thumbs-up to the tractor drivers. The roar of engines increased as half a dozen oversized tractors peeled away and headed toward designated sections of the grove. They all had big, fork-like attachments that could dig straight under the shallow roots of an orange tree. She watched the closest driver, the one who was positioned on the highest crest of the hill, where her most valuable trees swayed in the morning breeze. The driver tugged at the levers and carefully positioned the fork at the base of a tree. The tines sank into the earth and pushed through the roots with an audible ripping sound.

She couldn't take this. She rose to her feet and shot down the stairs toward the tractor, but Hemingway's arm closed around her like a steel band. "Don't let them see you sweat, Jenny. Head up. Shoulders back. We're going to get through this."

The revving of the tractor engine increased and the metal fork lifted the entire tree from the soil, its roots looking like pale strands of rope that flailed as they broke free of the soil.

"Let's go inside," Hemingway urged. "You don't have to watch."

She stayed motionless. "I won't run away from what's happening."

"Then come sit with me on the porch," Hemingway said. "It's going to be a long day."

She didn't resist as Hemingway tugged her toward the porch. She wished she could be anywhere else on the planet, but she wouldn't abandon her trees. She would stand vigil until the end.

THE TRACTORS DIDN'T LEAVE until sunset. Her ears were numb after hours of rumbling engines and the awful sound of tree limbs crashing to the ground.

Now everything was strangely silent. The grove was usually alive with evening sounds as the rustle of leaves mingled with the drone of crickets. Tonight, everything was brutally silent, with only the echo of the tractors ringing in her ears. She'd be hearing that sound for days. Years, probably.

What happened here wasn't her fault. Citrus canker was completely outside of her control. It had probably arrived on the feet of a bird or speck of dust on the wind.

It didn't matter how it got here, the trees were dead and she'd have no income for at least four years. She wouldn't be able to pay the mortgage and would lose everything. All because the state had an irrational law with no chance for appeal. How could she pay a million-dollar mortgage on her grove without a crop this year?

A Fabergé egg could do it.

Her eyes narrowed in determination. She was finished being polite and obeying the rules. She had meekly complied with the sheriff's request to keep silent about the egg, but her cooperation was over.

A faint smile hovered. It didn't matter what Wyatt or the sheriff wanted. She had solid legal grounds to claim that egg and was mad enough to do it.

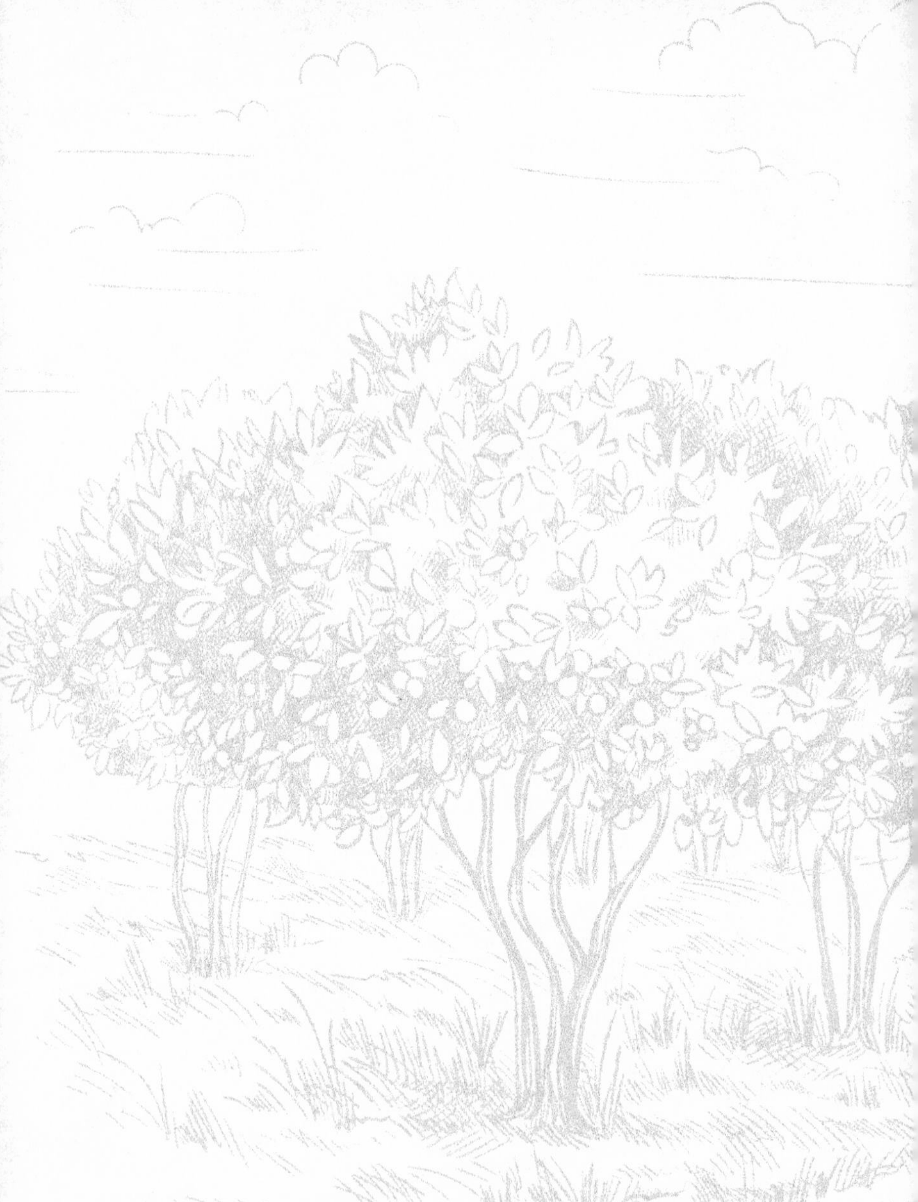

Chapter Twelve

Hemingway agreed with Jenny's decision to start the ninety-day clock for declaring ownership of the egg. No more playing nice with the state. They had found a treasure and were ready to claim it.

A high-end auction house like Christie's or Sotheby's would know the law and might even help them manage the flood of people likely to assert ownership. Jenny quickly decided to approach Christie's simply because the auction house had an office only four hours away in Miami.

By eight o'clock the morning after her grove was destroyed, she and Hemingway were on the road to Miami with their video evidence of the egg. Sprawling farmland in the middle of the state was mostly home to orange, grapefruit, and lemon trees, with occasional pastures for cattle. It was hard not to be jealous as they drove past miles of healthy orange groves.

Strawberry, avocado, and cabbage fields started showing up as they drove farther south, but it wasn't long until the urban sprawl of Miami encroached on the farmland. Jenny had allotted two hours of extra time for traffic, but even so they arrived ten minutes late for their appointment with an auction consultant.

Hemingway's eyes nearly popped out of his head when he saw her. Kristen Vargas looked like a cross between a Barbie doll and Betty Boop. She wore three-inch spike heels that clicked on the marble floor of the foyer and a flaring skirt that could have come straight out of a fifties Mouseketeer movie. She wore her black hair coiled up in twin rolls, ruby red lips, and cat-eye glasses.

"Hi, I'm Kristen," she said, reaching out to shake Hemingway's hand.

"And I'm dazzled," Hemingway responded, to which Kristen from Christie's blushed gorgeously. She ushered them into a private office, although could an office with see-through glass walls be considered private? The interior had little besides a flat glass table, a sleek laptop, and a few black leather club chairs.

"You have something interesting to show me?" Kristen asked.

"You might say that," Hemingway replied and set his laptop on the glass table. Kristen leaned in, and her jaw dropped open as she watched the three-minute video of Jenny holding a Fabergé egg.

"Oh yes," Kristen agreed in a breathless tone. "Yes, this is *very* interesting."

EXCITEMENT THRUMMED on the drive home because Kristen from Christie's agreed to guide them through the legal process for claiming lost property in the state of Florida, and would happily help them sell the egg should their claim prove successful.

"We need to celebrate," Hemingway said as they arrived back in Amity. It was almost seven o'clock in the evening and they'd missed dinner.

"The Brickhouse?" she asked, which was their standard place to go for a celebration. The restaurant was pricey, but they'd had a good day and such blessings weren't to be taken for granted. A platter of slow-roasted ribs with baked beans and cornbread was calling their name.

Jenny was practically faint with hunger when she eased the truck into a parking spot on the town square and started making her way to the Brickhouse. Hemingway got distracted by a couple of girls who'd snagged him outside the coffee shop, but Jenny hurried ahead to secure a table because the Brickhouse was the most popular gathering spot in town. The exposed brick walls and wide plank flooring created a wonderfully homey atmosphere despite the staggering prices. There was space for hundreds of people and the stage near the front often featured local bands and political speeches. Tonight, a local author was holding a book talk. The podium was already in place, with books mounded on a front table ready for purchase.

Jenny's eyes widened when she recognized the name of the author, and she hastily exited the restaurant. Hemingway was only a few yards away.

"I changed my mind," she said. "Let's stop for a hamburger on the way home."

Hemingway slanted a frown at her. "Jenny, one does not stop for a hamburger when smoked ribs from the Brickhouse are available. Must I explain everything to you?"

"It's crowded inside. Let's go."

She tried to sound casual, but Hemingway peered over her

shoulder into the restaurant. "No more crowded than usual," he said, then glanced at the sign in the window advertising the book talk scheduled to begin in ten minutes.

Hemingway's face transformed, a feral light coming into his face like a leopard stalking its prey.

"I'm going in," he said.

She tugged his arm. "Don't go. It's not worth it."

Hemingway shook her off and headed inside. She followed, hoping she wasn't going to be forced to act as a referee, but it might be necessary.

Tonight's speaker was Raymond Wakefield, Senator Wakefield's son whose career serving on corporate boards happened by riding on his father's coattails. Sitting on the Board of Trustees for the college where Hemingway once taught had been one of those cushy appointments.

When Hemingway was denied tenure, he had appealed to Raymond Wakefield, pointing out their long and productive association. Raymond declined to intervene, and Hemingway lost his job. He was still bitter about it, and nothing could irk Hemingway faster than seeing another of Raymond Wakefield's books crawling up the bestseller lists.

Because Hemingway was his ghostwriter.

That came to an abrupt end after Hemingway got fired from the college, and Raymond obviously found a new ghostwriter because tonight he was promoting yet another biography of his grandfather. This one focused on the late Karl Wakefield's career as a philanthropist.

Jenny hurried inside and slid into a booth beside Hemingway.

"Don't cause him any trouble," she warned. "There's no point in stirring up bad blood."

"I think there is," Hemingway said. "He signed off on my termination letter when he's never held a real job in his life, only cushy appointments earned by being his father's son. He pays ghostwriters to write his books. I've spent six years burning the midnight oil to write my novel. I open a vein that leads straight from my heart to capture the soul of Florida, and yet Raymond Wakefield thinks I deserved to be fired."

She peered through the crowded interior of the pub and spotted Raymond with his wife, the Baroness Claudia von Buhler, standing near the stage and speaking with the restaurant manager. They'd been married for fifteen years but the baroness still held on to her Austrian title, which seemed to please them both given how liberally they flaunted it.

As usual, Raymond and the baroness wore coordinating outfits. Was that some sort of European custom for married people? Or maybe it was a sign of Raymond's slavish loyalty to his wife, because Jenny couldn't imagine any red-blooded man choosing to wear a yellow polka-dot sweater. It contrasted with his full head of dark chestnut hair, surprisingly thick for a man in his mid-forties.

The waitress took their order, then Hemingway started grumbling about his nemesis. "Raymond is desperate to have another bestseller to worm his way back into the senator's good graces."

"I didn't realize there had been a falling out." She rarely emerged from the grove to hear local gossip, but Hemingway was close to the staff at Wakefield Manor.

"The senator caught Raymond skimming from the household accounts," Hemingway said with a smirk, and Jenny listened with drop-jawed amazement as Hemingway recounted the story. The senator spent most of his time in Washington, leaving Raymond at home to manage the estate. Every year at Christmas the senator gave the household staff, stable hands, and groundskeepers a $5,000 bonus. Raymond had been trimming the amount to $100 and pocketing the rest.

"They've got twenty full-time employees, so Raymond has been skimming almost a hundred thousand a year," Hemingway pointed out. "It's been going on for years, and the senator threatened to cut Raymond off if he didn't repay each staff member for the entire amount he stole. Raymond is probably hoping the senator will be mollified by another best-seller celebrating the family heritage."

Jenny stared at Raymond through the dim light of the restaurant. Raymond and the baroness seemed so worldly and sophisticated, jetting all over the world to ski in Switzerland and bask on islands in the Caribbean. How could a person enjoy those luxuries knowing it was stolen from hardworking household staff?

A few minutes later Raymond came up to the podium and began speaking, outlining the main points of the biography of his grandfather, the internationally renowned Karl Wakefield, whose contributions to finance, industry, and humanity deserved to be lauded through the ages. After making a fortune from the phosphate mine, he became ambassador to the United Nations and founded a charitable relief foundation that was still operating decades after the old man's death.

Karl Wakefield and his son Senator Max Wakefield were so well known in Pierce County that Raymond skipped the introductions and went straight to the heart of his latest biography of his grandfather.

"In America we consider the decade of the 1920s to be 'the roaring twenties' because of a healthy economy and feeling of optimism," Raymond said with a smoothly polished voice. "It was quite the opposite in Europe, which was pock-marked with war, hobbled with grief, and plagued by savage hunger."

Hemingway leaned close to Jenny. "That came straight out of his ghostwriter's mouth," he whispered, but Raymond was just getting warmed up.

"My grandfather founded the World Famine Commission in 1924. It sent fertilizer and farming equipment to war-torn areas of the world," Raymond said. "Although he shipped emergency rations of grain, his motto was always that if you give a man a fish, he eats today. Teach a man to fish, and he eats for a lifetime."

Hemingway snorted. "Karl Wakefield's motto was to get rich as fast as possible," he said loud enough for others at nearby tables to hear.

"Shh," she urged. "Don't embarrass him. His wife is here."

The baroness sat at a table near the stage, her sleek chignon and Hermes scarf looking incongruent with Florida's best barbecue joint.

Hemingway grumbled, but their food had arrived, and he was too busy slathering spicy barbecue sauce over the ribs to care anymore. They stopped listening to Raymond's speech and toasted their triumph in Miami with a locally brewed ale, then toasted it again with an imported lager.

All the while, Raymond lauded his grandfather's glorious history. This was the third book Raymond had "written" about Karl Wakefield. Hemingway wrote the first two books. One covered Karl Wakefield's impoverished childhood in the backwoods of Florida, then their change of fortune when the family discovered phosphate on their land. Hemingway's second ghostwritten book covered Karl's years as ambassador to the United Nations.

Today's book was about Karl's commitment to easing world hunger through his creation of the nonprofit World Famine Commission. Raymond outlined his grandfather's three-pronged approach to alleviate world hunger: the donation of farming tractors to developing nations, free access to fertilizer, and a network of agricultural consultants who travelled the world to help struggling nations embrace modern farming techniques. If the Nobel Peace Prize could be posthumously awarded, Jenny suspected Raymond would be gunning for his grandfather to win it.

When the time for questions arrived, Hemingway immediately called one out without waiting to be recognized. "Did you instruct your ghostwriter to omit your grandfather's communist sympathies?"

A few people turned to glare at them, but there was a lot of chuckling, too. Raymond cleared his throat and stood a little straighter. "I wrote every word of this biography," he insisted. "My grandfather's work with Russia—"

"With the Soviet Union," Hemingway corrected.

"My grandfather's work with Russia was entirely humanitarian," Raymond insisted. "Are you familiar with the Holodomor of 1932? We'll never know how many Russians starved to death because of—"

"How many *Ukrainians* starved," Hemingway corrected. "The Holodomor was a man-made famine that happened when Stalin took control of Ukrainian farms and seized their grain. The term 'Holodomor' comes from the Ukrainian words for hunger and extermination, and that's what Stalin did. Four million people died in that famine."

Raymond handled the tirade with admirable calm. He nodded his head sagely. "You are correct. The Holodomor inspired my grandfather's humanitarian efforts throughout the 1930s. It was Karl Wakefield's commitment to Ukraine that stopped a horrible situation from becoming even worse. My grandfather knew of the Holodomor. He wept at the photographs."

"That was big of him," Hemingway muttered under his

breath as he raised his hand to order another beer. Jenny suggested it was time to stop, but Hemingway correctly pointed out that they had yet to properly toast Kristen from Christie's. Jenny switched to ice water while Hemingway got another mug of beer.

"With luck, we shall soon be toasting a fortune from a long-lost Romanov treasure," he said, and Jenny raised her glass in agreement.

The Fabergé egg might be the only way she could keep her head above water now that she'd lost her orange trees, and they were about to launch their quest to win it.

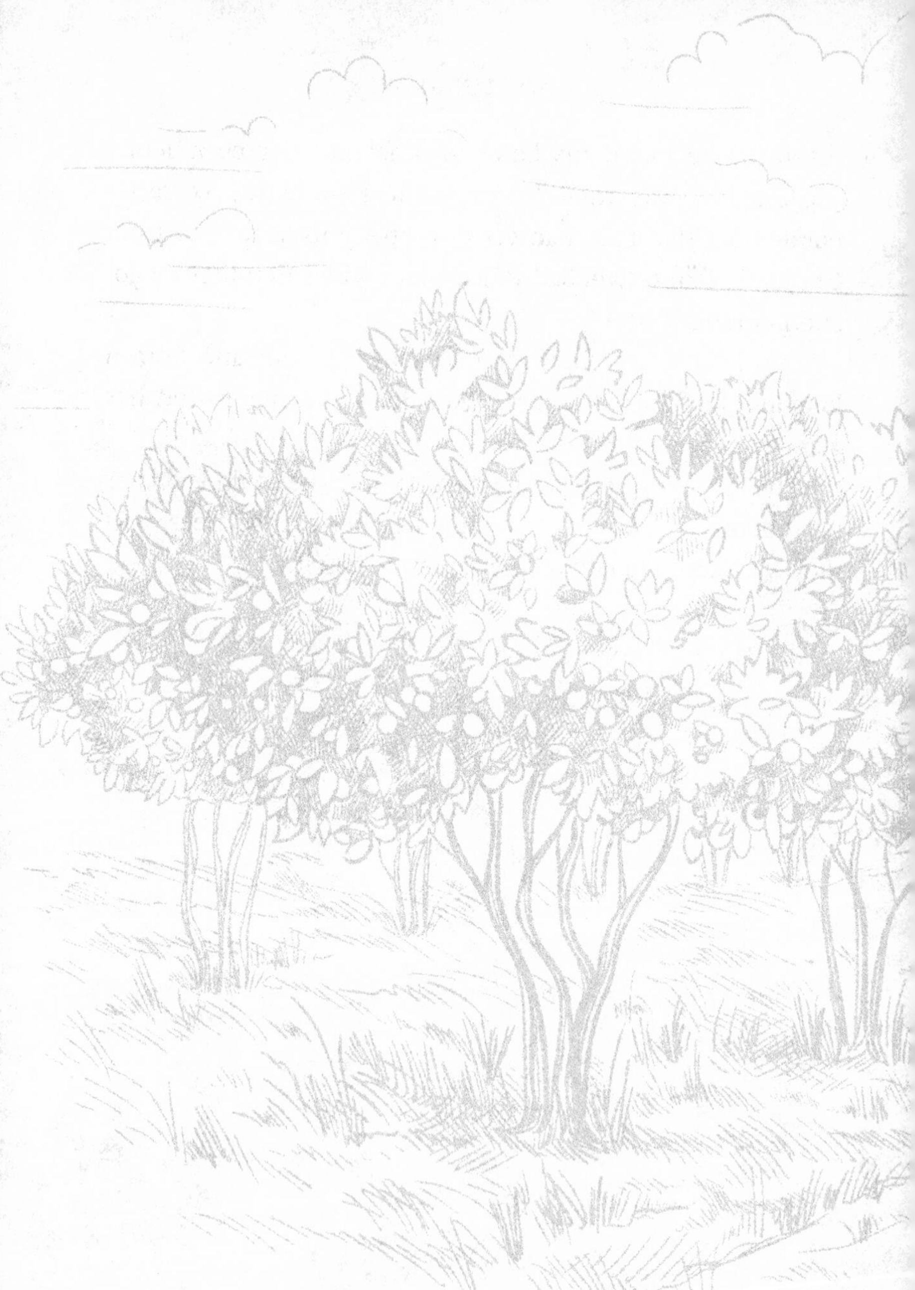

Chapter Thirteen

Wyatt's job in ag law enforcement had plenty of distasteful aspects, but overseeing the destruction of Jenny's orange grove had been the worst day of his career. Furthermore, he had yet to learn anything about the skeleton found on her land. Figuring out the identity of the dead woman and how she got into the hollow of a tree was the sheriff's job, not Wyatt's, but he was tired of waiting for answers. It was time to light a fire under the sheriff to get him moving.

His suspicion about the case gathering dust was confirmed when he asked the sheriff's administrative assistant who was researching the case.

"It's been assigned to Patrick Smith," she replied. "He's out on paternity leave for three more months."

Wyatt blanched. "Paternity leave?"

"Yes!" she said brightly. "His wife had twins last month. I think it's great the department lets men take paternity leave, don't you?"

"Sure, but who's investigating the skeleton until Patrick gets back?"

"I don't think anyone's investigating it. The case is kind of cold, you know?"

Not to Wyatt, or Jenny either. The Fabergé egg would remain locked in a vault until the skeleton was identified. It could take years unless someone convinced the sheriff to get moving on the case.

Wyatt spotted the sheriff through the window in his office door, and he was alone. Wyatt rapped twice and entered without waiting for a reply.

"Three months of paternity leave?" he asked tightly.

Caleb leaned back in his chair. He was built like a fireplug, with his belly straining at the buttons of his shirt. "Welcome to the twenty-first century. Don't worry, I've got Patrick's cases reassigned."

"What about the Summerlin Groves case?"

"Not a priority. It's a fifty-year-old cold case, and we're understaffed."

"What about the egg?"

Caleb sat back upright. "I asked one of those professors from the college to see if he could find out how it got here. He called it 'a provenance.' That's some foreign art term meaning the chain of custody for rare things. I don't know why they don't just say 'chain of custody.' Anyway, the professor said he might have time over spring break to start looking into it. Why the big rush?"

Because Jenny teeters on the edge of financial ruin, and that egg means a lot to her. The case wouldn't make progress while the sole detective was out on paternity leave and unpaid volunteers "might" have time to help out during spring break. Wyatt didn't have the funds or the authority to launch his own investigation into the identity of that skeleton, but he knew someone who did.

It was the same person who submitted the anonymous complaint about the disease on Jenny's grove.

PENNY DANVERS HAD NEVER BEEN a good fit for this town. In the highly competitive television news industry, on-air positions were hard to get and ambitious reporters often paid their dues in places like Amity before advancing to a major market. It hadn't taken Wyatt long to trace the IP address from the anonymous complaint back to the local television news station, and Penny was the most likely source.

The beige brick building housing the news station also contained Amity's city hall and only radio station. Penny had a private office, even though she had to share it with shelves of lighting equipment, tripods, and computer servers. She didn't even try to deny sending the complaints.

"Citrus canker is highly contagious," she said, the picture of innocence as she put her hand over her heart. "It was my civic duty to report it."

Penny covered the grove demolition for the evening news. Most of the people on site that day took no joy in the task, but Penny looked triumphant. Everyone knew that Hemingway had dumped her a few months earlier, and she seemed delighted to twist the knife to hurt both Hemingway and Jenny in one swift jab.

"You're familiar with Summerlin Groves," he said. "What's your theory about who the woman in the tree is?"

Penny warmed to the subject. "That woman died around

the same time the environmentalists started raising the alarm about the dangers of phosphate. Her skeleton was found a few miles from the biggest phosphate mine in the country. A coincidence?"

Wyatt mulled over the idea. He wasn't at liberty to share the biggest clue, the Fabergé egg that was still sitting in a locked storage vault, and yet, Penny's theory was a good one. "Have you reported that to Sheriff Eckert?"

"He's been useless," Penny said dismissively.

Wyatt nodded. "He's short-staffed and this is a very cold case, but *you* could do something."

Penny straightened, suddenly all business. "What have you got in mind?"

"A forensic artist. The skull is in good condition and we already know the woman's age and ethnicity. That's enough for a forensic artist to come up with an accurate rendering of what she looked like. And once you have *that* . . ."

Penny's eyes gleamed. If the sketch resulted in a solid lead, it would give Penny plenty of attention and maybe even the chance to solve a crime. It was the kind of story that could catapult a small-town reporter onto the national stage.

Penny stood and came around her desk to face him. "Can you pay for it?"

He shook his head. "This case is outside my purview. I'll bet the station would fund it."

"The station is cheap," Penny said. "All they care about is local weather and traffic reports. As if traffic is a big deal in a one-horse town with five stoplights."

Wyatt kept his expression carefully neutral. He and Penny shared similar frustrations with life in Amity. He'd been born and raised here and could criticize its shortcomings. Penny was an outsider and didn't have that right.

He strolled forward to brace a hand on the wall above Penny's glossy chestnut hair. "I get it, Penny," he said with deceptive calm. "When you look at Amity you see an aging town square with cracked sidewalks and empty storefronts. It's not big enough for a cinema or yoga studio or a decent Thai restaurant. The Friday night football game and church on Sunday morning is the only excitement all week. But if your car breaks down on the side of the road, someone will stop to help before you can even lift the hood. If you get sick, your neighbors will show up with a covered dish. These people work hard, pray harder, and raise the food that feeds people all over the world. This backwater town represents the heartbeat of America, and all those fancy urban hotspots would grind to a halt without it."

Penny's eyes glittered with cynicism. "You hate Amity as much as me."

Wyatt pushed himself away from the wall. Was it possible to love and loathe a place at the same time? Obviously it was, or he wouldn't feel so compelled to defend his hometown. Even though he never wanted to settle down here, he *respected* Amity.

"I'll exercise my right to remain silent regarding Amity, but a good investigative reporter would yank out their own eye teeth to discover the identity of the woman in that tree. It might even get you out of Amity."

"It will cost a fortune."

Wyatt shrugged. "How much is it worth for you to make a name for yourself?"

Penny's smile was wolfish, and he knew he'd come to the right place.

WYATT'S KNOWLEDGE of Fabergé eggs couldn't even fill a thimble, but the best place in Florida to learn more was right here in Amity. Karl Wakefield founded a museum to display his phenomenal personal collection of Russian art and antiquities. He claimed it was to share his bounty with the community, but mostly it was a tax write-off. Over the decades the museum became one of the best private museums in the country. The Wakefield Museum put Amity on the map, and its biggest attraction was two Fabergé eggs.

How did Karl get those eggs? How much did they cost and who did he buy them from? Somehow, the dead lady in the tree came into possession of a rare, missing Fabergé egg, and she'd probably been drawn to the area by Karl.

Wyatt turned into the museum's parking lot and let out a low whistle as he got out of his car. He'd been to this place a couple of times as a kid on school field trips, but never as an adult. The white limestone building reflected the subdued glamor of 1940s art deco design. Wide steps led up to an expansive portico, and inside was another a huge lobby built to host swanky receptions. Russian icons hanging on the interior walls looked oddly modern with their flat, unsmiling faces looking down on him as he walked toward the reception desk. It was a weekday and almost nobody was here.

To his surprise, he recognized the woman at the reception desk. It was Mrs. Hawkins, everyone's favorite fourth-grade teacher.

"I didn't realize you worked here," Wyatt said as he approached the chest-high counter.

"I volunteer three days a week," Mrs. Hawkins said. "I

always loved this place, and now that I'm retired, I get to be a part of it."

It *would* be a nice place to volunteer. The reception area was filled with a fortune in Renaissance tapestries and those gilded Russian icons. "What sort of work do they have you do?"

"Smile at guests as they come in."

Wyatt laughed. "That's it?"

She nodded. "It's a self-guided museum, so there's not much to do. The real reason they staff a reception desk is because it lowers the museum's insurance bill."

"This place carries a lot of insurance?"

Mrs. Hawkins sent him a pointed glance. "Those two Fabergé eggs are worth more than this entire building."

"Where are they?"

Mrs. Hawkins came around the counter and gestured him into the gallery. "I love showing them to people. I'm afraid one of them is on loan to another museum, but the Blackberry Winter Egg is here."

Although the gallery walls featured plenty of framed art, the star attraction was two display cases in the center of the room. The freestanding cases were tall enough to bring the eggs to shoulder height. One case was empty, but Wyatt walked to the other. Spot-lit from above and surrounded by bullet-proof glass on all sides, it gleamed with astonishing radiance.

The craftsmanship was staggering. Tiny clusters of blackberries and coiling vines were made of amethyst and jade, twining around an opal egg and looking shockingly realistic.

"I'll never tire of looking at it," Mrs. Hawkins said, her voice hushed with reverence. "So much beauty, so much artistry and love and wealth, all contained in that tiny egg that fits into the palm of my hand."

"Have you ever held it?" he asked.

Her trance was broken. "Oh my, don't be silly. Visitors are never allowed to hold the egg."

It wasn't exactly a denial, but he wouldn't push. "Where's the other one?"

Mrs. Hawkins glanced at the empty case. The flicker of annoyance was so fleeting he could have imagined it.

"Mr. Wakefield and his wife took it to Amsterdam for an exhibition. It's been out on loan for months."

"You're talking about Raymond Wakefield?"

Mrs. Hawkins nodded. "He's on the board of the museum, and he loves taking these eggs all over the world for special exhibitions." Mrs. Hawkins glanced both ways as if to assure herself they were alone in the gallery. Then she leaned in close to speak in a low voice. "Personally, I think he takes them on the road because he loves getting wined and dined all over the world. He only takes them to glamorous places, where he and the baroness can stay at luxury hotels and dine at Michelin-starred restaurants."

Mrs. Hawkins led him over to the empty case, where a photograph pasted to the side of the case showed the missing egg, a masterpiece of scarlet enamel that opened to reveal a golden palace inside.

"How does a person come into possession of one of these things?" he asked.

Her expression turned sadly cynical. "You have to know the right sort of people. You could be the richest person in the world, but this sort of treasure hardly ever goes up at auction. It's almost like the owners are in an exclusive club and they control who gets access to them. Raymond could tell you a lot more. I don't move in those kinds of circles."

But she came close. Mrs. Hawkins had been the daughter of the Wakefields' cook, but once upon a time she was

Senator Wakefield's sweetheart. Did Mrs. Hawkins ever look around at the fortune in treasures that filled this museum and wonder what her life could have been had she married Max Wakefield? Instead of an old apartment on the town square, she'd be living at the Wakefield mansion. Although Mrs. Hawkins never breathed a bad word about the senator, she didn't bother to hide her disdain for Raymond.

"How did old Karl Wakefield get these two eggs?"

"Probably some sort of back-room deal with the Soviets," she said dismissively. "The archivist might be able to shed more light on it."

He followed her back to the reception desk, where she placed a phone call to someone in the archives.

"Belinda will be out in a few minutes," Mrs. Hawkins said as she replaced the phone. Then she turned to the computer screen and didn't glance at him again.

Had he offended Mrs. Hawkins? Maybe probing into her knowledge of the Wakefield family had pricked an old, unhealed wound. If she still carried a fondness for the senator, why had she chosen to work in a place where she'd be surrounded by evidence of the Wakefield fortune everywhere she looked?

Most people probably had a long-ago love affair that never panned out. Those youthful flings rarely survived, but their memory could linger forever, a glorious season in the sun against which all other romances would be measured.

It was how he felt for Jenny. Remembering the intensity of those magical few months still carried a wistful, tender longing that was almost enjoyable in its anguish.

The archivist finally emerged, a middle-aged woman in a boxy beige suit who introduced herself as Belinda Cruz. "What can I help you with?"

"I'd like to learn more about the Fabergé eggs you have on

display," he said. "I'm especially interested in how the Wakefields got them and how much they paid."

"We don't have a whole lot," Belinda said as she led him into the archives. It was a grim, windowless room filled with worktables and metal cabinets. "One of the eggs was purchased abroad, and the other was a gift, so there isn't much of a paper trail."

Gifts? What kind of person could afford a gift of that magnitude? "Can you show me whatever you have?"

"Certainly." She began searching through a file drawer, and Wyatt took the opportunity to study the photos on the wall. Most featured Karl Wakefield with world leaders, and it was an impressive lot. How many people had photos standing in between Mahatma Gandhi and Albert Einstein? Others showed him with aging Hollywood stars. Charlie Chaplin and Paul Robeson…both men were known for harboring communist sympathies.

Then came the biggies. Karl Wakefield always considered his efforts to alleviate famine during the twenties and thirties in the Soviet Union to have been his proudest accomplishment, and his efforts were honored with receptions at the Kremlin. One photo showed a young Karl Wakefield shaking hands with Joseph Stalin, both men grinning broadly. Others showed Karl with Khrushchev and Brezhnev.

Joseph Stalin was probably history's biggest mass murderer of his own people, and a friendship with him wasn't something most people would be proud to flaunt.

"Karl never tried to hide this?" he asked Belinda as she closed the file drawer.

"The extent of Stalin's atrocities wasn't fully brought to light during Mr. Wakefield's lifetime," she said in what sounded like a well-rehearsed script. "The terms of his endowment to establish this museum require these photos to be publicly displayed, and we thought the archive was the best place."

The best to escape attention, anyway. He glanced at the slim file Belinda held. "This is the paperwork for the eggs?"

"It's all we've got. I'm afraid there's not much."

Wyatt settled into a chair and opened the file. Belinda wasn't kidding. The top document was an old mimeographed copy of a Russian form, dense with Cyrillic writing and impossible for Wyatt to read. An English translation was appended. The document was a customs declaration, stating that Karl Wakefield had legally purchased the Blackberry Winter Egg and paid all necessary taxes and fees to the Soviet government before leaving the country. The price was never mentioned. The other document was even shorter, just a simple Christmas card from the Kremlin, thanking Karl for his decades of service with "this modest gift of the Castle Egg."

Mrs. Hawkins's assertion about needing to know people in high places had never been more evident than these two forms. Was the dead woman in the tree one of those "people in high places"? The discovery of her body only a few miles from the home of an ardent collector of Fabergé eggs couldn't be a coincidence.

Other files contained paperwork for failed attempts to buy additional eggs. Both old Karl Wakefield and his grandson Raymond had been insatiable in their attempts to buy a third Fabergé egg, but never succeeded. Raymond seemed particularly fascinated with the glamor of the eggs. One entire file contained photographs of him at museums around the world posed alongside various Fabergé masterpieces, his expression one of awe and admiration. Nowhere in these files was any evidence that Senator Wakefield participated in the hunt for more eggs.

The only thing he learned for sure was that two of the Wakefields had an unquenchable thirst for Fabergé eggs stretching across half a century, and these treasures were almost impossible to win.

What would Raymond do when he learned Jenny had one?

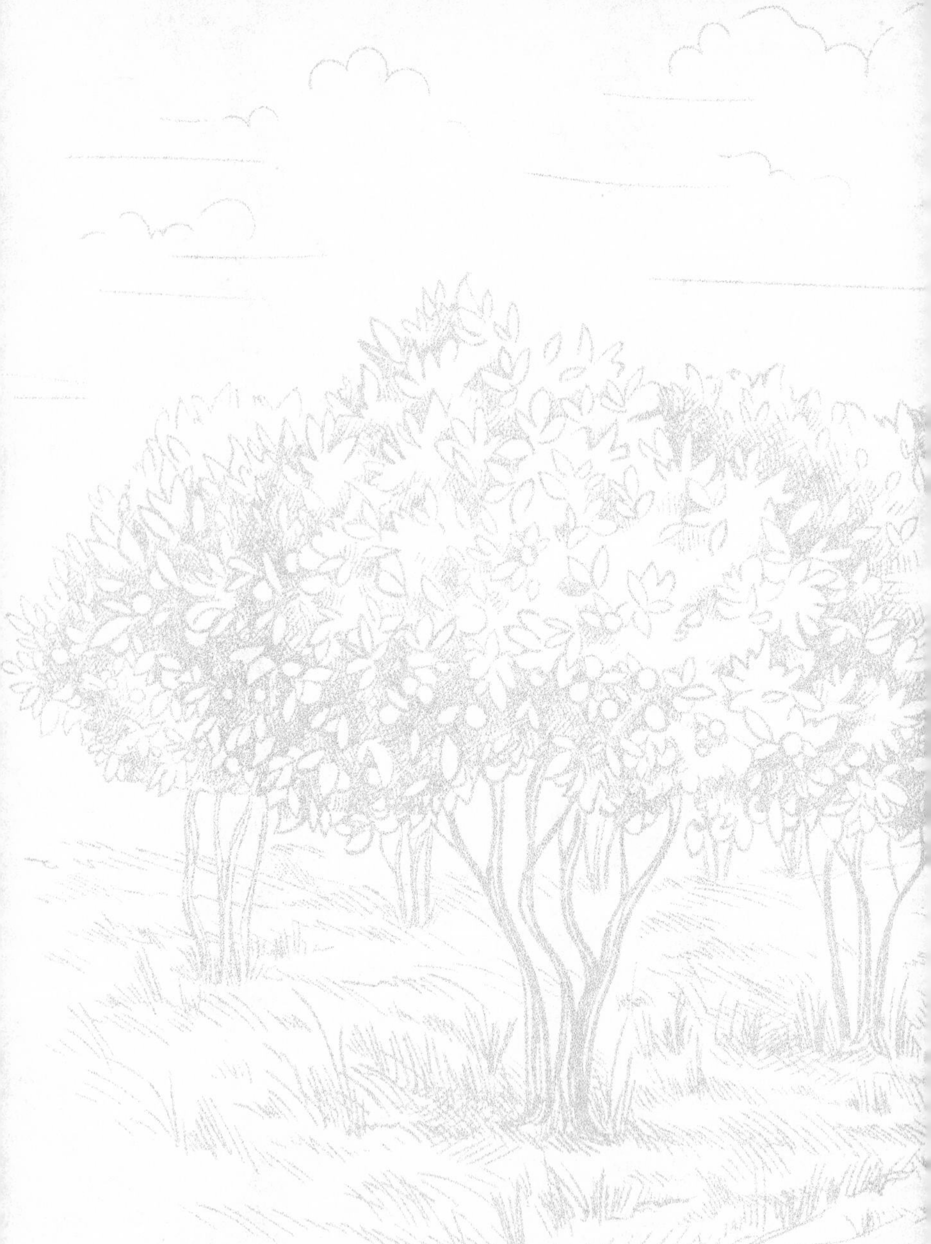

Chapter Fourteen

Wyatt didn't want to go through the rest of his life avoiding Jenny Summerlin like he'd been doing since the night his sister died. Jenny wasn't responsible for what happened to Lauren, and she'd had nothing but bad luck ever since that awful night. While he disapproved of how she'd hid the citrus canker, it was time to do something about the guilt that clobbered him each time he remembered her stricken expression as government tractors closed in on her grove.

The damaged gutter on the side of her house was a good excuse to check up on her. He could drive out to Jenny's place, fix the gutter, and wish her well, then put her safely in the rearview mirror of his life. His campaign to run for Commissioner of Agriculture had picked up surprising momentum, and he needed to pay more attention to it instead of worrying about Jenny.

It had been a week since her grove had been plowed down. His heart sank as he turned onto her property because it looked even worse than he remembered. It couldn't even be called a grove anymore. It was only a torn-up field of barren, lumpy dirt.

To his surprise, a state vehicle was already parked in front of the house. He'd known the department intended to send an agronomist out to make recommendations for getting the grove up and running again, and Heidi Larsen was already here. Heidi had a master's degree in plant science and a cute, flirtatious smile.

He cut the engine and stepped out of his truck, slipping on his sunglasses like a battle shield. This wasn't going to be easy, but it was time to extend an olive branch to Jenny.

Jenny and Hemingway were talking to Heidi over by the supply shed. He raised his arm in greeting, and even from fifty yards away it looked like every muscle in Jenny's body stiffened at the sight of him. She strode toward him, her face grim. He needed to lower the temperature and adopted a casual tone as she approached.

"It's good to see Heidi already out here," he said. "She's a pro at getting farms up and running. I'm guessing she's here to take soil samples?" That was usually the first step in a farm evaluation, but Jenny acted like she hadn't heard a word he said.

"What are you doing here?"

He nodded to the roofline of the farmhouse. "That gutter needs anchoring."

"Go away, Wyatt."

He shifted uneasily. Making conversation with attractive women had always been a struggle, but it used to be easy with Jenny. Now he felt as awkward and tongue-tied as ever. Maybe it was best to simply tell the truth.

"Jenny, I'm sorry about what happened—"

"What happened?" she interrupted. "You say that as

though you weren't the person who signed off on the paperwork."

"I was, and I'm sorry that I had to do it. And I'd like to fix that gutter for you."

She folded her arms and glared. "Tell me this, Wyatt. If I came over to your house to fix *your* sagging gutter or whatever else needed repair . . . would that mend everything that's gone wrong between us?"

He winced, her arrow finding its mark. "Some things can't ever be fixed," he finally said, and her eyes hardened.

"But that gutter can. Go fix it." She stomped up the porch steps and slammed the door without a backward glance.

He tamped down the urge to follow her inside and demand a full-blown, cards-on-the-table accounting over how she let him down after Lauren died. He tried to make things right regardless of what Jack did. They could be married now if Jenny hadn't been so irrationally fixated on this grove.

Instead, he swallowed back the frustration and hoisted the ladder from his truck, then climbed onto the roof to examine the gutter. At least, that was what he was *supposed* to be doing. Instead, he glared at Hemingway taking the state agronomist on an ATV tour of the property. Heidi clung to Hemingway's back like a barnacle, her laughter floating over the yard as the ATV rocked and bumped over the torn-up ground. It was annoying how easily Hemingway could flirt with any woman under the sun.

"English professor," he muttered under his breath, then went back to examining the damaged screws on the gutter. What kind of English professor did nothing but drink and flirt with women all day? Back when Wyatt was dating Jenny he'd been so suspicious of Hemingway that he ran a background check on him, and found that Hemingway had been fired from every job since college. Yes, Hemingway earned a doctorate in English Literature at the University of Iceland but got fired from a college in Reykjavik during his first year of teaching. Then he got fired from the Icelandic coast guard. In a country with a miniscule population, how bad did you have to be to get fired from the coast guard? Then he got ousted from a tenure-track position here in Florida, even though the students loved him. According to an online site that reviewed professors, Hemingway was wildly popular with the students, especially the female students. They said he was funny, irreverent, and as handsome as a Viking god.

That was the actual term they used. "Viking god." It made Wyatt want to rinse his eyes with bleach, but Hemingway seemed to have that effect on women.

Wyatt frowned at the series of rusted screws barely holding the gutter up, all of which needed to be replaced. He secured the gutter with a bunch of c-clamps, and the battery-operated drill made a satisfying grinding buzz as he removed the screws. This was the sort of job any man would do for a woman he cared about.

Once, long ago, he'd assumed he and Jenny would find their way to the altar just as easily as they'd slipped into a whirlwind love affair. By the end of their first date, he concluded she was the woman he was going to marry.

Not that their relationship had been perfect. Jenny always assumed he would move to the grove to raise a family here, which was their first problem. She never believed him when he reminded her that he'd only returned to Amity for a short stint after leaving the army. As soon as he passed the bar in Florida, he planned on leaving for a bigger challenge, like the job in Morocco or consulting on international trade. He never intended to settle down in Amity. The opportunities were too small, and life on an orange grove was too lonely. Where would their kids find friends?

Then there was Hemingway, the irresponsible and disrespectful womanizer. The *only* thing Hemingway had going for him was a quirk of fate that granted him symmetrical facial features so attractive it made otherwise intelligent women fall at his feet.

The pitch of the roof was steep and he crept carefully to place another bracket when a ringing cell phone from inside the house distracted him. He cocked his ear to listen.

"Hello?" Jenny said.

The window in the office must be open, because he could easily hear her. He had no business eavesdropping, but it would be rude to start the drilling when she was on the phone only a few yards away.

"I'm sorry, it's going to be tough to drive to Miami again," she said. The breeze picked up, obscuring whatever she said next. A screw rolled down the incline of the roof. He smacked it with his hand and almost lost his balance.

Idiot. If he died after falling off a roof on Summerlin Groves, his mother would never forgive him. Downstairs, Jenny started talking again.

"If you can email me the contract, I'll get it notarized and sent back to you."

The other person must be talking because Jenny was silent, and he waited. He ought to be ashamed for eavesdropping. It wasn't something an honest, straightforward person should be doing. He picked up the drill and started working again. Jenny could close the window if the noise bothered her.

It took an hour to replace the old brackets with rust-resistant hardware. He repaired a couple of loose shingles that needed it and scanned the rest of her roof to be sure it was in good condition. A few more snatches of Jenny's conversation leaked through the window. She'd given someone directions to Summerlin Groves and sounded profusely grateful about not having to drive all the way to Miami to sign some papers.

It took two trips to bring his equipment down to the ground. Jenny must have heard him folding up the ladder, because she came out, shading her eyes to look up at the roofline.

"The gutter is fixed," he said. It was cleaned out, secured, and her roof was in good shape, too.

"Thanks," she said, looking as uncomfortable as he felt.

"What's in Miami?"

Her eyes widened. "Nothing."

"Nothing?"

"Let me clarify. Nothing that's any of your business."

He shouldered the ladder and headed toward the truck. "Fair enough," he said. Jenny had gone back inside by the time he returned for the rest of his tools.

He hadn't succeeded in softening the arctic blast between them, but at least her gutter was no longer in danger of falling off. He'd done a lot of things on Jenny's behalf over the years. He'd warned her about her overdue taxes and gotten the district attorney off her back over that gun charge. He even convinced Kent McAllister to start letting her visit Sam again. She would never know any of it, but at least it helped dull the ache of regret whenever he thought of her.

No matter how long he lived, he would probably always revisit memories of the glorious few months he had with Jenny, and wonder if he could have somehow salvaged the wreck her brother made of their lives.

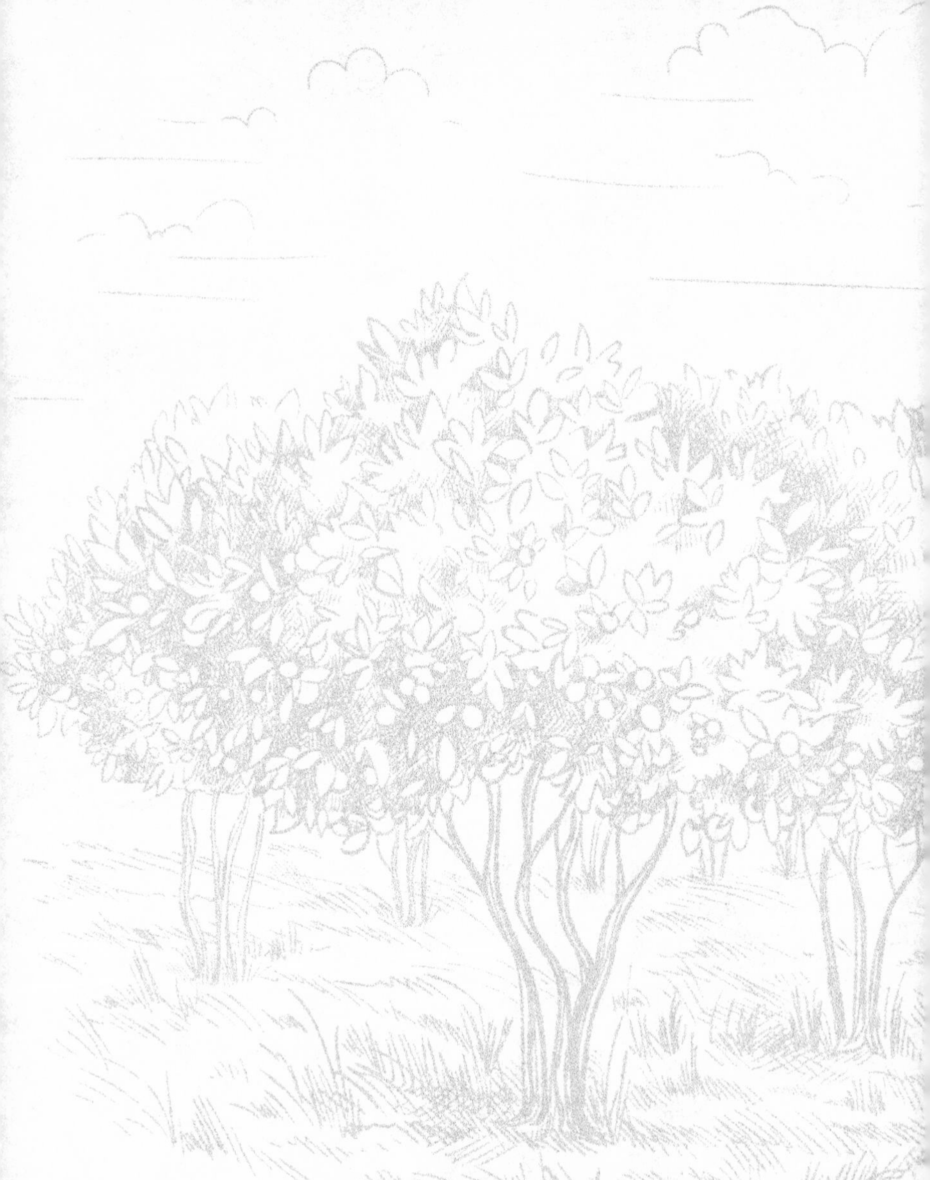

Chapter Fifteen

Jenny snapped awake in the middle of a nightmare.

In her dream, Kristen from Christie's arrived at the grove to discuss selling the Fabergé egg and brought the four Romanov daughters along for the meeting. It was impossible, but dreams were like that. Jenny sat at the farm table discussing the auction with Kristen while the four Romanov daughters watched from the kitchen, dressed in their ethereal white gowns, their faces expressionless. Jenny tried to offer them a cup of coffee, but they wouldn't look at her.

The dream was unnerving, even though she shouldn't feel guilty about claiming the egg. She wasn't robbing a grave; she was merely starting the process to determine the egg's legitimate owner.

Jenny sat on the porch swing with Hemingway to await Kristen's arrival. "Are you sure you want to pull the trigger on this?" he asked. "Once Kristen announces the discovery of the egg, our ninety-day clock starts."

Looking at the churned-up dirt in her lumpy, barren grove hardened her resolve. "I'm sure," she said, even though

Hemingway's question screwed her anxiety a little higher. Revealing the existence of the egg was going to infuriate the sheriff, but she couldn't afford to wait any longer.

Nervous apprehension still swirled as Kristen's four-door sedan rolled up the gravel driveway, clouds of limestone dust kicking up beneath the wheels as she drew near.

Once again, Kristen was fabulously attired in a flirty skirt that flared out beneath a belt that cinched her waist into enviable proportions. In light of her stiletto heels, Hemingway lent Kristen his arm as she gingerly tiptoed over the gravel drive and up the porch steps. Inside, Kristen's heels clicked on the plank floors as they headed back to the kitchen for something to drink after her long drive from Miami.

Kristen's eyes sparkled behind her cat-eye frames as she admired the kitchen. "What a charming carafe!" she enthused as Jenny poured a glass of iced tea. "Is it Steuben glass?"

The jug was what she and Jack used for Kool-Aid when they were kids. "I'm not sure. It's always been here."

"What about those vintage Waffle House signs I saw propped against the side of the barn? Are they original?"

"I don't know," Jenny said. "My grandfather collected them."

"It appears he had quite the eye for collectible southern folk art," Kristen said.

Her grandfather also had quite the eye for old margarine containers, broken radios, and crates filled with moldering issues of the *Saturday Evening Post*. After he died, Jack went on a binge inspired by *Antiques Roadshow* to search through Gus's junk for treasures. He started selling the good stuff through online auction sites before he died, but Jenny never pursued selling the rest.

"Shall we get down to business?" Kristen asked brightly, and Hemingway jumped up to pull out a chair at the farmhouse table. Kristen sat, then opened a sleek alligator-skin briefcase and removed a number of files stuffed with paperwork.

"Let's start with what our researchers have learned about the egg," Kristen said. "The Firebird Egg was commissioned by Czar Nicholas in 1896. One of our associates in Russia researched what is known about the fate of the egg, and it isn't pretty."

Jenny braced herself. The czarina kept the egg on a bookshelf in her private parlor at the Winter Palace. Nothing that happened to the czar's family or their possessions during the revolution was going to be a pretty story.

The first photograph Kristen showed them was of the Winter Palace in Saint Petersburg. The stately building had broken windows, blackened scorch marks, and the ground was littered with rubble.

"This was taken in October of 1917 right after the palace was stormed by the Bolsheviks," Kristen said. "The czar and his family were already in custody at a rural house in Ekaterinburg, so the palace was only guarded by a handful of troops, who were quickly overwhelmed. A mob broke through the barricades and streamed inside the palace. The looting was terrible, and the Firebird Egg was lost for ten years after that night."

"The first sighting of your egg happened in 1927," Kristen continued. "A Soviet official gave it to his mistress in Moscow. She eventually sold it back to the Kremlin a few years later, but not before she had herself photographed with it. Brace yourself. It's a very candid photo."

Kristen opened the file to reveal a black-and-white photograph, and Jenny blanched.

The woman looked a little like Greta Garbo. Her hair was bobbed fashionably short, her skin shockingly white against smoky, kohl-rimmed eyes. She balanced the egg on her head, opened to display the firebird with its spread wings. The woman had her own arms similarly extended in a mocking pose. She was topless, flaunting her bare breasts with a lewd expression.

"She certainly knew how to make an impression," Hemingway said wryly.

An inexplicable sadness weighed as Jenny stared at the photograph. That egg had been given by a man to a woman he adored. Maybe the czar was a bad leader, but he loved and cherished his wife. Had the world been different, that egg would have eventually gone to one of those four pretty daughters in their white dresses instead of serving as a trinket in an obscene photo.

Jenny fought to keep her voice composed. "You say she sold the egg back to the Soviet government?"

Kristen nodded. "In 1929 it appeared on an inventory of the Kremlin Armory, which is one of the oldest museums in Russia. They display antique weapons, jeweled crowns, and that sort of thing. It was the logical place for it to go, and the Russians still display a lot of Fabergé eggs as proof of the czar's decadence. The Firebird Egg was only on display for a few years before it disappeared from the inventory in 1935."

"Then what happened to it?" Hemingway asked.

Kristen leaned back in the chair and twirled a pen. "We don't have proof, but the egg disappeared at the same time that a diamond tiara and a fine Rembrandt painting vanished from the Armory Museum. The Rembrandt showed up in New York as part of an under-the-table business scheme between the Soviets and American communists sometimes called 'treasure into tractors.' I've spent the last week looking into the scheme, and I can't decide if it was an act of sheer heroism or rapacious greed. If I had to choose, I'd say it was a little of both."

Kristen outlined the "tractors into treasures" program that secretly began in the 1920s when the Russian economy was in shambles after a decade of war and revolution. Bridges and railroads had been destroyed. Horses that once pulled plows had been stolen, killed in the war, or eaten by starving people. Millions of farmworkers had died on the eastern front, and famine left thirty million Russians in danger of starvation.

There was no money to revitalize the agrarian economy, but there were empty castles brimming with artwork and jewels to be seized. Diamond tiaras, Gutenberg Bibles, and paintings by old masters all disappeared into the "treasures for tractors" scheme. At least ten Fabergé eggs were sold by the Soviets, then the cash was used to buy heavy farming equipment, fertilizer, and medicine. The Red Army went on a march through the countryside, gathering up what they could. Some of it was turned over to the Soviet government, some of it simply disappeared.

Jenny's gaze flicked to the sultry-eyed woman in the photograph. It looked as if the Firebird Egg was one of those priceless antiquities that got swept up during those terrible years of chaos. Kristen continued outlining her theory.

"The USSR wasn't recognized by the United States, which made trade with them illegal, but for the right price, some Americans were willing to help the Soviet Union get back up on its feet. The Soviets were desperate to buy farming equipment. Tractors, combines, grain elevators . . . they needed anything that could transform the war-torn fields into productive farmland. They also needed fertilizer and grain."

Jenny met Hemingway's knowing gaze. It sounded exactly like what the World Famine Commission had been created to do.

Karl Wakefield lived only a few miles away during those turbulent early years of the Soviet Union, and he never denied being a communist sympathizer. He might have been part of the "treasures for tractors" scheme. His phosphate mine was the largest producer of fertilizer in the nation, and Karl would have been ideally poised to make such a trade.

"What did the Rembrandt look like?" she asked Kristen. "The one that disappeared from the Kremlin at the same time as the Firebird Egg?"

"It was a self-portrait of the artist in middle age." Kristen leaned forward to tap her fingers on the laptop keyboard, then turned the screen so she and Hemingway could see. "Kremlin records indicate that its sale was used to buy ten Ford tractors. The deal was brokered by an anonymous American donor."

The tension in Jenny's neck eased. The Rembrandt on Kristen's laptop didn't look anything like the one hanging above Senator Wakefield's fireplace. "If these under-the-table deals saved people from starvation, it sounds like basic human decency," she said, hoping she didn't sound too defensive.

"The American agent took a ten percent commission to broker the deal," Kristen said. "Maybe his motives were humanitarian, but he also made a fortune from the trades."

Jenny swallowed back her distaste. The horrible photo of the nude woman with the Firebird Egg taunted her. How many times did stolen art need to change hands before it was clean again?

"Did your contact in Russia know the name of the American who brokered the deal?"

Kristen shook her head. "All we know is that the trading went on for decades. Lots of artwork was liquidated with that man's help, but he insisted on anonymity."

"Karl Wakefield liked art," Hemingway pointed out, and

he ought to know since he'd ghostwritten two biographies about him. Most of Hemingway's information came from Karl's adoring grandson Raymond, who would hear no ill about his esteemed ancestor. Getting rich by taking a cut from famine relief wasn't something most people would brag about.

Jenny suspected Karl was the anonymous American trader, meaning his descendants would have a legitimate claim on the egg, but her grandfather might have a claim, too.

"My grandfather was a collector," she said to Kristen. "He prowled through flea markets and estate sales and bought anything he thought might someday be valuable. I've never had an expert evaluate his collection. As long as you're here, would you mind taking a look?"

"I'd be happy to."

Kristen's high heels weren't going to survive walking across two acres of gravel pathways to the storage barns, so Hemingway revved up the ATV to drive them all over. The oversized buildings were made of galvanized steel and anchored to concrete pads. They were ugly, but Jenny had always been proud of them since Gus built them himself.

"Tell me more about your grandfather," Kristen said once they arrived at the first barn, straightening her mussed hair while Jenny worked a key in the padlock.

"He was born and raised here on the grove," she replied. The chain rattled as she pulled it off the door handles. She rolled the corrugated metal door to the side, releasing the familiar musty scent from the interior. "Gus was responsible for getting the grove financially sound. He rewired the farmhouse's electrical system and added the front porch. He built the outbuildings, too. He was an orange grower all his life."

"And quite a collector," Kristen said, peering inside at the rows of metal shelving stuffed with bric-a-brac. "Was he ever involved in the New York art scene? Or Paris? Many of the Russian aristocratic refugees ended up in Paris."

Jenny shook her head. "My grandfather had a tenth-grade education and never set foot outside the state of Florida. He liked vintage art, but mostly he was a hoarder. He was interested in quantity, not quality."

Hemingway switched on the light, illuminating the aisles of stacked metal shelving. The place didn't look too bad now that it was organized. The first aisle contained old electronics, television sets, radios, and record players. The second aisle was mainly dishes and kitchen equipment. Jack had grouped materials by type, which accounted for dozens of orange crates filled with cast-iron doorstops, antique clocks, and bookends, all of which had a cheap, mid-twentieth-century vibe.

Hemingway made himself at home on an antique barber chair with a chrome footrest while Jenny guided Kristen farther into the aisles.

"My brother thought these old hunting decoys might be worth something," she said, gesturing to dozens of carved wooden ducks. "And these crates are full of vinyl albums and turntables. Jack didn't know if they were worth anything or not."

Kristen's curious gaze scanned the shelves with keen intensity, but the slight wrinkle on her nose indicated she wasn't overly impressed. She was like a shark slicing through the dross, immediately pouncing on items that might be of value and dismissing the rest. She identified two duck decoys that might fetch a hundred dollars each, and the large collection of mismatched Fiestaware dishes that might fetch between ten and twenty dollars each . . . but nothing was valuable enough for taking to auction.

They spent an hour going through both storage barns

before returning to the farmhouse in defeat. Kristen went to freshen up in the bathroom before beginning the long drive back to Miami while Jenny and Hemingway made more iced tea.

"Can I get you something to drink before you go?" Jenny offered once Kristen returned, but she shook her head.

"It will just make me stop along the way," Kristen said. "All I need is your signature on the agreement to let us broker the egg. Then I'll start the process as soon as I get back to the office."

Jenny nodded and headed to the desk. She set her glass of iced tea down and laid out the pages of the contract. Why did contracts always have to be so wordy? She leaned over to read the small print while Kristen hovered uncomfortably close. It was disconcerting. Jenny shifted to move a little farther away.

"Um," Kristen said. "Can I take a look at that coaster you're using?"

The quaver in Kristen's voice sounded odd, and Jenny lifted her glass of iced tea to reveal the spiral metal coaster.

"Can I touch it?" Kristen asked.

Jenny nodded, and Kristen's expression morphed into wonder as she lifted the green coaster made of coiled metal. It was an unusual coaster because it had room for two cups. Whoever made it used a long, thick wire and coiled it from each side to create the identical matching coasters joined by a loop of metal.

Kristen carried it to the window for a better look, turning it over in her hands while holding back laughter.

"Jenny, this is a Bronze Age double-spiral pendant that is somewhere between three and four thousand years old."

"What?" she burst out. Maybe she hadn't heard correctly but Hemingway looked equally amazed as he listened to Kristen repeat herself.

"These spiral ornaments were common among the Tumulus people of central Europe a few thousand years ago. The ornament would have been a shiny bronze when it was made, but with age, the copper in the alloy has given it a green patina. Given the workmanship, I'd say it originated in the Baltic or maybe Polish region of Europe."

This seemed too bizarre to believe. Hemingway opened his laptop and began typing like mad, a little smile hovering on his face as he clicked through some images. He turned the screen so she could see, and sure enough, he'd quickly located several of those distinctive green spiral ornaments in museums throughout the world.

"And I've been using it for a coaster?" Jenny asked in horror.

Kristen set the green disk on the table and carefully blotted it with a tissue. "At least it's waterproof," she said. "This piece has been restored and treated, which is why it looks almost new. Restoring ancient metal is an expensive process that can't be done by amateurs. Whoever restored this knew its value and invested a lot in it. Do you know where it came from?"

"From my grandfather's junk collecting," Jenny said. "My brother wanted to toss it, but I've always liked it. How much do you think it's worth?"

Maybe it was crass to bring up money, but the mortgage payment was due soon and it was hard to think of anything else.

"Not as much as you might think," Kristen said. "I'd estimate around four or five thousand dollars. The Fabergé egg is far more valuable and carries the glamor of the doomed czar and his sad German wife . . . but this primitive bronze coil is so much more intriguing to me. It was probably worn by a tribal leader of great status and passed down for generations before getting lost to time."

"And now it's here," Hemingway said quietly.

"Yes," Kristen said in an equally reverent tone. "I wonder how it happened?"

Jenny had no explanation. Her grandfather was *not* a sophisticated art collector. Maybe he could have gotten lucky with a once-in-a-lifetime discovery of a Fabergé egg in a flea market, but lightning didn't strike the same place twice and she had no explanation how he could have come across such a treasure.

"All I know is, that coaster has been in this house as far back as I can remember," she said. "My grandfather used it as a coaster, too. We all did. My grandfather never suggested it was of any particular value. I don't think he knew."

Kristen scanned the interior of the farmhouse with new eyes. "Can I look around the house to see if I can spot anything else?"

"Please do!"

She and Hemingway opened every cupboard in the kitchen, setting out dishes and crockery, then putting them away as quickly as Kristen looked at them. They opened drawers, closets, pulled books from the shelves. Kristen moved fast. It didn't take her long to dismiss countless pieces of furniture and knickknacks. After going through the first floor with no additional treasures, they headed upstairs, where there wasn't much to be seen in the bedrooms aside from the clothes and ordinary furniture. It was dark by the time they finished, and their treasure hunt came up empty.

"It's getting too late to make the trip back to Miami," Kristen said. "Is there a decent hotel in town?"

"Not really, but you can have your pick of bedrooms if you'd like to stay here," Jenny offered. "I'll bet Hemingway will even catch you something for breakfast if you like catfish."

Kristen flushed and her eyes grew round in admiration. "Really? You catch your own fish?" she said with the same sort of astonishment as when she located that Bronze Age artifact.

"I can't promise catfish," Hemingway said. "Sometimes the best I can do is trout."

"I'm totally fine with trout," Kristen rushed to say. "I love trout. Or catfish. Or whatever you catch."

Jenny tried not to laugh at the way Kristen was falling under Hemingway's spell. Most women usually did.

Why couldn't Jenny be like most women? Life would have been easier if she could have fallen in love with Hemingway instead of getting wrapped up with Wyatt Rossiter and his gentle brown eyes and deep, strong compassion. Should she have taken his offer to run away to Morocco? They might have been happy there.

But Morocco was in the past, as was any hope of a life with Wyatt. She turned her attention to Kristen. A little more late-night prowling in the mudroom cabinets turned up an early-twentieth-century Coca-Cola bottle Kristen said would be worth around $2,000.

It was cause for a celebration. Or maybe they were just tired and looking for an excuse to quit working and enjoy each other's company. The difficulties of the past two years made Jenny appreciate the value of a lovely evening. They moved onto the front porch, opened a bottle of wine, and toasted their new friendship while watching the sun melt into the horizon of a glorious Florida evening.

TRUE TO HIS WORD, Hemingway caught catfish before dawn, and Jenny browned some cornmeal hushpuppies with fried green tomatoes for breakfast. Everything she cooked in the old cast iron skillet had a depth of flavor impossible to produce any other way. It had been used for the past four generations right here in this kitchen.

Kristen looked entirely different this morning. She hadn't brought an overnight bag, and without her bright red lipstick or hair shellacked into ruthless obedience, she seemed far more approachable as she padded around the farmhouse in a pair of Jenny's bedroom slippers.

Or perhaps it had been celebrating until after midnight that made everything feel mildly wonderful this morning. They sat at the Formica table in the kitchen nursing cups of strong black coffee, the remnants of breakfast still on the table.

"Once we make the announcement about the egg, your 90-day clock will start," Kristen said. "Are you certain you want to proceed? It might get you in trouble with your local cops."

The legs of Jenny's chair scraped as she rose to rinse the cast iron skillet. The sheriff asked, but couldn't *order* her to stay silent about the egg. It was time to take her life back, and the egg might be the key to doing it.

Confidence pumped in her veins as she met Kristen's gaze. "Let the countdown begin."

Chapter Sixteen

Jenny headed out to the equipment barn after bidding Kristen farewell. It was time to start leveling the ground to prepare it for saplings. She was oiling the tractor when her cell phone rang, showing Senator Wakefield's familiar number on the screen.

It was a little late for him to return her flurry of desperate telephone messages. It had been more than a week since her grove had been destroyed. She sighed, then dried her hands and reached for the phone.

"Yes," she said in a flat tone.

"Jenny," he greeted in a disconcertingly jovial voice.

"Senator."

Several uncomfortable seconds passed before he tried again. "Look . . . I'm sorry about what happened out at your grove. How are you doing?"

Her gaze trailed out the window. Dirt as far as the eye could see, and she didn't feel like talking about it. "What can I do for you, Senator?" She clenched the phone so hard her knuckles hurt, but she would be polite even if it killed her.

"Raymond and I are out running errands and would like to swing by your place. Are you up for a visit?"

"Why?"

"To see how my favorite goddaughter is doing. That, and maybe talk a little business."

It piqued her interest, and she agreed to meet with them.

She called Hemingway immediately. "The Senator and Raymond are on their way over, and I'd like you to be here. I'm curious about what they have to say, so be nice."

"I'm always nice," Hemingway tossed off before ending the phone call, probably still smarting over the incident at the Brickhouse.

Hemingway and Raymond Wakefield were opposites in all things. Hemingway lovingly crafted each sentence of the novel he'd been working on for six years, while Raymond paid ghostwriters to churn out laudatory books about his famous relatives. Hemingway kept in flawless shape through manual labor on the grove, while Raymond's enviable physique came compliments of downhill skiing in the Alps or piloting a sailboat around the Caribbean.

Ten minutes later she sat with Hemingway on the porch swing, slowly rocking as the senator's Range Rover approached the house. Raymond was driving, and he came around to the passenger side to help his father out of the car. As usual, Raymond looked like he'd just stepped out of a Ralph Lauren advertisement. Crisp white chinos, a navy sports jacket, and a lime green pocket square. His wife wasn't here, but Jenny would bet that the baroness wore lime green today.

"How are book sales?" Hemingway asked as the pair arrived at the base of the porch.

Raymond's mouth thinned. "Excellent. It seems I must reiterate your contractual obligation to remain silent on ghostwriting projects. Unless you want a lawsuit, you need to stop mouthing off in public."

The senator held up a placating hand. "Let's all calm down," he said. "We came here to express our sympathy about what happened and offer to buy you out. You've declined my offers in the past, but this one is a little different. You can keep the house, keep living here if you like; we're only interested in buying the land."

He gave a brusque nod to his son, who opened a briefcase and handed her a purchase proposal. She blinked in surprise. The offer was even more generous than in the past, which made no sense given the condition of her torn-up fields.

"What would you want with a ruined orange grove?" she asked.

"I want it for hunting," Raymond said. "Fox hunting demands a lot of territory, and since this land adjoins our property, we can transform it to a nice open space to give the horses free rein."

Jenny always thought Raymond's quarterly fox hunts were the ultimate in pretentious showmanship, but they'd been a tradition for generations at the Wakefield estate. Rich people from all over Florida brought their horses for the hunt, which didn't chase a fox at all, merely a carefully laid trail of scent from a lure.

Raymond's eyes gleamed as he scanned the land. "We can dig out a section and flood it, plant it with marsh grass, then build up a few hills with the excavated dirt. It will dramatically improve the riding experience. And as I said, you're more than welcome to keep the house and a few acres surrounding it. We only want the land for hunting."

Her life here revolved around growing oranges, not indulging Raymond's aristocratic pretensions. She handed the slip of paper back to Raymond. "Thanks for the offer, but I'm going to replant the grove."

Raymond refused to take the document. "Hang on to it," he said. "If you change your mind, you know how to contact us. And Jenny . . . I really am sorry for what happened here."

Hemingway placed a hand over his heart. "Your compassion is a model for us all."

Jenny held her breath as Raymond glowered, but the two men left without incident.

"Why do you keep needling him?" she asked once their car pulled on to the road. "One of these days he might make good on his threat to sue you over the ghostwriting thing."

"He won't," Hemingway said. "All it would do is shine a spotlight on the fact that he's no writer. I learned a lot while I was living at Wakefield Manor, doing interviews and listening to that pretentious snob ramble about his glorious family. Most of it was self-congratulatory blather, though he told me a few interesting stories. I put it all in the manuscript, then Raymond blew his stack when he saw it in there."

She cocked a brow. "Like what?"

Hemingway rocked the porch swing in silence for several moments before speaking. "Like the real reason the senator dumped Millicent Hawkins."

Jenny stopped rocking. She had always assumed the romance between the heir to the Wakefield fortune and the daughter of his family's cook was little more than a fleeting teenaged romance.

Not according to Hemingway.

"Raymond told me that his father wanted to run away with Millicent to France, where an interracial marriage wouldn't be so scandalous. When old Karl found out, he put an end to it. Karl had grand ambitions for his son, and wanted Max to reach the pinnacle of the American political scene.

That couldn't happen if he was married to a Black woman. When Max wouldn't budge, old Karl threatened to accuse Millicent's mother of theft and send her to jail. Max caved, and according to Raymond, he never got over it. Raymond refused to let me include it in the book. He said it would reflect badly on his own mother, and it's no secret that Max never really loved his wife."

True. Rumor had it the senator's marriage was the joining of two wealthy and politically powerful families, and he didn't seem too shattered after his wife passed away almost a decade ago.

Jenny lingered on the porch long after Hemingway returned to work, but the tale of two thwarted lovers remained in her mind. There were surely a million reasons love affairs died. What would have happened if Max and Millicent ran off to France? Maybe Karl's threats were empty, and they could have found a happy ending in France.

Maybe she and Wyatt could have been happy in Morocco.

The thought weighed heavily as she revved up the tractor and got to work preparing the soil. She was too practical to throw everything away and run off to Morocco . . . but a part of her would forever mourn the dream of Morocco that vanished before it ever had a chance to begin.

WYATT WAS a massive underdog in the race to become the state's next Commissioner of Agriculture. He had no money, no name recognition, and no experience navigating the world of politics, but his unique background won the grand prize of political advertising: free statewide media attention. Career politicians with their business suits and law degrees weren't as interesting as someone born, raised, and currently working in agricultural law enforcement. When a television news anchor from Miami asked for an interview, Wyatt chose his parents' feed store as the location since it showcased his deep roots in agriculture.

Answering the reporter's questions was easy because all he had to do was tell the truth. "Everyone else in the race is a professional politician," he told the reporter once the camera started rolling. "I grew up helping customers right here in my parents' feed store, and my first paying job was bailing hay on a cattle ranch. I'm the only one in the race who knows agriculture from the ground up."

His parents watched from their position behind the checkout counter, both beaming with pride. It was a friendly interview, and the journalist tossed him a number of softball questions, such as his first priority should he win the election.

"The state's zoning laws need to protect agriculture," he replied. "Every year we're losing more farms and ranches because the zoning laws favor development. I'm fighting to preserve our agricultural heritage rather than build another high-rise hotel. I'm aiming to protect pastureland, not parking lots."

It was the perfect closing line, and the reporter sensed it. She wished him luck, then signaled to the cameraman to stop filming.

"It will be on tonight's six and eleven o'clock newscast," she told him. "Are you able to get Miami broadcasts up here?"

His mother couldn't restrain herself any longer. "Our next-door neighbor has a satellite dish, and he's invited the whole street to come over and watch."

"You must be so proud," the reporter said politely.

Donna clasped a hand over her heart. "This is the best

thing that's happened to our family in years. It gives us all something to cheer for."

His mother continued to gush, and Wyatt didn't have the heart to stop her. His long-shot campaign was likely to come to a swift end after the primary in two weeks, but until then he would go along with anything his mother wanted.

It was why he arrived at his neighbor's viewing party wearing a T-shirt his mother had printed up with the slogan *Pastureland, not Parking Lots!* She brought enough T-shirts for everyone at the house party to wear. The whole crowd obligingly tugged on a T-shirt and posed for a group picture. In a few weeks this photo was likely to be nothing but an embarrassing reminder of his failed quest, but for now he was grateful his mother had found a spark of life again.

Donna gleefully recounted the Miami reporter's interview for his neighbors. "Howard and Tina Mayweather came into the store while the news lady was fixing her hair right before filming. The Mayweathers are having trouble with ticks on their hogs and asked Wyatt for a good delousing solution. They didn't even realize he was about to be interviewed for television! Wyatt walked them over to the pesticide aisle and told them what he knew about delousing. And you know what? The cameraman got the whole thing on tape!"

Everyone seemed to realize how important this was to Donna and gladly played along.

"Here it is!" his dad called out, hurrying to the television to crank up the volume.

A hush settled over the gathering as an exterior shot of the feed store filled the screen. The reporter enthusiastically recounted Wyatt's experience in agriculture, his service in the army, and his law enforcement background. They even showed a snippet of him explaining how to delouse a hog.

Most of the story featured a lengthy clip of Wyatt

explaining why he wanted to run: "Too many people use the commissioner's job as a launching pad to a higher office, so they cater to aerospace and tourism because that's where the money is. I intend to serve the folks who run fishing boats and cattle ranches and the people who make orange juice. I want the person sitting in Tallahassee to put those people *first*. Trust me, the space industry and the tourists are doing just fine."

Everyone in the room hooted and cheered. His parents hugged each other, and people clapped him on the back and shook his hand.

The news cut back to the reporter, now sitting in the television station with her practiced smile. "We certainly wish Captain Rossiter well in the primary just two weeks away. Coming up after the break, a rare treasure worth millions has been found on a central Florida orange grove. Stay tuned!"

Wyatt froze. Had he heard correctly? There couldn't be too many rare treasures turning up in orange groves. Jenny was under orders to remain silent about that egg, but she was bitter about what happened to her orange trees. Bitter enough to blow the whistle on that egg?

His mother had prepared a blowout meal of smoked ribs and wanted to lead folks over to dig in and celebrate on the back patio. While everyone else headed outside, Wyatt paced in the family room, praying the next story wasn't what he feared.

Jenny wouldn't *dare* . . . and yet, he feared she would.

The news came back on the television and cut to a reporter interviewing a lady who looked like a 1950s pinup model. Wyatt cranked up the volume, growing cold as the lady mentioned a Fabergé egg in mint condition. Photographs of the egg appeared on the screen and there could be no doubt. Jenny had spilled the beans about the egg.

The report switched back to the newscaster in the studio. "As to how this egg got from Russia to an orange grove in Florida?" the newscaster said. "It remains a mystery, but we invite you to submit your theories at our online webpage. Christie's is working with the owner to iron out legalities, and an auction is anticipated later in the year. John? Over to you for the evening traffic."

Wyatt stood motionless for a full minute. How could he possibly protect Jenny from the firestorm she'd just unleashed? A quick call to the sheriff's department confirmed they hadn't authorized Jenny to release news about the egg.

Wyatt couldn't shield Jenny from whatever retaliatory action the sheriff might throw at her, but he could warn her it was coming. As much as he wanted to keep Jenny in his past, he needed to warn her about this first thing in the morning.

JENNY SPENT the morning re-grading the soil, which was long, dirty, and stinky work. The air swirled with so much dirt and sand she could taste it. Her tailbone hurt from bouncing on a hard tractor seat and she longed for a shower.

The work put a lot of stress on the tractor, too. It was starting to backfire, but her grandfather taught her how to fix this kind of thing long ago. A good cleaning of the fuel injectors would probably do the trick.

She sat on an upended orange crate in the open doorway of the equipment garage to get started. The metal building was big enough for the tractor, the cherry picker, two pickup trucks, and the ATV. A pegboard filled with tools covered the wall above the worktable, and the space was brightly lit thanks to overhead florescent lights.

She was swiping a bit of steel wool at the crud built up around the rim of the fuel pump when the distant sound of a car engine came from the front of the grove.

She set the pump down, wiping her hands on a rag as a truck barreled down the front drive, stirring up clouds of dust behind its wheels. She mentally kicked herself for not closing the gate after Hemingway left for groceries this morning, but it was too late now.

Really too late. It was Wyatt, and his expression was stormy as he slammed the door of the truck. The only thing she'd done lately to annoy him was let Christie's make that announcement about the egg, but it was a biggie.

Wyatt glowered as he approached "Why did you talk to the press about that egg?"

"Me? I haven't. It was the auction house that made the announcement." It didn't stop the guilt from rising to the surface. She turned away from the accusation in his face and sat down to continue cleaning the fuel pump.

"You were instructed to keep news of that egg confidential," he said.

"I was *asked* to keep it quiet," she corrected. "I decided to proceed."

"Why?"

"Because according to the law, I need to give the public ninety days before I can sell the egg, and I got tired of waiting."

Wyatt's expression remained stony. "What you did could be considered obstruction of justice. Or tampering with evidence. It was a reckless and stupid thing to do."

She kept polishing the grime from the pump and tried to sound calm. "Has there been talk of doing that?"

"Not yet."

She glanced up in hope. "Is there likely to be?"

"Probably not," he conceded. "The courts are overloaded with current issues instead of cold cases of long-dead skeletons, but what you did was wrong. Don't you get that?"

She dropped the rag and stood up to face him. "I need the money, okay? I took out a huge mortgage on the grove and the first payment is due at the end of the quarter. The bank and I agreed on that date because it was when I was supposed to harvest my oranges, but thanks to someone plowing down my trees, I can't pay it. So yes. I'm moving as fast as I can to stake my claim for that egg."

"It's not yours, Jenny."

"It's been on my land for fifty years. My grandfather might have bought it. Or traded for it. Unless someone shows up and can prove ownership, I get it by default."

"Congratulations," Wyatt said. "I got word from Caleb that the sheriff's email system crashed thanks to the flood of loons coming out to claim it."

"Really?" she asked, trying not to wince. She'd expected as much, although she still clung to the slim hope that there wouldn't be too many claimants.

"Really. Hundreds are coming in from all over the country, and most are pure nonsense. Someone claimed to have lost it while camping. A guy from New York said it was stolen from his shop last year, even though it's been in that tree for half a century. One guy even said his Ouija board told him the egg belonged to his grandparents. Any hope we have of weeding out legitimate leads over the skeleton is now going to be tangled up with kooks and fortune hunters."

That was regrettable, but she wasn't going to lose her grove over it. "Wyatt, I need money. I can't lose the grove. It's the only thing I have left."

"The sad thing is that I think you really believe that. There are a million things you could do with your life if you could only break free of this place."

She didn't want to hear this. Wyatt had always looked down on her for wanting to follow in her family's footsteps, as though he was better than she because he'd seen something of the world.

"Why should I break free of this place? I love it here. My life is good."

"Your life is limited. Your family has been growing oranges on this plot of land for ninety years, and if you have your way, you'll be here for another ninety. Doing what? Growing oranges. I asked you for two years in Morocco. Two years! And you couldn't give it to me."

"Because I had a duty," she snapped.

He walked to her, standing so close she had to crane her neck to look up at him, and he was practically crackling with anger.

"Yes. You had a duty to a bunch of oranges. And where are those oranges now, Jenny?"

She whirled around to start putting tools away, so angry she could spit. Those oranges were sold to the OJ factory, where they'd been pulped, concentrated, and shipped out all over the world. Nobody gave her a Bronze Star or a Purple Heart for it. Maybe a glass of orange juice was a piddly thing to Wyatt, but she was proud of what she'd accomplished that terrible year Jack went crazy.

She whipped off her gloves to point a finger in his face. "There aren't many people who could have gotten the grove pruned, pollinated, and harvested after what Jack did. I didn't run away and I didn't collapse. I did my job, even though everyone in town treated me like kryptonite, like I'm carrying Jack's stink on me."

"I never treated you like that."

"Your mother did. The one time I saw her in the grocery store she acted like—"

"Don't criticize my mother," Wyatt interrupted.

"Then don't pretend she doesn't hate me." Donna had testified at a custody hearing that Jenny shouldn't have visitation with Sam. Donna's word carried weight because as a former social worker, she had plenty of experience with traumatized children, and the judge pounced on Donna's testimony as an excuse to award full custody to the McAllisters.

"That was why I wanted us to go to Morocco," he ground out, and she flinched just hearing the word. How many times had she wondered if going to Morocco would have been the right thing for them? They could be married now. Maybe even have kids . . . but it would have meant leaving the grove behind, and she would never give up Summerlin Groves for anyone.

"My grandfather always said not to let yesterday use up too much of today," she told Wyatt. "I'm not going to stand here and argue about your mother. I'm fighting for today. To get my grove back."

She pointed to the lumpy mounds of dirt. "I've got a lot of work to re-grade this land after your people destroyed my livelihood. Don't try to make me feel guilty over making a claim for that egg. I'm going to fight hard for it whether you approve of it or not."

WYATT SMOLDERED as he drove down the rural two-lane road back to town. There was a time when he had loved this drive because it meant he was going to see the woman he wanted to marry. Now the view was forever tainted with what happened that horrible night in July.

He hated fighting with Jenny. In the entire time they dated they hadn't fought a single time. Now all they did was yell and snap at each other when painful emotions rose to the surface.

For a few days after Lauren died, he still hoped for a future with Jenny. In the wake of the town's rage and his parents' tears, he felt Jenny slipping away from him and reached out for the long-shot hope that Morocco might be their salvation.

At the time, Wyatt's unique background in agriculture and the law prompted an unexpected job offer from United Phosphate & Fertilizer. The richest phosphate deposits in the world had just been discovered in Morocco, and the company was setting up a new operation in the small north African country. They needed an American lawyer on the scene who understood the fertilizer business and was tough enough to deal with dicey issues of international trade. The appointment would last two years and the company would pay him a fortune to do it.

Wyatt hadn't seriously considered the opportunity until Lauren died, but then it seemed the perfect solution to escape memories of Lauren that surrounded him in Amity. He wanted to take Jenny with him, strike out for the horizon, and never look back. They were two wounded souls who could start over somewhere completely new. After checking with United Phosphate to confirm the job offer was still on the table, he drove out to the grove to find Jenny.

He parked his car on the south side of the farmhouse where he wouldn't have to see the outbuilding where Lauren had been shot in the back. Jenny was mixing a tank of fertilizer at the pumping station when he approached. It was the first time they'd seen each other since Lauren's funeral.

"Wyatt, thanks for coming." Her voice was weak and timid. She took a moment to twist the spigot off and stood. Wearing faded jeans and a dingy white shirt, she looked as exhausted and haggard as he felt. "Wyatt, I'm so sorry . . ."

What happened wasn't Jenny's fault and she shouldn't apologize for the mess her brother had made of their lives. Wyatt just wanted to solve the problem and get out of Florida.

"Jenny, the United Phosphate job in Morocco is still on the table. I'm going to take it."

She sagged against the side of the water tank, sorrow clouding her pained blue eyes. "You're leaving?"

"I want you to come with me. Right now. Leave everything behind and we can start over on the other side of the world. Just you and me and the desert and a new start."

Jenny let out a stunned laugh of disbelief. "I can't just leave."

"Why not?"

She opened and closed her mouth a few times, as though trying to speak words that wouldn't come. She looked past the pumping station to the endless rows of orange trees beyond.

"I can't leave the grove," she finally said. "There's so much to do."

"Let someone else do it. Come with me and we can find a pastor to marry us. Then we buy a one-way ticket and start over in Morocco." No more memories of Lauren. No parents who hated Jenny and blamed her for what Jack did. Just a clean start beneath the hot baking skies of the desert.

"Wyatt, you're not thinking clearly. I have responsibilities here. I've got thirty acres under cultivation. Pruning season is next month—"

"Screw pruning season," he roared. "I love you! We belong together. Doesn't that mean anything to you?"

She held up her hands. "Yes, I want us to be together, but not in Morocco. Are you insane? I'm not leaving my grove."

"Ever?"

She got more and more panicked and threw her gloves on the ground. "Yes, I'm never leaving my grove. It's been in my family forever and I'm the only one left. I can't leave it because you want to go to Morocco on a whim."

A whim. Every word she said was a nail to his heart, and he lost his temper. He couldn't remember all the things he'd yelled that morning, or the angry words she'd hurled back . . . the only thing that was indelibly etched in his mind was that Jenny's undying love for a miserable orange grove would always mean more to her than anything he could offer. They'd be married now if she could have thrown off the shackles of that two-bit grove.

He silently steamed as he continued driving down the country lane, still angry over that Fabergé egg. He'd done what he'd come out here to do. Yelled at Jenny.

Was that all they were going to be to each other anymore? His car hit a pothole and he muttered a curse. He'd have to submit another work order to get it patched because the county had ignored his last request.

Why was he still running all over town to fix Jenny's problems? If Jenny understood her rights, she could have demanded the county patch any pothole this big, but this was the sort of thing normal civilians didn't realize. He would swallow his ire and go pound on the right doors to get the job finally completed.

And then he would be finished with Jenny. For good, this time.

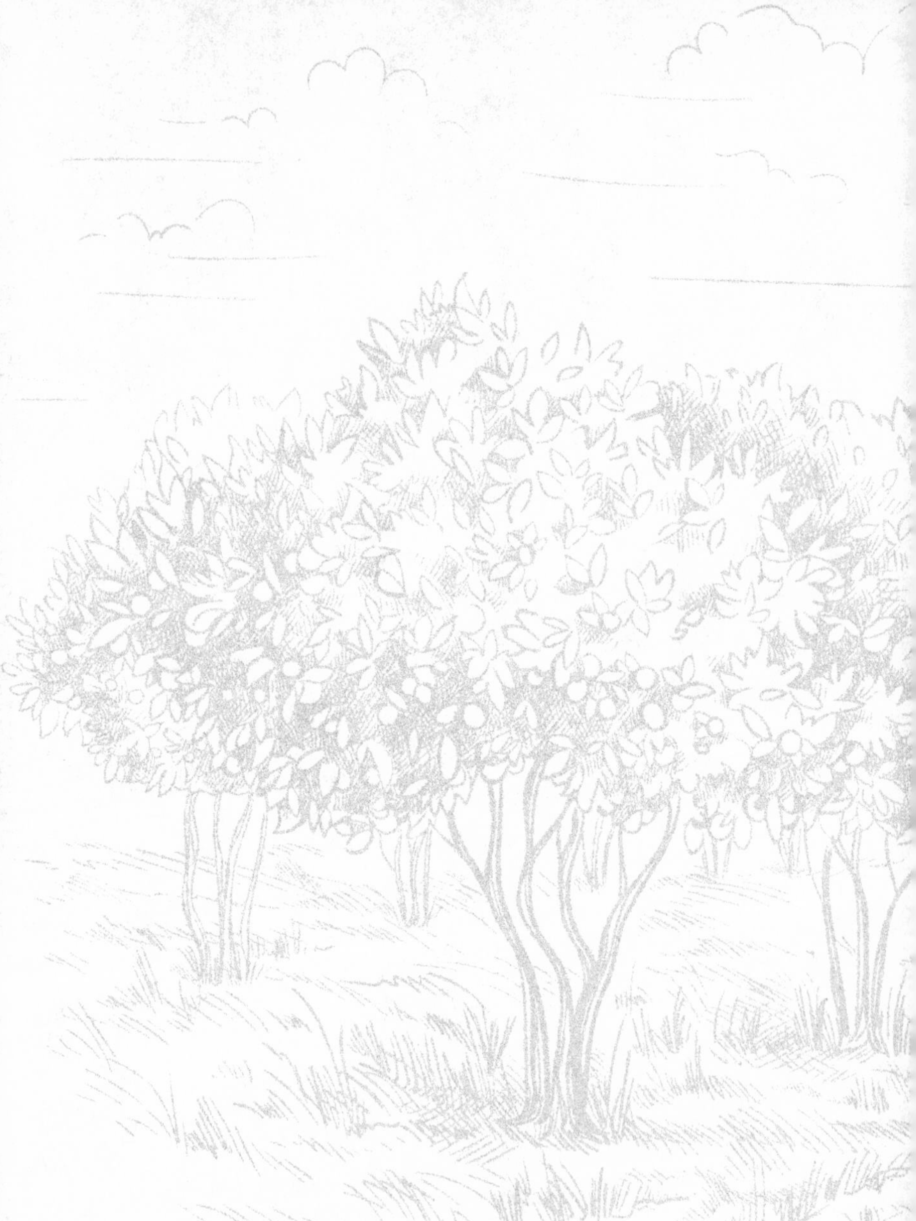

Chapter Seventeen

Jenny wore her grandfather's rubber overalls to muck out the drainage pipes at the river's edge. It was a wet, stinky, and dangerous job because this river had its fair share of poisonous snakes and alligators.

There weren't any alligators today, just the buzz from a pair of dragonflies as they zinged across the surface of the water. The river level was low, exposing soft mud banks and releasing the organic smell of silt. Mucking out the drainage pipes had to be done twice a year or they'd clog up and she'd have a soggy grove. It required wading several yards into the river, then squatting down to insert a long-handled hook into the end of the drainage pipes to drag out the gunk.

She hoisted a wad of drippy sludge toward the bank and dumped it. Specks of mud and algae spattered her face, but the goggles protected her eyes. She was heading back for another load when she spotted Hemingway hurrying toward the riverbank.

"We're about to have company," he called out. "Bad Penny is on her way over with a film crew."

Jenny used a sleeve to swipe mud from her jaw. "Tell her she can't film on the property."

"You might want to rethink that," he replied. "She commissioned a forensic artist to make a sketch of the woman from the tree and wants to show it to you. It should be interesting."

That *was* something worth getting out of the river to see. Jenny tossed the pole onto the bank. "Help me out," she said. Hemingway continued relaying information as he hauled her up the steep bank. Apparently, Penny called a few minutes ago and Hemingway had already opened the front gate for her.

"She wants to film your reaction to the sketch," Hemingway said. "Trust me, she's going to milk this for every drop of publicity she can wring from it."

Jenny peeled off her goggles. They probably left red marks imprinted on her face alongside the mud and sweat. Her grandfather's rubber overalls came up to her armpits, but there wasn't any time to change. The news van was already creeping up the front drive and Jenny waddled forward to meet them. She didn't care how she looked, she just wanted to see that sketch.

Penny was immaculate as she descended from the van, her shiny hair in a sleek, shoulder-length cut with expensive highlights. A crewmember followed behind her, hoisting a camera onto his shoulder.

"No filming," Jenny said.

Penny put on her poised, newscaster smile. "Are you sure? I brought a forensic sketch of the lady found in your cypress tree."

The paper fluttered in Penny's hand as she held it aloft, and even from here Jenny could see a remarkably lifelike sketch of a woman.

She *had* to see it, and there wasn't anything on the grove she needed to hide anymore. "Okay, go ahead and film. Let me see that picture."

Penny waited until the cameraman gave the signal, then she handed Jenny the sketch.

It was a charcoal drawing, and the lady was attractive. She had high cheekbones, a thin aquiline nose, and arched eyebrows plucked like they would have been in the 1950s. Her face was long and narrow.

"Do you recognize her?" Penny asked. "Is she someone from your family?"

"I've never seen her before," Jenny replied, still admiring the quality of the sketch. The hair was styled in a short, soft bob like a woman from the 1950s would have worn. The artist gave her no expression, but the high cheekbones and narrow chin made her universally attractive. Fine lines and a slight sag beneath her eyes hinted at her age, yet she still looked refined and healthy. How did a woman like this end up dead in that old cypress tree?

She passed the drawing to Hemingway, who had no answers either. They stared at the drawing so long that the cameraman stopped filming.

"Does she look like your grandmother?" Penny asked. "I understand your grandmother died sometime in the 1950s. Cancer? Where was she buried?"

Jenny raised her brows. "Are you suggesting my grandfather dumped his wife in a cypress tree instead of burying her? Because that's what it sounds like."

Penny was unfazed. "It's well known that your grandfather had mental disorders."

"I think the proper term is mental illness," Hemingway corrected.

Jenny wasn't so polite. "Actually, I think the term is *this isn't any of your business, Penny.*"

Penny easily shifted gears. "How is your quest to win the Fabergé egg coming along? I gather you're about three weeks into that ninety-day countdown."

Two weeks and five days, but who's counting? Jenny collected the rake, eager to finish mucking out the drainage pipe. "I'm not letting myself think about it yet."

"Did you hear that Raymond Wakefield has filed a claim on it?"

Jenny froze, the weight of disappointment making it hard to breathe. This was what she'd feared. The Wakefields had a long-standing interest in Fabergé eggs and might be able to scrounge up some kind of proof they were entitled to it.

"What's the basis for his claim?" she asked.

"The judge won't let outsiders review the application, but I thought you might know something about it."

All Jenny knew was that Raymond was likely to swoop in and win that egg and crush all Jenny's nascent hopes for getting out of debt. "Sorry, Penny, I don't know anything."

Hemingway waited until Penny climbed back into the van and the wheels started rolling before he talked, his voice deliberately casual.

"I think it's time to pay a visit to Raymond and find out why he thinks he has a claim to that egg. He won't resist being able to brag."

As always, Hemingway was right.

"BE NICE," Jenny warned Hemingway as she drove the truck toward the Wakefield estate. She needed Hemingway's insight into Wakefield family history in order to ask the right questions, but he could be such a wild card in his eternal quest to needle Raymond.

"Don't worry," Hemingway assured her. "I've got a few million reasons not to provoke him today . . . even though it's always fun," he added with a wink.

Jenny shared Hemingway's low opinion of Raymond. What sort of forty-five-year-old man had never been gainfully employed? Paying ghostwriters to churn out books could hardly be considered professional employment, nor did accepting vanity appointments to college boards. When he wasn't touring European resorts with the baroness, Raymond spent his days training his foxhounds for the quarterly hunts scheduled on the Wakefield estate.

After turning onto Wakefield property, Jenny turned the truck onto a gravel path leading to the dog kennels. The freestanding kennel building was built of the same honey-colored stones as the main house. A picket fence contained a dog run and two acres on which the hounds could play. Raymond stood to one side, watching the baying dogs chase after balls shot from a mechanical tennis-ball launcher. The dogs chased the balls with joyous abandon, then came bounding back to drop the balls into the machine's basket. On the rare occasion a dog's ball missed the basket, Raymond snapped his fingers until the dog performed the skill correctly.

Jenny leaned her forearms on the top rail of the fence to watch while Hemingway explained how the fox hunts worked.

"Raymond rides the lead horse and blasts the hunting horn, all in an elaborate game of let's-pretend-we're-a-British-aristocrat. He actually yells 'Tally-ho' whenever the dogs change direction. Can you believe it?"

"Shh, he might hear you," Jenny cautioned, because

Raymond stepped away from the machine that kept the dogs busy and strolled over to them.

"Jenny, Hemingway," he said with a cordial nod. "What brings you out this afternoon?"

There was no point in beating around the bush. Given the knowing gleam on Raymond's face, he already suspected.

"We heard rumors that you've filed a claim on the Fabergé egg," she said. "Just curious . . . can you tell us the basis for your application?" She clenched the top rail of the fence so hard her knuckles hurt, but she was proud of how calm she sounded.

"Easy," Raymond said. "My grandfather bought and paid for that egg back in 1952. I've got proof."

"What sort of proof?" Hemingway asked.

Raymond walked over to the ball launcher and turned it off. The dogs whimpered in disappointment at the abrupt halt to their game. Raymond's whistle pierced the air, and with a few hand gestures he directed the dogs toward the kennel.

They obeyed.

The sudden silence seemed ominous as Raymond returned to the fence, determination in his face. "As soon as I heard about the egg, I knew that my grandfather was the only person in Pierce County with the interest or ability to buy it. I searched through his old files and found paperwork for an insurance policy he bought in 1952 in anticipation of acquiring another Fabergé egg. I've got the insurance policy and the cancelled check he used to pay for it. He had the egg professionally appraised, and I've got the paperwork for that, too. The appraisal identifies it as the Firebird Egg. I also have a cancelled check for a large sum he wrote a month after the appraisal."

Jenny's mouth went dry, but she managed to get out her question. "Who was the check written to?"

"A trust that was administered by a bank here in Amity," Raymond said. "The bank has stonewalled me in getting access to those records, but the bank officer referred to the trust beneficiary as a 'she.' I suspect it was the woman in the tree."

Disappointment settled on Jenny because it sounded like a strong case. Raymond continued. "The woman in the tree obviously double-crossed my grandfather. Or maybe she intended to deliver the egg, but someone killed her before she could make good on it. All I know is that my grandfather was in the process of buying the Firebird Egg and wrote her a check that cleared. He didn't ever get the egg and ended up cancelling the insurance policy the following year. The egg was stolen from Karl Wakefield."

"Did the check written to the trust match the amount of the egg's appraisal?" Hemingway asked, and Raymond's eyes narrowed.

"That's irrelevant," he said dismissively.

It was *highly relevant.* There might be no connection at all between Karl's attempt to buy the Firebird Egg and the check he wrote to an unknown beneficiary. Rich people funded things all the time. That trust could have been set up for a charity or a mistress.

"Where was your father during all of this?" she asked, and Raymond waved a dismissive hand.

"My father was in India working in famine relief during those years. He doesn't know anything."

The three years the senator spent in India as a young man laid the basis for his reputation as a humanitarian and his future in politics. It coincided with the breakdown of his relationship with Millicent Hawkins . . . and Jenny had always wondered if it was a broken heart that sent the senator abroad rather than a purely humanitarian mission. All she knew for sure was that the senator was on the other side of the world when the lady in the tree died.

"How much was the check for?" Hemingway pressed.

"I told you that it's not relevant."

But it was obviously a huge, glaring hole in Raymond's claim or he would have gladly shared it with them.

Hemingway refused to show concern and sent a teasing smirk to Raymond. "I'm not sure you're right about that, but tally-ho, old boy."

Jenny had to smother her laughter as they left. She intended to do everything within her legal powers to win that egg. The problem was that Raymond was known to be a cheat, which meant she would keep hoping for the best, but brace herself for a fight.

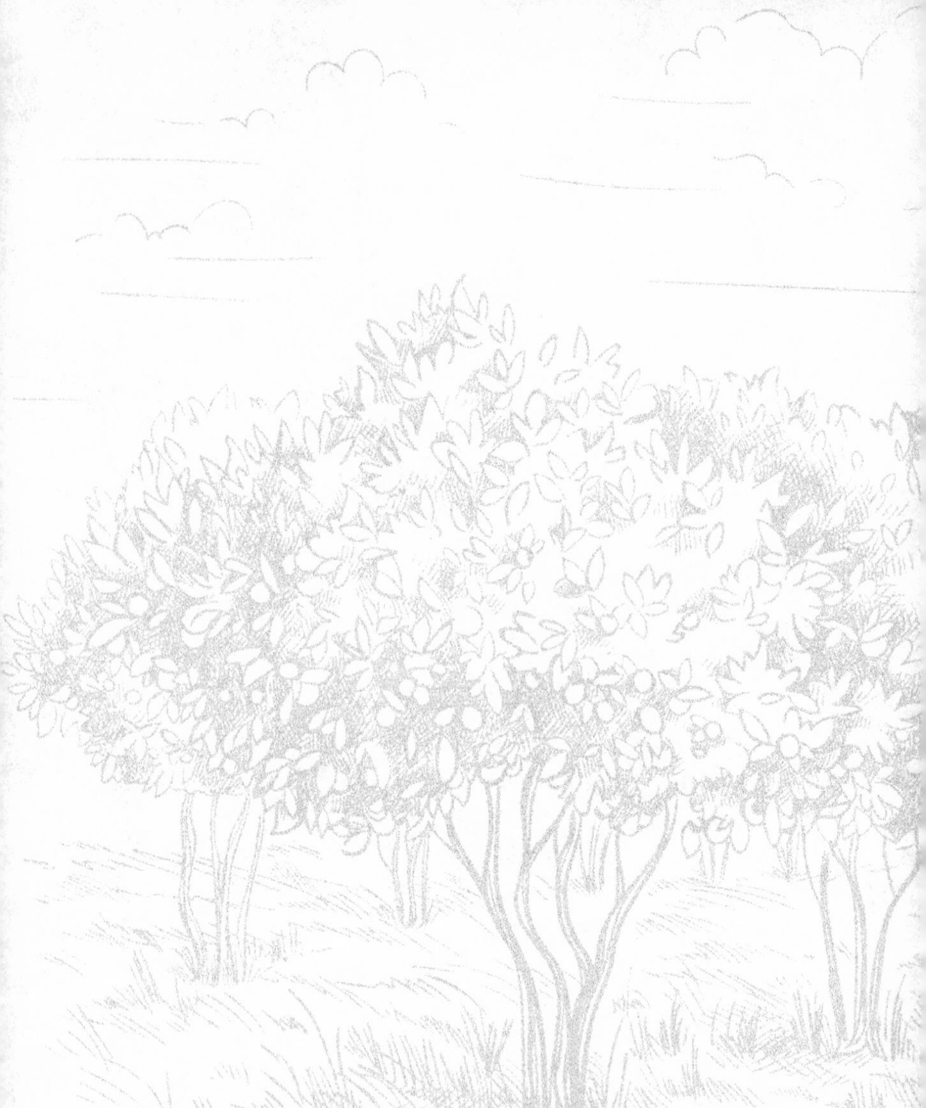

Chapter Eighteen

Wyatt tried not to let his nerves show as he circulated at the big bash Kent McAllister hosted to watch the crucial basketball game between the University of Florida and Florida State.

It was a coincidence that the party happened on the day of the primary election. Most of the people at the party probably had no idea the primary had been held today. Who voted in special election primaries? There had been only two farmers and a guy from the OJ plant lined up to cast a ballot at the elementary school when Wyatt voted this morning. The election results were due within the hour, then the leading candidates from each party would proceed to a one-on-one special election in June to become Florida's next Commissioner of Agriculture.

The evening was warm enough for the party to spill out onto the flagstone patio overlooking a sprawling pastureland, but Wyatt stuck close to the butler's pantry, where he stashed his laptop to periodically check election results as they trickled in. So far, he was making a respectable showing.

Eleven other candidates had thrown their hat in the ring, although most of the votes were split between Wyatt and the three professional politicians. The professionals had around fifteen percent each, while Wyatt hovered around twenty percent.

His heart started pounding faster. It was hard to believe, but the wind was now at his back. He might actually *win* this thing.

He closed the laptop, planning on joining the crowd watching the basketball game when a snazzy woman intercepted him in the hallway. It took a moment to place her as Dr. Lowenstein, the county medical examiner. He'd only ever seen her in a white lab coat; now she wore a red patent leather blazer with matching heels and shiny red lip gloss. She looked spectacular, if a little imposing.

"Hello, Wyatt," she said, greeting him with a kiss on his cheek.

He fought the temptation to wipe his cheek. He'd never been a huggy-kissy kind of guy, but he could pretend to be okay with it. Dr. Lowenstein looped her arm through his as they drifted into the main room where half the crowd watched the basketball game and the others held drinks and talked too loudly.

"Where have you been all this time?" she asked as she snagged a glass of wine from a circulating waiter. "I never see you around town anymore."

Was she making a pass at him? It felt like it because she hadn't let go of his arm and kept her gaze fastened on him as she sipped her wine. He glanced around for a way to extricate himself when Penny Danvers swooped down upon them.

"Dr. Lowenstein, have you seen the sketch of the skeleton found out at the Summerlin place?"

Even the name Summerlin caused a twinge deep inside.

He wished he could block his ears from hearing the discussion, but others gathered around, eager to hear the medical examiner's assessment of the sketch.

"I saw it," Dr. Lowenstein said.

"Will it help you identify who she is?" Penny wasn't on the clock, but a good journalist never turned off the instinct to drill for dirt.

"That's not my job," Dr. Lowenstein said. "I submitted the results of my medical examination to the sheriff's department, and the ball is with them now."

"But are they any closer to figuring out who she is?" someone else asked. "It seems strange that more people haven't come forward, especially with that Fabergé egg getting so much attention."

Speculation abounded as people started tossing out unfounded theories. "Jeb Bickner swears she's the spitting image of his mother," a bleached-blond woman announced. "He always said she ran off with a long-haul trucker when he was a kid, but now he thinks that's probably her in the tree."

Penny scoffed. "Jeb Bickner just wants to claim the Fabergé egg."

"I don't care who gets the egg, I just hope the Summerlins don't get to keep it," someone else said. "Jack was a scoundrel, and if Jenny gets a dime, it ought to go straight back to the McAllisters. After all, they're the ones raising that poor orphaned child."

"The McAllisters don't need the money," the bleached-blond woman said. "I'm sure they're praying the crazy gene didn't get passed down to the boy. Jack was crazy. So was his dad, and so was his granddad."

The conversation turned to a long-ago baseball game when Jack Summerlin got in a fistfight with the umpire, and Jenny bailed him out of jail.

The bleached-blond had plenty to say about that. "Maybe if she hadn't bailed him out, Jack would have learned how to control his temper."

Wyatt lowered his head. Jenny implied that the town's resentment toward the Summerlins ran pretty deep, but people rarely aired it in front of him. Could he blame them for dredging up old gossip? There'd been a time not so long ago when he savaged Jack Summerlin with just as much gusto, and never stopped to consider how it might have hurt Jenny.

He extricated his arm from Dr. Lowenstein and headed toward the butler's pantry to see if another batch of election results had come in. Anything was better than listening to gossip about the Summerlins.

A couple of caterers were inside the butler's pantry, filling trays with steak sliders and dipping sauce. Wyatt stepped inside the moment they left.

He hit the refresh key and watched the screen, holding his breath as new data populated the fields.

It was unbelievable. His lead had grown. He now had twenty-two percent of the vote and his nearest competitor was at sixteen percent. Could this really be happening?

"Wyatt, can I speak with you for a minute?" It was Dr. Lowenstein, standing in the open doorway. He closed the laptop so she couldn't see the screen and managed a polite smile.

"Yes, Dr. Lowenstein, what can I do for you?"

"Call me Rebecca," she prompted, smiling up at him, and now there could be no doubt that she was making a pass at him. She stepped farther into the pantry, blocking his escape. He cleared his throat and looked away.

"Rebecca," he said, scrambling for an excuse to escape. "I

really need to get back to the front room. I haven't had the chance to thank Mrs. McAllister for inviting me."

She laughed a little, causing squeaks from her patent leather jacket as she drew closer. "Relax. You don't have to be such an Eagle Scout all the time."

Jenny used to tease him about that. He never had a problem relaxing with Jenny, and this woman with the squeaky jacket held no appeal. Dr. Lowenstein was smart and attractive and successful, but she wasn't Jenny.

He scrambled for a graceful way to escape this awkward encounter. "I've got an early morning at the office tomorrow," he said. "I should probably head home—" He bumped into the laptop, tipping it off the shelf. He lunged for it, catching it just in time.

"What have you been looking at?" Dr. Lowenstein asked. "Don't tell me you've been watching a competing basketball game."

He had to tell her something, and the truth was always a good place to start. "There was an election today. I've been watching the results."

"Oh yes!" she said brightly. "*Pastures, not parking lots.* I love that slogan. Are the results in?"

"Not yet."

She brushed him aside and lifted the laptop screen. It wouldn't be gentlemanly to slam it down and tell her to mind her own business. The computer woke up and automatically reloaded.

"Hey, look," she said. "You won."

He gaped at the screen. His name had a checkmark beside it. Dr. Lowenstein gave a loud whoop and kissed him flat on the mouth. He pulled back, but she raced into the family room.

"Hey, everybody," she shouted. "Wyatt won the election! He's going to be our next Commissioner of Agriculture!"

He hurried after her. "No, not true," he hastened to add. "I've only won the primary. The big race is in June, and it will be a lot harder to win."

His words made no difference. Any excuse for a party, right? Cheers broke out and people lined up to shake his hand. Kent McAllister boomed his hearty congratulations and promised a hefty campaign contribution.

Wyatt couldn't stop smiling because winning the primary was huge. *Huge!* His mother was going to be over the moon and the next three months were going to be a whirlwind of activity.

Twenty minutes later he learned who his competitor would be, a state representative from Cape Canaveral named Mindy Bannerman. She was a career politician with over a million dollars in her chest, a background in aerospace law, and fifteen years advocating for the space industry. The Commissioner of Ag job was clearly a stepping-stone to higher office for her.

Mindy Bannerman would be tough to beat because in a statewide election, everyone could vote . . . including the city folks more interested in aerospace, tourism, and cheap land. She was favored to win the election, but if Wyatt could force her to start paying lip service to issues of agriculture, he'd consider it a win. He relaxed on the patio with Kent McAllister and some others from the ranching community to talk politics and savor his victory.

But just inside the open French doors, Penny Danvers gossiped about the forensic sketch and her visit to Summerlin Groves. It was distracting. Snippets of conversation kept floating his way and none of it was good.

Penny said something about Jenny wearing ugly rubber

overalls that came up to her armpits, looking like a yokel. Someone else mentioned white trash and trailer parks.

Wyatt's jaw clenched as anger simmered. Jenny Summerlin worked hard seven days a week. She labored with her hands, her back, and her brain while these women with professional manicures looked down their noses at her. How often did Jenny run into this sort of thing?

If his mother had been here, Donna would be joining in the small-minded evisceration of Jenny, and was he any better? The last time he'd seen Jenny they'd been yelling at each other and he hadn't believed her when she claimed people in town treated her like a pariah.

He needed to apologize. Their romance ended badly and they had no possibility of a future, but he didn't want her believing he stood with the small-minded people who didn't see her worth. Although their romance would never be more than a four-month idyl that briefly blazed during a glorious spring, it had been pure and wonderful; something he would forever cherish. He was a better man for having known Jenny, and she had left an imprint on his soul that would never fade.

Tomorrow he would head out to her grove and apologize for the things he'd said. When they were both old and gray, he wanted Jenny to know that she had once been adored.

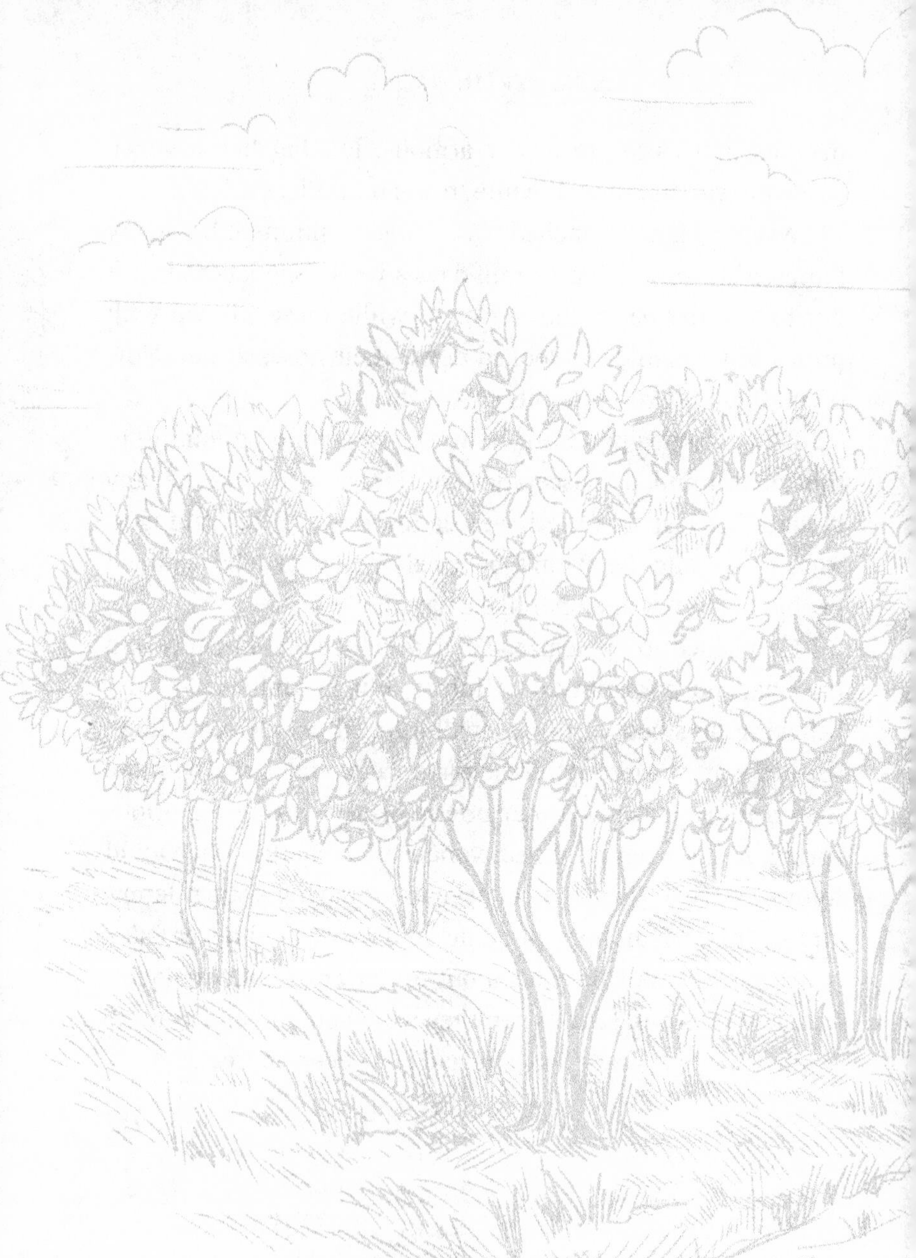

Chapter Nineteen

Elbert Davies was the kind of guy Jenny wished she'd had for a father. Or grandfather, for that matter. With his lean, weather-beaten face, Elbert exuded gentle wisdom as he walked the freshly churned north field of her grove on this chilly, misty morning.

He hunkered down to lift a handful of soil, squeezing and releasing it in his palm. "You've got good drainage here," he said. "See how the soil sticks for a few seconds, then crumbles apart? That's what you want. I'll mix a batch of custom fertilizer to stand up to your drainage, but I want to do a little liming of the soil first. Pretty soon you'll have thousands of saplings planted on this land, and I want a perfect romance between the saplings and the soil. A little chemical engineering will set the stage for it."

It was hard not to smile as she soaked up Elbert's folksy wisdom. Her grandfather mistrusted Elbert because he was a sales rep from United Phosphate, but Jenny sensed a kindred spirit in the gentlemanly old man. Elbert was famous for making house calls to people's property to help with fertilizing. Yes, he was the sales rep responsible for selling her the right blend of fertilizer, but what her paranoid grandfather never understood was that Elbert's success rode on *her* success. Elbert wanted the grove to thrive, and she loved having an older, wiser person to guide her through the challenging months ahead.

"A little lime mixed into the soil will get the earthworms excited," Elbert said. "An excited earthworm is a hungry worm, and that nice, aerated soil is going to feel good on the roots of your new saplings. Got me?"

"I got you," she agreed. Elbert brought the right spreader attachment to hook up to her tractor, but she didn't know how to adjust the spinner disks.

"Can you help me calibrate it?" she asked. "I've never used lime before and don't know what I'm doing."

Elbert clapped her on the shoulder. "That's why I'm here, Jenny."

Why did she suddenly feel the urge to cry? Elbert was just doing his job, but it had been a long time since someone she barely knew had been so purely nice to her. She drove the tractor out of the garage while Elbert waited at the industrial-sized spreader he'd brought from the fertilizer plant. It looked like a big metal dumpster on a trailer hitch. It was already topped off with chalky granules of lime, and ready to be dragged behind the tractor while the disks spun out a perfectly calibrated release of the grains.

From her position atop the tractor she could see all the way to the end of the drive, including the pickup truck that had just arrived outside the closed gate. It was Wyatt's truck, and his presence sapped her brief surge of happiness.

Wyatt gave two quick taps on his horn to get her attention. He'd probably think her a coward if she refused to see him.

Elbert was still adjusting the spinner disks, and she

assured him she'd be back in a few minutes. He cast a critical eye at the gathering clouds.

"It's best to get this lime added ahead of the rain," he said.

"I promise I'll be back before you need me," she answered, then jogged down to the end of the drive. By the time she arrived, Wyatt had his forearms casually braced atop the metal gate. He looked tense and uncomfortable, and there was no need for the scary sunglasses.

"What now?" she asked, a little breathless from the run. "Was there something nasty you forgot to say the last time you were out here?"

"No!" Wyatt said, surprising her with the urgency in his voice. He yanked the sunglasses off, piercing her with a look brimming with such aching regret that it made her take a step back.

"Jenny, I came to say I'm sorry. I'm sorry for every mean, rotten, small-minded thing I ever said to you. I'm sorry for disappearing during the past eighteen months. *Nineteen* months, now. I thought it was best for both of us, but I never considered how badly you must have been hurting because of the way people treated you. Are *still* treating you. I should have been there for you to lean on. You were as much a victim of what happened that night as me, and I'm sorry for bailing on you."

It sounded like the Wyatt she used to know, a man of kindness and open-hearted honesty. "What's gotten into you?" she said, almost afraid to ask.

He clasped the top rung of the gate, looking at her through sorrowful eyes. "I don't like the way things ended between us. I want you to know that I don't blame you for what happened, and I wish you nothing but the best. You're one of the finest people I've ever met, and I want you to know that."

She swallowed hard. "This is starting to sound like one of those 'have a good life' talks before the hero disappears forever. Is it?"

The corners of his eyes crinkled in a hint of humor. "Yeah, probably," he said, not even bothering to hide the affection in his tone. "My mother isn't ever going to get past what happened. I wish things were different, but everything is just . . . too complicated."

"You're probably right," she said as regret swelled inside.

"You've been a lot more gracious than I deserve," he said. "The last nineteen months have been the hardest of my life."

"Mine too," she whispered.

He gazed over her shoulder, scanning the barren fields with wistful eyes. "I hope you can get this grove up and running again. If anyone can make it happen, it's you."

She turned around to see what he was looking at. As far as the eye could see, there was nothing but churned-up fields of dirt. To the untutored eye it probably looked dreary and depressing, but she'd worked hard to get it looking this good. The soil had been tilled, aerated, and graded. New irrigation lines had been laid. Soon she would have lime churned into the soil and happy worms tunneling around.

"Someday this field of dirt is going to blossom again," she said. "It hasn't been easy, but it will be beautiful again."

His smile was tender and sad. "You should be proud of what you've accomplished here. *I'm* proud of you."

There was that lump in her throat again. This was becoming a lot harder than she expected. The warm support coming from him was an achingly familiar echo from the past, a strange combination of comfort and sorrow.

"We're adding lime today," she said, trying to sound cheerful. "Then another round of liquid fertilizer before we plant the saplings. The folks at the state agency have been really great about helping me get back on my feet again."

"Let me know if you have any troubles. I can pound on a few doors if the bureaucracy slows down."

She managed a nod. "Thanks, Wyatt. I'll be rooting for you in the election."

A bit of humor lightened his face. "Are you going to vote for me?"

"What are my alternatives?"

"A career politician from Cape Canaveral who's never gotten her hands dirty."

She laughed at that. "Then I'll *definitely* vote for you."

They locked eyes as their laughter faded. A cool wind swept down from above, and it might rain soon. Elbert was waiting for her, but all she wanted to do was keep gazing at Wyatt because at long last they were friends again. She had a few more seconds to bask in the sensation before he was going to get back in his truck and drive away from her forever.

"I need to head back to town," he said slowly but made no move to leave.

"And I need to get the field limed before it rains." She didn't move either.

He sighed, then reached across the gate to touch her shoulder, sending a shiver racing through her, because this was goodbye.

"Jenny, what happened between you and me will always be my biggest regret."

She didn't say anything as he returned to his truck, started the engine, and pulled away. Was this really going to be how they ended? Wyatt lifted a hand outside the truck's window to wave goodbye as he got back on the road.

She smiled and lifted her hand high in return, but inside her heart was breaking.

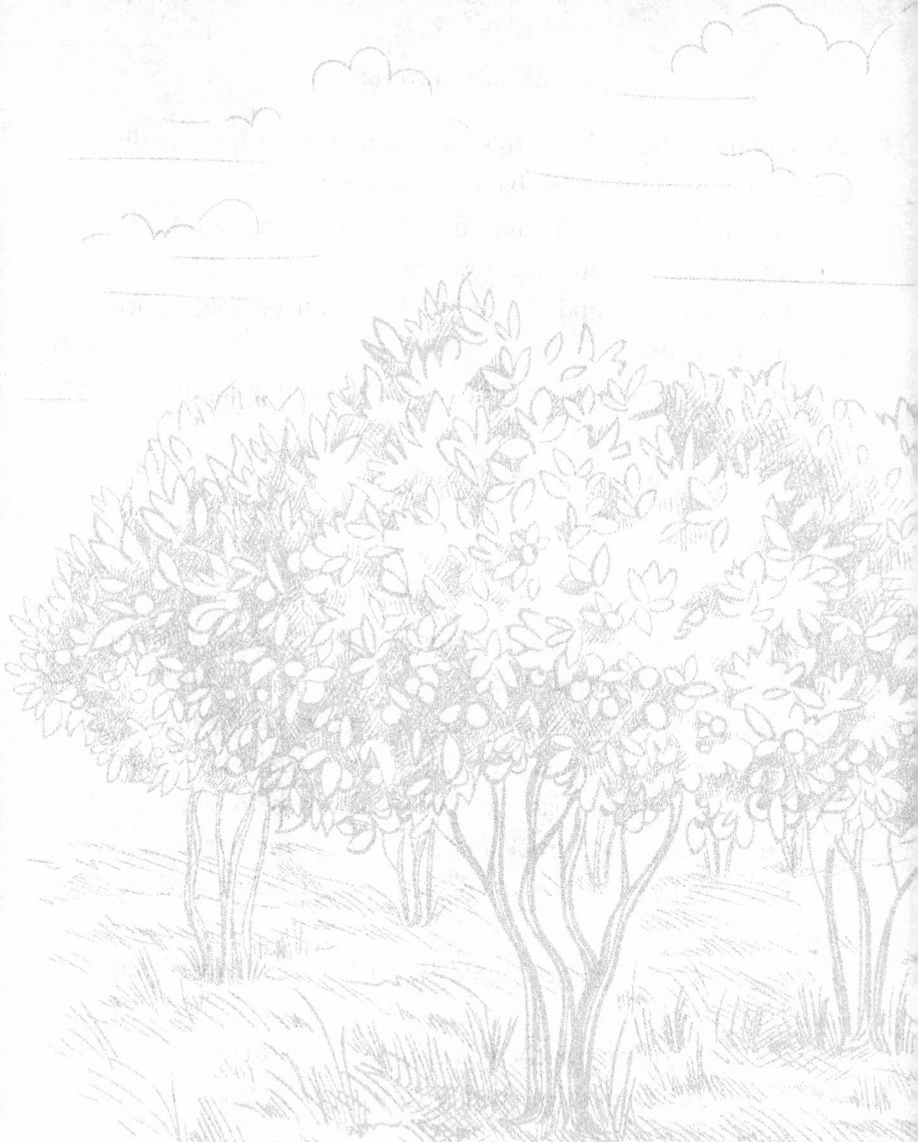

Chapter Twenty

A chilly March turned into a blustery April, and then the full heat and sun of Florida welcomed a glorious May.

Jenny used the two months to plant three thousand orange saplings. A hired crew did most of the manual labor, but she and Hemingway worked alongside them for ten hours a day to get the job done. The state of Florida had paid for the saplings and provided a low-interest loan to pay the workers, and soon the grove had saplings in tidy rows stretching as far as her eye could see.

Almost everything was going well. The saplings were shoulder-high and her grove was alive again. She'd been allowed to have every-other-weekend visitation with her nephew. The McAllisters still hovered nearby during the entire visit, but they were beginning to thaw and she had formed a real bond with Sam.

And most thrilling, there had yet to be a credible claimant for the Fabergé egg. Raymond Wakefield's claim had collapsed when the arbitration judge looked into it. The judge was able to subpoena the bank's records about the mysterious trust Karl Wakefield set up and funded at the same time he had the egg appraised. The judge learned the identity of the trust's anonymous beneficiary and ruled there was no connection between the trust and the Fabergé egg. He dismissed Raymond's claim *with prejudice*. That meant it couldn't be reopened, and no other credible claimant had emerged.

They were now seventy-five days into the ninety-day waiting period. She and Hemingway tracked the countdown on a calendar taped to the refrigerator. They gleefully celebrated each time they crossed another day off the calendar. It was amazing, but they were only fifteen days away from being able to claim ownership of that astounding treasure.

Life was back to normal.

Well, mostly normal. She hadn't seen Wyatt in all that time, and she'd adopted the embarrassing habit of talking to him in her mind. As she went about her day, she silently explained her chores to him, such as her struggles with the irrigation system or how she'd stopped an outbreak of aphids. In her mind, Wyatt always answered. They could carry on friendly conversations for hours. Even friendly arguments, such as when she confessed to getting mad at Hemingway when he went AWOL during the week she set aside for mulching.

Careful, Jenny, imaginary-Wyatt cautioned. *Hemingway has been fired from every job he's ever had.*

Typical Wyatt. She explained that Hemingway only slacked off when he really loathed a task, and that he'd held amazing jobs all over the world and what was she? Someone who knew how to grow citrus and nothing else. Then imaginary-Wyatt told her to quit beating herself up and get back to work, but he always chuckled as he said it.

Her daily mental chats with Wyatt were ridiculous, but she missed him and had no intention of stopping their lovely conversations. It could be lonely out on the grove. Loneliness was something she was accustomed to, though she still didn't like it.

Maybe that was why she'd been so eager to host a group of college students studying agriculture. The eight students from Purdue University arrived on the first of May along with their professor to spend the afternoon learning about the orange business. These future farmers were participating in an immersion class traveling the state of Florida to learn about citrus groves, cattle ranches, and greenhouse farms.

She started at the pumping station to explain her irrigation system, then she led them to the front acres to show them something far more interesting. She hunkered down before a Valencia orange sapling and pointed to a knobby joint a few inches above the soil.

"This is the bud union," she explained. "I grow for the juice industry, so all my orange saplings are grafted onto lemon rootstock. Lemon trees are the thirstiest of all citrus plants. I want my oranges to be as juicy as possible, so almost all the orange trees you see in Florida are grown on the roots of lemon trees. Orange growers from California laugh at us. They say if you want to eat a Florida orange, you'd better get into a bathtub first because you'll get drenched when you cut into it."

"That's right," a good-looking student from California said. He had the blond hair and tanned skin of a typical surfer dude, and he'd grown up on a California orange grove. Jenny was already impressed by his keen insight into the differences in their groves.

"Our oranges aren't as juicy, but they're a lot prettier," he said.

"Maybe," Jenny admitted as she stood, brushing the grit from her hands.

"*Maybe?*" the California kid challenged.

"Yeah, maybe," she said, barely able to contain her laughter. She'd never confess that California oranges were both prettier and more flavorful, too. Even in Florida everyone ate California oranges. The arid valleys of central California grew oranges with a smooth, sweet interior and beautifully colored orange skin, which was what grocery store shoppers wanted. Florida oranges were small, thin-skinned, and splotchy, but appearance didn't matter since they went straight to the juicing factory. *Nobody* could top Florida for great-tasting and inexpensive orange juice.

It was a joy having her grove back. Each day she awoke to gaze at her fields blanketed with healthy orange saplings and thanked God she had the faith to weather the crisis. There would be more challenges in the years ahead, and success wasn't guaranteed, but farmers had always been the original entrepreneurs. Who else would look at a field of dirt and plan, work, and pray that a marketable crop would show up at the end of the season? These few hours with the rising generation of new farmers invigorated her hope for the future.

At two o'clock, the bus arrived to take the students to the next stop on their tour of the state.

"On our way to Tampa, we're going to drive past the Wakefield ranch," the professor said. "Who remembers what the Wakefields are famous for?"

Most people in America would probably point to Senator Wakefield and his thirty-six years in the U.S. Senate, but these were students majoring in Agriculture. A girl with long red braids in the front row supplied the right answer.

"Didn't one of them start the World Famine Commission?"

"Correct," the professor said. "Karl Wakefield founded the commission in 1924. Back then they mostly shipped fertilizer and equipment around the world to ease hunger, but now the commission is doing their best to diversify agriculture all over the world."

The kid from California had plenty to say. "My dad said Karl Wakefield was a communist. That his son probably is, too."

The professor bristled at the California kid's tone of mild contempt. "The communists were the good guys during the early part of the twentieth century," the professor insisted. "The communists cared about the starving peasants in Russia, while our capitalist system let the Dust Bowl and the Depression happen."

Jenny didn't necessarily agree with the professor, but she appreciated his vocal defense of the Wakefields.

The professor continued bemoaning the injustice done to Karl Wakefield because of his communist sympathies, although most of the students no longer listened. The Cold War was ancient history for them, about as relevant to their lives as a horse and buggy. They were about halfway through the grove when the girl with red braids noticed a detail Jenny hadn't discussed.

"Is that part of your irrigation system?" she asked with a nod toward a small concrete pad with pipes and a metal door on it. The remnant of her grandfather's Cold War paranoia wasn't something Jenny was proud about.

"No, that's something else," she replied dismissively, walking toward the bus and hoping the girl would leave it alone.

Jenny had considered getting rid of the fallout shelter when she replanted the grove, but in the end, she hadn't had the heart for it. Maybe it was respect for tradition, or a lingering hint of her grandfather's prepper paranoia, but she'd decided to keep it.

That didn't mean she wanted to brag about it. She accompanied the group to the bus and waved goodbye as the ag students set off for Tampa to tour a strawberry farm.

It had been a good day.

Strike that . . . it had been a *wonderful* day. The weather was perfect, her saplings were thriving, and she got to spend a few hours with a bunch of young future farmers. God had provided her with an abundance of blessings if she would only recognize them rather than bemoaning her troubles.

She savored the loamy scent of the soil as she strolled back to the farmhouse, where Hemingway read the newspaper on the porch.

He set the paper aside as she approached. "Kristen from Christie's called," he said, and Jenny's breath froze. If Kristen had good news, Hemingway wouldn't look so grim.

"And?"

"She left a message on both our phones, asking us to call her back. I could tell by her voice it isn't good news. We need to call her back."

Her legs suddenly felt like leaden weights as she trudged up the porch steps. There were only fifteen days left on the ninety-day waiting period to claim the egg, but it didn't matter how close they came to the expiration of the deadline. The moment a credible claimant came forward, a judge would swoop in and start an arbitration process to determine true ownership.

"Let's go inside and call her back," Jenny said.

JENNY SET her cell phone on the kitchen counter with the

speaker turned on so Hemingway could listen in. It didn't take long for Kristen to answer.

"Hey, Jenny." The tone of Kristen's voice said it all. It was regretful and apologetic, as though she dreaded this phone call, too.

"What's up?" Jenny asked, her heart thumping against her ribcage. She stared at the ninety-day calendar taped to the refrigerator. The hopeful checkmarks ticking off the days seemed to mock her now.

"I'm afraid someone has come forward with a strong claim on the Fabergé egg," Kristen said. "All the supporting paperwork he submitted is starting to check out. It's from a guy in Texas named Clement Cooper. His grandfather started a small-town museum of curiosities in the 1950s and was looking for interesting things to display. Someone approached him with what he thought was a real Fabergé egg. The grandfather paid five hundred dollars for it, but the seller disappeared with his money."

"Only five hundred dollars?" Jenny asked skeptically.

"Yeah," Kristen said. "That's around five thousand in today's money, but still insanely cheap for a real Fabergé. The guy lost his money and ended up collecting rare cereal boxes for his museum. You know, the original Corn Flakes box, a complete run of Wheaties boxes, that sort of thing. They've got a really cute website."

Jenny met Hemingway's skeptical gaze. Who would sell a Fabergé egg to a small-town collector of cereal boxes? It didn't sound credible at all.

"Any insight on the person who tried to sell the egg?"

"Some Russian lady," Kristen replied. "He thinks she was using a fake name. She claimed she was desperate for money, and that's why she was willing to sell it so cheap. I know the story sounds strange, but the guy from Texas has a ton of paperwork to back it up. He's got a handwritten receipt for the egg. After the lady absconded with the egg, the grandfather filed a police report in Bryan, Texas. I've looked at the police report. It's from 1952 and includes a sketch of the egg, and it looks just like the Firebird Egg. One of our lawyers called the Bryan Police Department, and they've authenticated the report."

Jenny bowed her head. If there was a police report from 1952, it was starting to sound real. Bizarre and ridiculous, but not something that could be easily dismissed.

"You think he has a good case?" Jenny asked.

"I'm afraid so," Kristen said. "Our legal team says it looks like a slam dunk in favor of the Texas guy. They're going to turn it over to a judge to start the arbitration process."

She felt so ill she couldn't even speak, but Hemingway leaned forward. "Hey, Kristen, can you send us a copy of those old police documents?"

"Sure," Kristen chirped. "I'll send them over right away. And Jenny . . . I'm really sorry."

"Yeah, me too," she said on a shaky breath.

Twenty minutes later, Kristen's email with several attachments arrived and Jenny printed them out. The police report was photocopied from a reel of microfilm in the police archives of Bryan, Texas. It included the "receipt" for the egg, which was handwritten on a piece of notebook paper. The museum owner wrote the terms of the agreement, then it was signed in a spindly, feminine hand.

The seller's name was Svetlana Jones, and it was dated February 10, 1952.

Then came the police report where Mr. Cooper handwrote his side of the story:

I put an ad in the newspaper looking to buy interesting artifacts for my history museum. A Russian lady came to my house and offered to sell a jeweled egg of blue enamel with sapphires and diamonds all over it. She said it was a real Fabergé egg and worth a lot. She was scared and nervous. She said she wanted to defect to America and needed the money quick. I felt sorry for her and made the deal so she wouldn't have to go back to the Soviet Union. I gave her $150 on the spot but needed to wait for the bank to open on Monday to get the rest. We met there and I paid her the rest of the money. She was supposed to go get the egg and promised to bring it to my house, but she never showed up. I don't know if she snookered me or if she got in trouble with the commies. I'm worried about her.

Mr. Cooper's complaint concluded with a crude sketch of an egg that looked like the one from her cypress tree.

There was also a clipping from a local newspaper announcing the pending acquisition of a Fabergé egg to appear at the Bryan Cereal Museum. It included a photograph of Clement Cooper, a grinning old man wearing overalls and a plaid shirt.

Hemingway rubbed his hands together while Jenny stared at the documents, every dream of restoring the grove with a huge infusion of cash beginning to crumble. There was no way all these old microfilmed files could have been faked. The old man from the cereal box museum really did buy the egg. He had a receipt, and now his grandson was going to claim it.

The police thought "Svetlana Jones" was either a fake name or she was a con artist. Could using a fake name make this sales agreement invalid? It seemed such a piddly detail, but forty million dollars was riding on the authenticity of this deal.

"I don't know what to do," she said.

Hemingway opened the refrigerator and poured them both a tall glass of iced tea, then sighed as he took a seat beside her. "I think we should get a lawyer," he said.

"I can't afford a lawyer." She couldn't afford to pay her mortgage, let alone hire a lawyer to gamble on a long-shot hope of overturning the Texas claimant. Why even bother trying? Lawyers didn't give away advice for free.

But Wyatt might.

She and Wyatt had parted on friendly terms. Would he be willing to help her?

A slow smile curved her mouth. She was about to find out!

Chapter Twenty-One

"Jenny Summerlin just called," Veronica said. "She wants a meeting with you."

Wyatt rocked back in his office chair, abandoning the statistical reports as his administrative assistant peered at him through her spectacles.

It had been two months since he'd seen Jenny that bittersweet day when they declared a truce in her barren, freshly plowed field of dirt. On that day he was certain they had no possible future together, even though he hadn't been able to stop wishing it were otherwise. Even now, just hearing her name stirred a longing.

"Did she say what she wanted?"

"Nope," Veronica replied. "She said it's a private matter."

A spark of hope flared. If Jenny regretted the way they'd ended their last conversation as much as he, maybe it wasn't too late to reconsider things. His mother was getting better. Even if she wasn't, he couldn't live the rest of his life to please his mother. Maybe Jenny could forgive him for the way he turned his back on her. Maybe they could find a way forward after all . . .

"I can see her during the lunch hour," he suggested, and Veronica nodded before pulling the door closed behind her.

How was he supposed to go back to compiling statistics on beef exports now that his concentration had been shot to pieces? His office was spotless because he'd already been preparing to resign. If he didn't win the election next month, he still intended to leave town. He'd given his parents two years. It was time to break out of the shackles of rural Florida and strike out for the horizon like he'd always planned.

He stared out the window at Route 17. He could hop on that road and start driving, taking it all the way up to Washington D.C., where he could work for the military or any one of a million agencies that needed a lawyer who understood ag or the environment. Even now he could taste the freedom....

Jenny's cactus garden soaked up the sunlight coming through the window.

Okay, that cactus garden had to go before she got here. It might make her think he'd been obsessing over her by keeping it all this time. He opened the cupboard in his credenza and found a space to hide it. A few swipes with a paper towel got rid of the water stain where the bowl had been.

It was hard to regain his concentration while toying with fantasies about Jenny. Was she here to start things up again? Could he risk it?

At five minutes after the noon hour, he heard her arrive in Veronica's office and his heartbeat surged. When his desk phone rang, he reached a single finger out to touch the speaker button.

"Yeah?" He ought to get a medal for how calm he sounded.

"Jenny and Hemingway are here to see you."

Hope crashed back to earth like a pricked helium balloon. Jenny wouldn't have brought Hemingway if she was here to rekindle their relationship. No wonder Veronica sounded cheerful. The entire female population of Pierce County perked up whenever Hemingway strolled into view.

"Show them in." It had been idiotic to get his hopes up. He grabbed a can of soda from the mini-fridge and opened it to have something to do with his hands.

Jenny wore a pair of nice khaki slacks with a black blazer. For Jenny, it was as close to business attire as she came. Hemingway was still a slob in a ratty old T-shirt.

Wyatt ignored him as he sent Jenny a polite nod. "Jenny. Have a seat."

She thanked him and set a file on his desk. "You remember that Fabergé egg we found on the grove?"

As if he could forget. "I do. How's the ninety-day clock coming?"

"Not so good," she said. "Someone with a strong claim has come forward."

Ah, Jenny. If only he could draw her into a hug and soothe that tragic look on her face. Hemingway's annoying presence made that impossible, and maybe it was for the best. He listened as she filled in the details of the other claimant, laying some documents on the table.

"The police think 'Svetlana Jones' might be a fake name," Jenny said. "If it is, would that invalidate this sales agreement?"

Her cautiously optimistic expression hurt to see. The Texas guy's claim was strong and pretending otherwise would only give her false hope. Svetlana Jones could call herself whatever she liked so long as she had legal right to the egg.

"The deal was agreed on and money changed hands. It's going to be hard to overturn this."

If Jenny was disappointed, it didn't show. "I think she's probably the lady in the tree."

"Possibly," he said. He wasn't used to seeing Jenny in business attire, and she looked terrific. She could have been anything she wanted to be, but she remained dedicated to that grove and never lifted her eyes to consider the possibility of something more for her life. *Something with him.*

He cleared his throat. "What do you want from me?"

"I know it seems foolish," she began. "I shouldn't have put so much stock in that egg, but we were *so* close. We were fifteen days away. Fifteen days! I want a lawyer to tell me that this person from Texas isn't going to snatch it all away."

He'd do anything if he could give her a slim bit of hope. He sighed and picked up a photocopy of the handwritten sales agreement. He scanned the handwriting, the date, the emblem at the top of the page.

Then he saw it. His eyes widened and a hint of a smile tugged. "This was written on a World Famine Commission notepad."

"What?" Jenny gasped. She snatched the page, and he pointed to the logo at the top. The capital letters *WFC* were so elegantly written it was hard to even read them, but it was the logo used by the charitable organization in the mid-twentieth century. Their logo was far more streamlined today, so perhaps it wasn't surprising that Jenny overlooked it.

"My guess is that your mystery woman was affiliated with the World Famine Commission," Wyatt said. "She used one of their notepads to write this agreement."

"Why was she in Texas?" Hemingway asked, and Jenny supplied the answer.

"Because Bryan, Texas is home to Texas A&M, one of the

best ag schools in the nation. The WFC did a lot of consulting work with ag schools in the 1950s."

Wyatt rubbed his hands together, warming to the topic as his theory took shape. "The World Famine Commission has always been under the umbrella of United Phosphate & Fertilizer," he continued. "It would be the logical place to start tracking this woman down, but their archives are closed to the public. They're always fearing that reporters or environmentalists are poking around to cause trouble."

Jenny's smile was radiant. "Lucky for me I happen to have a lunch appointment with Kent McAllister, the CEO of United Phosphate, this weekend."

JENNY NOW HAD lunch with the McAllisters every other Saturday so she could visit with Sam. Two years ago, her relationship with the McAllisters was filled with threats of lawsuits and restraining orders. Now it had evolved into a cautious friendship as they came together to help raise Sam.

Their lunches took place at the McAllister ranch so Jenny could visit Sam in his own home, which was much more relaxed than the public park where they initially met. Now she played with Sam for a while in their backyard, tending the "magic tree" that had finally been transplanted to a sunny spot where Sam was looking after it.

After visiting with Sam for an hour, she relaxed on the flagstone patio with her nephew and the McAllisters for lunch.

"I wonder if it might be possible for me to gain access to the archives over at United Phosphate," she tentatively began.

Mr. McAllister steepled his hands as he settled into his

slingback chair. "What for? Most of it is just business and legal reports."

There was no reason to lie or dissemble. "I'd like to see records from the World Famine Commission back during the 1950s. I think there might be a connection to the woman found on my property."

"We generally don't open the archives to the public," Mr. McAllister began before his wife interceded.

"Kent, why don't you pull some strings to let Jenny inside?" Mrs. McAllister prompted. "It seems harmless."

Mr. McAllister shifted uneasily. "Our archives are closed to the public for good reason. I can't tell you how many times we've had undercover journalists or ecoterrorists doing anything they can to undermine the company. If farmers don't have phosphate, the world's food supply will plummet, and millions of people all over the world would be in danger of starvation, but at least the environmentalists can be happy they don't have to look at a strip mine."

Jenny kept her tone polite. "You know I'm not like that."

Mr. McAllister shook his head. "If we make exceptions for you, we have to do it for everyone."

"I'm not 'everyone.' I'm Sam's aunt and someone who is keenly interested in protecting our family and American agriculture. You can trust me."

Mr. McAllister pierced her with a hard stare, the unfriendly sort of scrutinizing laser she hadn't seen in months. What was he protecting? And didn't he realize that by digging in so fiercely it made her a little suspicious?

Maybe he sensed her train of thought, because he finally sent her a conciliatory smile. "Okay, you convinced me. I'll make an appointment for you to meet with our archivist on Monday."

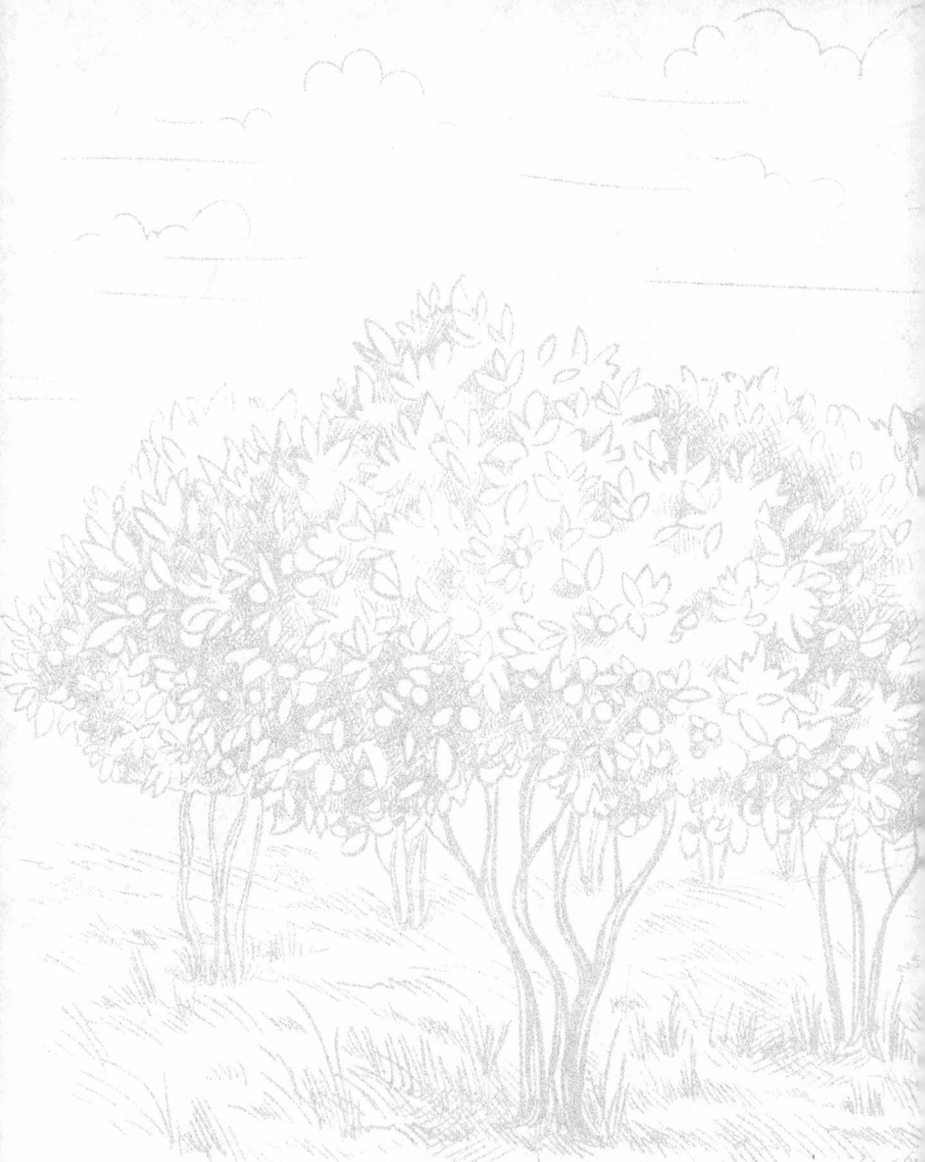

Chapter Twenty-Two

A smile tugged at Wyatt's mouth as he drove to United Phosphate to meet Jenny because she wanted his help plowing through old records in search of their mystery woman. He liked doing favors for Jenny, whether it was pulling a few strings to get a pothole filled or helping her discover the identity of that woman in the tree. With luck, today he'd be able to see the names of all the people working for the World Famine Commission in the 1950s and start narrowing down their search.

United Phosphate's headquarters reflected the unfortunate architectural styles of the Depression era. The building was four stories of brown brick with no ornamentation and only slits for windows. A few picnic tables of poured concrete were arranged on the grassy lawn beside the parking lot, and Jenny sat at one of them.

She stood as he drew near, gazing at him in surprise. "You got a haircut," she said.

Heat gathered beneath his collar. He'd spent a ridiculous amount at a salon recommended by his campaign consultant, but a televised debate was coming up, and he didn't want to look like a hick from the sticks.

"I went to Orlando for it," he confessed. After decades of paying less than ten dollars for a trim at a barbershop, he was stuck in a chair for thirty minutes as a stylist trimmed, razored, blow-dried, and put some glossy gunk in his hair. He even bought a bottle of the gunk because it *did* look pretty good.

They fell into step as they walked toward the building. His hand bumped hers and he jerked it away. Once, they had been joined at the hip wherever they went. Today an invisible barrier still hovered between them, but awareness of her nearness charged the air with electricity.

He opened the heavy front door for her, a blast of air conditioning hitting them as they stepped inside. They'd arrived fifteen minutes ahead of their appointment with the archivist, and the secretary refused to let them in early.

"Sorry," she said apologetically. "We can't let visitors loiter unattended. Mr. Gillingham should be back from lunch soon. Have you seen the new exhibit about United Phosphate's history? It opened last month, and we've already had a lot of school groups come learn about all the good things phosphate has done for the world. Why don't you take a look while you wait?"

Any company engaged in strip mining needed something to burnish their reputation, and United Phosphate spared no expense on their impressive exhibit. It filled an entire wing of the first floor and still smelled of fresh paint and new carpet. It featured professionally lit displays, and touchscreens mounted on the walls invited viewers to select short videos on United Phosphate's contributions to the health and welfare of people all over the world.

He pretended great fascination in the corporate timeline

of United Phosphate, but all the while he was intensely conscious of Jenny standing only inches away. Every nerve ending longed to bridge the few inches dividing them and draw her into his arms.

Instead, he dutifully kept his hands to himself as Jenny stepped forward to a touchscreen and launched a video.

A grandfatherly voice narrated the company's role in American agriculture. *"We're committed to feeding the world. From the plains of America's breadbasket, to the ranches of the west, United Phosphate & Fertilizer has provided the nutrition our soil needs to make this land prosper."*

The screen showed bird's-eye views of rippling waves of grain and the orderly rows of an apple orchard. Then the video showed canvas sacks of grain spilling into baskets while smiling children from India looked on, their happy faces grateful as aid workers unloaded relief supplies. The grandfatherly narrator continued.

"Throughout the twentieth century, when the world was in need, United Phosphate came to the rescue, shipping fertilizer to the parched fields around the globe. In partnership with the World Famine Commission, millions of dollars have been spent providing fertilizer to struggling nations around the world."

Wyatt stepped behind Jenny and set his hands around her middle, holding his breath and praying she wouldn't shake him off.

She didn't. Instead, she covered his hands with her own as she slowly moved toward the next series of display panels. A black-and-white photograph showed Eleanor Roosevelt cutting a ribbon at a ceremony. Then there was a photo of Karl Wakefield shaking hands with President Truman while a bunch of executives stood in the background.

"*Look!*" Jenny said, pointing at the photograph of Karl Wakefield with President Truman.

"What?" he asked.

Jenny pointed at the group of people behind Karl. "There she is! The woman from the tree."

Wyatt took a second look. Karl Wakefield and President Truman shook hands next to the flag of the United Nations while a group of men stood to the side, watching in approval. There was only one woman in the group. Attractive, well dressed, probably in her mid-forties.

And yes, she looked exactly like the artist's sketch of the woman found in the cypress tree.

"Do you think it's her?" Jenny asked, and Wyatt managed a stunned nod. The resemblance was startling. It took a moment to find his tongue as excitement mounted.

"Whoever put this exhibit together might know who she is," he said. Their odds of identifying the woman from the tree had just skyrocketed.

"Come on, let's go find out what the archivist knows about that photograph."

He grabbed Jenny's hand and they hurried back toward the archive. Had holding hands with a woman ever felt more electrifying? The thrill of the hunt united them as they set off in search of that unknown woman's name.

The archivist was a retired army officer who once guarded employment records at the Pentagon. Now he protected the secrecy of United Phosphate with as much diligence. The wiry old man scowled as he stood in the doorway of the archives.

"Are you seriously wanting me to pull ten years of employment records?" he growled the moment they entered.

"We changed our mind," Wyatt said. "We only need information about a picture in the exhibit down the hall. The one with President Truman."

Instantly, a grin split the old man's face. "Oh, the Truman

photo! I found that one myself. I fought hard to get it in the exhibit. Truman was a great president. He never got the credit he deserved. Come on in."

Who knew the key to this crusty old man's heart was through President Truman? Inside the archives was a bleak room lined with metal cabinets, microfilm drawers, and map cases. They sat at an oak worktable while Mr. Gillingham opened a rattling metal drawer, pawing through files and mumbling about how Truman got unfairly blamed for firing General MacArthur when it was clearly the right thing to do. Wyatt didn't care about President Truman's legacy, he just wanted to know the names of the people in the photo.

It didn't take long for Gillingham to pull the file on the Truman photo and set it on the worktable. Wyatt held his breath as he opened the file to reveal a large glossy copy of the Truman photograph on top of the stack.

The next page noted the location, event, and names of the witnesses. His heart thumped as he scanned the paragraph of names and landed on the only woman.

Svetlana Markova, the Soviet representative to the World Famine Commission.

"Hello, Svetlana," he said, his voice heavy with marvel and excitement. Jenny squealed and threw her arms around his neck. He laughed and returned her embrace, pulling back to kiss her . . . then she extricated herself from him before he got carried away.

"Sorry," she stammered. "I just got so excited."

"Don't apologize." He was excited, too. They still weren't free to, well . . . start things up again, but for the split second it had felt like old times. He adjusted the collar of his uniform and cleared his throat.

"I should get back to work," he said. Never had he felt less inclined to head back to the office. Who wanted to dive into statistics for cabbage and cucumber regulations when a long-unsolved Russian mystery was coming to the fore and Jenny looked at him like he was a hero?

Jenny picked up the page with the names. "And I've got a name I need to hunt down."

Maybe it was his imagination, but Jenny seemed as sorry to be parting as he.

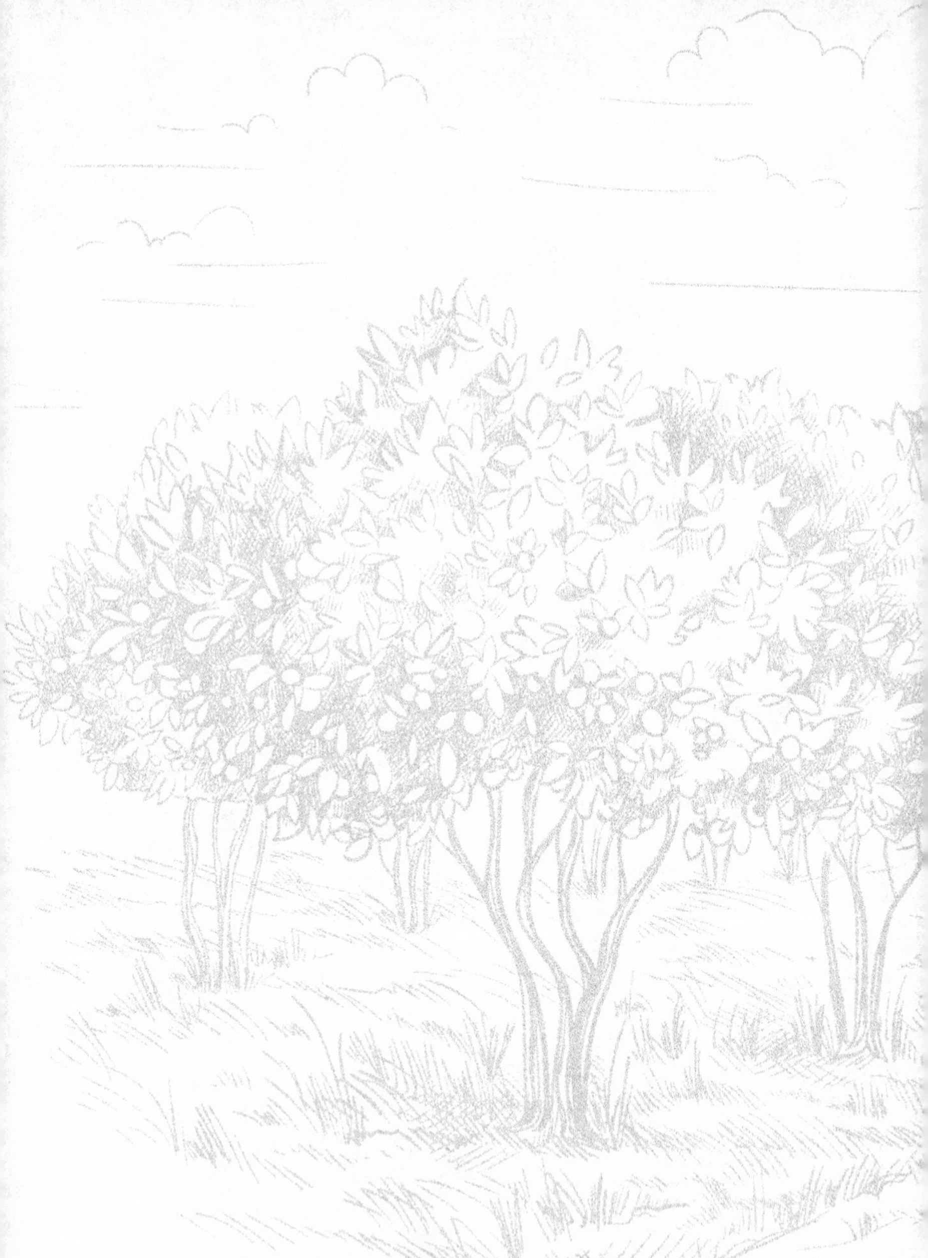

Chapter Twenty-Three

Jenny and Hemingway burned the midnight oil searching the internet for clues about Svetlana Markova. Although the internet was rich with cat photos and what people had for lunch, data about foreign visitors from the 1950s was almost completely absent. They quickly concluded that genealogy databases were their best bet for catching sight of the enigmatic Svetlana Markova. A quick search of the free online databases led nowhere except dead ends, but they were novices at understanding complicated genealogy archives and weren't ready to admit defeat.

"People who belong to genealogy clubs are a friendly bunch," Jenny said. "What if we put out a public call for help locating Svetlana Markova?"

It proved easy enough to do. It only took Jenny a few minutes to create an anonymous profile at FamilyOrigin, the biggest online genealogy website. The site had a place to post questions and tap the collective wisdom of a huge brigade of amateur genealogists.

She typed in Svetlana's name, an approximate year of

birth, and her likely birthplace somewhere in the Soviet Union. It was almost midnight. The glow from the large computer monitor provided the only illumination as she and Hemingway stared at the information she'd just keyed in about Svetlana.

"Do we dare?" she asked Hemingway, her finger hovering over the enter key. Once she posted this question, Svetlana's name would be out in the world and it might help them get more information, but it was just as likely to poke a sleeping dragon . . . a sleeping dragon who wanted the return of a missing Fabergé egg.

"We need to know more about her," Hemingway said. He leaned across the keyboard and tapped the enter key.

It was done. Now all they could do was wait.

OVER THE NEXT two days Jenny fielded eight responses on the genealogy website. Her heartrate galloped each time she clicked on a new message, but so far, they'd come up empty. All eight helpful genealogy buffs asked for additional information such as Svetlana's church affiliation, the name of her parents, and other questions Jenny had no hope of knowing. After the initial flurry of replies to her query, the responses trickled to a halt.

On Thursday morning she set off to inspect the grove for pests. It was an ordinary day until she spotted an alligator killing one of Hemingway's chickens.

Again. It was only a six-footer, but alligators lost their fear of humans when they were getting fed. This was the third time it had nabbed one of Hemingway's chickens, so Jenny got a rifle and took care of business. It wouldn't be safe to bring Sam to the grove for weekend visits if there was an alligator that had lost its fear of people.

The freshly killed alligator was at the base of a huge cypress tree, where the knobby roots would make it impossible to bury. She swallowed her distaste and dragged it to a sandy patch an acre away for burial. She'd only dug a few feet when water began pooling in the bottom of the hole. The high water table that made Florida so good for growing oranges also made it hard to bury things.

Could that be why Svetlana's body ended up in the cypress tree?

Jenny jabbed the point of the shovel into the dirt and eyed the gap in the line of cypress trees where the old cypress once stood. The entire grove had a high water table. It was why their house couldn't have a basement and why the fallout shelter stank so bad. Digging a hole deep enough for a human body would be almost impossible. Stashing a body in the hollow of a cypress tree suddenly made sense.

She yanked the shovel out and began digging again, flinging another load of sodden mud out of the hole, and wondered how her grandfather handled the water problem when he dug the fallout shelter. He had been so clever, but crazy, too. He wasted most of his adult life preparing for a war that never happened. From a distance of three generations, it was easy to poke fun at Cold War paranoia and "the red menace." The duck-and-cover videos with old-timey narration instructing school children to hide under their desks to protect them from a nuclear bomb seemed so quaintly foolish.

And yet, the four Romanov daughters, dressed in their white gowns and dainty gloves, probably wouldn't think it quaintly foolish. They experienced the fury of the red menace up close.

The slamming of a car door made her jump, and her heart

almost stopped at the sight of Wyatt's truck parked at the end of the field.

What a disaster. She and Wyatt had been getting along so well, but a dead alligator lay a few yards away and it wasn't hunting season. As the chief law enforcement officer in the county, Wyatt was the guy who enforced hunting laws. He was in uniform, too.

She glanced behind her, relieved to see the gator carcass completely hidden by palmetto fronds, but flies were starting to gather and it didn't smell too sweet.

A hint of a smile lifted the corner of his mouth as Wyatt headed toward her. "What are you up to this afternoon?" he asked, glancing at the hole with curiosity.

She fidgeted. "Oh, just digging a hole. Seeing how deep I can get before I hit water."

"Thinking of putting in another well?" He started walking around the area, as though assessing it for the viability of a new well. Skepticism was written on his face, and Jenny needed to stop him from looking around.

"Did you have any luck getting more information on Svetlana?"

"I did," he said, still scanning the area. "According to her visa application, she was the Soviet representative to the World Famine Commission from 1946 to 1952. She disappeared in 1952. That's all I could find."

Wyatt glanced behind her again, where the buzz of flies was getting louder. "I think there might be a dead animal back there."

"Don't worry about it. Vultures will clean up anything too awful. Let's go back to the house and discuss what to do next."

Jenny tried to coax him away from the palmettos, but he angled around her and took a few steps closer.

Then he cursed and reared back, grabbing her arm. "Get out of here, Jenny! There's an alligator over there."

She cleared her throat. "Really?"

"Yeah, really. Hurry up." He started tugging her toward the house, but then he froze and looked back toward the hole she had been digging.

"It's dead, isn't it." It was a statement, not a question.

"Well, you were the one who saw it. Did it look dead to you?"

He grabbed her shovel and crept back into the scrub, a hand on his service weapon. He peered through the palmettos for several moments, then extended the shovel to push the fronds aside before turning away in disgust. "Jenny, please tell me you didn't shoot an alligator."

"Did you actually see a bullet hole?"

"Two of them," he snapped. He threw the shovel down to prop his hands on his hips. "You know shooting alligators out of season is against the law. You still have a few more months on your probation, and if you get caught violating, you'll have a felony conviction slung around your neck for the rest of your life."

She didn't realize Wyatt knew about her mortifying gun conviction from shooting in the air when a trespasser wouldn't leave the grove. She didn't want to discuss it, but at least she had a good excuse for what she did today.

"Your colleagues at the county government weren't any help when I called to report a nuisance gator, so I handled the problem on my own."

The smell from the alligator was getting worse and the longer it remained exposed to the heat, the nastier it would be. She picked up the shovel and walked back to the hole. "Want to help me bury it?"

"No, I don't want to help you bury it," he snapped. "Shooting alligators out of season is illegal and you should have thought of that before you shot a protected animal."

He kept his back turned on her as she dug in silence. He probably didn't want to soil his eyes by looking at anything that whiffed of illegality, but Jenny could never afford to be so puritanical. Alligators swarmed all over the state because city dwellers thought they were quaint and only allowed two months of hunting a year.

After a few minutes of stony silence, Wyatt broke the standoff. "Who at the county government wouldn't help you?" he asked quietly. He still kept his back to her, but his voice had gentled.

"I reported it to Sheriff Eckert. He said six-footers weren't considered a nuisance."

"And you felt otherwise?"

"It's killed three of Hemingway's chickens."

Wyatt turned toward her, the ire draining from him. "That makes it a nuisance," he said. "Speaking of Hemingway, why isn't he out here helping you?"

She hoisted another load of sloppy mud out of the hole. Hemingway had gone AWOL again, which he often did when he wasn't in the mood to work.

"Gone fishing," she said simply. "I'm on my own today. Unless you want to help, of course."

"Forget it, Jenny. I might be willing to look the other way, but I'm not going to lift a finger to help."

She hid a smile as she kept digging. "Okay, Mr. Law and Order." She actually liked that he was a rule-follower. In a world of uncertainty, Wyatt Rossiter was as good as they came.

WYATT MADE himself at home in the kitchen while Jenny took a quick shower after burying the alligator. He braced both hands on the farmhouse sink while gazing outside to the fields beyond. Didn't Jenny understand the danger she'd put herself in by using a gun to kill an alligator? She escaped a felony charge two years ago by the skin of her teeth, and if she got a second violation, he wouldn't be able to save her this time.

Ten minutes later Jenny came springing down the staircase. Dressed in faded jeans and a white tank top without a speck of makeup, she looked fresh, wholesome, and exactly what he'd always wanted in a woman. Her cornsilk hair was twisted up into a knot, held only by a pencil stuck into it. It would be so easy to pluck the pencil out and admire the waterfall of hair pooling around her shoulders. He had to cross his arms to block the temptation.

She hopped onto the sofa and hugged her knees to her chest. "Tell me more about your election," she prompted, her face alive with curiosity. "Do you get nervous before any of those interviews you do? Because if you do, it doesn't show. I get so proud every time I see you on TV."

"First I want to talk about the gun," he said. "Shooting an alligator out of season could land you in a world of hurt if the district attorney learns you did it while you're still on probation."

She cocked her head. "How do you know so much about that gun charge, anyway?"

He looked away and shrugged. "It's a matter of public

record." He wasn't about to add that he had to call in a lot of favors to get the district attorney to back off from proceeding to a messy public trial. With Jack dead, Jenny was the only Summerlin left for the town to hate, and prosecuting her for a gun charge would bring the D.A. a lot of free publicity.

"Don't worry," Jenny said lightly. "My probation is almost over."

He took a seat on the coffee table, leaning forward to look directly into her eyes. He didn't want to alarm her, but she needed to understand how serious this was. "Jenny, if you get caught again, it will be a second conviction, and things won't go so easy on you."

The nonchalant expression on her face vanished. Her eyes darted around as she processed her thoughts. "Did you . . . were you the one who got the D.A. to back down?"

Of course he was the one who got the D.A. to back down. "He was being irrational. Tempers were still hot after what happened, and I merely pointed out that it was your first offense and you shouldn't be punished for what Jack did."

She hugged her knees tighter and kept staring at him. "Last year someone put a note in my box warning that my property taxes were late. Did you have anything to do with that?"

He couldn't in good conscience deny it. He dropped that note in her mailbox in the middle of the night so she wouldn't spot him, then checked the county records a week later to be sure she carried through and paid her taxes.

"I knew it was a tough time for you, so I sent a reminder. It was what anyone would do."

She unfolded her legs and leaned forward, setting a hand on his knee. "Don't belittle this," she said. "I could have lost the grove if you hadn't done that."

"You were grieving."

"So were you."

True, but keeping a watchful eye over Jenny gave him a sense of purpose. A reason to shake off the grief and protect the woman he loved. Watching over her from afar hadn't been without pain. Each time he inserted himself back into Summerlin Groves it was like ripping a bandage off a still-tender wound, awakening a rush of regret and longing for what might have been.

She got off the couch and started to pace. "Kent McAllister," she said, nervous tension coiled in her voice. "He threatened to sue for a restraining order if I kept trying to see Sam. And then last February he did an about-face when I didn't even ask."

He nodded. "You once told me how adrift you felt after your grandfather died and there wasn't anyone from an older generation to lean on. I relayed that to the McAllisters, and they were smart enough to understand."

Her eyes softened into two huge pools of feeling as she gazed at him. It was the way Jenny used to look at him and it tugged at every primitive instinct he kept tightly under control.

"What else did you do?" she asked. "Did you have the county fix those potholes outside the gate?"

He closed the distance between them, standing close enough to breathe the lemony scent of her soap. "Everyone hates potholes," he whispered.

He traced a thumb along the sides of her face, and she didn't pull away. Temptation won and he reached for the pencil anchoring her hair and tossed it aside. It clattered on the floor and then her silken waves tumbled over his fingers. *At last.* At last he could sink his fingers into this glorious mess of beautiful hair. It was what he'd fantasized about doing every single time he'd seen her in the past two years. He tilted her face up, holding his breath as he gave her a gentle, sweet, nibbling kiss.

They were tentative at first, then he delved deeper and kissed her with everything he had in him. Jenny fit against him like a puzzle piece and his arms clamped around her.

She drew back, a little breathless. "I was so blind," she said. "All along it felt like I had a guardian angel. How could I have been so stupid—"

"Shh," he said, putting a finger on her mouth. Why should she have known? For over a year he crossed to the other side of the street whenever he saw her. He'd been too ashamed to speak to her, too weak to confront their demons. "Shh," he murmured again, then leaned down to continue kissing her.

It was a dangerous kiss. Starting things up again could break Jenny's heart or send his mother's fragile recovery spinning out of control. He kissed Jenny's forehead, her temples, the side of her neck . . . then he simply hugged her tight, staring out the window to see thousands of orange saplings blanketing the fields.

He would go insane if he had to live out here in the middle of nowhere. "Jenny . . . could you ever leave the grove?"

Her answer came so fast it was painful to hear. "No, I'll never leave. This is where I belong."

He disentangled from her and walked over to plop down on the sofa. For no apparent reason, every muscle in his body felt immensely heavy. Jenny's glance was pained as she joined him, curling up on the opposite end of the sofa and looking at him with confusion.

"That's not a surprise for you, is it?"

"Not really," he admitted. "I'm almost certain to lose the election next month, but even so, I won't be staying here much longer. Once my mother is on an even keel, I'll be moving on."

She flinched a little. "Where will you go?"

"To the bottom of my soul I wish I could move to Tallahassee and be the next Commissioner of Agriculture. My chances of that happening are miniscule, but I could still take the job in Morocco. Or Alaska. They always need people who understand environmental law up there. All my life I've wanted to strike out for the horizon. To test my wits against a new challenge."

"Would the job in Tallahassee do that?"

He gulped back a spurt of laughter and gazed up at the ceiling, a world of possibility opening before him. "A term in the Capitol with a hundred-million-dollar budget? The power to help shape ag and fishing and ranching all across the state? Jenny, I would give anything for it."

"*Oh, Wyatt,*" she said on a breath filled with longing. "That's the first time I've seen you really smile in two years. Just for a moment I saw the old Wyatt again."

He sobered. Had he really been that miserable these past two years? The world was ablaze with good things, but he'd been letting the bad blot out the sun. It was easier to be optimistic when Jenny was with him.

"It's probably stupid to keep hoping I can win," he admitted, "but I can't stop dreaming about having that job. In a way it feels like my entire life has been in preparation for it. Working on a ranch as a teenager and helping my parents at the store. Getting my law degree, doing environmental stuff for the army . . . but especially watching you go through all the triumphs and sorrows that come with owning your own grove. Yeah, I want to win this election."

Jenny rolled forward to nudge his shoulder. "Then I'll help make it happen."

Before he could respond, her desktop computer dinged and she sprang off the sofa. "It's probably nothing," she said as she wiggled her mouse to wake up the monitor, but her eyes soon widened. Whatever just popped up on her computer must be interesting because she seemed completely spellbound.

He stood. "What is it?"

She made a few choked sounds as though unable to draw a breath or form a sentence. All she could do was gesture to the monitor and he hurried to her side.

The screen was filled with a full-color image of Svetlana Markova sitting on the porch swing at Summerlin Groves and grinning at the camera as if she hadn't a care in the world.

Wyatt's heart began to thud. The photograph was attached to a message at a genealogy website with a single question in the subject line: *Is this the Svetlana you are looking for?*

WYATT LISTENED as Jenny explained the genealogy website and how she'd been fielding responses ever since posting her question three days earlier, but this was the first response of substance, and it was a doozy.

The message came from an anonymous profile that had been created only an hour ago under the name "HistoryGeek."

The woman in the photograph had the same high cheekbones and arching dark brows as the lady in the Truman photograph, although her clothes were starkly different. Instead of a formal suit, she wore a plain white blouse knotted at her waist, a pair of capri slacks, and ballet flats as she smiled from the porch swing. It had a very fifties aura, with a touch of Audrey Hepburn.

The room suddenly felt warm, and he tugged the top couple buttons on his uniform open. "Can anyone else see this message?" he asked, and Jenny shook her head.

"He sent this to me privately. I'm worried he might be . . ."

Her voice trailed off, but he knew what she feared. HistoryGeek might be related to Svetlana and have a claim to the Fabergé egg. He could even be someone involved in her death. Wyatt stared at the blinking cursor, knowing that HistoryGeek had just sent this message and was probably waiting for a response.

"Ask him how he knows Svetlana," he prompted.

Jenny keyed in the question and hit the send button.

The reply came quickly: *I didn't personally know her, but I know a lot about her. Can I come to your grove to discuss?*

"No!" Wyatt said. "We don't know who this person is. And how does he know you live on a grove?"

"It's all over my FamilyOrigin profile."

Wyatt let out an aggravated sigh. If he'd been here when she created this account he would never have let her dump all that personal information onto the web for the whole world to see, but it was too late now.

"Ask if he's in Florida," Wyatt said.

Jenny typed in the question, and the reply immediately popped up: *Tampa. I could be over in an hour and a half.*

Wyatt started pacing. "I don't like this. We don't know who this guy is, and he obviously doesn't want you to know. Otherwise he wouldn't be using an anonymous account."

"I know," Jenny admitted. "But we can't let him get away because I want to know everything he has."

"Let me take the keyboard," Wyatt suggested, and she

instantly vacated the chair. He settled his hands over the keyboard and typed: *Can you tell me how you got interested in Svetlana Markova?*

The reply came two minutes later. *I'd prefer not to put things in writing. Can we meet? I'll gladly tell you everything I know about her.*

Wyatt swiveled in the chair to look at Jenny. "Don't let him out here," he warned. "There's something off about this."

"What about meeting him in a public place? The Brickhouse?"

It was a good suggestion because the Brickhouse was always crowded. He turned back to the keyboard and typed: *Let's meet at the Brickhouse on Amity's town square.*

This time there was a long pause before HistoryGeek finally replied: *Sorry. I'm a vegan.*

Now Wyatt was certain there was something weird about this guy, and quickly typed a reply. *How about the Green Goddess?* It was the only vegan restaurant in the entire county, but it still didn't appeal to the guy on the other end of the conversation.

Sorry. The metal chairs at the Green Goddess give me a backache. I can drive out to your grove and we can talk there. I'll even bring a vegan dinner for us to share.

This guy was clearly familiar with Amity because, yes, the Green Goddess had awful chairs. His frustration mounted. HistoryGeek knew where Jenny lived, and Wyatt needed to get to the bottom of this.

"The only place we're going to meet this guy is the Sheriff's Department," he told Jenny. "I can get us a private room."

Jenny nodded. "Go ahead and suggest it."

He did. This time there was a long pause . . . almost five minutes before a reply popped up.

Okay, I'll meet you at the Brickhouse. I'll just have iced tea.

The Brickhouse would be safe. It was crowded, and half the clientele was probably armed. Only an idiot would try something there.

He met Jenny's gaze. "I'll go with you. Are you in?"

She nodded, and Wyatt keyed in a response. *I'll book a table under the name HistoryGeek for six o'clock tonight.*

Chapter Twenty-Four

Thankfully, Hemingway answered his phone when Jenny called with the news and was eager to join them at the Brickhouse. Wyatt was being overly cautious and wanted Hemingway to hang out at the Brickhouse bar all afternoon to be on the lookout for indication of a setup. It would be easy for HistoryGeek to know what Jenny looked like because her face had been on a newscast when the grove got plowed under last February, but he probably wouldn't recognize Hemingway.

Jenny waited with Wyatt in the public library on the other side of the town square, monitoring periodic messages from Hemingway. There'd been no sign of any strangers arriving at the Brickhouse all afternoon, but the text they were waiting for came exactly ten minutes before six o'clock.

> A dweeby guy just showed up and asked for the HistoryGeek table. No sign of companions.

"Let's go," Wyatt said and propped his arm out to escort her to the restaurant.

Nerves created an ache in her gut. As always, it was crowded at the Brickhouse. She instinctively surveyed the crowd, spotting Hemingway at the bar as Wyatt asked the hostess to point out the "HistoryGeek table."

She did, and Jenny scrutinized the skinny guy with thick glasses at a corner booth. HistoryGeek caught her gaze and sent her a goofy grin and a wave.

"Okay, let's go," Wyatt said.

Something about the gangly man looked familiar, though she couldn't place him. He stood as they drew near. He had a buzz cut and horn-rimmed glasses, but mostly she just noticed how short he was. *Really* short.

Recognition dawned. "You're the guy who trespassed on my land," she burst out, and he winced. This idiot nearly got her convicted of a felony gun charge because he wouldn't leave when she asked him to.

"To be fair, I wasn't actually trespassing," HistoryGeek pointed out. "I was standing on the path leading to the river, which is an easement recognized by the state for public use, so I was technically within my rights to be there."

True, there was a tiny easement on Summerlin Groves. It gave her a break on property taxes to allow public access to the river, but hardly anyone except a few county officials knew about it.

Jenny lowered her voice because half the town was here tonight. "You got me charged with a felony."

"Hold on," Wyatt said, grabbing her arm. "This is the guy you shot at?"

"*I shot in the air*," she hissed. "He was poking into my business and wouldn't leave when I asked him to."

The dweeby guy held up both hands, palms out in the

universal call for peace. "Hey, I didn't want to report it, but the postman saw it and told the sheriff, so I was kind of backed into it. Can we sit down and talk? There's something I want to show you."

HistoryGeek had already caused her way too many problems to want to break bread with him, but she needed to pick his brain about Svetlana. She slid into the booth and Wyatt sat beside her.

Hemingway left the bar and strolled over, extending his hand toward HistoryGeek. "Can I join you?"

"He's with us," Jenny told HistoryGeek. "And yes, he is joining us."

As soon as they were all seated, HistoryGeek placed a slim leather wallet on the table and flipped it open. An FBI badge gleamed up from the table.

She sucked in a quick breath. The other side of the wallet had an identification card with his photo and name.

"Special Agent Robert Crenshaw from the Tampa office of the FBI," he identified himself.

Wyatt took the badge, examining it closely. The badge must have passed muster because he set it back on the table and introduced himself as Captain Wyatt Rossiter of the Department of Agricultural Law Enforcement.

Special Agent Crenshaw looked awfully puny for a hefty job in the FBI. On television, FBI agents were always brawny guys who wore their bulletproof vests and shoulder holsters with a manly confidence. This guy could be the captain of a high school chess club.

"You don't look like an FBI agent," she said, and the guy sagged.

"I get it," he said grimly. "All my life I've been five feet tall with bad eyesight. That's not easy for a man. It doesn't matter how fit or how smart I am. I speak Russian, German, and Kazakh, but all you noticed about me was that I was short."

"I'm sorry," she admitted, a little embarrassed because it was true. "I don't understand why you're interested in this or why you showed up at my grove right after my brother died."

He looked directly at her. "Ma'am, I have an interest in FBI history. The Summerlins and Wakefields represent a fascinating chapter in the FBI's involvement in the Cold War. I really did just want the chance to ask you about some old family photographs."

The first time he barged onto her property had been two weeks after Jack died, and she had no interest in anything he said. Now her only interest was the woman in the cypress tree.

"Where did you get that picture of Svetlana Markova?"

"I bought it from your brother," he replied. "He sold stuff from your grandfather's storage barns on eBay. I kept careful watch, and anytime he sold something that dated from the 1950s, I bought it. Old farm registers and outdated technical equipment. I bought an entire crate of broken old cameras and video machines. One of the cameras still had a roll of undeveloped film inside. Svetlana was in a lot of those photos."

"How did you learn her name?" Wyatt asked.

A waitress arrived before Crenshaw could answer. "Hi, y'all," she said, setting tall glasses of ice water on the table. "Can I get you started with some appetizers? We've got Cajun-dipped alligator tail on special."

Crenshaw looked a little repulsed at the prospect and ordered fried mushrooms for the table.

"Are you really a vegan?" she asked him after the waitress left. It looked like he could use a little protein and a few days in the sun.

"Yeah, I really am. I wish we could have met out at your grove because you've got some really interesting things out there." He dug into his jacket pocket and removed a photograph that he tossed down onto the table.

It was a photograph of the concrete slab, pipes, and doorway leading to her grandfather's fallout shelter. Very few people would even recognize it as a fallout shelter, but Crenshaw's face had a knowing expression as he waited for her to speak.

She returned his stare. "If you think I'm going to be the first one to talk, you're wrong."

"Have you ever been down there?" Crenshaw asked.

How did the government find out about this? Her grandfather had been so paranoid about people finding the location of his fallout shelter that he'd hired an out-of-state crew to help him build it. He warned them never to tell anyone about it lest desperate people try to take possession of it after Armageddon. Embarrassing, but true.

"It stinks down there," she said. "I haven't been down in ages."

"Stale air always smells bad," Crenshaw said. "I would love to get inside and have a look around."

Wyatt was completely baffled. "What on earth are you people talking about?"

"My grandfather's fallout shelter," she said, wishing she didn't come from such an odd, paranoid family. "I want to know why it's any business of the FBI."

"This fallout shelter was used for years as a rendezvous where confidential information was handed over to the Soviets," Crenshaw said.

She snorted. Her grandfather built that bunker because he *feared* the Soviets, not because he was working with them. Her grandfather couldn't have been a spy . . . could he? Her mind still grappled with the question as Crenshaw continued talking.

"I've got a stack of old photographs of Svetlana with your grandfather. There are a lot of other fascinating pictures of the Summerlins and the Wakefields that might have clues to what happened in 1952. I'll show them to you in exchange for getting down into that bunker."

It was tempting, but Wyatt refused to budge. "Why is the FBI interested in this? You showed up at the grove right after Jack died, and long before Svetlana's body surfaced. I want to know why."

"The FBI monitored old Karl Wakefield for decades," Crenshaw replied. "We believed he was more than just a Soviet sympathizer, but was an actual spy. Whenever he went to Moscow on World Famine Commission business, our government had eyes on him and he knew that. We bugged his homes in New York and Florida. We even bugged his private airplane and his apartment in Moscow. Decades went by and we couldn't find out how he was slipping information to the Soviets. We eventually learned he was passing his information to your grandfather, who met with the Soviet contact in the Summerlin fallout shelter to trade information. It was the only place they were certain wasn't bugged or could be spied on."

It was hard to even draw a full breath. Her brilliant, paranoid grandfather had been part of a *spy ring*? Disillusionment swirled and it was hard to keep concentrating as Crenshaw continued speaking.

"The plan worked for years until the Soviet handler flipped." Agent Crenshaw removed a photo from inside his jacket and tossed it on the table. It was the photo of Svetlana, smiling while sitting on the farmhouse porch.

"She was one of ours," he said, a look of unabashed admiration on his face. "Her name was Svetlana Markova. She came to this country as a Soviet representative to the World Famine Commission, and the Kremlin ordered her to get information out of Karl Wakefield. She offered Karl all sorts of Russian treasures in exchange for confidential information. Sometimes she brought things for Gus Summerlin, too."

Jenny's mind whirled with the implications. Could that explain the Bronze Age spiral pendant she mistook for a coaster?

Crenshaw gazed into the distance as he explained. "Svetlana was a loyal communist when she arrived, but over time, that changed. She became disillusioned with the Soviet worker's paradise. She rejected the atheism that was force-fed to all good communists, and started attending church. She was even baptized. Then she contacted the FBI, wanting to defect, but we convinced her to maintain the status quo so we could control what she sent the Soviets. We promised to help her defect in exchange for spying on Karl Wakefield. She agreed and risked her life in doing it. Everything was working perfectly until she stopped communicating with us. It was as if she'd dropped off the face of the earth . . . until the day a skeleton turned up on Summerlin Groves."

Agent Crenshaw pierced her with a probing stare. The face Jenny initially thought looked goofy and weak had transformed into grim and determined.

She didn't want to ask but had to. "Do you think my grandfather killed her?"

"That's what I'm here to find out. Show me his bunker, and I'll show you everything else I have on your grandfather and the Wakefields. It's interesting stuff."

"This doesn't make sense," she said. "Why would my grandfather be so paranoid about a Soviet attack if he was helping Karl pass messages to them?"

"Everyone feared the Soviets back then," Hemingway said. "Maybe he wanted a foot in both camps."

"If you can't beat them, join them?" she asked.

"Something like that," Crenshaw said. "The frustrating thing about history is that we'll never really know for sure. We get these tiny glimpses into the past and try to piece them together into some semblance of meaning. Some of those puzzle pieces might be down in that bunker."

She exhaled a frustrated breath. "I think you'll be disappointed. My brother already cleaned it out of anything valuable or interesting."

Agent Crenshaw's face softened into a wistful expression. "I want to see the room where it happened. It would be like stepping into a time capsule from a different world . . . a more dangerous, uncertain world when two superpowers stood on the brink, eye-to-eye, waiting for one to flinch. That bunker on your grove was part of the equation. How about it? I'll bring my stack of old Summerlin family pictures in exchange for getting a peek at that bunker."

"Agreed," she said instantly. She had to know if her grandfather had any role in this, and with each new detail, she feared he did.

Wyatt still seemed suspicious. "Why are you so fired up about all this? What's your goal?"

Agent Crenshaw picked up the photo of Svetlana, a charming woman smiling on the Summerlin porch swing.

"This woman was one of ours," he said in a voice vibrating with passion. "She didn't deserve to end up dumped in a cypress tree, and I intend to find out who did it."

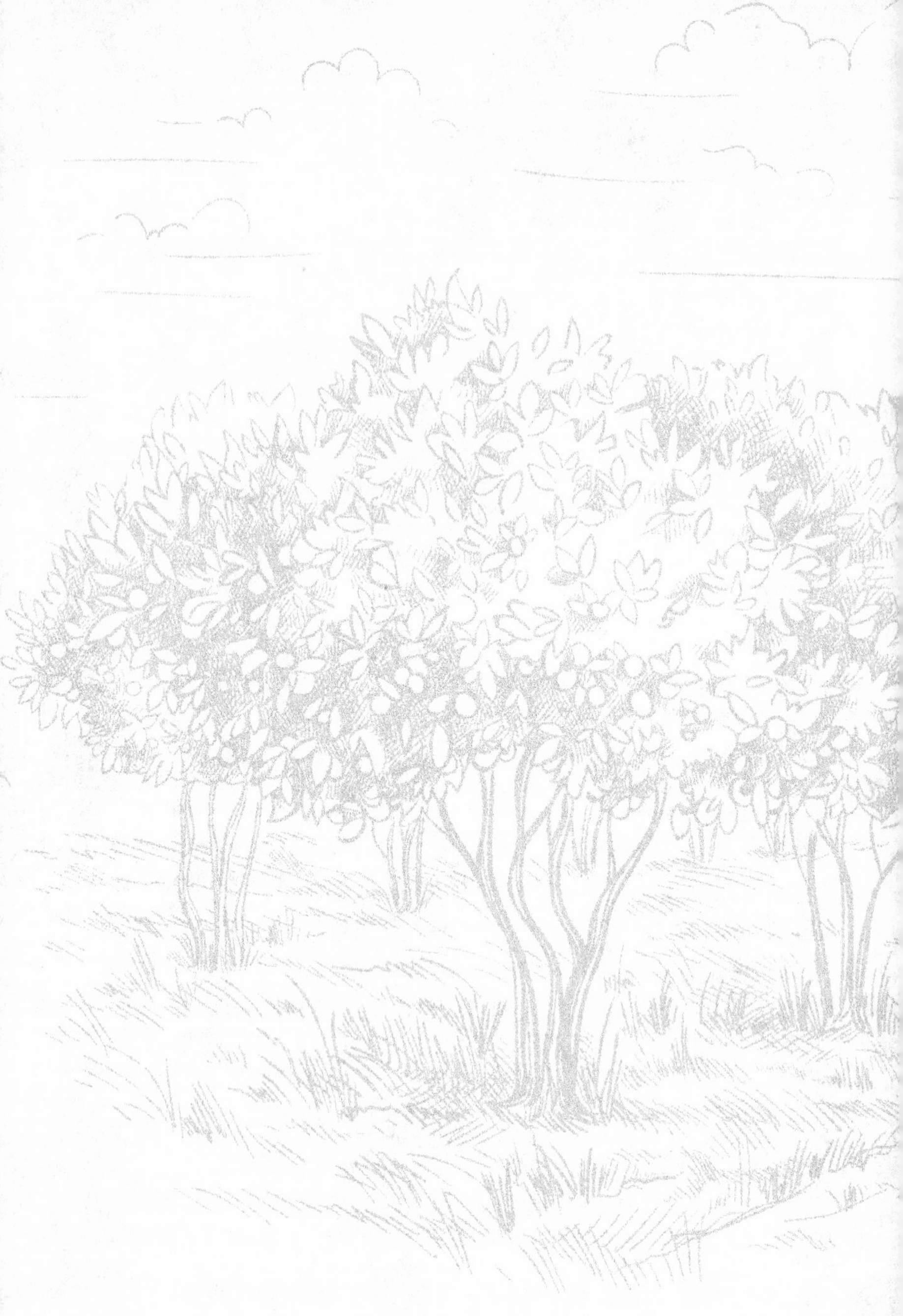

Chapter Twenty-Five

Special Agent Crenshaw's interest in Cold War espionage was a sideline to his actual job at the FBI, which was to investigate bank fraud. The FBI allowed Crenshaw to pursue his passion for Cold War history, provided he used no government time or resources. Crenshaw was testifying in a criminal court case all next week, so their meeting to start piecing together clues about Svetlana's demise would have to wait until the following weekend.

It gave Wyatt plenty of time to prepare for his looming debate with Mindy Bannerman, his political opponent from Cape Canaveral. Wyatt's experience in agriculture was light-years ahead of Mindy's, but any statewide political issue was fair game for the debate, so Wyatt took a week's leave of absence from his job to study. He arrived at the grove every morning to spend the day with Jenny, who had gladly volunteered to be his study partner. She found a list of the top twenty concerns of Floridians and had checked out a stack of library books to help him cram.

It felt like he was back in college, except in college he'd

never been infatuated with a study partner. He spent almost as much time flirting with Jenny as he did studying. They'd spend twenty minutes reviewing zoning laws, then they'd flop onto the sofa for an epic session of kissing. Twenty minutes on school funding, then they'd waste time giving each other foot rubs. In the evenings they cooked together in the farmhouse kitchen, dined by candlelight, then curled up to watch old movies.

This afternoon's topic was highway construction. Jenny had spread a blanket down near the river and he lay with his head in her lap while she read aloud. A quiet joy filled him as he listened to her read about the tensile strength of concrete. On this last cool afternoon of spring, as he gazed up at the slow dance of clouds overhead, there was nowhere else on earth he'd rather be.

And in those long, lazy spring days, he fell in love with her all over again.

"Why do you care about this so much?" he asked one evening as they studied a proposed bill about irrigation law. The porch swing creaked as she leaned forward to toss the pamphlet on the stack of study books.

"I want you to win," she said in her sunniest voice. Sometimes Jenny's ridiculous optimism was charming, but he didn't have much of a shot at winning this election. His opponent now had three million dollars in her campaign war-chest, while he'd raised a paltry sixty thousand. She'd won endorsements from the tourism, construction, real estate, and aerospace industries. The number of people employed in those industries dwarfed the number of people who earned a living from ag, but everyone got a vote, which meant the race was likely to be an embarrassing landslide.

He gently rocked the porch swing, an arm around Jenny as he trailed his fingers through her hair. "Winning means I'd have to move to Tallahassee," he said softly. "And that would spell the end for you and me."

Jenny would never live in a big city like Tallahassee. There were no orange groves or cattle ranches, no endless pastures as far as the eye could see. Her smile faded, replaced with a wistfulness that was hard to look at because he was to blame.

He stood to watch the blazing sunset. The gathering of clouds on the horizon was purple, amber, and violet. It was a typical Florida sunset, where the combination of heat, humidity, and fading light created these nightly spectacles.

He leaned against a column as Jenny hugged him from behind, propping her chin on his shoulder to watch the sun melt into the horizon. "I wish you could be happy here," she said, her voice quiet. "You're all wings, and I'm all roots."

He turned to press a kiss into her palm. There was no need for him to add anything else because they both knew it was true.

JENNY SAVORED every moment of helping Wyatt prepare for his debate. Raising oranges was a solitary task, but getting Wyatt prepped for the debate was a satisfying joint effort. By the end of the week they'd worked their way through a stack of books about Florida's economy and headed back to the public library to check out more. A late-afternoon downpour started shortly after they arrived. Rather than venturing through the rain, they retreated to the top floor of the library to study while waiting it out.

Nobody was up here, and it was quiet except for the thud of rain pelting the roof like a cascade of pennies. They claimed a shabby sofa tucked in the far corner and stacked their books on the nearby table. Wyatt stretched an arm along the back of the sofa and she hopped up beside him, a book about beach erosion at the ready.

She flipped it open. "So! Tell me the three strategies to manage coastal erosion," she prompted. This one ought to be easy because she'd read him an article from the newspaper on the topic only last night.

Wyatt kissed the side of her jaw. "Retreat, accommodation, and protection," he murmured, then his lips trailed behind the shell of her ear, nibbling.

"Very good," she teased. "Do you have any proposals regarding . . ." She glanced down at the page because what he was doing with his lips sent shivers throughout her entire body and she had to clear her throat. "Do you have any proposals regarding government programs to protect the coastline?"

He gave a perfectly crafted response involving seawalls and restoration efforts. A shiver raced through her as his fingers traced through her hair and she scooted to the far side of the sofa to grab another book. He clearly didn't need help mastering coastal erosion, and maybe rural education would be a properly sober topic that was both important and likely to come up at the debate.

Wyatt adjusted his position on the far end of the sofa and pulled her feet onto his lap. She'd already kicked off her boots so he could rub her stocking feet, and he casually gave her a foot massage while covering everything from school tax rates to elder care.

They remained in the library even after the rain trickled to a halt. Everything was going swimmingly until he brought up Hemingway. "When is he going to do something with his life?" Wyatt asked. "He's been fired from every job he's ever had."

"I haven't fired him," she defended.

"It will happen eventually," Wyatt warned. "He's over-educated and under-employed. You've got a blind spot where he's concerned."

She pulled her feet away. "Why do you dislike him so much? Hemingway has my back and will never turn on me."

"I don't trust him. What's a college professor doing hanging out on an orange grove?"

Someone as ambitious as Wyatt probably couldn't understand. Wyatt's competitive instincts couldn't resist looking for the next mountain to climb or dragon to slay.

"Hemingway is happy here," she said simply. "He loves literature, but being a college professor is about raising grant money and speaking at conferences. He wasn't a good fit."

"He got fired from the coast guard."

She nudged him with her toe. "Would you want to serve in the Icelandic Coast Guard?"

She had him on that one and he grinned, conceding defeat by scooping up her feet to continue her foot massage. They had just launched into a discussion of highway construction when an electronic tapping on the library's intercom startled her.

"Patrons, the library will be closing in ten minutes. Please bring any items you wish to check out to the circulation desk at this time."

She met Wyatt's gaze as he gave her feet a final rub. "Let's go," he said, although she suspected he was as sorry to leave as she.

The air outside was warm and sticky from the rain. Wyatt opened the trunk of his car to dump the books inside. It was six o'clock and she was hungry. The Brickhouse was just across the street.

"Do you want to get something to eat?" she asked after he closed the trunk. "There isn't a line at the Brickhouse yet."

"Sorry," Wyatt said. "I've got a, um . . . I've got an event."

"An event?" The way he stumbled over the words was odd. "What kind of event?"

"Just a thing," Wyatt said, not meeting her eyes as he unlocked the passenger door for her.

She moved in front of the door, preventing him from opening it. "What kind of 'thing'?"

"It's a fundraiser," he said, a flush gathering on his cheeks. "Kent McAllister is hosting it out at his ranch. I haven't had much luck raising money yet, and there might still be time to buy a little advertising."

She brightened. "Don't be embarrassed, I think it's wonderful. Can I come?"

Wyatt gazed off into the distance. A long pause stretched between them, broken by laughter from some teenagers throwing frisbees on the town square. There was only one reason Jenny could think of to explain why he wouldn't want her there.

"Wyatt? I'd like to come to the fundraiser, if that's okay with you."

More silence. Tension gathering around his mouth signaled his discomfort. It would be easy to pretend she didn't care and go home to have a beer with Hemingway, but she *did* care and this *did* hurt. She crossed her arms and waited.

"My parents are going to be there," he finally said.

It was surprising that he'd admitted it, but at least it was out in the open now. "And they wouldn't want you to be seen with a leper like me."

"Jenny, don't be that way. The race for the commissioner's office has been the one thing to give my mother a glimpse of daylight since Lauren died. *The one thing*. Don't ask me to take that away from her."

"And my showing up at the fundraiser will do that?"

He sighed with a look of resignation. "Yes, Jenny, it will. I'm sorry, but there it is."

Okay. It wasn't like Jenny didn't have two years of experience feeling like a pariah in this town. Donna Rossiter had more cause than anyone to despise the Summerlins, but was it going to last forever?

"Does she know we're seeing each other again?"

"No."

It was like a punch to the chest. These last weeks of her relationship with Wyatt had been fresh and new and exhilarating. It was understandable that his mother might disapprove, and it was time to learn how bad the situation was.

She nodded across the street toward the Brickhouse. "Let's go get something to eat and we can talk about it."

"I don't have time," Wyatt said.

She reached for his hand, drawing him toward the row of outdoor cafés and shops. "Then let's go to the ice cream parlor to get a soda for the ride to the grove."

He withdrew his hand and refused to budge. She turned to face him. "Are you embarrassed to be seen with me?"

"I'm not embarrassed—"

She cut him off. "Then why can't we walk down the street holding hands?"

"It's a small town, Jenny."

And word would leak back to his mother. No wonder he wanted to hide out on the top floor of the library where nobody ever went. She stepped forward, keeping her voice low because this conversation was mortifying and there were people around. "I never did anything bad to your mother, and I'm tired of hiding from the world over what Jack did."

Wyatt's voice was tense. "Let's do this *after* the election, okay? Our dating again is going to be a tough nut for her to swallow."

The words stung, all the more painful because they were true. Jack's crime was a millstone that would forever drag her down in some people's eyes, including Wyatt's mother.

Wyatt walked around the car and opened the passenger door from the inside. "If you want me to drive you back to the grove, we need to leave now."

She fumed as she slid into the seat. Wyatt's jaw was clenched as he silently began driving her home. Finally she couldn't take it anymore and spoke in a quiet tone.

"My grandfather always said 'don't let yesterday use up too much of today.' He was right. I'm finished doing penance for what Jack did. I've moved on. I have a good life ahead of me. Sometimes I still come across a picture or memento that reminds me of the good times with Jack and the wound rips open all over again. It cuts especially deep because my defenses were down. That's okay. I pause, I grieve . . . and then life goes on."

"Try saying that to a woman who's lost her only daughter."

She didn't have anything to say to Donna Rossiter, a woman whose grief now smothered the people around her. Jenny couldn't begin to imagine what Donna had endured, but she was finished trying.

It was a long, sullen, and silent drive home.

Chapter Twenty-Six

Jenny rarely woke up in an angry mood, but her argument with Wyatt had made it hard to sleep. It cycled through her mind and she repeatedly woke up from the same dream in which she argued with him again. Sometimes they were in the grove and sometimes on the town square, but always she was shouting at his back as he walked away from her.

The other reason she'd been too restless to sleep was the Fabergé egg. The ninety days were up and the final ruling on its ownership would be announced today. The judge had already dismissed Raymond Wakefield's claim as unsubstantiated. Now Jenny's only competition was the guy in Texas, and according to Kristen, he was almost certain to win.

Jenny rolled from bed, still tired, and yanked on a pair of jeans and work boots. She and Hemingway were inspecting the saplings for insect damage today, which meant walking the entire length of the grove and stopping every few yards to spot-check the trees. It was a long but easy task, giving her plenty of opportunity to vent about Wyatt.

"Doesn't he understand how beautiful life on the grove could be?" she asked. "He would love it out here if he'd only give it a chance. He's *never* done that. In all the years we've known each other, he never gave this place a fair shake."

Hemingway squatted down to check the base of a sapling for root weevils while Jenny inspected leaves for aphids. Acres of bountiful farmland surrounded her, and yet they could get to town in less than ten minutes. It was the best of both worlds and Wyatt would see that if he wasn't so stubborn.

"You think Wyatt doesn't know what living on a farm is like?" Hemingway asked.

"He *thinks* he knows. He used to work summers on groves and ranches, but he's never actually lived on one." Even when they were dating, Wyatt resisted the prospect of living on the grove if they got married. He worried about where their kids would go trick-or-treating, as if that was somehow the measure of a home. When she was little, Gus helped them carve jack-o'-lanterns to set on the front porch. They'd illuminate them with candles, huddle on the front steps, and toss seed corn to the deer and armadillos that came out at dusk. Real bats zoomed in the air, snatching insects and making their Halloween every bit as magical as the kids enjoyed in town.

The phone in her pocket vibrated, and she pulled it out to check the screen. Kristen from Christie's. Her mouth went dry, and she tilted the phone so Hemingway could see.

He stood and wiped his hands on a rag, his face serious. "Better answer it."

The next sixty seconds were going to change the course of her life and her fingers shook as she opened her phone. "Hello?"

"Hey, Jenny." Kristen's voice had a slow, saggy quality. It ached with so much compassion that Jenny knew what to expect, but the words still hurt. "The arbitration judge has made his ruling. He says the guy from Texas has proven his case and will get the egg."

The last bit of hope that a judge might save her flickered out and died. Her gaze strayed to the gap in the line of cypress trees in the distance.

"It's final, then?"

"It's final, but you have the right to appeal."

An appeal would only drag out the inevitable, and she tried to find the humor in the situation. "So a Fabergé egg is going to a guy who runs a cereal box museum."

Kristen gave a sad snort. "Yeah, the cereal box guy is going to get it. But hey! When I called to tell him, he sounded really decent about it. I think he's worried that you might appeal, and he wants this thing to move along quickly, so he's offering you a ten percent finder's fee if you're willing to settle now."

"Ten percent?" Hope surged and she met Hemingway's gaze. Ten percent of forty million was still a fortune, and Hemingway looked as thunderstruck as she felt, as though the world had just tilted off its axis.

"Yeah," Kristen said. "After taxes and the auction commission, I expect you'll each get about a million dollars. Are you interested?"

The phone fell out of her hand, but Hemingway snatched it before it landed in the dirt. "We're interested!" he shouted into the phone.

"Yes," Jenny said, her breath shaking with laughter. "Yes, yes, *yes*!" Tears pricked at the backs of her eyes because she would have plenty to pay the monthly mortgage and fix her truck. No more pinning her hopes on a long-shot quest to win an improbable court case.

"Great!" Kristen said brightly. "I'll email you the paperwork to accept the finder's fee, and then we can get moving."

The phone call ended and Jenny squealed in delight. Hemingway let out a Viking war whoop of victory, scooping her up and whirling her around in the middle of the grove. The moment her feet touched the ground they tore off toward the house, running at full speed, laughing and giggling like children. They had won. It wasn't tens of millions of dollars, but it was still a fantastic windfall that would get her out of debt and give Hemingway the chance to do anything in the world.

They didn't even kick off their muddy shoes once inside, they simply ran to the computer. Jenny wiggled the mouse, wondering how long it would take for Kristen's documents to arrive.

She smiled so wide it was hard to speak. "The first thing I'm going to buy is a computer that doesn't take forever to boot up!"

"No way," Hemingway laughed. "Fix your kitchen. Get rid of that ancient stove with the metal coils. How can a man cook on that thing?"

"Really? I like that old stove."

"Up your standards, woman!" Hemingway roared. "Get a decent gas stove with a built-in griddle."

The joy of an imaginary spending spree kept them both talking over each other for the next few minutes until Kristen's email arrived. The contract for the finder's fee was breathtakingly straightforward, as was the timeline for the impending auction.

The most surprising item on the timeline was that Kristen wanted to host a fancy gala to formally introduce the Firebird Egg to the world. It was to be a red-carpet event with people in ball gowns and tuxedos, the international press, the whole nine yards. Jenny and Hemingway were both invited. They were each allowed to bring a guest, but they'd probably end up going together. If Wyatt wouldn't take her to a fundraising barbecue, she wouldn't take him to the fancy gala.

In her heart, she'd known their renewed fling was likely to end badly, although she didn't regret it. She and Wyatt had leaned on each other a lot over the past month. Even these past two weeks when she put her life on hold to help him practice for the debate was something she would remember fondly. It was within her power to decide how she wanted to remember their affair, and she would focus on the good.

She and Wyatt weren't going to get across the finish line together, but she loved that he was willing to put his pride and reputation on the line to fight for the farmers. She cared for him and intended to be there for his big debate tonight.

Hemingway was skeptical. "You really want to go to his debate? After the way he treated you?"

"Oh, don't be such a killjoy," Jenny told Hemingway in mock exasperation. "This may be the happiest day of my life. We just won a huge victory with the egg. We have healthy new orange trees. I love Wyatt and want to support him during his big debate."

Hemingway still looked doubtful, but nothing was going to dissuade her from attending that debate.

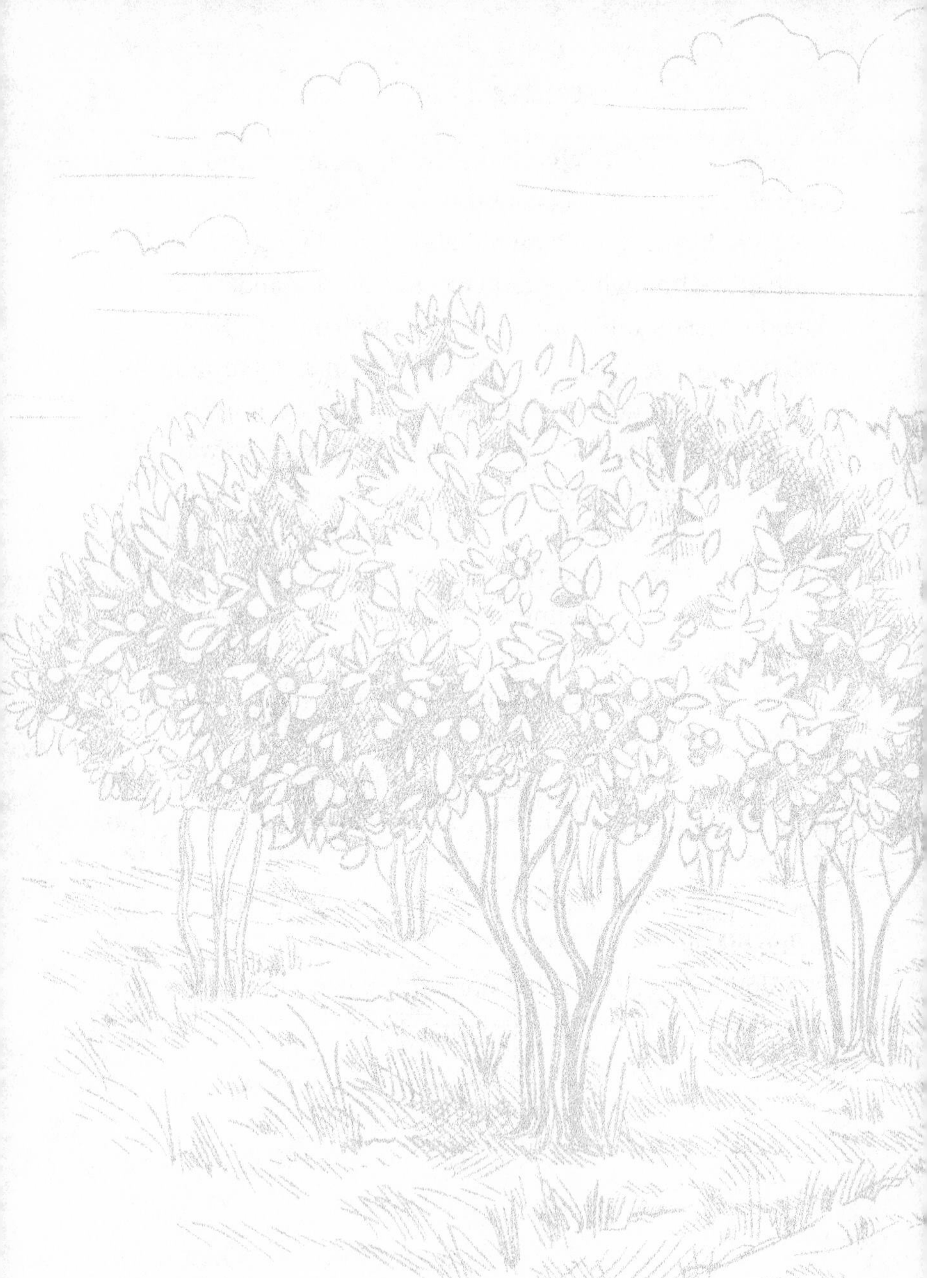

Chapter Twenty-Seven

Hemingway's words hovered in Jenny's mind during the one-hour drive to Sumpter County, the site of Wyatt's debate with Mindy Bannerman. Maybe she was headed for trouble, but that didn't stop her from wanting to support Wyatt.

The debate was on the grounds of the largest dairy farm in Sumpter County. About a hundred people had already gathered at the Lundberg Dairy Farm by the time she arrived. Most were milling around the grounds, but a few sat in the rows of plastic chairs set up in front of the debate platform. An outdoor lighting crew hung light diffusers, reflectors, and tripods with impressive microphones because the debate was going to be televised on a public access station, broadcast over the internet, and picked up on two ag radio stations.

Everything was far more elaborate than she'd anticipated, and she scanned the venue in search of Wyatt. This place was huge! The dairy barn housed six hundred cows. There were outbuildings, feed pits, storage tanks, and an insulated milk silo as big as the ones at the OJ factory. The air smelled like sweet hay mingled with musty scents from the animals. Oversized fans built into the barn walls kept the air moving so it didn't smell too bad, and she'd always liked the earthy smell of animals.

She rounded the calf pen and spotted Wyatt with a bunch of people clustered around him. He looked tanned, rugged, and fit. A crew member clipped a microphone to his white safari shirt. Wyatt's sleeves were rolled up, exposing his tanned forearms, and it looked like he belonged out here. *He looks perfect*, and that fancy haircut he got in Orlando had been worth every dollar. A lady with a headset read last-minute instructions to him from a clipboard.

Oh, Wyatt. It was hard to contain the pride brimming inside as she strode forward, eager to wish him luck, but he raised his eyes and spotted her.

He frowned and gave a quick shake of his head.

She froze. His parents stood nearby, and Wyatt's quick flash of warning said it all. If Jenny came any closer, she risked a confrontation with his mother and this evening was already stressful enough for him without that.

His reaction hurt worse than a slap, but she sent him a quick nod and retreated to blend in with the sound technicians before Donna could see her. This wasn't the time to rock the boat.

She choked down a bitter laugh as she walked. It was stupid to let this hurt her feelings. Of all the tragedies she'd survived in the past two years, this didn't come close to the top of the list. It was a snub, nothing more. Not like getting an orange grove plowed under. Not like having a brother blow his stack and kill two innocent women or witnessing her nephew become an orphan.

This was only a little snub.

From a man she adored, but oh well.

She picked her way across the lumpy yard to the other side of the dairy barn where Mindy Bannerman stood with her team. A couple of campaign consultants in business suits stood nearby and a makeup lady dabbed powder on Mindy's face. It probably took half a can of hairspray to keep Mindy's jaw-length bob so perfect in the humidity of the summer evening.

A campaign consultant whipped through a series of index cards, firing off questions, which Mindy answered like a rattling machine gun.

Price of beef? Check. Number of people employed by ag in Florida? Check. The three major challenges in accessing groundwater? Check, check, and check. Mindy had been doing her homework because she spouted the statistics with ease and gave a brilliant analysis of the problems of urban encroachment on farmland prices.

"All *we* really care about is the price of home rentals in Tallahassee," Mindy's husband joked to the campaign consultant, which elicited good-natured chuckles from her entire team.

Then someone from the news crew beckoned Mindy to the stage, where both candidates were needed for a sound check.

Jenny remained by the barn to watch. It was never quiet on a dairy farm. The cows inside the barn lowed and let out an occasional bellow. The drone of insects and chatter of evening birds were a constant in the background. The sounds would surely add a touch of rural ambiance for the radio and television crowd.

Mindy headed toward the stage. It looked like she tried to dress down with khaki slacks and a white safari shirt, but she hadn't been able to resist the high-heeled ankle boots, which looked terrific until she tried to cross the muddy path. Her husband lent an arm as they navigated around the lumpy terrain.

How much did cute ankle boots like that cost? Jenny glanced down at her square-toed cowboy boots of scuffed leather with a one-inch stacked heel. She'd always liked them until she saw Mindy Bannerman's classy ankle boots.

Two pairs of shoes approached, and she looked up, almost choking on her breath as she spotted Wyatt's parents a few feet away.

"Oh, h-hi," she stammered.

"Hello," Donna said tightly. "Jenny, I think it would be best if you left. Wyatt doesn't want you here tonight."

She blinked. "Did he tell you that?"

"He didn't need to," Donna said. "We all saw his expression the moment he spotted you. This is the most important night of his life, and you are a needless distraction."

That was blunt, but also probably true. If Wyatt had to choose between his mother or Jenny, so far he had an unbroken track record of siding with Donna.

She straightened her shoulders and managed a dignified nod. "I don't want to cause any trouble. I'll get out of your way."

There was no thaw in Donna's expression and Jenny didn't wait for one as she headed toward the parking lot behind the barn.

She would eat nails before letting Wyatt's mother scare her off tonight. A bunch of dairy workers had lined up along the back fence to watch the debate, and she would join them. Neither Wyatt nor his parents could see her back here behind the tables filled with telecommunication equipment. The sound check was still underway and she could hear everything. The television monitor on the table provided a closeup of the people on stage.

"Can I join you?" she asked a weathered dairyman, who scooted to the side so she could brace her forearms along the top rail of the fence.

The plastic chairs in front of the stage were soon filled. With the exception of the well-heeled campaign crew from Mindy Bannerman, most of the audience looked like farmers or ranchers from the surrounding counties. Up on stage, Wyatt and Mindy stood next to each other, chatting congenially during the last few minutes before the big show.

A debate moderator stepped up to welcome the crowd. Wyatt and Mindy moved to stand behind their respective podiums.

"Welcome to Lundberg Dairy Farm on this warm summer evening," the debate moderator said, then proceeded to read the rules and introduce the candidates. Jenny stared at Wyatt, the strong column of his neck looking tanned against his white shirt. Over the past few weeks, she had snuggled against that neck, kissing it and laughing as she tossed debate questions his way.

Now she huddled at the back fence to hide from his mother.

It didn't matter. The TV monitor on the camera crew's table was only a few yards in front of her, and she had an even better view of him than those people on the hard plastic chairs up front.

She brightened as the announcer read Wyatt's name and qualifications. Each candidate was greeted with polite applause from the audience; then the debate began.

Both sides were well prepared. Both sides spoke eloquently and with polish, but to Jenny's mind, Wyatt seemed more appealing when he recounted his very first job bailing hay at fifteen, then helping out at his parents' feed store from the time he was sixteen.

Rather than drawing on personal experience, Mindy's opening statement was an elegant homage to the American farmer and the nobility of producing food for the world. She even reserved special praise for the Lundberg Dairy Farm and their commitment to grass-fed dairy cows.

"Yeah, but I saw her drinking almond milk before the debate," the guy standing next to Jenny muttered, and another worker had some choice comments about the pricey bottle of vitamin-infused water her husband carried.

Once the debate moved into the main questions, both candidates performed well. If she was honest, Jenny would call it a draw, but Wyatt clearly had support from the dairy workers lined up along the fence. They supplied running commentary that kept Jenny's mind distracted from the ache in her heart. Wyatt would be leaving central Florida regardless of if he won or lost. Why couldn't she be enough for him? Hadn't they been happy these past few weeks?

As expected, the debate soon veered away from agriculture to delve into tourism and other industries in the state. The future Commissioner of Agriculture would be a member of the governor's cabinet, so all questions were fair game.

Then came a question that no one saw coming.

"Captain Rossiter," the debate moderator said in an unusually somber tone, "gun violence is a concern for us all. Your own sister fell victim to the blast from a semi-automatic pistol during a domestic dispute. Would you care to speak to your position on gun control?"

It was a kick in the gut. Jenny held her breath as the camera zoomed in on Wyatt's face. He looked thrown off balance. His Adam's apple bobbed as he absorbed the impact of the question. She clenched the railing of the fence, anxious for Wyatt to get on with it.

"No," he finally said. "My sister's murder is the last thing I'll ever want to discuss."

He stepped back from the podium and gathered a breath. The dairymen beside her grumbled in sympathy and it seemed to take forever as Wyatt cleared his throat a few times. He glanced at his parents sitting in the front row, and that was a mistake.

Donna had buried her face in her hands. Wyatt came out from behind the podium, as if prepared to go to his mother's side, but Wyatt's dad gestured for him to continue the debate.

Wyatt returned to the podium but kept his head bowed, hands clutching the rim of the stand. Her heart thudded. Politically speaking, it was probably good to let people see some genuine emotion from Wyatt. This wretched pause could be forgiven, provided he could come up with a good, strong response to the question.

Sweat rolled down Jenny's back and she fanned herself. Why hadn't she anticipated a question like this and prepared him for it?

Wyatt finally lifted his head, his expression tight as he stared at the camera. *Come on*, she silently urged. He had been performing so brilliantly until now.

"I don't have anything else to add," Wyatt finally said.

There was another awkward pause until the moderator smoothed it over. "Representative Bannerman? Would you like to take a position on gun control?"

"Of course," she said in a respectfully compassionate voice. "My sympathies are with the entire Rossiter family. Florida's farmers and ranchers face unique challenges in rural areas where they sometimes encounter dangerous wildlife and have a right to defend themselves. This doesn't preclude the need for sensible gun control throughout the state."

Mindy kept speaking, but Jenny barely listened. Donna

still hadn't lifted her head and Wyatt's expression was tragic as he helplessly watched his mother from the stage.

To make matters worse, Mindy knocked the gun control answer out of the park. She was poised, fair-minded, and pitch-perfect.

Closing comments were next, and Jenny prayed Wyatt could regain command of his arguments. The rules for the closing statements were simple: Each candidate was allotted three minutes to speak on whatever topic they wished.

Maybe Wyatt could somehow pull a rabbit out of a hat and salvage his disastrous non-answer on gun control, but his closing comments were a word-for-word recitation of the speech she'd practiced with him a dozen times.

The excruciating debate was over and Jenny slipped away before the moderator finished his closing remarks. The worst thing would be for Wyatt to see that she'd stayed and witnessed his poor performance.

She tortured herself on the drive home by listening to commentary on the ag radio station that broadcasted the debate. Both announcers agreed Wyatt fumbled the gun-control question but did well enough otherwise. Both men appeared surprised with Mindy Bannerman's impressive command of the subject matter, although Jenny thought her answers mostly amounted to rattling off a bunch of statistics. Any high school kid could memorize stats.

She turned off the radio and drove in silence.

Why hadn't Wyatt ever stood up to his mother on her behalf? When push came to shove, he always sided with Donna, and that would probably never change no matter how much she wished otherwise.

WYATT DROVE his parents to their home while listening to a country music station. He had no interest in the commentary from ag radio, nor did he want to discuss his debate performance, or worse, his botched answer to the gun-control question.

But there was a topic burning in his mind, and after arriving home and watching his mother head upstairs for bed, he motioned his dad out to the backyard to discuss it.

This yard was a masterpiece, the envy of the neighborhood. It had an expansive deck with plenty of benches, two large picnic tables, and a fire pit. It had been the perfect place for his parents' lively weekend picnics. The oversized grassy lawn had once been the site of neighborhood flag-football games and Cub Scout camping. His dad had been the scout master and his mother taught the kids how to roast corn in open pits and identify birds by their call. During his teenage years, this was the house where everyone came to hang out. Creating this magical home and garden was his mother's greatest triumph.

Now the picnic tables were unused, the barrels that once brimmed with his mother's potted herbs were empty, and the lawn overgrown.

"I wished you would have let Jenny sit with you during the debate."

His father released a heavy sigh as he took a seat on a bench, staring out into the darkened yard. "Your mother couldn't . . . Wyatt, she's not ready yet."

"Will she ever be ready?"

His dad shrugged, his face drawn with anguish. Neither one of them wanted this conversation, but it had to happen.

"Dad, I've got two women in my life who I love. Mom is one of them. What's happening right now isn't Jenny's fault. Mom is the only one who can fix it."

Ed stared at a couple of fireflies flickering in the darkened yard. The night air was warm and damp, its heavy mugginess weighing on them both.

"It's not easy being caught in the middle," Ed finally said. "As you get older, you'll come up against all kinds of things that pull your loyalties in different directions. A boss who wants the time you'd rather spend with your family. Commitments to your kids warring with obligations to the church or your job, and there's always a cost to choose one over the other. I know Donna isn't rational right now, but I promised her for better or for worse. Lately it's been a whole lot of worse, but I made a vow."

Wyatt let it sink in, then asked the most painful question of all. "Are you saying that if I marry Jenny, you'll always side with Mom?"

His dad's eyes crinkled at the corners, and he looked grief-stricken all over again. "Don't make me say it."

Wyatt clapped a hand on Ed's knee before rising. "Don't worry, Dad. I get it."

He understood his father's message perfectly. If Wyatt chose Jenny, it was going to cost him *both* his parents.

JENNY STARED at the pitched ceiling above her bed, unable to sleep. She should have asked Wyatt's permission before showing up at the debate. It was a shame that she needed to, but maybe her appearance had thrown him off his game and caused him to flub that last question.

She rolled over and punched her pillow. What happened wasn't her fault and she shouldn't blame herself that Wyatt couldn't stand up to his mother.

The ultimate irony was that Jenny desperately admired Wyatt's parents. Anyone would want parents like Donna and Ed. They hosted backyard picnics for everyone in the neighborhood and their Christmas decorations lit up the entire street. Donna used to bake Wyatt a birthday cake in the shape of a football and his sister got a butterfly cake. Their Fourth of July celebrations featured backyard barbecues with sparklers and fireworks, not emergency drills and stories about the Bataan Death March.

Yes, Gus Summerlin really did use patriotic holidays to scare her and Jack with stuff like that. If her own mother had lived, things would have been different. Jenny would have learned how to bake charming cakes instead of learning to skin a deer.

A clattering noise sounded outside her window and she lifted her head, listening, because that didn't sound like an animal.

Then something pinged on the actual window glass and she sprang off the mattress to peek outside. The silhouette of a man stood down below, flinging pebbles at her window.

It was too tall to be Hemingway, and those shoulders belonged to Wyatt. She lifted the window sash.

"Quit throwing things at my window!"

"You didn't answer your phone," Wyatt said.

That was because she'd put it on silent mode, but she wouldn't have answered his call anyway. "What are you doing down there? How did you get onto the property?"

"I jumped the gate. You need better security out here, Jenny."

Did he really come all this way to lecture her at two o'clock in the morning? "My security is fine. My taste in men is questionable."

"I know, and I'm sorry." Wyatt's voice brimmed with regret. "I should have asked you to the debate. I was wrong. You've been a pillar of strength helping me study, and I blew it. Jenny, I'm sorry."

"Are you drunk?" It sounded like it. Wyatt was normally so restrained and composed, not loud and agonized in the middle of the night.

"No! I'm just heartsick and mad and feel like I've lost the election because of that stupid gun-control question. You're the only person I wanted to commiserate with, but I ended up with my parents because . . . Well, because they need me."

And she didn't. Jenny had been completely self-sufficient for years, but did that mean she had to take a back seat forever? Sometimes it got old being the pillar of strength.

"Quit pestering me at two o'clock in the morning," she called down. "I've got a full day tomorrow and you're interfering with my sleep."

"What's going on tomorrow?"

"Crenshaw," she replied. "He's coming out with that roll of pictures he found in my grandfather's old camera."

Talking about Crenshaw stirred her anger anew. She'd put her entire life on hold to help Wyatt with that debate. No progress had been made in figuring out how Svetlana got in the tree, and Wyatt was still down below being needy.

"Can you come down and let me in?" he hollered. "Come downstairs and let's talk."

"Forget it. It's been a long day." Frankly, she'd endured long days ever since her grove got plowed under, another sin to lay at Wyatt's feet. Maybe it wasn't fair to hold it against him, but she wasn't in the mood for fair and lifted her arms to close the window.

"Wait!" Wyatt called out. "If you can't let me in, then let me shout it out. Jenny, I love you. You're the most important person in the world to me, and I haven't been showing that to you. I love your optimism and tenacity and your great big, generous heart. Jenny . . . you've made me a better man. Even tonight, when I blew the debate and hurt my parents and disappointed a million voters, you're the person I want to commiserate with because everything is brighter when I'm with you. In a few hours the sun is going to rise on another day, and you are going to saddle up and greet it in a good mood."

"Is that a problem for you?"

"No! I love that you can do that. Come on, Jenny . . . let me in. I know you're pissed at me and I deserve it. Let me hold you."

As if that would solve anything. "You sided with your mother."

"I did and I'm sorry."

"Look behind you," she said, pointing to the acres of land. "You sided with the state and tore down my grove."

"I hate that law," he said, a little of the warrior coming out in his voice. "It's why I'm on fire to win this election. The first thing I would do is strike that eradication law from the books. It should have been scrapped years ago. Jenny, even when the worst happened, you didn't let it beat you down. You keep springing back to the surface to face another day."

She sagged against the window frame. "Lately all I do is lose my battles."

He started laughing. Laughing! "Don't you know that's why I love you? It's because you never give up. Even on the darkest night you figure out a way to spot the sunshine, and Jenny, that's worth all the gold in Fort Knox. Come downstairs and let me hold you."

It was tempting, but she didn't have the energy to be his sunshine tonight. "I'm going back to bed. Crenshaw is coming tomorrow and I need to get some sleep."

"What time? I want to be here."

She was still mad at him but had never been good at holding a grudge. Nursing grudges only kept wounds from healing, and besides, she wanted him. From the moment she saw Wyatt sauntering across the parking lot at the OJ processing plant two years ago, she'd wanted him.

"Ten o'clock tomorrow morning, and don't be late," she shouted down, then slammed the window closed.

Her heart still thudded as she lay back on the pillow, but she couldn't stop the smile from forming. Wyatt still loved her, and she could have him back if she wanted.

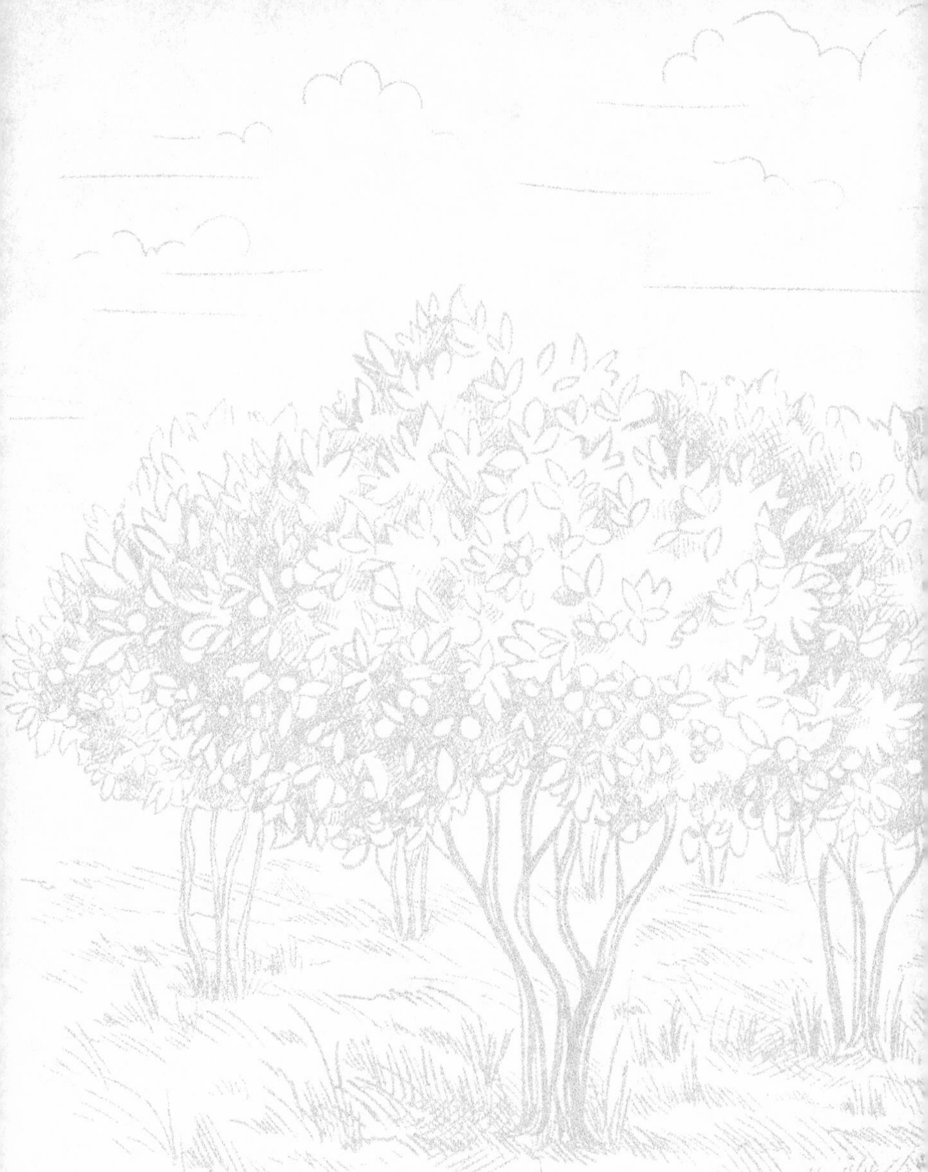

Chapter Twenty-Eight

True to his word, Agent Crenshaw showed up at the grove with the old photographs from her grandfather's camera. Jenny held the door wide to welcome him inside.

"I love old houses like this," Agent Crenshaw said as he stepped inside the farmhouse, gazing all around to admire the front room. She sent Wyatt a fleeting glance of triumph, as if to say that at least *somebody* appreciated the grove. Wyatt had arrived ten minutes earlier, still looking a little tired and glum about the debate, but with his sleeves rolled up and ready to help. Hemingway had joined them, too.

"Did you bring the pictures?" Wyatt asked Crenshaw.

"I did, but first I want to see the fallout shelter," Crenshaw said. "A deal is a deal."

And she promised to show it to him, even though she hated that place. Jenny's earliest memories were the mandatory emergency drills her grandfather insisted on to prepare against a great Soviet attack. Whenever the air-raid siren shrieked across the grove, the entire family had five minutes to gather necessities and hightail it to the fallout shelter, where they hunkered down for a full hour. What kind of nutcase subjected little kids to that? Jenny practically wet her pants each time the air-raid siren shattered the calm, never knowing if it was a drill or the real thing. The smell was the worst. Stale air mingled with the stink of damp concrete and musty linens as they huddled by the light of a battery-operated lantern.

Jenny walked with Crenshaw down a sandy aisle of orange saplings toward the shelter. Wyatt and Hemingway trailed behind. The entrance to the shelter was embedded in a concrete pad, requiring a crowbar to lift the heavy metal door. Wyatt and Hemingway worked together to get the lid up, then Jenny led the way down, her boots clanging on the metal steps leading into the shelter.

She carried a lantern, casting shadows from the florescent glow of the bulb. The concrete floor had cracked with age and eerie shadows highlighted the ridges in the barrel-ceiling that always reminded her of a hollowed-out ribcage. Two sets of bunkbeds lined one wall, and a chrome-plated dining table and vinyl chairs were pushed against the other.

Her grandfather warned that if the Russians ever bombed them, they'd be living down here for two weeks while radioactive fallout settled. Metal shelves still held cans of baked beans, condensed milk, and bags of dehydrated food. It was decades-old by now, and surely a health hazard.

Crenshaw looked spellbound as he scanned the interior, as though he'd just stepped into a different time. She could find no joy in imagining the treason her grandfather might have committed down here.

Wyatt's nose wrinkled as he moved past the rows of canned goods, a first aid kit, and a basket of leaky old batteries to examine a stack of moldering board games. It was embarrassing to come from a family that put such stock into preparing for a great Soviet attack that never came. She turned her attention away, pretending to study a stack of old books.

Most were cheap paperbacks, but one looked different. The thick volume was beautifully embossed with gold lettering against the rich dark leather. It was Tolstoy's *War and Peace*. It didn't belong among the comic books and dime store westerns, and things that didn't add up should be examined carefully.

"Wyatt, can you bring the lantern over?" There was a handwritten inscription inside the front cover, and Wyatt lifted the lantern while Jenny read the message aloud.

> *To my friend Gus. I hope you enjoy the great Russian classic. Perhaps someday when we live in a more peaceful world, you and I shall meet again and raise a toast to our colorful lives.*
>
> *Until then, may God be with you, and please remember me fondly.*
>
> *Svetlana*
>
> *January 1952*

Her heart thudded. Beside her, Crenshaw gazed at the inscription. "This is the first time I've actually heard directly from her," he said, his own voice awed. "She sounds . . . friendly."

Friendly was such a pale word for the mystery of a woman carrying a Fabergé egg who came to a bad end in a Florida orange grove. Colorful life, indeed. The inscription had a wistful tone, as though Svetlana knew their friendship was nearing an end.

Oh Svetlana, what happened to you? Jenny could only pray her grandfather didn't have anything to do with the brave woman's demise. Everything about this dank and dim fallout shelter reeked of sadness.

"I'll wait for you outside," she said to Crenshaw, anxious to escape this underground burrow and see the photos Crenshaw found in her grandfather's old camera.

And perhaps find answers to the mystery of Svetlana's relationship to Summerlin Groves.

WYATT PRODDED Crenshaw along after a few more minutes exploring Gus Summerlin's bolt hole and was grateful for the deep lungful of fresh air the moment he emerged back into the sunlight.

Back at the farmhouse, Hemingway took the prime position next to Crenshaw on the sofa. As the ghostwriter for biographies about old Karl Wakefield, Hemingway had plenty of insight into Wakefield family history and could help identify the people in the old photos. Crenshaw set a large manila envelope on the coffee table and opened the flap. All the photographs had been enlarged to an 8-x-11-inch format for easy viewing.

"That's my grandfather," Jenny said of the first picture on the top of the stack. The color photo showed a gangly young man in overalls with no shirt underneath. He looked about thirty years old and leaned proudly against a vintage pickup truck in mint condition. Gus Summerlin looked wiry and strong, with a cocksure lopsided smile. The farmhouse in the background needed a fresh coat of paint and the shrubs could use a trim, but everything else looked the same, even the porch swing.

The next photo showed Svetlana next to Gus as they stood in front of the truck. It was probably taken the same day as the first picture because Gus wore the same grubby overalls, but this time he held up a string of freshly caught trout. They were laughing, looking relaxed and happy together.

Another photo showed Gus holding a huge trout, aiming its opened jaws toward Svetlana, who laughed while holding her hands out to protect her face.

"They were clearly friends," Agent Crenshaw said, which was undeniable, and a bit of tension unknotted from Wyatt's neck. Whoever killed Svetlana, it probably wasn't Gus Summerlin, and that would give Jenny peace of mind.

The next batch of pictures was starkly different. A dozen people mingled outdoors, all dressed for horseback riding in preparation for one of the famous Wakefield fox hunts. A middle-aged Karl Wakefield was clearly recognizable, wearing jodhpurs and riding boots like all the other posh riders. A young man who might be Max Wakefield was there too, dressed for riding and grinning ear to ear.

"Could that really be Senator Wakefield?" Jenny marveled. "He looks so young, so different."

The senator was probably still in high school when this picture was taken. Wyatt only knew Senator Wakefield as an elder statesman. This younger version seemed so drastically different, and it couldn't be explained just by his youth. In the photo, Max looked happy and exuberant as he gazed at something just beyond the frame.

Wyatt moved to the next picture and blanched. It showed Mrs. Hawkins, his fourth-grade teacher. Only she wasn't Mrs. Hawkins back then, she was Millicent O'Grady, the teenaged daughter of the Wakefields' cook. Millicent was dressed in a black-and-white maid's uniform, holding a silver tray loaded with goblets before one of the horse riders.

"I didn't realize Mrs. Hawkins worked at the house, too."

"Oh yes," Hemingway told him. "Her mother was the cook, and Millicent helped out whenever the Wakefields hosted a big bash. Somewhere along the line Millicent and Max became an item, quite a shock to 1950s society, but they never hid it. They even went to their senior prom together."

"They certainly did," Agent Crenshaw said, flipping to the next photographs.

They were prom photos of Max Wakefield and Millicent O'Grady. Millicent wore a pale gown with a modest neckline and full skirt flaring from her trim waist. A corsage of a lavender orchid was pinned on her shoulder. Max wore a white tuxedo jacket with a bow tie and a matching boutonniere on his lapel. They stood on the front steps of the Wakefield mansion, arm in arm, smiling directly at the camera. There were several photos of them taken from different angles, and Karl Wakefield appeared in one of them. Karl's relaxed expression was proof he knew of his son's relationship and was at ease with it.

Then there were a batch of photos that looked like a Thanksgiving celebration here at the farmhouse, and Svetlana was in most of them. One photo showed Svetlana in the kitchen dicing apples while Gus Summerlin stuffed a turkey. Gus wore a heavy flannel shirt, and Svetlana sported a chunky sweater with her sleeves pushed up, revealing a delicate wristwatch.

Wyatt leaned in closer. "That looks like the same watch found in the cypress tree."

Hemingway took the photo for a closer look while Wyatt turned to the next photo. It showed the Thanksgiving table with Gus at the head, the turkey before him and ready for carving. Bowls brimming with mashed potatoes and green beans filled the center of the table, and everyone smiled for the camera.

"Oh look, that's my dad!" Jenny said, pointing to a boy around six or seven years old. "I can tell by the ears. And the lady who looks like Doris Day is my grandmother. She died of cancer in 1954, so I've never seen many pictures of her."

Svetlana was at the table, sitting next to Max Wakefield. Everyone wore casual clothes except for Max, whose starched shirt and bow tie seemed out of place. There were five people around the table, but place settings for six.

"Who took the picture?" Wyatt asked.

"That's what I want to know," Agent Crenshaw said, looking at Jenny. "Do you have any other relatives who were likely to have been there?"

Jenny said there weren't, but soon came up with a theory. "Could the photographer be Millicent Hawkins?" she asked. Technically her name was Millicent O'Grady when these photos were taken, although he and Jenny always knew her as Mrs. Hawkins.

Hemingway chimed in. "Millicent's mother would have cooked the Thanksgiving meal at the Wakefield estate, so there probably wasn't a holiday dinner at Millicent's home. And the fact that Max was here at the grove? He looks awfully spiffy compared to everyone else . . . like he left one party to be at another he'd rather attend."

Wyatt stared hard at that empty place setting. It surely belonged to whoever took the photograph. "It couldn't have been Millicent Hawkins," he concluded.

"Why not?" Agent Crenshaw asked.

"Right after the medical examiner's report came out, I asked Mrs. Hawkins if she could think of a middle-aged woman from Russia who socialized with either the Summerlins or the Wakefields. She said she couldn't, and I believe her."

Wyatt spread the photos across the table, scanning them quickly. "There isn't a single picture here of Mrs. Hawkins in the same frame as Svetlana. They didn't know each other."

Hemingway didn't seem convinced. He picked up the photo of the Thanksgiving feast with one empty chair. "Max is looking straight at the photographer with a rapt expression on his face. Kind of like he was in love with the photographer."

"It couldn't have been Millicent because she never knew Svetlana," Wyatt insisted. The only photos with Millicent in them were the prom pictures and the riding party at the Wakefield estate where she served the drinks. Svetlana didn't appear in either batch. The two women were never in the frame at the same time.

Agent Crenshaw picked up a photo of Max holding Millicent snug against him right before setting off for the prom and pointed to Millicent's wrist. "She's wearing Svetlana's watch."

Wyatt's mouth went dry. Yes, the delicate watch on Millicent's wrist looked like the one Svetlana wore, but it was not necessarily the same. That was the style for ladies' watches in the early fifties.

Agent Crenshaw laid out all the prom photos, five in all. "The only jewelry Millicent is wearing in most of these pictures are a pair of pearl earrings, except in this final photo. Suddenly the watch appears on her wrist. My hunch is that Svetlana was the photographer, and she loaned Millicent the watch right before they set off for the prom."

"So what?" he demanded. "Maybe Svetlana loaned Millicent the watch. It was obviously returned before Svetlana ended up dead in the tree, so it doesn't prove anything."

Except that Mrs. Hawkins lied when she said she didn't know anyone matching the description of the lady in the tree.

He locked eyes with Crenshaw, who didn't look away, but his expression saddened. Did Crenshaw know something he wasn't sharing? Wyatt's heart sped up and his mouth went dry.

"This doesn't prove anything," he stressed again.

"Not yet," Agent Crenshaw said. "But now that you know the name of the woman in the tree, it's time to ask Mrs. Hawkins if she remembers Svetlana Markova. I can't do it because she doesn't know or trust me. Svetlana was well-known to both Gus Summerlin and the Wakefields. We have proof right here. If Mrs. Hawkins claims not to remember Svetlana, she's lying, and that means she's hiding something."

Wyatt's worry turned into anger. "Are you suggesting Mrs. Hawkins could have had something to do with whatever happened to Svetlana? *Because of a watch?*"

Agent Crenshaw merely shrugged. "I think that woman knows a lot more than she's ever told anyone." He began gathering the photographs into a stack and replaced them in the envelope. He met Jenny's gaze.

"You have access to Senator Wakefield. You can get onto his estate and ask him questions about what we're seeing in these photos. I'd like to be there when you meet with him. I want to see his expression when you ask if he remembers Svetlana Markova."

Jenny nodded. "The Wakefield fox hunt happens four times a year, and there's one coming up next weekend. The senator is always in town for that. That would be a good opportunity."

"It would," Agent Crenshaw said, then turned his attention to Wyatt. "You have a good relationship with Mrs.

Hawkins. I'll leave it to you to ask her if she ever knew Svetlana Markova. If you don't want to ask her, the FBI can do it."

"I'll do it," Wyatt replied grimly. "Let me have one of the photographs to see if it jogs her memory."

Crenshaw gave him the one of Svetlana smiling in the porch swing at the grove. "I suggest we coordinate our questioning of Mrs. Hawkins and the senator to occur at the same time so they can't tip each other off to get their stories straight."

Wyatt nodded hesitantly. It was hard to imagine that everyone's favorite small-town, fourth-grade teacher could have had any role in Svetlana's death, but it was almost a certainty that she had known Svetlana.

The question was, would she still lie when confronted with these photographs?

Chapter Twenty-Nine

Jenny prayed that the Senator wouldn't deny knowing Svetlana Markova. There could be plenty of reasons he hadn't been forthcoming earlier in the year when he denied knowing anybody matching the description of the woman in the tree. Fifty years was a long time. Svetlana was a visitor in America, and maybe he assumed that she'd simply returned to the Soviet Union. Even so, anxiety made the muscles in her neck ache as she drove to the Wakefield estate.

"I hope you're not afraid of dogs," Jenny said to Crenshaw, who was sitting in the passenger seat as her pickup rounded the bend. The Wakefield Manor stood at the end of a long drive, and even from here, the baying of the hounds pierced the air and ratcheted her already tense nerves even tighter.

Agent Crenshaw winced a little. "They're not my favorite thing in the world."

Raymond's pack of English foxhounds had already been released from the kennel to roam in the fenced pasture beside the house, barking and snuffling and baying. The throaty dog-howls sounded intimidating even to Jenny.

Trucks and horse trailers crowded the drive, and the quarterly fox hunt was about to get underway. Early morning mist swirled above the grassy lawn and a dozen riders in traditional red hunting garb were already mounted while others loitered near the refreshment table.

How different this seemed from the photographs from the 1950s, where staff served the riders from silver trays. Today, the staff no longer wore those fussy black-and-white dresses but simple buff slacks with white polo shirts. She recognized Mrs. Darby, the housekeeper who'd been with the family for years, setting out a tray of warm cranberry muffins.

Jenny approached. "Is Senator Wakefield available?"

Mrs. Darby straightened. "Yes, but he's not taking visitors today. He's heading off to Washington this afternoon."

"I'd just like to say hello," she said. *And ask him if he remembers Svetlana Markova*, she silently added to herself.

"He'll be out to say a few words before the hunt starts," Mrs. Darby said. "I'll let him know you're here." The housekeeper carefully waded through the pack of snuffling, anxious hounds while Jenny leaned against the fence with Agent Crenshaw.

"Remember, say nothing about the photographs," Agent Crenshaw said. "Give him the chance to talk himself into a corner. I'll let you do all the talking, but I'll be listening.

Raymond trotted his horse toward them. With tall black boots, a red jacket, and a white cravat expertly tied around his throat, he looked like he could have just stepped out of the eighteenth century as he tipped his head toward her.

"Jenny, come to watch the hunt?"

She nodded. "It's been a while since I've seen one, and it's always an impressive sight."

Raymond flushed with pride. "Indeed. The baroness and I laid the scent before dawn, and the hounds are raring to go."

He glanced behind her shoulder and his entire body tensed. "Father," Raymond said stiffly.

Jenny turned to see Senator Wakefield arriving at the stables. He couldn't have missed his son's greeting but didn't even glance at or acknowledge Raymond in any way as he walked to the refreshment table. The other riders noticed the senator's arrival and began leading their horses a little closer.

The senator raised a glass. "Friends!" he called out in a healthy, robust voice. "Welcome to the famous quarterly Wakefield hunt. This year marks our seventy-fifth anniversary of the hunt, a celebration of sportsmanship, comradery, and tradition. As you follow the hounds, give thanks for the natural splendor of the Florida countryside. Be kind to your horses and to each other, give thanks for the good weather, and ride safely. Carry on!"

The gate was opened and the blast of a trumpet released the hounds, who howled in delight as they raced toward the line of oaks in the distance. Then the ground vibrated from the thunderous stampede of horses' hooves as the riders followed.

"Quite a show," Agent Crenshaw said. He visibly relaxed once the dogs were gone, their barks fading into the distance.

The senator stared at the riders as they rounded a bend of mounded haystacks and galloped toward a line of trees. It took almost a minute before the ground stopped vibrating. The senator had been witnessing these awe-inspiring hunts all the way back to his youth, but he still seemed entranced as he stared after the riders.

"Keeping it up is all Raymond's doing," he said softly.

"You must be very proud," Jenny said. It didn't matter that foxhunting was a snobby, rich person's sport. Raising these hounds and preparing the course was still a lot of work.

"Am I?" he said, but perhaps she imagined the tragic look

in his eye because a moment later he sent her a grandfatherly smile.

"What brings you out so bright and early?" he asked. "Raymond has been hosting these hunts for a decade, but I haven't seen you here in years."

This was it. This was what she'd been dreading from the moment she saw the photographs of a blissfully young and hopeful Max Wakefield smiling alongside Svetlana.

"I wanted to catch you before you headed off to Washington," she said, a chill racing through her in the damp morning air. "We finally got a positive identification on the woman in the cypress tree. Her name was Svetlana Markova. Does it ring a bell?"

Please don't deny it, she silently prayed.

The senator's grandfatherly expression didn't change. No flicker of surprise, no hint of fear. "Svetlana," he said slowly. "That's a very distinctive name. I don't think I've ever met anyone named Svetlana."

A weight settled on her chest because the senator's denial had just skyrocketed the odds that he was somehow involved in Svetlana's demise.

"You're sure?" she prompted. "You never knew anyone named Svetlana Markova?"

Again, his patient expression didn't waver as the senator peered down at her. "Never," he lightly said. "Who was she? And how did they identify her?"

It took effort to block the disappointment from showing on her face. There could still be a legitimate reason for him to deny knowing Svetlana. Maybe she went by a different name when she was here. Maybe he was protecting someone. Jenny parsed her words carefully, trying to coax the senator's memory.

"She came from the Soviet Union. She worked for your

father's charity . . . the World Famine Commission. She disappeared in 1952, but before then she travelled all over America, learning whatever she could about modern agriculture. She seemed like a nice person."

The senator patted her on the shoulder. "Well, I'm glad you finally have a name to go with your mystery lady. She's been dead a long time, so you needn't sound so sad. And now you must excuse me; I have a flight to catch."

Jenny watched him depart, wondering if all politicians found it so easy to lie. The senator's firm denial of ever knowing Svetlana Markova didn't bode well, and the FBI now had a prime suspect for who killed one of their agents all those years ago.

WYATT'S first duty this morning was to question Mrs. Hawkins about Svetlana. It was odd to call on her so early in the morning, but it needed to happen at the same time Jenny would be questioning Senator Wakefield. Instead of his uniform, he wore ordinary street clothes and used his own vehicle to drive to her house. He didn't want her feeling like she was being interrogated or that she was a suspect.

Because she isn't. There was no earthly way Mrs. Hawkins could have had anything to do with Svetlana's downfall.

Wyatt rang the doorbell for the second-floor apartment. A patter of footsteps sounded moments later, and then the door opened. Mrs. Hawkins was already dressed in a nice blazer with a Wakefield Museum name tag pinned to her lapel.

"Hello, Wyatt," she said in surprise. "What brings you out so early?"

"I've got a few questions about the skeleton that was

found on Summerlin Groves. It looks like you're heading out to the museum, but have you got a few minutes?"

If Mrs. Hawkins was surprised or nervous, she gave no hint of it as she held the door wide and beckoned him inside. He followed her up a narrow staircase to her second-story home. As always, it smelled like lavender. It reminded him of her fourth-grade classroom, where she kept potted lavender plants and taught the class how to care for them.

Morning sunshine streamed through the front windows, and Dr. Hawkins nodded a greeting from the dinette table where he'd been reading a newspaper.

"This won't take long," Wyatt said, refusing the invitation for a cup of coffee. "The authorities have finally identified the skeleton found on Jenny's property. Her name was Svetlana Markova. Do either of you remember her?"

Mrs. Hawkins seemed taken aback. She caught her breath and glanced away, but after a moment she shook her head. "That name doesn't sound familiar. Do you remember anyone, Alvin?"

"Can't say that I do," Dr. Hawkins replied. Mrs. Hawkins met her husband in college, and he didn't move to Amity until several years after Svetlana had died.

"Here's a photograph of her," Wyatt said, opening his folder to reveal the enlarged photo. It was the one of Svetlana sitting on the farmhouse porch swing, laughing and looking straight at the photographer.

Mrs. Hawkins blanched. She swallowed a few times, then smoothed all expression from her face. She made no effort to touch or look at the photo again.

"Is that what she looked like?" she finally asked.

A chair creaked as Dr. Hawkins stood and crossed the room, peering at the photograph. "Pretty lady," he said.

"She was," Wyatt confirmed. "Mrs. Hawkins? You're sure you don't remember her?"

"No, Wyatt. I don't remember her." She hadn't looked at the photo again, and her voice didn't sound quite as confident as before. It sounded weak and shaken, and perhaps a little sad.

"What year did you say she died?" Dr. Hawkins asked.

"We think it was in the spring or summer of 1952."

"Hmmm," Dr. Hawkins said, walking toward a hallway closet. He began pawing through boxes and holiday decorations on closet shelves.

"What are you looking for?" Mrs. Hawkins asked, a hint of frustration in her voice.

"I'm trying to help you remember," her husband replied. "You collected so many things from that year. That was your senior year, right? There might be something in your high school memorabilia box."

Dr. Hawkins nudged a stepstool out and climbed up to reach the top shelf.

"Stop it, Alvin," Mrs. Hawkins scolded. "You're going to get yourself killed!"

The old man reached both arms up to wiggle a bulky cardboard box from the top shelf. Wyatt reached up to help bring it down while Dr. Hawkins quietly chuckled.

"Why did you save all this stuff if you aren't ever going to look at it?" Dr. Hawkins set the box on the dining table, then lifted the cardboard cover. Notebooks, papers, and knickknacks filled the box.

"Look at this, Millicent!" Dr. Hawkins lifted up a pair of roller skates. He flicked a wheel that squeaked and wobbled as it rotated.

Mrs. Hawkins smothered a laugh. "I'd risk my life if I tried to roller skate now, but I used to be pretty good."

Dr. Hawkins grabbed the school yearbook from 1952 and opened it to the index. “Nobody named Markova in here,” he said. “I guess she wasn’t a teacher, then.”

“I already told you that,” Mrs. Hawkins said, back to being surly and frustrated. “I’m sorry, Wyatt. I have no idea who that woman was. Simply no idea.”

The box was stuffed with old report cards, a plaque from the debate club, and a scrapbook. Dr. Hawkins began flipping through yellowed newspaper clippings, but Mrs. Hawkins gazed at something in the box with pained fondness.

It was a clear orb about the size of a grapefruit snug against the corner of the box. Mrs. Hawkins lifted it out, her hands tender as she cradled it. A perfectly preserved flower rested inside.

It was the corsage from her high school prom. Wyatt instantly recognized it from the old prom photos because it was so unique: a violet orchid with a spray of tiny lavender buds behind it.

“I went to the science teacher to figure out how to save this,” she said. “I was afraid it wouldn’t work, but I did everything he told me. I dried the blooms in silica gel, then mixed up the resin and made the mold.”

She cradled the preserved orchid in her hands, gazing at it in awe. “And here it is, fifty years later, just as pretty as it was back then. Perfect.”

The violet orchid was forever young, suspended in the clear orb and surrounded by lavender buds. Dr. Hawkins stopped pawing through the box, watching his wife with an expression of tentative worry. Wyatt could barely breathe. Mrs. Hawkins blinked suspiciously fast as she set the preserved orchid back in its corner of the box.

“There now,” she whispered, almost as if she was talking to the blossom.

She shook the melancholy away as she loaded the yearbook and report cards back into the box, stacking them up with ruthless efficiency, her expression both determined and tragic.

Dr. Hawkins set an arm around her shoulders. "It's okay, babe. You're gonna be okay."

There could be no doubt of their affection as Mrs. Hawkins leaned on her husband, accepting comfort over a long-ago love affair that ended badly. A range of expressions crossed the old woman's face before she pulled out of her husband's embrace.

"You know what?" she asked, her voice suddenly bright with resolve. She returned to the box of memories and removed the orchid. "Wyatt, how about you give this to Senator Wakefield the next time you see him? I don't need it anymore. Tell Max he can keep it or toss it or do whatever he likes with it. It's time for me to let it go."

She extended the orchid, but Wyatt was hesitant to take it. "Are you sure?"

"I'm sure," she said, even as she smiled through a sheen of tears. He felt like a cad taking it from her, but Mrs. Hawkins seemed determined to sound cheerful.

"So, you've got that special election coming up, right?" Her voice was artificially bright.

He nodded. "It's tomorrow."

"Alvin and I will be sure to vote for you. I'm going to be late for work unless we get a move on, right?"

Wyatt left with the preserved orchid in its clear resin orb and wished to the bottom of his soul Mrs. Hawkins hadn't tried so hard to act like everything was normal. It wasn't. She was a bad liar and it looked like her heart was splitting in half when she gave him her old corsage from a long-ago high school prom.

Mrs. Hawkins failed the test. Now he needed to meet with Jenny to learn if the senator did, too.

WYATT HAD to put in a full day at the office before driving out to the grove to compare notes with Jenny. Crenshaw had returned to Tampa, so they were on their own for piecing together what they'd learned.

Darkness shrouded the rural country road. There weren't any streetlamps or cheerfully lit shops or restaurants to light the way to her home . . . just the beams from two headlights illuminating mile after mile of blank countryside. Why did the perfect woman have to live in the middle of nowhere?

If he left Jenny to chase his dreams, he would probably end up like Mrs. Hawkins, cradling an orchid trapped in resin and wondering what might have been. Or in his case, a cactus garden he'd never been able to let go.

He stopped his truck beside the closed gate outside the grove and hopped out to press the button on the panel. "I'm here," he said into the tinny speaker. "Can you open the gate?"

A moment later the metal gates creaked open and he drove through. It was probably his imagination, but they sounded like the gates of a prison cell as they closed behind him.

He shouldn't read too much into it. He was upset and despondent because the fourth-grade teacher he'd always idolized looked him in the face and lied. At best, she was protecting someone. At worst, she played a part in a murder.

Jenny stood on the front porch, wearing jeans and a white T-shirt and looking like every red-blooded male's fantasy of sexy, strong femininity. She was dressed exactly as she'd been the first time he saw her outside the orange juice plant. He fell halfway in love with her that day, and it had only deepened with time.

He rolled down the passenger window. "Let's go for a drive." If he had to stay here, he'd suffocate.

Jenny's hair bounced as she sprang down the steps and slid into the truck. "Where are we going?"

Anywhere but here, he silently thought. "I'm in the mood for a drive."

They left the grove and Jenny summarized her meeting with the senator. Max Wakefield flat out denied knowing anyone named Svetlana, exactly as Mrs. Hawkins had. Senator Wakefield was good at deception, Mrs. Hawkins was lousy at it, but they were both lying.

It was depressing, and Wyatt kept driving until they reached Amity. Most of the town square was dark because everything except the Brickhouse closed at six o'clock. He passed the center of town, the library, and the road leading to the high school where they'd both graduated. He knew each of these streets as well as the back of his hand. Youthful dreams of venturing to Morocco or Tallahassee would remain just that. Dreams. Youthful, magnificent, thwarted dreams.

Only the hum of the engine and hiss of wheels sounded as they headed north of Amity. This was some of the prettiest sections of the county. It was too dark to see much of the horse farm behind a white fence lining the road, but for once he knew exactly where he was going.

Jenny probably did, too. There was a time when these stolen moments outside of town had been the best hours of his life.

He slowed the pickup as he approached the turn-off. The gravel lane was buckled, pitted, and so narrow that twigs slapped the sides of the pickup. He navigated around a ridge of exposed granite, then parked beside the old tupelo tree. He stared straight ahead, letting the engine idle.

"You remembered," she finally said.

The corner of his mouth lifted. "I remember everything."

Once upon a time this was the spot where they came to be alone, to escape her brother or the noise from other people's parties at his condo. How many warm summer evenings had they lain in the pickup bed on this exact spot to marvel at the millions of stars scattered above? It had been a blissful time. Now his heart was heavy, battered by two years of grief and shame over how he'd treated Jenny. The raft of unanswered questions about Svetlana swirled in his mind. He took a sobering breath and stared straight ahead while he spoke.

"I don't know what happened to drive the senator and Mrs. Hawkins apart all those years ago, but I saw the photographs. They loved each other. Even now, fifty years after they went their separate ways, they're still protecting each other. They know what happened, and yet they're keeping the secret. Why? I think they're both good people."

"So was Svetlana," Jenny said.

Everything hurt. Mrs. Hawkins was harboring secrets. His mother was clinically depressed and might never come out of it. He'd lost the love of his life, even though she sat two feet away. He was on the cusp of losing the election for a job he desperately wanted.

"Oh, Jenny," he said. In a perfect world he could give her a Fabergé egg and snap his fingers to restore her orange grove and cure his mother. Those things weren't possible, but it was time to make some hard choices.

"Jenny, I love you," he said simply. "When I am old and gray, I will still love you."

"Do you?" she asked. "Because it hasn't felt like it."

He looked away.

"I should have brought you to the debate. I shouldn't have abandoned you because of what Jack did. These last couple of years have been harder on you than on me, and I should have been there for you."

"Wyatt, don't make me find the strength to cheer you up." She gave him a gentle shove. "Weeper."

He stifled a spurt of laughter, but the humor vanished quickly. "I'm going to lose the election tomorrow," he said, hating to admit the truth. He didn't want to live on an orange grove, but if that was the price for winning Jenny, he was willing to pay it.

He turned off the ignition. "Come on. Let's go look at the stars."

They both got out and headed to the rear of the truck. After lowering the tailgate, he climbed inside and spread a blanket.

Jenny clambered in beside him. They simply lay on their backs, held hands, and gazed at the stars overhead. His sister's life had been snuffed out too soon and nothing could ever change that, but he couldn't crawl into the grave with her. It was time to live the life he chose for himself, not the one Jack Summerlin inflicted on him. He wanted Jenny to be his wife. They belonged together. Joy and relief bloomed inside, even though it meant letting go of other dreams.

"I want us to be together," he said. "Life can change in an instant, and I don't want to spend another hour with distance between us."

She rolled onto her side to face him. "I can't go through the rest of my life hiding from your mother."

"You won't go through another day. I want us to be together. I'm willing to live in that old farmhouse on your grove if you'll have me."

She propped up on an elbow. "What are you asking?"

Leave it to Jenny to be blunt and direct. He sat up and took both her hands in his. "I want a future with you. I want a wife, and kids, and years of waking up beside you, even if it's in the middle of an orange grove. Jenny, will you marry me?"

"You could really live on the grove?" Her voice held a world of hope, and it was humbling to see how desperately she wanted this. He would give it to her.

"Yes, Jenny," he said, tracing his fingers along the side of her jaw. "On the grove. If you'll marry me, I'll settle down wherever you will be."

Her smile was blinding in its radiance. "Yes, Wyatt. I love you and want us to be married."

They held each other as the moon rose in the night sky. Overhead, a million stars scattered across the sky, and they were only two insignificant people in God's vast universe, and yet he'd never felt more grounded and certain. They were on the right path. It was the springtime of their lives and anything was possible.

An overwhelming sense of quiet joy bloomed inside. It was a transcendent experience, almost divine. Overhead, the luminous ribbon of the Milky Way arched across the sky, huge and vast and beautiful. A shimmering feeling of enchantment hovered in the air.

"Do you feel it, Jenny?"

She squeezed his hand. He had no explanation for this immense feeling of happiness, only that it was blessed and wonderful and fleeting. It couldn't last, but he knew it to be an echo of Eden.

"We should go to church in the morning," she said.

He instantly agreed. This fleeting sense of awe would be gone soon, but it needed to be honored and acknowledged. God never promised him a life without loss or pain, but glimpses of divine blessings were all around if he remembered to look for them.

He would not forget again.

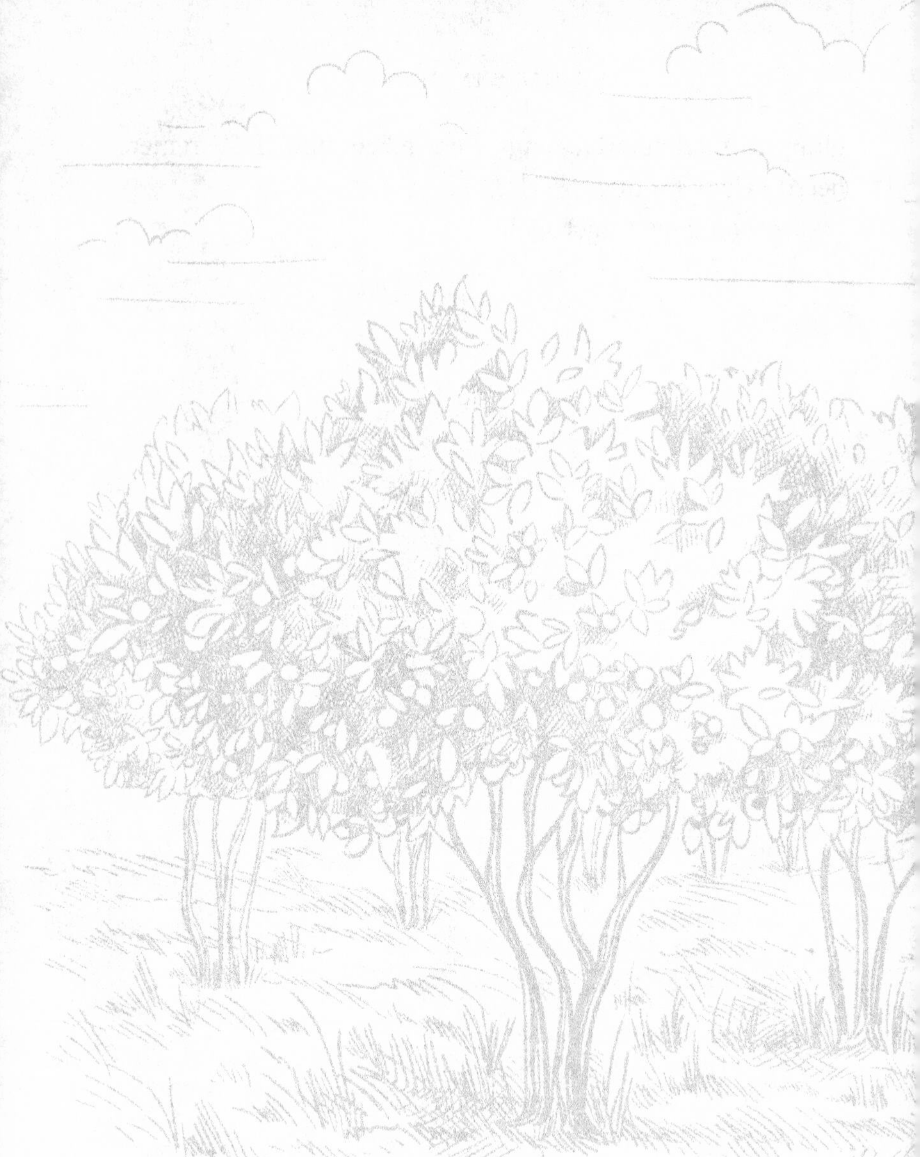

Chapter Thirty

Jenny lay beside Wyatt in the back of the pickup until dawn lit the eastern sky. For most of the night they talked and dreamed, though at some point they finally slipped into a light doze.

They awoke to a gaggle of marsh wrens whistling in the trees. She almost feared the arrival of daylight would dissolve their newfound intimacy, like the sun burning away the morning mist.

Her muscles ached as she rolled into a sitting position to look down at Wyatt, who still stretched out on his back, staring at the sky.

"I don't want the night to end," he said. They were both bleary-eyed and achy, but happy.

"It's election day," she said, tracing the back of his hand, and he gave her the world's bleakest smile.

"Yeah. It's gonna be embarrassing."

She leaned down to plant a quick kiss on his mouth, determined to put a bright face on this. "You made that lady from

Cape Canaveral publicly commit to farmland zoning reform, so in a way, you've already won."

"Hmmm," he grumbled, but his eyes fairly worshipped her. They were in love and they were together. No matter how bad a beating he took at the polls today, nothing was going to pull them apart.

They began their day at church, kneeling in prayer and gratitude for having found each other again. Then Wyatt drove her to the grove. They were both grubby after a night in the back of the pickup, and constantly bumped elbows while vying for use of the sink in her compact bathroom. Wyatt's gaze continually travelled over the old, cracked tiles as he brushed his teeth, probably already thinking of ways to knock out walls and make this space more livable for the two of them.

That was fine with her. He'd agreed to move to the grove! He was going to give it a chance, and that was all she could ask. She couldn't stop smiling as they cleaned up, and then Wyatt drove them to the elementary school to cast their votes.

The parking lot was surprisingly full for an off-year election. Inside, the cafeteria had been set up with patriotic bunting draped over the tables. The elderly man who staffed the check-in table didn't recognize Wyatt as he handed each of them a ballot, but others in the cafeteria did. A few people even wandered over to shake Wyatt's hand and wish him luck.

Their footsteps echoed along the vacant corridor as they headed to the cafeteria,

Jenny slid behind one of the privacy screens set up on a table that served as a makeshift voting booth. Her heart squeezed with pride as she darkened the circle beside Wyatt's name. Wyatt might consider this a humiliating day, but his bold campaign had forced Mindy Bannerman to make promises for ag reform, and that alone was a victory.

The entire process took less than three minutes, then they headed outside, where the glare of sunlight was blinding after the dim hallways of the school, and Wyatt surprised her with a question.

"My parents are hosting an election night party to watch the results come in," he said. "Would you like to come?"

She shaded her eyes to look up at him. "Are you sure?"

"I'm sure," he affirmed. "We're getting married. You and I are now a team, and if my mom can't accept that, we'll watch the results come in from your place."

The last thing any woman wanted was to drive a wedge into her man's family. Wyatt loved his parents and it wasn't fair that he was being forced into this position . . .but this was Donna's decision, not Wyatt's.

"Of course I'd like to come," she said. "This day is going to be stressful enough without announcing our engagement yet. Can we keep that part quiet for a while?" She wanted to savor their engagement before confronting the inevitable storm of disapproval from Donna.

Wyatt agreed, which was a relief, because she was going to be as welcome as the thirteenth fairy at Sleeping Beauty's christening.

WYATT CALLED his parents to let them know he was bringing Jenny. His dad took the call, and the news didn't go over well.

"Are you sure that's a good idea?" his father asked, his voice heavy with concern.

"Yeah, I am," he said. "Can you break the news to Mom? If it's not okay, call and let me know and we'll watch the election results from Jenny's place."

That was pretty definitive, but he was done denying Jenny. The ball was in Donna's court.

"I'll call if it's going to be a problem," his dad said.

That call never came, and at six o'clock he and Jenny drove to his parents' house. An old Garth Brooks song crooned on the radio to cover the awkward silence, but the jittery shaking of Jenny's leg was a dead giveaway she was anxious.

"Relax," he said as he slowed his car to parallel park on the leafy street across from the house. Cars were already lined up down the street, and his uncle's van was parked in the driveway.

"That's my Uncle Brian getting out of the van," he said. "You'll like Brian. He and his wife run a photography studio over in Tampa." His aunt and uncle sent him a friendly wave, then their teenaged kids got out of the van. Ethan landed on the ground with a flying leap, then went to the back of the van, while his sister, still all coltish arms and legs, followed.

Brian opened the back of the van, and Wyatt's heart stilled. They were unloading Lauren's hope chest.

Wyatt jogged ahead to intercept him. "What's going on?"

Brian straightened after setting the chest back on the driveway. "Donna called me last week asking for the chest back, and I promised to bring it over the next time I was in town. We don't mind, do we, Becks?"

Becky nodded vigorously. "We totally don't mind. Your mom can have it back. Forever, if she wants."

"I'm sorry if we jumped the gun," Brian said.

Wyatt swallowed back his frustration as Jenny drew near, gazing at the hope chest in curiosity. There wasn't time to explain because his mother was already heading down the drive.

"Welcome, welcome," she said to the Tampa gang, although her eyes devoured the hope chest. She leaned down to run a hand across the cedar lid like she was greeting a long-lost friend. She deliberately ignored Jenny.

Wyatt enfolded Jenny's hand in his. "Brian, Cindy, this is Jenny Summerlin. She runs an orange grove south of town."

If Brian or his aunt were surprised, they hid it well as they greeted Jenny, then introduced their children. Jenny responded in kind, but Donna ignored them all as she knelt to open the chest, taking inventory of the items inside.

His dad finally came outside to draw Donna away from the chest so Wyatt and Brian could carry it inside.

"Let's set this down in the study for now," he said to Brian. The party was already underway and there'd be time to lug it upstairs later. The chest landed with a thud in the darkened study. Brian headed into the main room, leaving Wyatt alone with Jenny.

"Come here, Mrs. Rossiter," he murmured, drawing her into his arms. Sounds from the party down the hall leaked through the open door, but he wanted to savor these last few moments with Jenny before joining the others. He cradled her face in his hands, kissing her long and deep as she melted against him. How long should they keep their engagement secret? It was Jenny's call, but tonight was their first step in getting his mother accustomed to the reality of their relationship.

"Ready?" he asked, and she gave him a brave nod before leaving the study.

Her hand tightened in his as they neared the kitchen. Who wouldn't be nervous about walking into the lion's den?

And yet, Jenny's natural buoyancy sprang to the surface as

soon as she recognized Elbert Davies, the kindly old fertilizer salesman who knew half the people in the county. They joined others in the family room, where the television was tuned to a cable access news station waiting for the election results that would start reporting later tonight. He linked hands with Jenny as they mingled with others. There wasn't going to be any doubt about where she stood in his affections after tonight.

Donna was doing her best to appear cheerful even as she continued to ignore Jenny. "Can I get anyone more chili?" she asked as she gathered a few empty bowls. "Don't be shy. It's going to be a long night."

Truer words were never spoken. At seven o'clock the first results began trickling in. Although the vote for Commissioner of Agriculture had been the only item on the local ballot, other places in the state had special elections for school board replacements, tax assessments, and a judge who had died in office near Jacksonville.

The early returns for the ag race weren't good. Mindy Bannerman jumped to a fifteen-point lead, but only six percent of the vote was in.

"Don't anyone start panicking," Donna said. "Before this night is through my son will be planning his move to Tallahassee."

"That's right," Brian said. "The cities always report first, so of course the Cape Canaveral lady is ahead. Pretty soon the rural votes will start reporting."

"Absolutely," Elbert said. Then the old fertilizer salesman unwittingly poked a sore spot when he made a comment to Jenny. "If the election goes in Wyatt's favor, maybe you could move to Tallahassee and work at an orchard up there."

"Jenny wouldn't want to move to Tallahassee," Donna instantly said. "It's too far north to grow oranges."

Elbert continued, oblivious to the landmine he was stumbling into. "They have orchards up near Tallahassee. Peaches. I think even pears or apples could grow up there. It wouldn't be too hard to shift your focus if you want to stay in the business."

"Don't be ridiculous," Donna said. "No woman should follow a man unless she's got a ring on her finger."

Wyatt held his breath as everyone in the room turned to stare at Jenny's left hand and she shifted uneasily. "I'll probably be staying in oranges," she said. "Pierce County suits me just fine."

"Hey, aren't you getting married?" Becky asked. The young girl's expression was quizzical as she glanced between Wyatt and Jenny. He couldn't flat out lie to everyone in the room, but he needed to buy time.

"What makes you say that?" he asked carefully, looking at Becky but monitoring his mother in the corner of his eye.

"I heard you calling her 'Mrs. Rossiter' in the study. I just figured you were getting married. Wait! Are you *already* married?"

"No!" he said. Donna looked ready to faint, and he hurried to reassure her. "Mom, I'm not married."

"Then why did you call her Mrs. Rossiter?" Donna asked.

Wyatt turned to Jenny, who looked like a deer caught in the headlights. He wouldn't announce their engagement without her consent. Donna still looked like she was going to be ill.

Jenny slid a little closer to his side, and everyone in the room gaped at them. "Yeah, we're getting married," she admitted.

The moment of stunned silence was followed by some tepid applause. Most of the people here seemed happy for him, but plenty sent worried glances in Donna's direction.

Old Elbert Davies approached them first, drawing Jenny into a hug. "Congratulations," he said warmly. "A good marriage is the greatest blessing anyone can have. I'm glad you two are on your way."

Others crowded around, but in the far corner, his parents sat quietly, his mom staring at the carpet with a blank expression.

Then, amazingly, Ed patted Donna's hand and left her. He managed a smile for the two of them as he approached. "Congratulations, son. And Jenny. The two of you are well-matched."

"Oh, Ed, I really appreciate that," Jenny said, her voice a little wobbly.

Wyatt pulled his dad into a hug. "Thanks, Dad," he choked out but kept his eyes on Donna. A few of the neighborhood women stood beside her, looking like they didn't know if they should offer her congratulations or condolences.

He kept Jenny anchored by his side as more well-wishers came forward to congratulate them. His dad soon rejoined Donna, who busied herself loading the dishwasher. The amount of noise she made banging and slamming around in the kitchen wasn't a good omen.

He wouldn't try to pacify her. It wouldn't work, and it was time to move forward with the life he wanted with Jenny. It's what Lauren would have wanted for him.

He smiled down at Jenny. "Want something to drink?"

She declined and nodded toward the television. "It looks like more results are coming in."

Mindy Bannerman's lead was widening, but it didn't matter. He might have lost an election, but he'd won a wife. Donna hadn't yet rejoined the party. After straightening up the kitchen, she headed upstairs, his dad close behind.

That was okay. His mother deserved privacy while

working through this, and Jenny deserved his support. They both were exactly where they ought to be.

The party continued while election results trickled in. By eight o'clock Wyatt was behind by twenty-three percentage points. The announcer pointed out that it was too early for Mindy Bannerman to start celebrating because she was the natural choice to sweep the city vote, most of which had already reported. Rural county results always trickled in last.

By nine o'clock her lead shrank to twelve, and by ten o'clock he was only down by six points, with eighty percent of the precincts reporting. "Come on, rural Florida," Uncle Brian shouted at the television set. "We're counting on you to turn this thing around!"

A few neighbors from elsewhere on the street dropped in as the end drew near. Even though he'd known most of these people all his life, losing would still be embarrassing. Nobody wanted an audience when they failed, but at least it wasn't a complete shutout. He was doing way better than he had any right to expect.

Tension coiled, making it impossible to sit. Too many people were casting surreptitious looks at him. He sprang to his feet and drew Jenny up with him. "Let's go outside."

She seemed to understand and followed without question. The steady hum of crickets in the backyard was a relief after the boisterous atmosphere inside. He walked to the tire hanging from the old oak tree and held it steady while Jenny climbed into it.

"My dad kept this swing so his grandkids can play on it," he said, giving her a gentle nudge. He nodded to the supply shed bordering the line of trees that framed the yard.

"We built that shed together," he said. Actually, the entire family built the shed. Wyatt had been twelve and Lauren only nine. His dad could have easily built the prefabricated shed on his own, but he wanted his kids to learn, so it took three weekends in which the whole family worked to assemble it.

"The hardest part for me was nailing the wall joist in place. I botched it three or four times, and Dad was always patient as he pulled the nails and had me try again until I got it right."

"Your dad is a good man," Jenny said.

His mom was too, though Jenny had seen precious little of that from Donna recently. His mom had been there for every hour of the shed project and insisted Lauren help, too. Lauren was a girly-girl, but Donna wanted Lauren to learn to take care of herself.

This had been a great place to grow up. He'd always imagined a big backyard like this where he'd show his own kids how to build a shed or host backyard barbecues for everyone on the street. He never wanted to live on an orange grove far away from neighbors, but they would make it work. He pushed Jenny on the tire swing, wondering how much money they could cobble together to upgrade the bathrooms in the farmhouse.

A cheer went up from inside the house, and his father opened the porch door. "The race is getting closer," Ed called out. "You're only down by two, with ninety percent reporting."

Wyatt's heart began to thud. How many percentage points could he eke out of those last remaining rural counties? The population was puny compared to the cities, yet he was sweeping the rural vote and it might be enough.

Jenny clambered out of the swing. "Let's head back inside," Jenny urged, her expression looking cautiously optimistic.

His gut felt a little queasy as he followed her inside. The television blared the weather report for tomorrow, but everyone's gaze fastened on the numbers scrolling along the bottom of the screen. It currently reported on the local races, with the statewide elections up next.

The weather report was over, and the feed cut to the announcer at the desk.

"Okay, folks, it's all over," the announcer said. "The state of Florida has just elected a political outsider from the rural heartland to be our next Commissioner of Agriculture. Congratulations to incoming Commissioner Wyatt Rossiter."

A roar broke out, arms hugging him. Was this really happening? All around him people cheered and clapped, but he stared at Jenny, dumbstruck.

"Congratulations," she said, and he broke away from the others to clasp her to him.

He was moving to Tallahassee.

He was moving to Tallahassee! This was unbelievably wonderful, and the most surprising moment of his life.

"Looks like you're moving to the big city, son!" his father boomed, and his mother beamed.

Jenny's smile was brave. Not radiant, not elated, just . . . brave.

Not everyone here was overjoyed with his win.

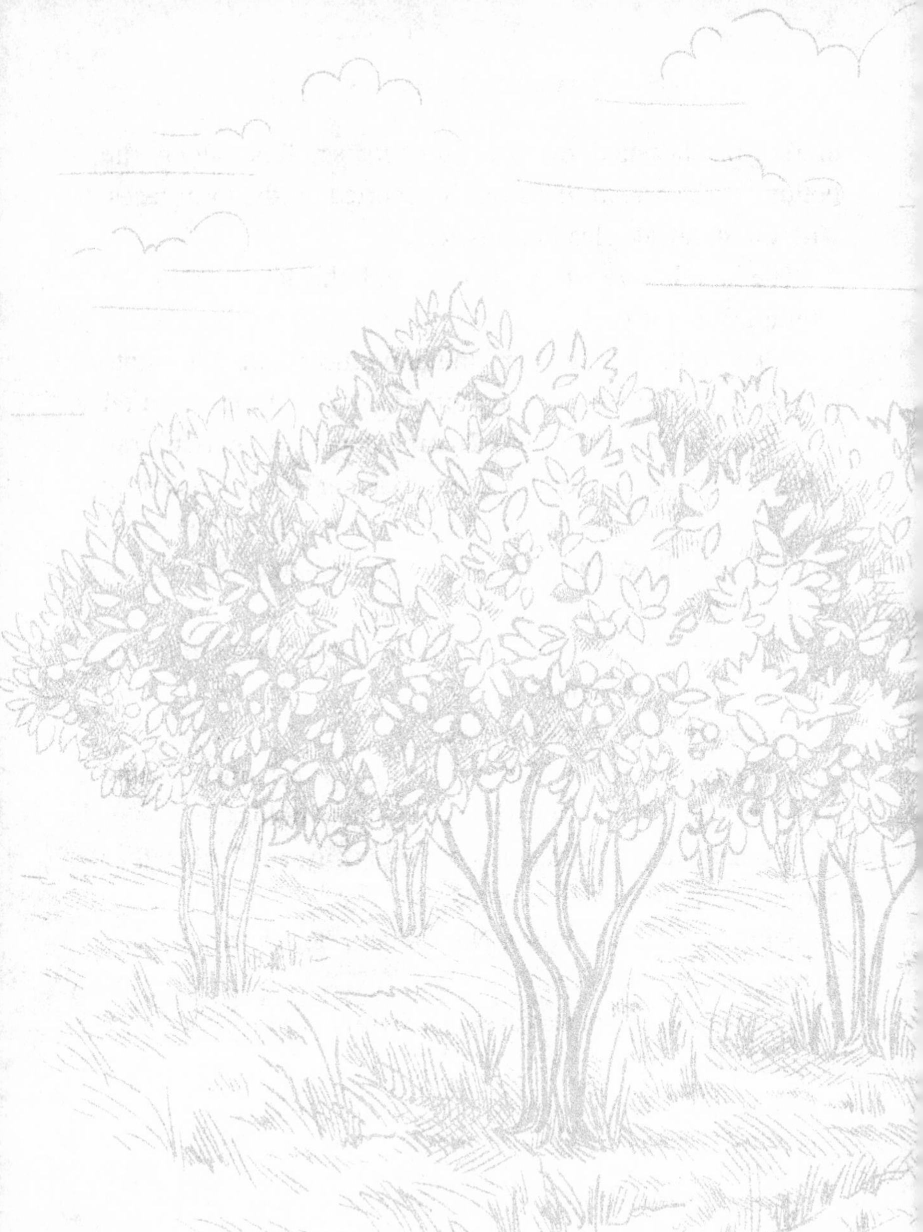

Chapter Thirty-One

Jenny was still flabbergasted by Wyatt's victory as they left his parents' house a little after midnight. She hadn't had a private moment with him after people crowded around and his phone started ringing incessantly. Congratulatory telephone calls started pouring in from all over the state. Even the governor called.

But now all was quiet as they drove through the dark of night back to the grove. Wyatt unlocked the farmhouse door, then they both went inside to plop onto the sofa in the front room, sitting in dazed exhaustion as the reality of the situation sank in.

"I'm expected to be in Tallahassee a week from today," Wyatt said. "That means I've got a million things to do at the office tomorrow."

"Can't someone else handle things?"

He shook his head. "I'm the only one who can write the staff's annual reviews, and their pay raises depend on it. I've got to sign off on a bunch of budget stuff. And train a replacement."

Jenny traced the back of Wyatt's hand as he kept rambling. It was odd how a person could feel joy and despair at the same time. Wyatt had staked everything on this unlikely dream, and amazingly, it was about to come true. She would roll up her sleeves and lift him up to the best of her ability. . . joyously and without regret, no matter how much the next few days would hurt.

"I'll have to rent a truck to pack up a bunch of stuff for the move," Wyatt said. "I don't know how I'm going to get it all done before Monday."

They both faced a monster week ahead. Wyatt had to end one job and start another. Preparations for selling the Fabergé egg were going into high gear and would be launched with a red-carpet gala this weekend.

Oh, and she had a wedding to plan and a grove to look after.

"You go to the office and I'll start packing your condo," she said. "I'll even run a load up to Tallahassee for you."

"*Oh, Jenny,*" he breathed and held her tighter.

Wyatt had been willing to move to the grove for her. Could she move to Tallahassee for him? It was only three hundred miles away, but it might as well be Morocco. Managing an orange grove couldn't be handled remotely, and Hemingway wasn't reliable enough to be the only one on the ground. She would have to choose, and going to Tallahassee would expose her deepest, most shameful secret:

Beneath all her bravado, Jenny wasn't capable of doing anything with her life except growing oranges.

JENNY HEADED to Wyatt's condo the next morning to help him pack. They started with a quick survey of his belongings to estimate how many packing boxes to buy. She counted the pictures on the walls and measured the books on his shelves. The decorative pewter tankard with the hinged lid still sat on the top shelf, exactly where it had been the night of their first date. She refrained from touching it as she continued measuring his books, though she desperately wanted to know if he had kept that note.

They got an hour of work done before Wyatt needed to leave for the office. As soon as the door closed behind him, the tankard beckoned, and Jenny couldn't help herself.

She held her breath and reached for the tankard. The pewter was cold and she trembled as she tilted the heavy lid, and *yes* . . . the note was still inside! She opened the slip of paper and savored the words all over again.

Today I changed a tire with the woman I'm going to marry.

A rush of affection bloomed inside. After all this time, even during those awful months they'd been apart, he still hadn't gotten rid of this note. She was about to replace the tankard on the shelf when footsteps sounded outside the condo. Keys jangled and the door abruptly opened.

"What are you doing?" Donna asked, her face cold.

Jenny hugged the tankard to her chest. "I'm helping Wyatt pack up."

The sour expression on Donna's face didn't bode well. Wyatt's dad stood right behind her, frowning. Donna pushed inside the condo and tossed her handbag on the kitchen counter.

"We're here now and can take over. You don't need to stay."

Jenny drew an unsteady breath and clutched the tankard even tighter. It was tempting to thrust Wyatt's note at Donna, tangible proof of her son's devotion, but it would be spiteful. Fighting over Wyatt wasn't the way to solve this. And yet, being deferential to Donna's suffering hadn't done any good either.

She set the tankard down and met Donna's steely glare. "If I live to be a hundred, I will never be able to apologize enough for the crime Jack committed against Lauren and your entire family."

"Agreed," Donna said.

"So I'm going to stop trying. Stop slinking away. I will be forever grateful that you raised Wyatt to be the strong and compassionate man that he is, but I won't take orders from you. The only person that can order me out of this condo is Wyatt himself."

Twin splotches of anger colored Donna's cheekbones as she reached for her phone and started dialing. Jenny pounced, covering Donna's hand to stop her.

"Don't do this," she warned. "Don't make Wyatt choose. He's got enough on his mind without playing referee between us. He loves you. He'd do just about anything for you, and the past two years is proof of that."

Donna jerked her hand away. "You're not married yet," she said. "I'll bet you're not even planning on joining him in Tallahassee, are you?"

The question hung in the air like an accusation, and it was painful because Jenny had strategized all night long about how to manage a long-distance marriage. The coldness in Donna's eyes was proof the older woman knew the truth.

Jenny tried to calm the thud of her heart as she gathered a

breath. "It isn't easy to be hated," she said. "A lot of people turned away from me over what Jack did, but I can't let their opinion of me become my reality. I love Wyatt and will do whatever I can to support him. You can stay and help me pack or you can go, but I won't let you drive me away."

The wall of anger coming off Donna showed a tiny crack. Not much, but any softening would be welcome. Donna set her phone down and smoothed the bitterness from her face.

"Why don't you consider putting the engagement on hold while Wyatt establishes himself in Tallahassee?"

It wasn't an entirely bad idea, except that if she let Donna start working a wedge between her and Wyatt, the rift would surely grow.

Impulsively, Jenny headed to the kitchen and knelt to open the lower cupboard. Where was that silly cake pan? Pots and metal lids clanged as she reached all the way to the back of the cupboard. Utensils skittered across the tile floor when she dragged a copper tin from beneath a pile of mismatched plastic containers. She latched on to the football-shaped cake tin and held it before her.

"Wyatt brags about the football cakes you made for him as a kid," Jenny said. "I *love* that you did that for him. I barely remember my mom, but she used to bake me cakes, too." She set the tin on the counter with a tiny click. "She used to braid my hair and make finger shadows on the wall. She sang me to sleep when I was afraid of thunderstorms. She died when I was eight, so I never learned how to bake or cook. The best I can do is open a can of soup."

Donna scoffed and looked away, but she was listening. *She was listening*, and Jenny couldn't afford to let this moment go to waste.

"After she died, I used to play dress-up in her clothes. They still smelled like her. I used to imagine her voice comforting me when I was lonely. I wished she had been there to teach me how to cook or put on makeup . . . or bake a football-shaped cake. What I'm trying to say is that I know what it's like to have a hole in my life. We both do. I hope that maybe someday you will . . ." Jenny lifted the cake tin again. "That maybe someday you'll teach me how to make one of these football cakes."

Donna cleared her throat and began collecting the spilled plastic containers. Her mouth was in a fierce frown, and Ed watched cautiously from the other side of the kitchen.

"Yes, maybe we can do that for Wyatt's birthday," Donna choked out.

Ed sent Jenny a look of gratitude, and his voice was warm with approval. "I think that would be a fine idea. I know Wyatt would like that. *Very* much."

Donna helped put the kitchen back together after Jenny's mad rummaging through the cupboards. She even initiated a stiff hug and an air kiss before she and Ed left.

It wasn't the most promising start to a new relationship, but it was a beginning.

JENNY WAS STILL in a good mood over the tentative truce with Donna as she drove back to the grove, but it evaporated the moment she turned onto her property.

Hemingway had neglected to wrap the saplings on the front twenty acres. She slammed on the brakes and got out of the truck, gaping in disbelief at the grove. Hemingway hadn't wrapped a single tree. Covering the trunks with white protective wraps was the best way to protect saplings from heat stress. It was the only thing she'd asked him to do all week, and he still hadn't done it.

Maybe she shouldn't grouse at him. She'd been so distracted with helping Wyatt that she hadn't been paying enough attention to her grove. Maybe Hemingway just needed more guidance. Or maybe he didn't realize how important it was?

No! Hemingway knew what he was supposed to do, and he'd been slacking off. She parked the truck and strode toward his trailer, getting more annoyed by the minute. The strains of Jimmy Buffett came from inside the trailer, so he was obviously home and lazing off in the middle of the day. She banged on the door and waited.

The music clicked off, and soft, feminine giggles came from inside. Hemingway sported a guilty grin and a shirtless torso when he finally opened the door. "Hey, Jenny."

She peeked behind him to see a woman rolling off his bed, her messy chestnut hair obscuring her face, but those fabulously expensive highlights belonged to Penny Danvers.

Jenny shot Hemingway a glare. "Really? I've got hundreds of saplings that haven't been wrapped so that you could roll around with Bad Penny?"

Penny flipped her hair back. "Don't be bitter. It makes you sound jealous."

"I'm bitter because you stabbed us in the back over the citrus canker. Sending that anonymous complaint was a low blow, Penny."

The words made no dent on the other woman's smug expression. At least Hemingway had the decency to tug on a shirt. He scrambled to button it while making excuses.

"Actually, Penny came here on business," he said. "Raymond Wakefield is kicking up a fuss and trying to pin Svetlana's demise on Mrs. Hawkins. He might try to pull something at the gala to embarrass her. Penny came here to warn us."

"Raymond wants the judge to reopen his claim for the egg," Penny added. "He's threatening to expose everyone's favorite fourth-grade teacher as a grifter who scammed the egg from his grandfather. Do you know what he means by that?"

Raymond's claim rested on the fact that his grandfather briefly owned an insurance policy for the Firebird Egg in 1952. The old man funded a trust with an unknown beneficiary around the same time, which Raymond thought was proof of something. The arbitration judge got a thorough look at that old trust and ruled it completely irrelevant to the egg.

"It means Raymond has a bad case of sour grapes," Jenny said.

"Apparently, they're sour enough for him to have hired an expensive new lawyer from Orlando," Penny said. "A gardener out at Wakefield Estates heard a rip-roaring argument between Raymond and the senator. Raymond is incensed his father won't fight for the egg and is blaming everything on Millicent Hawkins."

Maybe Millicent's name was included in the old documents. Why else would Raymond be so sure she was a grifter? Raymond was an intelligent man and probably had *something* on Mrs. Hawkins or he wouldn't be pushing so hard.

She sighed and turned away to gaze out at the grove. Everything was changing so quickly. Wyatt wanted her to move to Tallahassee, but how could she leave if she couldn't trust Hemingway to get off his duff and wrap the trees? She wanted to get married, but her future in-laws could barely tolerate her.

She met Hemingway's gaze. "I keep thinking about what Svetlana wrote in the book she gave my grandfather. *'Perhaps someday when we live in a more peaceful world, you and I shall meet again and raise a toast to our colorful lives.'* When are we going to live in that world? I'm tired of having to swim upstream all the time."

Hemingway gave a sad smile. "Someone should let Mrs. Hawkins know about Raymond's accusations because it wouldn't be fair to let her show up at the gala without a warning."

"She's invited?"

Hemingway nodded. "All the volunteer staff at the museum are invited." The gala was going to be hosted at the Wakefield Museum, a perfect venue because they already had two Fabergé eggs and a grand collection of Russian art.

"I'll take care of it," she said. Jenny barely knew Mrs. Hawkins anymore, but Wyatt could deliver the message. She sent a pointed look out the door at the naked saplings. "When were you planning on wrapping those trees? I've already done my half."

Hemingway had the grace to look embarrassed. "Oh yeah, I was going to do that today. Don't worry. I'll get it done before the weekend. Promise!"

She nodded and turned away. Hemingway used to work so hard on the grove . . . until he found something more interesting, and Bad Penny obviously had a lot to offer. For now, Jenny needed to head back into town. She wasn't happy about disturbing Wyatt while he was trying to juggle a million balls at once, but if Mrs. Hawkins was in danger, he'd want to know.

Chapter Thirty-Two

Wyatt spent the afternoon scrambling to wrap up his duties until his secretary buzzed his phone. Veronica sounded apologetic for the interruption.

"I know you're swamped, but Jenny Summerlin is here to see you. Shall I send her away?"

"No!" Wyatt said, halfway leaping out of his chair. Jenny was still waffling about moving to Tallahassee, and it worried him. He had approximately five million things to handle before leaving town, but at the top of that list was convincing Jenny to come with him. With luck, she was here to fling herself into his arms, proclaim she couldn't bear to be parted from him, and would move to Tallahassee.

The reality was far more mundane.

"I'm sorry to disturb you," Jenny said as she closed the door. "Raymond Wakefield is being a pest, and you need to know about it."

So, Jenny wasn't here to throw caution to the wind and ride with him into the sunset. She had only a bizarre story of

Raymond's latest scheme to get the Firebird Egg by proving that Mrs. Hawkins scammed his grandfather out of the egg.

Wyatt leaned back in his chair as Jenny finished reporting what she knew. "I don't know exactly what Raymond has up his sleeve, but he's hired a lawyer and is convinced Mrs. Hawkins is behind the disappearance of the egg. I think you should warn her about this since she's going to the gala on Saturday night."

It was a good idea and Wyatt immediately placed a telephone call to the Hawkinses' home. Although Raymond would make a fool of himself if he insulted Mrs. Hawkins in public, she shouldn't have to endure that sort of embarrassment.

"There's no answer," he said as he hung up the phone, admiring Jenny perched on the side of his credenza.

"Nice cactus garden," she observed. "Is it going with you to Tallahassee?"

"Of course."

"I'm surprised you still have it," she said, looking pleased.

"You shouldn't be. I've always been the sentimental type." He stood to draw her into his arms, pressing a trail of kisses along her jaw. "Any thoughts on moving to Tallahassee with me?"

She made a low growl of frustration but ended it with a choked laugh. "Why did you have to make everything so complicated by winning that election?"

Her voice was laden with affection and he laughed along with her. This was all his fault. He was the one changing the rules by leaving town and asking her to walk away from her home, her job, and everything she'd ever known.

"I know I'm asking a lot of you," he said, pulling back to lock gazes with her. "There are three years remaining on the term I've just been elected to. That's a long time to live apart or delay a marriage."

"Do I have to make this decision now? You only won the election yesterday, and this is a lot to think about. Oh, your mother came by the condo this morning, and guess what?"

"What?"

"She's going to teach me how to make one of those cakes shaped like a football. She definitely softened up a little since last night. Isn't that great?"

It *was* great, but he didn't miss how cleanly Jenny changed the subject of moving to Tallahassee. He sat in his desk chair, tugged Jenny onto his lap, and listened to her apologize that she was a lousy cook. She went on to say she was a klutz about almost everything if it didn't involve growing oranges. Jenny was so self-assured until the moment she set a foot off the grove. Then her insecurities came to the fore. Why hadn't he ever noticed that before now?

He put in another call to Mrs. Hawkins and let the phone ring while he nuzzled the side of Jenny's neck with a trail of kisses. The phone lay forgotten on the credenza even as it continued ringing at the Hawkins house.

"Maybe we can get out of here early and go shop for an engagement ring," he said between nibbles. "What kind do you want?"

He'd buy her the Hope Diamond if he could, but she wanted a plain gold wedding band. He slid his hands over her hips and continued kissing her.

"Hello?" A curious voice sounded from the telephone receiver.

Wyatt gulped back his surprise and snatched up the receiver. "Dr. Hawkins?" he asked, because it was clearly a man's voice on the other end.

"No, this is Marcus, his son. Who's calling, please?"

"Wyatt Rossiter. I was hoping to speak with your mother." He tilted the receiver out so Jenny could listen in.

A warm laugh sounded on the other end. "You're too late. My parents just set off on their anniversary trip this morning. It will be forty-five years next October."

That was odd. Mrs. Hawkins told him she had booked a cruise to celebrate her anniversary later in the year, not now. "Where is she going?"

Marcus sounded a little bemused when he replied. "Originally they planned on a seven-day cruise to Alaska, but all of a sudden they grabbed their passports and are heading to Europe."

Wyatt's heart began to thud. "Where in Europe?" Not all countries had extradition treaties with the United States, but his brain was too frazzled to remember the safe havens.

"They're starting in Paris," Marcus said. "They packed enough to last for months and are planning to wander wherever the mood takes them. I came over to pick up their cat and take him to my place."

They were fleeing the country. The moment Wyatt mentioned Svetlana's name, Mrs. Hawkins must have known the authorities were closing in on what happened back in 1952. Fleeing was a sure sign of a guilty conscience.

Raymond might be on to something after all.

"Okay, thanks, Marcus," Wyatt said, trying to sound calm as he hung up the telephone. Asking Marcus where Mrs. Hawkins went was a mistake. He was still an officer of the law and couldn't claim ignorance. He had no proof she was fleeing arrest or hiding from the law, but this didn't look good.

Jenny set a gentle hand on his back. "Wyatt? What's wrong?"

A million thoughts whirled as he battled the uncomfortable sensation of wanting to protect a possible suspect in a crime. Something like this needed to be handled carefully, with all parties lawyered up and aware of their rights.

"I think we need to talk to the senator and find out what Raymond has up his sleeve."

WYATT HAD to wait until Thursday before Senator Wakefield got back from Washington. Returning Mrs. Hawkins's preserved orchid was the perfect opportunity to coax the senator into discussing his long-ago relationship with Millicent.

Wyatt drove while Jenny sat in the passenger seat with the preserved orchid in a sack beside her.

"What are you planning to wear to the gala?" he asked Jenny, because in all the time they'd known each other, he had never once seen her in a dress.

"Something from my mom," she said. "A little black dress never goes out of style, and I've already tried it on. It fits."

Jenny had been living close to the bone ever since her brother lost his head and destroyed their lives. She shouldn't have to wear a recycled dress on the biggest night of her life.

"Are you sure? I'll take you shopping if you want something new."

A gorgeous flush colored Jenny's cheeks and she looked as pretty as he'd ever seen her. "I used to play dress-up in my mother's old clothes," she said. "My favorite was the little black dress with the sweetheart neckline. I've been waiting for decades to wear that dress for real. You'll see."

He grinned, because the confidence brimming in Jenny's voice boded well, and he couldn't wait to see her all gussied up. Right now, she looked tanned and healthy, the sun starting to bleach her yellowy hair a lighter shade for summer. It spilled over one shoulder in a long, sexy fall and he itched to pull to the side of the road and indulge himself by running his hands through the silky strands.

The sight of Mrs. Hawkins's orchid on her lap brought him back to reality. The coming discussion with the senator was going to be exquisitely awful. Who wanted to pick and prod at an old man about the woman he once loved and lost?

He slowed the truck as they neared the Wakefield estate. "Drive straight up to the front door," Jenny prompted. "Raymond is usually out back with the dogs at this time of day, so let's not alert him that we're here."

Wyatt parked and escorted Jenny to the grand entrance. To his dismay, Raymond answered the door, his wife right beside him.

"We're here to see the senator," Jenny said. "He agreed to meet us at ten o'clock."

Raymond blocked their entry. "I heard about that. May I ask your business?"

Wyatt lifted the canvas sack. "We have a gift from an old friend we'd like to give him."

"You can give it to us and we'll pass it on," Raymond's wife said in her faintly accented voice. The baroness looked typically elegant with her hair in a smooth French chignon and a blue paisley scarf knotted around her throat.

Wyatt shook his head. "We'd like to give it directly to the senator, Claudia." There was no way he would call her "baroness" or kowtow to a foreign title.

Raymond and his wife practically seethed with curiosity but stepped back to allow them inside. "He's in the main room," Raymond said, leading the way to a gathering room that was both lavish and comfortable at the same time. It had the rustic grandeur of a royal Scottish hunting lodge with a massive stone fireplace, timber beams on the ceiling, and comfortable leather seating. The only thing that looked out of place was the Kashmiri tapestry that warmed one wall, a memento of Senator Wakefield's years in India helping with famine relief.

The senator rose from a chair and cast a newspaper aside. "Jenny!" he boomed. "How are the saplings? Last time I drove past the grove they looked spectacular."

Jenny stepped forward and kissed the old man's cheek. "They've been thirsty and keeping me busy, but I wouldn't have it any other way."

"Excellent," the senator said. "I still wish I could have bought you out, though I'm glad you're back on your feet again."

"What's this about a gift?" Raymond asked.

Wyatt ignored the question and kept his gaze fastened on the senator. "The gala to introduce the Firebird Egg to the world is this weekend, and then the auction will be next month in Miami. Do you anticipate bidding on the egg?"

The senator stifled a laugh. "Good heavens, no. That sort of grandiose thing interested my father, never me."

"But, Dad, it probably belongs to us." Raymond's voice was equal parts grievance and urgency. "The gala is going to drum up publicity and try to cement the idea that it belongs to some nobody in Texas."

"He is going to put it in a *cereal box* museum!" the baroness said, her voice aghast.

"What kind of man dedicates his life to cereal boxes?" Raymond asked. "He has no class, no heritage, and no right to a Fabergé egg."

"The arbitration judge ruled otherwise," Jenny pointed out.

Raymond's gaze narrowed. "A treasure of incalculable

value, one that symbolizes the immortal love between Czar Nicholas and the woman he adored . . . yet a backwater judge thinks it belongs in a cereal box museum."

"Actually, Mr. Cooper intends to sell it," Jenny said.

That still wasn't good enough for Raymond. "Only a vulgarian would cash out a prize like that, and you're helping him. I heard about that ten percent cut you're trying to get as a finder's fee. I'm warning you not to proceed with that silly gala or the auction, because I won't take it lying down."

"You will be very sorry if you do," the baroness warned.

The senator lost all patience. "For pity's sake, the two of you have been implying things for weeks. If you have a good claim to the egg, spit it out. Right now."

Wyatt blinked at the anger simmering in the older man's voice. It was at odds with his carefully cultivated grandfatherly image, and even Raymond seemed a little cowed, though he didn't back down.

"I've got proof that my grandfather legally bought the egg. I'd rather not show my cards prematurely. This is best handled quietly before a judge, but if you let this silly gala and auction go forward, you will regret it. That's all I'm going to say on the matter."

Senator Wakefield let out an exaggerated sigh and went to the sideboard to pour himself a drink from a decanted bottle of wine. "Jenny? Wyatt? Can I offer you anything? I think we could all use something to lower the temperature."

The senator was back to his congenial self. Wyatt and Jenny both declined the drink, but it was time to return the orchid.

"I saw Millicent Hawkins recently," he said, handing the canvas sack to the senator. "She asked me to give this to you."

He watched carefully as the senator lifted the clear orb from the bag, the orchid still pristine and perfect inside. Fifty years had passed, but the senator seemed to instantly recognize the bloom. He carried it to the window, where the sunlight illuminated the orchid, forever suspended in the sphere. His expression softened as he gazed at the orchid, and it was as if he'd been transported to a different world . . . a better one, where teenaged dreams could come true.

"I remember this corsage," he said softly. "I had it special-ordered because Millicent loved lavender. She always wanted to see the lavender fields of France."

The baroness stepped closer to admire the bloom. "Yes, it's quite lovely."

The senator bowed his head and spoke in a reverent tone. "It was a perfect night. Our world was young and innocent and the fires of spring blazed with hope. It was Millicent's first grand ball, and I picked this flower because it was beautiful and flawless. An orchid looks as if God wanted to create something to represent purity and elegance in a single bloom."

Raymond visibly cringed. "It's only a flower, Dad. You're embarrassing yourself."

A steely look hardened in the senator's eyes. "You know what, son? You got the woman you wanted. I didn't, so shut up when I'm talking."

The smackdown lashed through the air like a whip. Raymond's mouth thinned as the senator stormed from the room, the orchid still in his hand. He slammed the door so hard everyone jumped. Raymond looked furious, and the baroness was coolly annoyed as she peered at Jenny.

"Satisfied?" the baroness said. "All you did was stir up old memories that are best forgotten. Millicent Hawkins was no angel, and it's a shame the senator hasn't figured that out yet. You should be grateful to us for trying to stop the auction."

"Oh, I still intend to stop the auction," Raymond asserted. "I can do it, too."

Wyatt shook his head. "The judge dismissed your claim *with prejudice*. You can't refile, and you're dead in the water."

Raymond fumed as he looked at his wife. "You know what? I've been trying to spare Dad the embarrassment, but maybe we should let it all come out."

"Yes," the baroness said in her chilling voice. "Let it all come out."

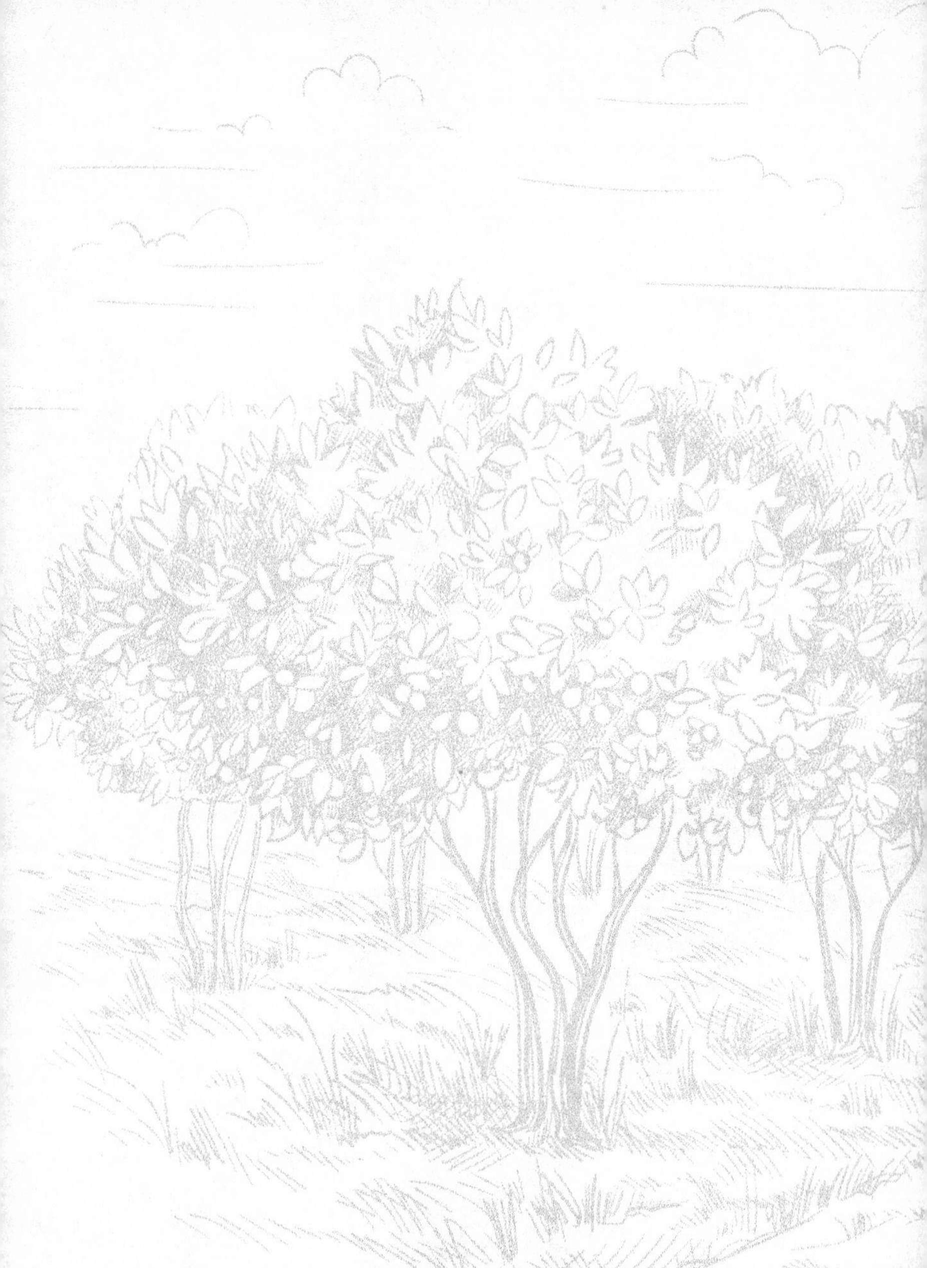

Chapter Thirty-Three

Jenny booked an appointment at the only hair salon in Amity to get an updo for the big gala on Saturday night. It took almost an hour to blow-dry her hair and twist half of it up into a coil at the crown of her head while letting the rest of it fall in soft, romantic waves down her back.

"You look like a movie star!" the hairdresser enthused as she released the final lock of summery-blond hair from the curling iron.

"It's probably going to last five minutes in the humidity," Jenny said, but she couldn't stop smiling. She'd never had her hair professionally arranged before and now she understood why women did it.

The stylist assured her that a generous shellacking with hairspray would keep it all in place. Her updo still looked good two hours later when Jenny stepped into her mother's little black dress and lifted the straps over her shoulders. She had to contort into three different angles to pull the zipper up in the back, but she got the job done.

Wyatt's expression when she answered the door was priceless. He gaped as his eyes travelled from her fancy hair, down the timeless elegance of the dress, and to her brand-new shiny high heels.

"I'm the luckiest man in the world," he finally said.

Wyatt looked pretty spectacular too in a spiffy tuxedo with a bow tie. She took his arm as he helped her down the porch stairs.

Nervous energy made her chatty. "We should hurry because Kristen said the cereal box guy from Texas is here and I'd like to meet him. Hemingway is already there. He's taking Bad Penny as his date, and they went early since she's covering the gala for the station."

"Did he find a tux?" Wyatt asked as they got into his truck.

"Hemingway? Of course not. He's wearing a Russian Cossack shirt, a fancy one with embroidery around the neck and a sash tied around his waist. They wear them for weddings over there, but it only cost Hemingway twenty dollars at a costume store in Orlando."

The Russian themes were going to be heavy tonight, so Hemingway could get away with the dashing outfit. Wyatt still sent a pointed glare at the saplings as they left the grove, most of which were still unwrapped.

She rushed to defend Hemingway. "It rained yesterday, so he couldn't finish the job."

"And yet he had time to go to Orlando to buy a Cossack shirt."

Hemingway wasn't perfect, but she'd never fire him. They'd been through too much together. Hopefully they would soon each earn a hefty sum from the finder's fee, provided Raymond was bluffing and lacked enough new evidence to reopen the ownership of the egg.

She was still worrying about it as they arrived at the museum, which was decked out like glamorous events she'd seen on television. A red carpet blanketed the front steps and banners with the old Romanov family crest flanked either side of the doors. Bad Penny stood with a camera crew outside the museum, and she looked fantastic in a skin-tight emerald gown with an ornate gold choker covering her throat. Penny cast a dismissive smirk at Jenny's simple black dress. Jenny wore no jewelry, but the best accessory was the man beside her, six-feet-two-inches of raw masculinity. She lifted her chin and sported a proud smile as she walked beside Wyatt, Florida's next Commissioner of Agriculture, toward the museum.

Hemingway hurried down the steps to join them. The Cossack shirt was perfect for the grand spectacle of the night, but his face looked worried.

"I've been watching Raymond for hours," Hemingway said. "He's got a lawyer with him, and he and the baroness are cackling with delight. They definitely have something up their sleeve. Oh, and I met the cereal box guy. I think Wyatt is about to have some competition."

Bad Penny called out for Hemingway's help, and he flashed Wyatt an irreverent wink before he left them.

"What's that supposed to mean?" Wyatt asked.

"Who knows? Let's head inside." She wasn't used to walking in high heels and was grateful for Wyatt's arm as they walked up the steps.

Raymond stood just inside the museum doors. His black tuxedo was offset with a fabulous bronze silk vest, but the rail-thin man beside him wore an ordinary business suit. He carried a brief case and scrutinized them through owlish eyes.

Raymond dipped a stiff nod as she approached. "Jenny, Wyatt . . . this is Harrison Griggs, my lawyer and advocate helping ensure my patrimony is not illegally sold in a premature auction."

Who used words like *patrimony* anymore? Wyatt introduced himself to Mr. Griggs, noting that he was also a lawyer, here to protect Jenny's legal interests. The battle lines were drawn, but at least all parties sounded civilized.

Inside, standing cocktail tables topped with white linen filled the lobby. Each table had flickering votive candles, white roses, and lilies of the valley because they were the favorite flowers of Czarina Alexandra. Soon this foyer would be crowded with socialites, politicians, and even a few celebrities, but for now it was empty except for staff making last-minute preparations.

Raymond followed them farther inside, still uttering warnings. "If you think you and the Marlboro Man are going to screw me out of the egg, you need to think again."

The Marlboro Man? Jenny had no idea who he could be speaking of until she spotted Kristen from Christie's at the far end of the lobby, standing beside a tall gentleman wearing a tuxedo and a wide-brimmed cowboy hat.

Oh my . . . Yes, the Marlboro Man had come to life. Kristen beckoned her over. "Jenny, this is Mr. Clement Cooper from the cereal museum."

This was the cereal box guy? She stifled a laugh as he winked at her and lifted his hat. "Pleased to meet you, ma'am," he said in a baritone voice so deep it practically made the room vibrate. "I'm grateful you found that egg and that we came to an agreement without a catawampus."

She grinned. "I am, too."

It turned out that Clement Cooper was actually *Professor* Clement Cooper, or "Coop" as he asked her to call him, and he taught agriculture at Texas A&M.

"Why did I think you ran a cereal box museum?" Wyatt asked, and Coop laughed while Kristen looked embarrassed.

"Bless her heart," he said with a good-natured nod to Kristen. "When some people hear the word 'cereal' they automatically think of breakfast. My father's museum celebrates cereal grains and the breadbasket of America. Most kids grow up worshipping Superman or James Bond, but the real heroes of this world are the people who get up to work seven days a week, no matter the weather or the ache in their bones. We've got exhibits on the history of farming, surviving the Dust Bowl, and a science wing to teach about modern topics. And of course, we've got the cereal box display," he teased. "We put 'em up on the website because the kids love them."

Kristen tugged on her arm. "Do you want to see the egg? It will be under wraps until the grand unveiling later tonight, but we can sneak a peek before everyone starts arriving."

"Oh yes!" Jenny clung to Wyatt as they followed Kristen, who unlocked the doors to the main gallery where the other two eggs were housed in display cases with plenty of room for guests to admire them from all angles. The Firebird Egg had been given the most prominent position. Hidden from the world for almost a century, it now perched on a velvet pedestal, professionally lit from above, a tiny fragment of history ready to make its reentry into the world.

The last time Jenny saw this egg it was in a plastic bowl lined with a terrycloth towel. How long ago that seemed now.

"Do you know why Svetlana picked your dad to sell the egg to?" she asked Coop. "Or why she never returned with it?"

Coop nodded. "My dad got overly excited about that egg. The Russian lady asked him to stay quiet, but he couldn't help himself and called the newspaper. I think she got spooked by the attention. If she was a Soviet trying to defect, I can't say that I blame her for taking off."

It was a logical explanation. A wistful sensation bloomed as Jenny gazed at the egg, glittering on its bed of velvet. It had once been cradled in the czarina's hands. Stolen from a palace by revolutionary soldiers and carried by countless others over the decades. Svetlana herself had smuggled that egg on her person before it was hidden in the cypress tree.

Guests began gathering in the lobby behind the closed gallery door, but she remained entranced, staring at the egg as Wyatt chatted with Professor Cooper.

The door opened and Senator Wakefield entered, followed by his son and the baroness. The baroness wore a strapless ball gown made from the same coppery-bronze silk as Raymond's vest. As ever, a matching pair.

The owlish lawyer was with them, which didn't bode well. What was Mr. Griggs carrying in that briefcase?

Kristen reached toward the stack of programs from a nearby table. "Senator, I thought you might like to know the events of the evening. We'll start with cocktails in the lobby, then there will be a ten-minute video my firm prepared about the Firebird Egg and its journey from the Winter Palace to an orange grove in Florida. Finally, we'll unlock the doors to this room for the grand unveiling of the Firebird Egg."

"Yeah, none of that is going to happen," Raymond said. The owlish lawyer set his briefcase on a standing cocktail table and rifled through some files.

"Dad, I didn't want to do this here but you gave me no choice," Raymond continued. "I am revoking the auction house's right to sell this egg and am declaring it Wakefield property."

Mr. Griggs handed a fat legal document to Kristen. "You are hereby served official notice of a pending lawsuit for ownership of the item known as the Firebird Egg."

Wyatt glared at him in annoyance. "Raymond, you have no standing to sue, and the judge has already dismissed your claim with prejudice. You can't re-file."

"It is a new complaint," the owlish lawyer said. "It is based on deliberate fraud on the part of Millicent Hawkins, formerly Millicent O'Grady, who conspired with Gus Summerlin to deprive the Wakefield family of their rightful ownership of the aforementioned Firebird Egg."

A low growl emanated from the senator's throat and he glared at Raymond. "You've got a lot of nerve," he said, his voice vibrating with anger.

Raymond held up his palms in placating fashion. "Dad, I didn't want this to happen here, but you kept siding with them, and I needed to serve the auction house before they went any further down this illegal path."

A voice chimed in from the other side of the room. "How did Millicent Hawkins conspire to steal the egg?"

Jenny whirled to see Bad Penny standing just inside the open door. A video guy behind her had his camera rolling. The senator must have neglected to lock the door when he entered, giving Penny the chance to barge in and hear everything.

"Turn that thing off," the senator ordered, pointing at the videographer. "I do *not* consent to being filmed."

Bad Penny's grin was smug. "Sorry, Senator, this is a newsworthy event and the public has a right to know. How did Millicent Hawkins conspire to steal the egg?"

Senator Wakefield shoved Penny aside to grab the camera from the videographer's shoulder and then hurled it against the wall. It smacked with a loud crash, scattering bits and pieces across the marble floor.

"That was a ten-thousand-dollar camera!" Penny shouted.

"Send me the bill," the senator snapped. Elegantly dressed guests crowded the open doorway, some carrying flutes of champagne, all looking fascinated. The senator ignored them and pointed a finger in Raymond's face. "I want you to withdraw this ridiculous lawsuit immediately.

Millicent O'Grady is as pure as the driven snow. She was then, and she is now."

"Dad, stop talking," Raymond said in an urgent voice. "Millicent was bad news. You made a lucky escape, okay? I found a lot of stuff in Karl's old paperwork. Let's go to my office with my lawyer, and I promise you will support me when you see what I've got."

Jenny had never seen Raymond so confident or so grim. Whatever he had must be serious, because even the senator looked uneasy.

"Everyone, return to the lobby," he ordered the bystanders in the open doorway. "The museum is private property, and this is a closed-door meeting."

Most of the guests instinctively took a few steps back, but Bad Penny didn't budge until the senator grabbed her elbow and propelled her backward. He slammed the door and twisted the lock, then returned to the table, his eyes glittering with rage.

"You've got two minutes," he told Raymond in a low voice.

Raymond nodded and accepted the challenge. "My grandfather had a safe-deposit box at the bank that had a one-hundred-year lease. I've got power of attorney to handle estate business, so I was able to get into it and go through his old papers."

"I revoked your power of attorney after I caught you skimming from the servants' Christmas bonuses!"

Raymond winced at the public disclosure of his embezzlement but recovered quickly. "You never let the bank know, so I was able to get into it. I found an affidavit from your father swearing that he witnessed Millicent O'Grady attempt to steal the Firebird Egg from a woman named Svetlana Markova. In the struggle, Svetlana fell down the staircase at the Wakefield estate and broke her neck. It was an accident, so it was manslaughter instead of murder, but she did it, Dad. Millicent killed Svetlana, then your father paid Gus Summerlin a thousand dollars to dispose of the body."

Jenny's stomach lurched because it had the ring of truth. Her grandfather always got irrationally angry whenever he caught her playing near those cypress trees. It wasn't because the exposed roots made it dangerous, it was because he knew what was hidden inside that ancient tree.

A hint of sympathy softened Raymond's features. "I'm sorry, Dad. I know you cared for her, but she killed that woman. Karl paid for the egg, and Millicent tried to steal it. I didn't want to bring this all out, but you didn't leave me any choice."

Raymond tried to hand his father the affidavit, though the senator wouldn't touch it. The faded document had old-fashioned typeface and the raised stamp of a notary.

Wyatt took it, frowning as he read. Jenny wouldn't know how to judge the validity of a legal document, but Wyatt's gaze travelled across each line of the old page. The senator watched as Wyatt read, fear in his expression as he awaited Wyatt's verdict.

"Well?" the senator asked when Wyatt set the paper on a table. "Does it look authentic?"

"It's authentic," Wyatt said. "It was notarized and witnessed by two people. One is long dead, but old William Longacre is still alive. I think he retired to Orlando. I suppose we could get him down here to validate his signature. This doesn't look good for Mrs. Hawkins."

"She high-tailed it to France a few days ago," Raymond said. "That sounds like a guilty conscience."

The hint of a smile played around the Senator's lips.

"France?" he asked. At Raymond's nod, the older man's eyes grew wistful.

"I hope she's happy," he murmured. "She always wanted to see the lavender fields of France. Ah, Millicent. What a woman."

His voice brimmed with fondness, but something didn't make sense. Jenny turned to Raymond with the question. "If Millicent risked her life to grapple on a staircase for the egg, why would she let it be buried with the body?"

"Because that document is a complete and total lie," Senator Wakefield said. "Millicent didn't kill Svetlana. I did."

Raymond shook his head. "Don't try to protect her. You had been in India for over a year when Svetlana died."

The senator gave a sad smile. "I went to India the week after she died, and my father pulled a lot of strings to give me a false alibi. He swore he could 'fix' everything, and he did. He changed the dates on my passport. He created fake paperwork for the World Famine Commission to back up his story. I had no idea he cooked up this affidavit framing Millicent because I was on the other side of the world when he did it."

He swallowed hard, and the anger in his expression faded, grief coming to the fore. Jenny ached to reach out to him, but there was nothing she could do to stop this trainwreck from happening. He walked to the gallery entrance, unlocked the bolt, and opened the door.

Bad Penny was on the other side, holding a digital audio recorder high. Given her triumphant expression, she'd captured every word, and yet the senator didn't seem to care. The lobby was filled with the glittering set of socialites. The chatter died as Senator Wakefield opened both double doors and gestured people forward. Most of them sensed something important was unfolding and stopped mingling to stare in fascination.

"It was an accident," the senator announced in a voice loud enough for all to hear.

Wyatt stepped forward. "You have no obligation to keep talking," he said. "In fact, I'd advise you to stop, and get a lawyer."

By now there was a semi-circle forming around them. Coop stood with Kristen, and he doffed his cowboy hat. Bad Penny's face glowed with anticipation as she held her recorder a little closer.

"I don't need a lawyer since it's time to tell the truth. My father figured out that Svetlana had betrayed him. Julius and Ethel Rosenberg had just been sentenced to death in the electric chair because they were caught passing information to the Soviets, and my father feared he would be next if Svetlana wasn't stopped. She was working with the FBI to lead him into a trap, and the Fabergé egg was the bait. He lured Svetlana to the house, desperate to silence her by any means necessary. I think he intended to bribe her, but she couldn't be bribed. I heard yelling and shouting behind his closed study door and went to investigate. Svetlana came running out, and my father ordered me to stop her."

"Dad, you need to quit talking," Raymond ordered, looking sick and panicked. "Stop talking *now.*"

Senator Wakefield's mouth twisted as he eyed his son. "The weight of shame can destroy a man's soul. How can I blame you for a dishonorable life when I've carried secrets that are even worse?"

The senator let out a heavy sigh and his shoulders sagged. "I didn't even know why I was ordered to stop Svetlana. I was nineteen years old and my father was terrified. She raced toward the front door and I tackled her from behind, sending us both to the granite floor in our front hall. Her neck was at a bad angle when I got up. She wasn't breathing."

Jenny stood frozen, unable to move. Everyone clustered near the open gallery doors looked just as dumbfounded.

"Millicent was in the house that day and saw us trying to revive Svetlana. My father ordered her to leave, and she did. We went back to working on Svetlana, but nothing we tried worked. Within an hour she was cold and we had to dispose of the body. We couldn't bury her on our land because the hunting dogs would have found her." The senator met Jenny's gaze, and her heart squeezed.

"I called your grandfather. He came over with his brand-new pickup truck."

"Oh no," she whispered. Her grandfather had looked so proud of that truck in the old photos. Her clever, hardworking grandfather who raised her and always did the best he could . . . including warning her away from the cypress trees and the terrible secret he *knew* they hid.

She dimly heard the senator continue, describing how they initially tried to bury Svetlana in the grove but the water table made it impossible. They found a high hollow in an old cypress tree and dumped her inside, planning on moving her once they had a better plan.

"We chucked everything she had into that tree," the senator continued, his face starting to twist with regret. "I remember that her arm was extended, almost as if she was reaching up to get out. She had a little gold watch on her wrist. She'd loaned it to Millicent the night of the prom because Millie's parents were strict about getting home on time. When I saw Svetlana's hand reaching out of that tree . . ."

His voice choked off. The crowd was silent, but Bad Penny had her recorder rolling. There would be no escape from this story.

"Gus tucked her arm back down and covered her with

leaves and dirt. She had been wearing a denim jacket that day," he continued. "The kind that have a pocket on the inside. That was probably where she had the egg, but we never looked for it. Gus and I didn't even know about it, we just wanted to get everything over with as fast as we could."

Flesh decayed quickly in the sweltering Florida heat, and they both dreaded the prospect of extracting the body and the risks of transporting her to bury her somewhere else. They ultimately decided to leave her there.

"My father was grateful for Millicent's silence and set up a twenty-thousand-dollar trust to send her to college. Then he got me out of the country and falsified the dates of my service to the famine commission. If Svetlana's body ever surfaced, I could use those papers to prove I was in India when she disappeared."

His voice choked up again. "I always wanted to give Millicent the world. We should have run away to France when we were young and everything was still possible. After what happened in the grove I couldn't even look her in the face again. She deserved better than a man like me. I went to India hoping it would cure my soul, but only shining sunlight into its darkest spaces can do that. I've always been afraid to do that. Not anymore."

He looked at Wyatt. "You're still a sworn officer of the law until Monday morning. You'd better get on the phone and call the sheriff."

"Already done," Bad Penny chimed, and to Jenny's revulsion it looked like the cameraman was on the phone, reporting everything.

Wyatt moved in close to the senator. "I doubt they will arrest you," he said. "I suggest you go home, get a lawyer, and negotiate this when tempers have calmed down."

Raymond butted in. "Dad, I didn't know. I swear! I never would have done this if I'd known . . ."

"Are you going to drop your ridiculous lawsuit claiming Millicent had anything to do with this?"

"Um, yeah . . . probably. But why did she flee the country if she was innocent?"

There was a painful longing in the senator's voice as he replied. "She did it to protect me. As soon as Svetlana was identified, she worried the truth would come out and didn't want to be forced to testify against me. She sent me the orchid as her last goodbye." He gazed into the distance and a little smile floated around his mouth. "I hope Dr. Hawkins will take her to France where she can finally see every lavender field, every old castle and cathedral, every perfume factory and vineyard and Parisian café that I should have taken her to see long ago."

He snapped out of his reverie and gestured for Kristen. "There's no reason the gala can't continue," he said. "I don't know what's ahead for me, but I would like you to update your video about how the egg got into that tree. Svetlana Markova was a remarkable woman and deserves a place in history. And now I shall take Wyatt's advice to go contact my lawyer."

Jenny swallowed back the lump in her throat as she watched the senator leave through a rear entrance. The guests who'd clustered around the gallery door began chattering, trying to make sense of the strange information they'd heard, but Bad Penny would have it all figured out in short order. She was going to gleefully report it on the eleven o'clock news, and by tomorrow morning she would have her first national news story.

THE SENATOR WAS SUPPOSED to deliver the welcoming remarks for the gala, but that obviously wasn't going to happen. Kristen did a bang-up job stepping in to fill his shoes, improvising a quick speech to welcome guests to "this historic night." A string quartet commenced playing and waiters circulated with hors d'oeuvres and flutes of champagne.

The lights dimmed and the video about the history of the egg began playing on the screen, but Jenny didn't have the heart to watch. She'd already seen the video, and everything about finding the egg in that cypress tree now seemed unbearably sad after coming to know the tragic end to Svetlana's life.

She walked to the outside balcony with Wyatt, gazing at the fairy lights strung through the trees. Torches flickered and gardenia blossoms perfumed the night air, but everything seemed desperately sad. Wyatt slid behind her, folding his arms around her middle and drawing her back against him.

"I hate how this is ending," she said. "People like Svetlana . . . they don't deserve to end like that. She was so brave, and I'm sorry she never got a chance to escape into America like she'd hoped."

"She had a few good years here," he said. "Now that her story is out, she won't ever be forgotten."

She rotated in his arms to look up at him. "What will happen to the senator?"

Wyatt sighed. "He'll be allowed to plead to manslaughter. The state could never have proved anything without his confession, and the evidence is consistent with his story. It's a clearcut case of involuntary manslaughter, so they won't try to up the charges."

"Will there be jail time?"

"I doubt it," Wyatt said. "He'll probably get community service and a fine, and hopefully some peace of mind for making a clean breast of it." Svetlana, Gus, and Max Wakefield had all been friends, and yet Svetlana ended up dead and the other two men lived with guilty consciences for the rest of their lives. The inscription Svetlana wrote in the book never seemed more poignant. *Perhaps someday when we live in a more peaceful world, you and I shall meet again and raise a toast to our colorful lives.*

They never got that chance. Svetlana's fight to seek freedom in America made Jenny's anxiety about leaving home pale in comparison. Wyatt was her future, not the grove. Moving to Tallahassee wasn't the life she would have chosen for herself, but it could be a good one. Maybe even a great one.

Tallahassee can be a beautiful place.

The sentiment popped into Jenny's mind from nowhere, but it had an affectionate tone and a Russian accent. It was as if Svetlana herself had just delivered a message.

Jenny rotated to face Wyatt and reached up to curl her arms around his neck. "Is the invitation to join you in Tallahassee still good?"

Wyatt's eyes warmed in pleased surprise. "Still good. Morning, noon, and night. Come to Tallahassee with me, Mrs. Rossiter."

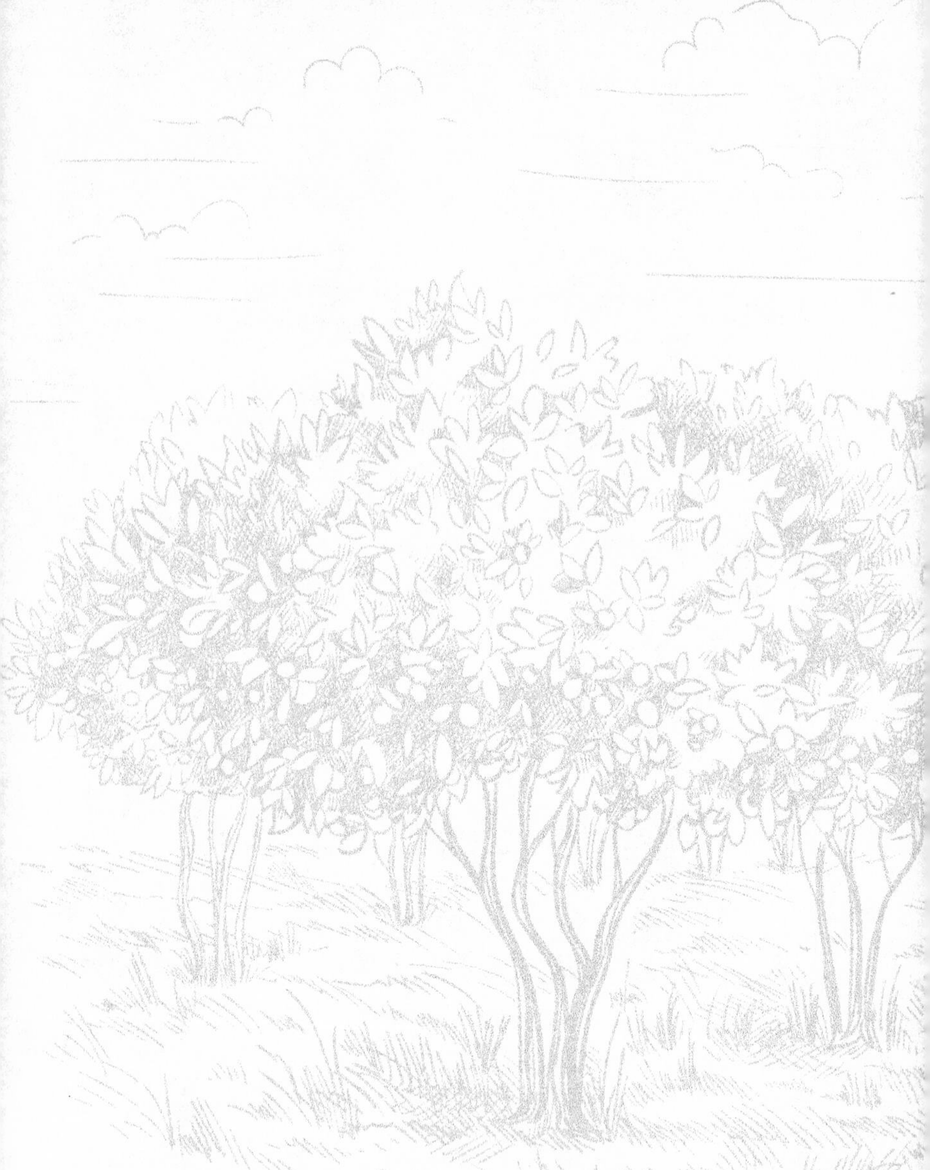

Chapter Thirty-Four

Tallahassee, Florida
Four years later

Jenny was nervous about seeing Hemingway for the first time since she had to fire him two years earlier. He would probably be decent about it, but Hemingway was a wild card so it was impossible to be sure.

"Don't worry," Wyatt soothed as they headed toward a local bookstore a few blocks from the Florida State campus. "You did Hemingway the biggest favor of his life when you kicked him off the grove."

Maybe, but she still regretted it. After the Firebird Egg sold at auction, she and Hemingway each got a little over a million dollars once the taxes and fees were paid. Hemingway still wanted to work on the grove, but he got lazy and neglected anything he didn't feel like doing, such as handling the grove's paperwork. The worst was when he let their contract with the OJ plant lapse because he rarely bothered to open the mail. It meant Jenny had to take a week of leave from her job in Tallahassee to drive down and mend fences with the guys at the plant.

After getting fired, Hemingway packed his bags and left Pierce County without a word. She worried herself sick for weeks and resorted to calling Bad Penny to find out what happened to him.

“He’s working on a shrimp boat down in the Florida Keys,” Penny had told her. “I think he’s dating the owner’s daughter. Who knows? Anyway, he still claims to be writing the great American novel.”

That was two years ago, and as usual, Penny was right. Hemingway’s novel was finally published last year. It was on the *New York Times* bestseller list for months and was short-listed for a Pulitzer. Who could have guessed that the novel embodying the spirit of rural America would finally be written by a guy from Iceland?

The sun had set and streetlamps illuminated the avenue of quaint shops. Jenny squeezed Wyatt’s hand as they strolled past a sidewalk café, a candle shop, and an over-priced antique store. The bookshop where Hemingway was doing an author-signing was straight ahead, and her steps slowed.

“Come on, don’t be nervous,” Wyatt coaxed. “Hemingway isn’t the type to hold a grudge.”

Neither was she. It wasn’t a confrontation with Hemingway she feared, it was seeing a glimpse of her old life that was going to be painful. She still owned the grove, but now spent the majority of her life in Tallahassee. Almost all the changes she’d been through since marrying Wyatt had been marvelous, but a part of her would always miss living on the grove.

The signboard propped outside the bookstore showed a photo of Hemingway with a long list of cities for his book tour. Stacks of his novel filled the window display, its cover showing the silhouette of a lone man fishing by a river.

On the other side of the plate-glass window, the warmly lit bookstore was crowded with shoppers and a line had formed at Hemingway's table. He looked tanned and healthy and fit. Mercifully, he'd put on a shirt. With Hemingway, things like that couldn't be taken for granted. It looked like he was enjoying himself with a couple of college girls standing before his table, their young faces alive as they preened and flirted. Hemingway returned their flirtation with a roguish grin.

She missed him. She and Hemingway had walked through fire together and come out on the other side with a few dings, but mostly whole and healthy and stronger for having known each other.

Wyatt must have sensed the rush of nostalgia that threatened to drag her back into the past, and he leaned down to kiss her cheek. "Thank you for coming to Tallahassee," he whispered before straightening to gaze through the bookstore window.

"I wouldn't have it any other way," she said. Moving here had been difficult, but major life changes usually were. And so far, the good things that came from marrying Wyatt vastly outweighed the sacrifices. The orange grove had once been her only world and she tried to cram everything else that mattered onto those lonely thirty acres. It wasn't until she moved to Tallahassee that she realized how limiting it had become.

The grove gave her priceless insight into farming and perseverance. Now instead of growing oranges, she used that knowledge for the World Famine Commission. She worked in an office where she raised funds, hired experts, and figured out how to turn difficult soil all over the world into productive farmland. Most of it was done from here in Tallahassee, but she flew to various parts of the world a few times a year for conferences or as an adviser in grove management.

"Come on, let's go inside," she said and snagged a copy of Hemingway's novel off the front table. The college girls still had him captivated, so she headed to the cashier to buy the book while Wyatt went for a cup of coffee.

The line at Hemingway's table continued to get longer. There was no chance for a private chat, so she joined the end of the line to wait. The college girls had moved on, but Hemingway was just as congenial to the matronly lady buying the book for her husband, an avid fly-fisherman. After the lady went on her way, Hemingway stood and glanced around the store as though looking for someone, but came up disappointed. He was about to greet the next customer when he spotted her.

"Jenny!" he said and beckoned her forward, ignoring the line of people in front of her.

"I'll wait my turn," she called up to him.

"Nonsense, woman," he groused, coming around the table to join her at the back of the line. "We haven't seen each other in two years. Am I forgiven?"

"You miserable Viking," she teased. "I just spent thirty dollars on your book. What do you think?"

His laughter was warm and familiar as she stepped into his hug. "I was worried you might be travelling and couldn't come tonight," he said. "How do you like working for the World Famine Commission?"

"It's good. I'm on my way to Morocco next month to speak at a conference on Mediterranean citrus." She and Wyatt were finally going to see Morocco after all. What an irony that it would be because of her job, not his. He had managed to clear his calendar for two weeks and they planned on stealing time to camp beneath the hot desert skies.

Wyatt soon joined them, and Hemingway congratulated him on getting elected to another term as Commissioner of Agriculture. It was nice to see the two men finally being decent to each other, but her gaze strayed to the cover of Hemingway's book. The silhouette of the lone man fishing in a lazy river reminded her of home.

Wyatt's reelection meant they had another four years in Tallahassee, and she would spread her wings to make the most of them. And if she occasionally missed the grove? Well, she still had access to the closed-circuit security cameras and sometimes tuned in to watch the sun rising above the grove in the early morning hours as the breeze rustled the leaves. The trees were healthy and tall now and stretched in orderly rows toward the horizon. This year they produced their first crop of oranges since they'd been planted, and she proudly watched the harvest from afar.

They still came back to the farmhouse each year at Christmas. Maybe she and Wyatt would return for good someday, or maybe they'd stay in Tallahassee forever. No matter what happened, Jenny would make the most out of every day . . . but her favorite sound on earth would always be the squeak of the porch swing while gazing out at her grove.

The line to meet Hemingway was getting longer, and this wasn't the place for a reunion. "What are you doing after your signing is over?" she asked. "There's a pub down the street that serves great smoked brisket. Want to join us?"

"Absolutely," he instantly replied. He signed her book and she gave him directions to the pub.

Though she would never admit it, the brisket at the new place was even better than at the Brickhouse. She and Wyatt already had platters of brisket, baked beans, and cornbread by the time Hemingway joined them half an hour later. They laughed about old times, and naturally, the conversation soon turned to Svetlana, the senator, and all the other people they'd known in Amity.

As expected, Senator Wakefield resigned from the senate and pled guilty to involuntary manslaughter. He'd been given a fine and performed community service, which most people thought was fair. Millicent Hawkins and her husband never returned to Amity. Rumor had it they relocated to be near their daughter in Orlando, but Jenny wondered if Mrs. Hawkins was finally ready to put Max behind her forever.

As for Svetlana, they all agreed her story deserved to be commemorated.

"Have you ever thought of writing a book about her?" she asked Hemingway, who shifted in annoyance.

"You sound like my agent," he said. "Every month she nags me about it. I don't know what I'll write next. I've toyed with some ideas, but nothing has gelled yet and I'm in no hurry."

Expecting Hemingway to do anything he didn't want to do was hopeless. Still, she hoped he'd find a way to write Svetlana's story so she would be remembered as more than just a woman found in a tree. One hot July evening many years ago, a lightning strike hit an old cypress tree and split it wide open. In the years since, Jenny had often wondered if it was the hand of God that caused that bolt of lightning, leading them to discover Svetlana's body and her amazing story.

Decades after her death, Svetlana's example inspired Jenny to break free and explore the world. Last year she read the copy of *War and Peace* that Svetlana had given her grandfather. It was a magnificent novel, but the most moving passage in the entire volume was the handwritten note Svetlana penned on the title page:

Perhaps someday when we live in a more peaceful world, you and I shall meet again and raise a toast to our colorful lives. Until then, may God be with you, and please remember me fondly.

Svetlana never lived to see that more peaceful world, but the three of them around this table had been blessed beyond all measure. They had good food, friendship, faith, and a mission in life.

She lifted her glass. "In honor of Svetlana," she said. "I'm grateful that our paths crossed with her, and hope that somewhere up there she is smiling down on us and knows that her life made a difference."

They clinked their glasses and raised a toast in honor of Svetlana's colorful life.

Author's Note

This book was set in 2005, shortly before Florida rescinded the policy requiring the destruction of orange groves infected with citrus canker.

American communist sympathizers did indeed supply agricultural equipment to the Soviets in the decades following the Russian Revolution. The deals were brokered under the table due to prohibitions against trade with the Soviet Union. Priceless treasures seized from the czar and other aristocratic estates paid for these deals.

The Firebird Egg described in this book is entirely fictional. The last time an imperial Fabergé egg surfaced was in 2012 when a scrap dealer recognized the value of a pretty golden egg that had languished in his house for years. Known as the "Third Imperial Easter Egg," it sold at auction for $33 million.

At the time of this novel's publication, six imperial Fabergé eggs remain lost to history.

Questions for Discussion

1. At the beginning of the novel, Jenny burned an acre of her trees in an attempt to hide the citrus canker. In doing so, she violated the spirit of state's policy. Did she have a moral obligation to obey that policy? Even if she knew it to be ill-advised?

2. Shortly after his sister's death, Wyatt tries to convince Jenny to run away with him to Morocco. Had she agreed, what do you predict would have happened?

3. Why do you think Wyatt and Hemingway never got along?

4. The truth of Svetlana's death would never have been known if the senator had not disclosed it. Was it okay with you that he got away with a slap on the wrist? How much responsibility does he bear for participating in his father's cover-up?

5. Amity, Florida is a fictional small town. Some of the characters love small town life while others find it stifling. Have

you ever lived in a small town? What are your thoughts on such a life compared to living in a big city?

6. Donna reflects on the following: "We live in an imperfect world, and can never really be happy because our hearts remember the echo of Eden." Do you think there is any truth in this?

7. When Mrs. Hawkins retrieves the preserved orchid from her senior prom, it is obvious her husband knows what it is. Should she have gotten rid of it when she married?

8. Do you think Donna will ever be able to accept Jenny as a daughter-in-law?

9. After Wyatt wins the election, Jenny toys with the prospect of having a long-distance marriage. What are the benefits and drawbacks of such a marriage?

10. Raymond Wakefield is the son and grandson of highly successful men, yet has contributed little to the world based on his own merit. How often does this happen among children of vast privilege? What can be done to insure such children grow up to become admirable people?

11. Do you think Jenny is happy in Tallahassee? How can a person who embarks on an unwelcome move reconcile themselves to their new home?

Connect with Elizabeth

To learn more about Elizabeth Camden and her books, visit her website at elizabethcamden.com/ and on Facebook (link: https://www.facebook.com/ElizabethCamden)

The best way to learn about Elizabeth's upcoming books, recommended reading, and more cool news is to sign up for her monthly newsletter at https://elizabethcamden.com/offi cial-elizabeth-camden-newsletter

If you liked this novel, you might enjoy Elizabeth Camden's historical novels. They are all set in gilded age America and feature a mix of romance, mystery, and a touch of inspiration.

Good starting novels to explore Elizabeth's backlist include:

The Spice King

Gray Delacroix has dedicated his life to building an acclaimed global spice empire, but it has come at a cost. Resolved to salvage his family before they spiral out of control, he returns to his ancestral home for good after years of traveling the world.

As a junior botanist for the Smithsonian, Annabelle Larkin has been charged with the impossible task of gaining access to the notoriously private Delacroix plant collection. If she fails, she will be out of a job and the family farm in Kansas will go under. She has no idea that in gaining entrance to the Delacroix world, she will unwittingly step into a web of dangerous political intrigue far beyond her experience.

Against the Tide

Lydia Pallas spends her days within sight of the bustling Boston Harbor, where her skill with languages has landed her an enviable position as a translator for the U.S. Navy. Her talents bring her to the attention of Alexander Banebridge, a mysterious man in need of a translator. Driven by a campaign to end the opium trade, Bane is coolly analytical and relentless in his quest. He cannot afford to fall for Lydia and must fight the bittersweet love growing between them.

Determined to prove her worth, Lydia soon discovers that carrying out Bane's mission will test her wits and her courage to the very limits.

A Dangerous Legacy

Lucy Drake's mastery of Morse code has made her a valuable asset to the American news agencies as a telegrapher. But the sudden arrival of Sir Colin Beckwith at rival British news agency Reuters puts her hard-earned livelihood at risk. Newly arrived from London, Colin is talented, handsome, and insufferably charming.

Despite their rivalry, Lucy realizes Colin's connections could be just what her family needs to turn the tide of their long legal battle over the fortune they were swindled out of forty years ago. When she negotiates an unlikely alliance with him, neither of them realizes how far the web of treachery they're wading into will take them.

Printed in the USA
CPSIA information can be obtained
at www.ICGtesting.com
LVHW040147240924
791976LV00004B/37

9 781733 222549